In the Next Moment Everything Will Change

In the Next Moment Everything Will Change

An Exploration of Love, Time Travel and the Prism of Narrative

Daniel Caulfield

Copyright ©2023 by Daniel Caulfield

All rights reserved.

No part of this publication may be reproduced, distributed, or transmitted in any form or by any means, including photocopying, recording, or other electronic or mechanical methods, without the prior written permission of the publisher, except as permitted by U.S. copyright law. For permission requests, contact the author directly @ dcaulfield@pm.me.

The story, all names, characters, and incidents portrayed in this production are fictitious. No identification with actual persons (living or deceased), places, buildings, and products is intended or should be inferred.

Cover design by Daniel Caulfield. Writer sketch by Gordon Johnson.

First edition 2023

For my mother and father,
whose unwavering faith, kindness and love
taught me to never give up.

In the Next
Moment Everything
Will Change

Part One

The 500-Tab Time Portal

Don't bother Max's cows. Let them moo in peace.

— Sign at the Woodstock festival in support of Max Yasgur, as reported in the New York Times, August 16, 1969

1

I 'd been at the cabin for about a month and a half when my mother broke the news to me that Laura had moved on. She was dating a writer, my mother told me, and she gave me his name. I looked him up and he'd only published one book. It was a memoir, a story about growing up emotionally and sexually crippled after a childhood affair with a middle-aged woman, and about the twenty or thirty years of therapy that it took to finally put his life back together and move on. It got decent reviews, and it smarted a little to read them. But I told myself that a memoirist is only a writer in the small sense, one who doesn't possess the creative drive and the longing for truth and perfection it takes to produce a work of fiction. And while my mother made a big deal about the great reviews and the sales of the boyfriend's novel, which had even managed to poke its head up high enough to appear on the *New York Times* bestsellers list for a week or two, I found it suspicious that this guy was finally cured of his trauma only as he became old enough to date middle-aged women without raising eyebrows.

Of course, the greater irony, in my mind, was that Laura had paid for our divorce and moved across the country to reinvent herself and now she was shacked up with my on-brand doppelganger. Her memoirist boyfriend was quite obviously another man who had spent the best years of his life trying to write his way out of the prison of a great first chapter. As a therapist herself—almost a doctor, as my mother interjected whenever I complained about the way Laura portrayed me—it was hard for me to believe either coincidence escaped her.

The really troubling thing that came through in my conversations with my mother was the way Laura kept telling her how worried about me she was. Laura still talked about me with the same degree of affection, if my mother was to be believed, and that gave my mother a degree of hope for reconciliation, but in the conversational anecdotes my mother reported, Laura was talking about me as though I had gone completely off the rails. Her story had a new hero now, a memoirist, and my character was being reimagined as someone I didn't recognize. I was no longer a struggling artist of prodigious writing ability with actual glimmers of genius—that comfortable character we had written together over the years. Almost overnight, I had been reimagined as a middle-aged failure whose one small critical success was a single short story that had been followed only by mounting desperation, and eventually by anger, drugs, and what Laura liked to call conspiracy theories but which were all well-documented by the exhaustive research that stole my attention in the hours I should have been writing.

It was like she was purposely ignoring the fact that I had taken some calculated risks in order to create the time I needed to finish my novel and build a life she might want to return to. I was working under the impression that's why she had left in the first place—to light a fire underneath me and because she knew that if anything would push me to finally complete the novel, it would be her. It was frustrating that she couldn't see my hero's journey for what it was. Instead, she was transforming me into a device, a backstory, an opaque and distant figure without solid lines to form a container. It felt like a betrayal, and though it is often painful to visit ourselves where we exist trapped in the minds of those we love, this was something far more pronounced. It left me feeling like I might disappear.

2

Before Laura left and I lost my job and met the abbot and entered into the period I like to think of as my life on the lam, I had a colleague who was always insisting that dramatic tension could be created through juxtaposition. I hated that word. As far as I was concerned, it was sophomoric and cloying and had I any idea Laura would end up dating a memoirist, I would've thought it belonged in the *New York Times* with her new boyfriend's book review. But my colleague thought he was Columbus. He had discovered a new device. He named it *juxtapositive tension*, and he proudly planted his flag. He published an article in a virtually unknown literary journal, and somehow the publication lifted him out of the lowly 101s. And while I had never seen him successfully use the device in any of his own fiction which was mostly about birds—and not that lovely, British variety of bird which is perfectly capable of creating tension all on its own—he was soon filling his students' heads with the nonsense of juxtapositive tension in advanced composition classes and turning his nose up whenever I nodded in his direction as we crossed paths in the halls.

When I met "the abbot," I had to reflect back on the writer of bird fiction and eat a small meal of crow. I'd been stranded on the hard shoulder of a northeastern interstate, hitchhiking west, and the abbot pulled over to offer me a ride. He was driving a red Ferrari. It was the same model Tom Selleck used to drive in that *Magnum P.I.* show from the eighties, and when he introduced himself as a man of the cloth, I thought, "*Motherfucker*. It's a clear case of juxtapositive tension!" So while referring to him here as "the abbot" rather than "Abbott" will likely make you think I'm one of those unreliable narrators a little down the road, I want to make sure you understand why I was so easily drawn into the abbot's story. Was it not for the way the holy title of "abbot" chaffed against the grand material opulence of the Ferrari and pricked at the tenderness surrounding my wounded ego, I may have had more resistance to him. But the juxtaposition formed a riddle that both caught my interest and stung me with humiliation. A lever in my brain was pulled back and held for a moment, shaking. Its release sent things hurtling forward, bouncing around in my head and setting off bells and bumpers and flashing lights as if in a pinball machine, leaving me hypnotized, and straining to determine how things were going to pan out.

I shook the abbot's hand, gave him my name and buckled into the passenger seat, immune to the normal cynicism that would have pegged him as a fabricated character, a man wanting to impress me as memorable if only for the duration of a ride.

"Well then, David," he said. "How the hell are you?" He had that salesman's way of repeating a person's name.

I told him everything was fantastic and left him to discern the sarcasm. I was a forty-six-year-old man standing on the side of a highway with a backpack. Things were obviously not going great.

"What do you make of this weather, David?" He gestured at the sun rising between the mountains through the car's open top, "Shaping up to be a scorcher, isn't it?"

I followed his hand with my eyes and nodded. "How far west are you heading?" I asked.

"Well, David," he said. He applied some pressure with his foot and the Ferrari's engine sang, high-pitched and musical, and then he released the clutch and the tires chirped and we lurched forward, pulling off the shoulder and onto the highway. "That's actually not the easiest question to answer." His voice had become low and confidential and a little sad. "You see, I lost my wife a while back."

"I'm sorry," I said.

"No, no. Don't be sorry," the abbot said. "You'll have to excuse my poor choice of words. My wife isn't actually dead. We got separated, you see? It was a while ago, but as far as I know she's still out there somewhere. I'm still trying to find her."

"I see," I said, though I felt like I was only getting more confused.

"Lucille," he said. "That's her name." His salted mustache stretched out over a sad smile. Slight dimples pocked his cheeks. "I guess if you want to put a name to where I'm heading, you could just say I'm heading to Lucille."

"To Lucille?" I said. Now I was the one repeating names.

"Lucille," he said back.

I felt myself soften a little each time he said his wife's name. There was tenderness and regret in his voice that hit me in a place I recognized. I guess that was because in my own way, I was like him. This would've been about four months after Laura left me, and it would still be a couple of months before I found myself alone in the cabin with my mother telling me that Laura was shacking up with a memoirist. I desperately wanted her back. She had gone missing of her own accord, of course, and my problem wasn't that I didn't know where to find Laura. I could've gotten in touch with her just by dialing my phone. My problem was that Laura didn't want me coming to find her. She was on her own now, and perhaps even better off in the world for her distance from me, but I still yearned for Laura the same way the abbot's voice told me he yearned for Lucille and, despite the small differences in our situations, this shared sense of loss and sadness opened my heart to him.

I tried to learn more about Lucille, but the abbot became evasive when I pressed him on the subject. His answers were disconnected anecdotes and curious character sketches. I sensed an underlying structure like he was approaching something important, but it was impossible to join any three points in a straight line. I found it compelling, and I hated that. I kept thinking about my colleague's big discovery and wincing. Then, after a hundred or so miles when I finally found an opening to broach the subject of the abbot's religious title, he claimed I'd simply misunderstood him. "No sir-ree, kid," he said, "Abbott is a proper noun, with a capital *A* and two *T*s."

I took a moment to appreciate the twist in plot. I accepted the joint he was passing me—maybe it was our second or third—and I dragged deep and blew a plume of smoke out the open Targa top, thinking that the weed was getting the best of me. A man driving around in a bright red Ferrari, referring to himself as an abbot, I thought—as *the* abbot? It was such a ludicrous idea I almost giggled to myself. Maybe I was even a little bit proud that I'd come up with it.

"There was a time—many years ago, mind you—when my students and peers may have referred to me as the abbot," he said, adding something about the way intuition sometimes smoothed over the potholes in a story. I passed the joint back to him and he took a last hit before flicking the roach out of the T-top. "Call me any way you please, kid," he said. "Abbott or the abbot. Either one is fine."

His name was just the beginning of my confusion. He explained how it connected to his father's early life as a comedian, to McCarthyism, to blacklisting, to subterranean jazz clubs on the lower east side of Manhattan where his mother sang, to burlesque shows and gentlemen's clubs.

"My father was a buffoon, see? He was the muscle of a comic duo, the worker, the proletariat. That's what drove him to Marxism if you get my meaning. So of course he gave me the name of a straight man. He was trying to save me."

He continued like this. I felt like I was studying his family history through a kaleidoscope. I saw a young kid growing up on Manhattan's Lower East Side, a victim of bullies who didn't like his name. Then I was looking at an adolescent riding his bike along the Harlem River to train boxing at Gleason's Gym. Now he was older, a golden gloves champion and a deep admirer of Muhammad Ali.

I've placed those events in order, but they weren't delivered that way. They were scattered before me like the stars of a constellation and I was left to connect the dots into an identifiable figure. The story of Abbott's father and mother bestowed him with his name. From the name came bullies and boxing which led him to Ali. When it came time for Abbott to enroll in selective service, that same string of causation left him resenting his draft card and propelled him toward the peace movement. Muhammad Ali had refused induction into the army two years earlier and the champion's stance had left a powerful impression on the young Abbott. It was a long series of events that reeked of predetermination and would eventually land Abbott at Woodstock and lead to the disappearance of Lucille.

"And later, see, that same watercourse path that began with my father's Marxism and my straight-man's name would also pave my way out of the institution."

I started to formulate a question but, before I could ask him if by "institution" he meant some limiting construct of society or a secure building made of block and steel, he'd already moved on.

"My mother died the spring before the Woodstock Festival," he continued. My father was destroyed by my mother's death. He got into bed after the funeral and refused to eat. Three weeks later, I was sitting in my childhood apartment alone. I was an orphan at eighteen."

As the summer of 1969 stretched on, Abbott began to feel like the world had left him no quarter to find peace. Images from Vietnam were flooding the TV. All around the country, peaceful protests were turning violent. In July, lower Manhattan erupted into the Stonewall Riots and he only needed to walk out his door to find himself in the middle of a combat zone. The whole world was splitting apart at the seams. When he picked up an August edition of the *Village Voice* and saw an advertisement for three days of peace and music in upstate New York, he was certain fate had intervened. He wasn't going to Vietnam or heading off to Chicago to fight police in the street. He was going to Woodstock. Abbott lit his draft card on fire and with it still burning in the amber glow of his father's ashtray he locked the door of his childhood home behind him for what would be the last time. At the bottom of the stairs, he walked a few blocks west, descended to the metro, rode the subway north to its terminal stop at 242nd Street and headed for the thruway.

Two days later, he was standing in a crowded field in Bethel, New York, with five sheets of acid in his pocket. "It was the brown stuff," he said. "All day long, I was selling it for a dollar a tab. And then sometime after dark, Ravi Shankar took the stage."

Abbott grew excited as he described the scene to me. At one point he reached his hand out of the Ferrari's open roof and closed it in a tight fist, pulling something invisible out of the air. He held it in the space between us for a moment before letting it go. While Abbott listened to Ravi play the sitar, he contemplated the interconnectedness of all things. For the first time in recent memory, he felt right with the world.

"Something shifted during Ravi's set," he said.

When I pressed him to be more specific, he began describing the beauty of the crowd. They were just people like him, he assured me, but somehow the festival and the music had transformed them into something greater than people.

"Greater than people?" I prodded.

"Waveforms," he said, "holograms, avatars—like that. And I could see something else. Each one of them was animated by a force that existed somewhere far away and outside of themselves. We were all reflections, transmissions from the same, distant source, connected by a ribbon of energy, and all of us were floating about one giant, galactic maypole."

He turned toward me and I glanced at his face without meeting his eyes. I wasn't sure what I was feeling. All the juxtapositive tension that had drawn me forward was resolving. I thought I was beginning to get a bead on Abbott. Maybe I was worried that he would turn

14

out to be just one more stock character in a world that seemed to have lost its ability to produce anything new. He seemed unaware that, in the years since Woodstock, his far-out ideas had saturated modern consciousness to the point of becoming platitudes.

"I can see that you're doubting me," he said.

"It's not that," I said.

"Listen to me, kid," he said. "The feeling I had—it was of being right on the very edge of something. Right on the cusp. Do you understand?"

I'd spent half my life feeling like I was right on the edge of something, and yet nothing ever seemed to change. I told Abbott as much, and he conceded that life was often like that—his life as well. But he insisted this moment was different.

It was a singular moment, he explained. Fertile. Hints of the miraculous were everywhere. Food and water were scant, but there was no aggression or competition. The scene was night and day from the life he'd left behind, from the images of war on TV and the chaos he'd been witnessing in the city. Everything at the festival was shared, and the more things were shared the more they seemed to multiply.

"The solution to my worries and fears and my sense of alienation, was simple," he said. "When I let go of my ego and connected with the eternal part of me, I could see another path opening up."

He shifted his Ferrari into a higher gear and let the clutch out and it sang down a long, winding grade of maybe six percent.

"Do you hear what I'm saying?" he asked.

"I do," I said.

I turned and watched his thinning, salt-and-pepper hair tousle in the wind. It wasn't just his red Ferrari that had materialized straight out of 1980s television. Abbott himself resembled Thomas Magnum. I hadn't caught it before—and sure, he was an aged and slightly insane version of the character, one who had lost a few inches of height and gained a few around the waist—but Magnum was there. His voice even had that Magnum quality, a range that could hit every emotional note with tonal perfection.

"You're not really here," he said. "Not the way you think. None of us are."

He shifted his gaze from the road and stared directly at me. I noticed that his eyeballs were beginning to bulge. Each iris had become a small land mass surrounded at all sides by a white sea. For a moment I thought he was having a mental episode and I wondered if I was in danger. But then, just like that, the intensity passed and he began to tell me about a stand of aspen somewhere out west. He described thousands of acres of trees interconnected beneath the ground in a spider-web network of fungal wire.

"We're just like that forest," he said, "all of us appear unique and separate, but beneath the surface we're connected to the same energy. You see? We're all generated from the same source code. We think we're separate, but we're cut out of the same fabric and strung together like a hundred thousand gingerbread men." He glanced at me one more time to make certain I was listening and then he went on with his story, relating the next stretch of events with more equanimity. His voice became reflective and internal.

"Things got progressively stranger," he said. "Ravi played, and his sitar commanded us all to dance. I could see that Ravi's fingers had tapped into the network, and now his music traveled from the great source and it spoke privately to every soul. With each note of his sitar,

I realized that his music already existed in me. Ravi was helping me remember something.

"And then, at some point, I noticed it was raining. It must have been raining for hours without me noticing, but suddenly I became conscious of the rain. I'd never noticed this before, but I could see that each drop of rain contained its own rainbow—not its own, of course—each drop had the ability—no kid, not the ability. It was more like an *imperative*, a *directive,* to reflect the essence of the Great Source. Do you understand, David? The light was divided into hundreds of thousands of different tones and hues and combinations of color. Each one was unique, and only when they came together could they create the harmony of that original, pure, white essence from which all things and all music are born."

Abbott didn't know for how long it had been raining when a man of the rainbow approached him and held out a dollar and asked him for a dose. That's when he reached into his pocket and realized that the five sheets of brown acid he'd tucked into the pocket of his cut-offs had been saturated by the rain and that five-hundred-dollars worth of lysergic acid diethylamide had been absorbed by his genitals.

He told me he had three coherent thoughts before his consciousness disintegrated. The first was that he at least wished he had worn underwear. He thought he would've been more comfortable riding out a grand mal LSD trip with a good pair of tight-fitting underwear. Then he had a regret. He recalled the invitation of an attractive but intense young woman who had knelt before him and tugged lightly at the frayed legs of his cut-offs just before the rain. She had been trying to coax him, in her own words, "to shed the shackles of society and dance uninhibited in the light of freedom." If he had only accepted her offer, he would not have been in his present predicament with five-hundred doses of LSD surging through his brain.

He could almost sense that alternate timeline traveling beside him. He watched himself stripping naked and copulating as the dry earth turned to mud, and he reached out toward that other self as if that parallel reality were a rope dragged by a passing ship and he was drifting in a sea of rain and storm and clay. He reached out and the line passed through his fingers. The ship slipped into the distance with the rope slithering behind in its wake.

His last coherent thought was that there was no changing the past or preventing the future. Then he heard three clear knocks of the divine on a golden door that rose out of the earth before him. He walked over, twisted a doorknob he must have imagined, and went marching into the light.

3

As usual, my mother was having a hard time seeing the bright side of things.

While Abbott gassed up and bought some coffee and Mars bars, I stole a few minutes to return her calls, which I had been avoiding for days, and to smoke a cigarette. I'd been trying to limit my smoking to the one cigarette a day that I really enjoyed.

I regretted lighting up almost immediately. I could never enjoy a cigarette while I was on the phone with my mother. I began doubting everything I heard myself say, even as I tried to convince my mother that the recent series of catastrophes that had befallen me was fortuitous.

"Laura will see things differently when I finish my novel," I told her.

"Novel?" she said, "It's one chapter, David. It's been one chapter for twenty years. And now you don't even have that little part-time job at the college to keep you afloat?"

She took a moment to sigh, and I wanted to tell her once again that the college where I used to teach, part-time as an adjunct, was considered to be very close to bush-league. But we had been through that debate enough times over the years for me to know better. And now that I'd been fired, the point was pretty much moot anyhow.

"I'm just worried about you, David," she said. "A man your age should have his own transportation, not be out hitchhiking across the country like some sort of vagrant. Why don't you take a bus?"

I told her that buses were more dangerous than hitchhiking these days. Packed full of real vagrants, and criminals just out of prison, and addicts and drunks.

"I don't know, David," she said. "Do you think maybe it's time to put that novel aside for a while and focus on the important things?"

I took a long drag off my cigarette and looked up at the afternoon sky, which was actually very pretty. I exhaled. For a few moments, neither of us spoke. I listened to the silence on the other end of the phone and the hum of the highway.

"This man I'm traveling with," I said, "He lost his wife years ago, and I think he still misses her. He seems to think they'll find each other again. He's never stopped looking for her."

She didn't answer for a few seconds. I took another drag and exhaled. My mother had lost my father a few years before, and she still looked for him every day of her life, not for real like Abbott was looking for Lucille, but in coincidences and synchronicities and signs from beyond.

"Are you smoking?" she asked. "I thought you gave that up."

"Ma," I said, "It's just one."

"That's how it always starts," she said. "Do I need to start worrying about you, David? Laura mentioned something about drugs, but she didn't want to go into it. She still calls me now and then, you know."

"That was just to help me write, Ma," I said. "It's not like I was out partying."

I took a last drag, rolled the cherry out of my cigarette, and flicked the filter into the trash. I was sitting at a picnic table under a tree. The picnic table was that typical deep brown color, and whoever had placed it picturesquely under that tree had never considered how quickly and completely it would be plastered in bird shit.

"Are you sure this guy is alright, David?"

"He's a good guy," I said. "You remember that TV show you used to like? *Magnum P.I.*? This guy has a Ferrari like that, except it needs a tune-up. He looks kind of like Magnum too. Just a little older."

"Leave it to you," she said. "You lose everything. You have the sheriff's department knocking on my door with a bench warrant for God knows what, and that Mister McGee always trying to track you down. And in spite of everything, you're out riding around in a Ferrari."

"It's just a misunderstanding, Ma. Taxes and stuff."

"A misunderstanding?" she repeated.

"It's not like I robbed a bank," I said. "Things will cool down. I'll finish my book and it'll all be fine."

I could see Abbott returning the nozzle to the pump and screwing on his gas cap. I hated lying to my mother. I wanted to either tell her the truth or get off the phone.

"Anyway, I should go, Ma," I said.

"Okay David," she said, "I don't mean to be harsh. You know I'm always rooting for you. Just get somewhere safe and figure the rest out later. My friend Elaine says Arizona is very pretty. Maybe you'll end up there."

"I've heard that too," I said.

I looked over and Abbott was in his car with a Mars bar, the wrapper peeled back like a banana. He waved to me."

"David," she said.

"Yeah, Ma?"

"Tell your friend I hope he finds his wife."

"I'll tell him," I said.

"I always liked that Magnum you know."

"I know, Ma."

We were both silent again.

"David?" she said. "Are you still there?"

"I'm here," I said.

"I wasn't going to say anything, but you know how I told you Laura called?" Her voice was shaky all of a sudden. "I just remember how she always seemed to keep you... I don't know... focused. I know you two had your problems—all marriages do—but there was never anything like this when you were living together."

"Ma," I said. "What's going on? She told you something I should know about?"

"Maybe you're right about finishing your novel, David. I can tell that she still loves you. And you know I always say that where there's love, there's hope."

"I know, Ma," I said.

But it always irritated me when she thought some simple slogan could somehow change the course of my life on a dime. I let the conversation rest in silence for a respectful few seconds and then told her I loved her and ended the call.

Over at the pump, Abbott was squeezing the last of his Mars bar into his mouth, and while he wolfed it down I used the time to take inventory of my life. I wanted another cigarette. Why, I wondered, did I never learn to save my one daily cigarette until after I talked to my mother? Leave it to her to bring up Laura at the end of a conversation. Now I'd be wound up in self-loathing for the rest of the afternoon, thinking about all the ways I was to blame, and about all the time I'd wasted under my enduring delusion that a short story I'd been struggling to novelize since my twenties was forever on the cusp of becoming a great novel. That twenty years of frustration had ruined everything for us, and now I'd spend the night missing Laura and regretting that I'd ever written anything at all. The worst of it would be imagining Laura's narrative in which I was undoubtedly cast as a delusional narcissist who had lured her with perfect, shiny love and left her swimming with a hook through her cheek when she just wanted to be reeled in or released. I knew how to attract, Laura would tell me, but I didn't know how to love—and this was why my novel would forever remain unfinished.

I would often reinvent Laura in my head and talk to her as if she were there beside me. Laura was the expert after all—a therapist and almost a doctor, as my mother liked to remind me, though she never gave Laura any trouble about how many years becoming a doctor was taking her. The fact was that Laura was brilliant, always the better writer of the two of us. And her characterization of me was the spool that any good novelist would begin to wrap a narrative around. Most of her observations made sense, but I could never grasp my character's motivation for not moving forward in life. Even when I dug deep into it during my imaginary conversations with Laura, it seemed that my self-concept would have to completely unravel before that part made any sense at all. A proper treatment would have run the length of a novel, and the core issue, baked right into Laura's plot, was my endless struggle to ever write more than one good chapter.

Abbott tapped the horn a couple of times and ended my rumination. I looked at him and felt a wave of hope pass through me. I was starting to like Abbott, and I was looking forward to getting back on the road and continuing our conversation. But as soon as I started to stand from my place on the table a state police cruiser shot into the station and pulled between us.

I sat back down and lit up a second cigarette and tried to appear casual.

The trooper's door opened and closed and a standard-issue hat rose above the roof of the car on the other side.

"Whoowee! Is that a 308-GTS?" the trooper shouted to Abbott. His voice raised a few notes above the official tone, which I thought was a positive sign. "That's the Magnum car, isn't it?"

Abbott didn't miss a beat. "Does the pope shit in the woods?" he asked. He didn't wait for an answer. He turned the engine over and gunned it, let it come down almost to idle, and then gunned it again.

"I used to dream about owning that car when I was a kid," the trooper said over the sound of the engine, one hand cupped to the side of his mouth to make himself audible.

"Who didn't?" Abbott yelled back. He wound out the engine again and let it fall back to idle. "Why don't you come live in my guest house? You can run my security. I'll let you drive it any time you want."

The trooper smiled at the *Magnum P.I.* reference, childlike as the engine screamed again. Abbott released the clutch and the Ferrari lurched back from the cruiser. For a moment I thought he was going to abandon me, but he shot forward, cut the wheel, and pulled up to the table.

"Come on," he said, "Get rid of that thing. What are you waiting for?"

It was a fair question, but I didn't waste any time thinking about it just then. I planted my cigarette in a big white turd, hopped off the table, vaulted into the car and, as the engine screamed again, I pulled my seat belt forward and buckled in.

4

We tore out of the gas station and headed west. I could almost hear Mike Post's theme song to Magnum P.I. playing in the background. In an episode of Magnum, this would've been the part where Tom Selleck started speaking in voiceover. "I know what you're thinking," he would say, "and you're right." Then, while we took in a bird's eye view of his Ferrari cruising along the beaches of Oahu, he would elaborate. He would talk about the far-fetched inconsistencies in whatever case he was working, and the little voice inside him that was telling him that things didn't quite add up.

But that's not what I was thinking—not the way Magnum would've been suggesting. I was thinking about my mother and about Laura and about Mr. McGee, who was another one of my problems I'll have to get into, and who just wouldn't leave me alone. I was trying to track a life that had gone way off course back to the first wrong turn. It was Abbott who had me thinking this way, and it was because he told his story like a man for whom everything added up through time, all the way to the present moment. Even with a set of plot points that challenged credibility, he spoke with such ease and confidence that one completely unrelated thing seemed to lead naturally to the next. It had the feeling of a story that was going somewhere and that was the element that my life lacked.

To recall a time when my life had any sort of direction, I had to go back at least as far as the publication of "The First Chapter." The story had been written after Laura and I met at a workshop. We were both going to be writers back then, and we spent those first weeks together, loving each other and gazing into each other's eyes and smiling like fools. I was young, and at the time I thought life all but guaranteed that this was a phenomenon that would continue to repeat itself. I could see love affairs, glorious and torrid and inspiring, stretching out to the horizon. The first chapter, I thought—wasn't it always the best chapter?—the whole book ahead, full of possibilities and implicit promises that never had to be kept. A good first chapter could suggest a thousand different novels. Why should a beginning have to be spoiled by an ending?

After I returned home, I spent months consuming the first chapters of every tome I had ever wanted to read but had doubted my resolve to finish. I devoured them. I lugged huge stacks of books from the library and back again. The librarians first regarded me with suspicion and then—I thought—with a sort of competitive envy in the form of raised right eyebrows that suggested my appetite was overreaching if not an outright put-on. I was manic. And I wanted to tell them, "I only read first chapters!" But who would've understood? It would have been just one more point of derision by a group of people who couldn't fathom the world of infinite potential and were ill-equipped to handle it. These were, after all, people devoid of curiosity and wonder and imagination, people who had to follow every path to its pre-scripted conclusion. They lived—I was certain—as if hypnotized and under a spell that would only be released by the two words I never planned to see: *The End*.

"The First Chapter" was my manifesto. The first sentence was a play on the famous first line of *Anna Karenina*. "Every story begins differently; all narratives conclude with the same lie," I wrote. It was an allusion that went completely unrecognized. "The First Chapter" went on in a way that suggested that all stories were not fabrications of reality but a sort of pruning process by which the fabric of reality was reduced to a single spool. Fiction, after all, had trained us to believe the most dangerous lie in human existence—that narrative structures have truth. We had become dependent on these lies, building lives and identities around them, and our sacrifice had been the truth of no-truth. We were no longer comfortable to dwell in pure potentiality. We clung to facts and fabrications as if swinging vine to vine over an abyss in which we didn't know how to swim. We felt safe perhaps—though fear and insecurity would always undermine the foundations of structures built on lies—but the grand illusion that delivered our narrative security asked for the nirvana of the unfinished masterpiece in trade.

I should say that *I* thought "The First Chapter" suggested all of that. The critics, though they loved it, didn't see it that way. The critics celebrated the return of "a timely and precious sort of narrator who has not been so well drawn since Dostoyevsky." I was compared—and, truth be told, it was me in that story—to Raskolnikov and The Underground Man. They psychoanalyzed me as "so unhinged by philosophical ideas and the intellectualization of emotion as to be, in all practicality, a weathervane for the challenges of a generation for which all things are relative." It was as if to say that I was not a genius who wrote like the greats, but a confused kid who inhabited the minds of their most profoundly deranged characters. Without exception, they all saw "The First Chapter," not as the brave new form of a short story it was intended to be, but as the beginning of a promising novel. Not a single critic understood that my short story was never supposed to have an ending. They began to review the novel they imagined before it had even been written. It was heralded as a zeitgeist, as "dystopian and potentially Orwellian in scope..." and as "a testament to the destructive power of a growing nihilism..."

Had I any sense of humor back then, I would've seen the poetry in all of this. The critics were finishing the novel for me. They were living in potential reality. "The First Chapter" was doing what all great first chapters were supposed to do. But the mistake I made was that I had imagined the story as a completed work. They had called my bluff. I had seen the last period as an endpoint. I had, myself, committed the great sin of narration. I believed my story about non-truth contained a deep and specific truth, and so instead of sitting back and enjoying myself as the story fractured into an infinity of imagined novels, I fretted about its reception because I thought I had been misunderstood.

And then, I couldn't help wondering if the world knew me better than I knew myself. I went back and read *Crime and Punishment* and *Notes from the Underground* in their entirety. I felt implicated and ego-wounded and destined for tragedy. The world, it seemed, was trying to write me into a damning narrative and, the way I saw it, I was the only one capable of writing my way out of it.

Meanwhile, I was signed by an agent, and my agent found a publisher who was clamoring for the rest of the novel and was willing to pay through the nose for it. For a cash-strapped, love-struck kid with few other prospects, it was money in the bank. I was offered a handsome advance and I accepted. A few months later, I married Laura. Our first chapter was perfect, beautiful. Our hearts were in every word. We rented a place together and I set up my word processor in a corner to write, and nothing came. Years passed. Laura moved ahead with her life, went back to school. I took an adjunct position to supplement the advance money which was running thin. But with my novel and with us, things stagnated. Rather than write more chapters, we argued until our love was erased and then we rewrote that first beautiful chapter over again. It was a good chapter, full of sweetness and dreams and bursting with potential, but it grew more tired and tedious with every rework. When Laura began to catch on that I had no second chapter in me, I put a down payment on a house with what remained of my advance money as an attempt at subterfuge. The story that would bring me together with Abbott, along with everything that happened afterward, began to write itself.

I didn't even have to lift a finger.

5

The northeast was behind us now. We were heading west on that stretch of road somewhere around Pittsburgh, where the mountains settle down and the hills begin rolling and the land ripples until you hit the plains. The roads become long and straight with very few towns, and the towns that are there are mostly just a string of whistle stops parenthesized by the Appalachians and the Rockies or, if you travel by air, maybe by just a tarmac on either coast.

Abbott was taking full advantage of the ease of navigation. He had one knee bracing the wheel, and he was breaking up his marijuana so that we would make this transition to "the open country" as free men, in body and in mind—or he said something to that effect. When the joint was rolled, he pulled out a gold Zippo from the pocket of his blazer, and then he snapped the lighter open and lit it with one fluid movement of his hand. He set the joint ablaze, took a few quick sips, and passed it my way.

I took a big pull of smoke and locked it down, exhaled, and then I felt the beauty of the scenery rush in as if I'd never seen shadow and sunlight before.

"I've been sailing through life on the winds of cognitive dissonance," I sighed, realizing too late that it was a completely pretentious and nonsensical thing to say. But Abbott thought on it anyway.

"Those sorts of troubles, kid, they usually come with a history of shooting albatrosses."

I laughed—Abbott may have been as stoned as I was. For some reason, I looked up at the sky. I suppose I was half expecting to see an albatross or some other synchronistic sign that things were about to change. In my head, I heard the first few bars of another Mike Post theme song. The song was from that show where a school teacher and an FBI agent are presented with a superhero costume by an alien spacecraft, but they lose the instruction manual and the school teacher is always falling out of the sky in mid-flight and tumbling through the dust with a defeated look on his face. I could almost see him up there in his red suit, flying along beside us, ricocheting off trees and overpasses, clipping road signs, making a general fool of himself. I passed the joint back to Abbott and he put it to his lips and drank it in. He dragged so deep that his back arched and his head tilted back.

"Good song," he said, without releasing his breath.

"*Great* song," I said back. I tapped out a few beats on the side of the door and then let him press the joint into my fingers. "Wait, you hear that too?"

Abbott retrieved his Zippo off the dash, slipped it into his breast pocket and gave the volume dial a long, slow turn. He looked directly into my eyes, nodding his head as I passed the joint back his way with my lungs still full of smoke. It registered that he'd been playing a collection of Mike Post themes since we'd left the gas station. I hadn't imagined the *Magnum P.I.* theme song. Abbott must have slipped the tape into the stereo, inspired by the state cop's recognition of his car.

Now I could remember hearing *The Rockford Files* theme too, and a few others I couldn't put my finger on. The tape had probably cycled two or three times, the tunes blending with the sounds of the wind and the tires. I'd only thought they'd been the work of my imagination.

Abbott was excited that I recognized the song. He was really taken with the moment.

"*Just like the light of the new day...*" he started singing, holding an imaginary microphone and looking directly into my eyes.

I'm sure it sounds uncomfortable, but something about the idea of an aging Tom Selleck singing the theme song to *The Greatest American Hero* captivated my attention and I couldn't look away. Besides that, he was nailing it. Abbott had a first-rate set of pipes.

"*It hit me from out of the blue,*" he continued. He took a moment to break eye contact and salute the blue sky with the imaginary microphone, timing his return to now semi-uncomfortable eye contact perfectly with the last two lines of the verse. I began to feel what I think is usually described as, "a swelling in the heart."

"*Breaking me out of the spell I was in*
Making all of my wishes come true..."

The synthesizer began gathering energy for the triumphant refrain. I exhaled and my smoke rushed toward Abbott's face, but before it reached him it was sucked up through the open targa top and there was only clear air between us. The smoke was behind us now, rising toward the sun and dispersing into the blue sky, and I felt my soul soar with it. I began hammering out the beat on the outside of the door and, though I have a voice that can hit about three notes with any confidence and has about a half an octave of range, I belted out the refrain with Abbott because it didn't feel like there was any other reasonable thing to do:

"Believe it or not, I'm walking on air
I never thought I could feel so free...eee...eee
Flyin' away on a wing and a prayer
Who could it be?
Believe it or not,
it's just me..."

Abbott took another hit off the joint as the song ran through its final verse. "That's right, kid. That's right," he said. "Now you got it." He took another rip off the joint and held onto it, raising it in the air like a chef who had just tasted something exquisite, and then he exhaled and handed it back to me.

For a few moments, it felt like we had it all figured out—new places, new lives, new chapters—it was going to be great. I held the joint as the song went through its last refrain and now it was me I saw flying alongside the car. I was right where the grassy section met the forest. I was dodging trees and slaloming the poles that held the road signs. I watched as my imagined-self accelerated ahead of the Ferrari and crossed into the other lane to dart around oncoming tractor-trailer trucks with complex aerial maneuvers that betrayed a pure, internal joy.

There was no keeping me down. The suit had come with no instruction manual. It had been the source of confusion and frustration and heartbreak and I had wanted to give up so many times, but there I was—I had stuck through it and I had mastered it anyway. I was walking on air. I was free of all the old burdens of mental habit that had left me paralyzed with self-doubt, and I had come to grips with the suit and with myself and I had learned to use it in this world for which both it and I sometimes seemed so ill-fitted.

I took another look at myself. The stunts were becoming more complex by the minute. The suit and my creative mind had merged and we had moved beyond inhibition to something beautiful.

I looked so happy.

I put the joint to my lips, and it was right as I inhaled that I felt the heaviness enter the car. In that instant, it was as if all the levity and hope that had been circulating a moment before vanished without a trace. I wondered if the drug had turned on me like it sometimes did, but that wasn't it. It was something different, something I recognized from my younger years when I used to hitchhike regularly and perfect strangers would often, in the middle of ordinary conversations, feel compelled to confess to horrible things.

I turned to Abbott.

"I have to ask you something," he said. He shut the stereo off and moved both hands to the wheel. "You can get rid of that thing. I'm done with it."

"Sure," I said.

I blew the smoke out of my lungs and then flicked the roach up through the open Targa top. It rose for a moment and then the wind ignited it and it shot back like a rocket. I readied myself for Abbott's confession. This moment seemed to repeat endlessly throughout my life, and I could never find the heart to shut it down. I was a magnet for lunatics.

"Ask away," I said.

Abbott swallowed and cleared his throat. "You ever hear of Schrödinger's cat?"

I had a vague recollection of the theoretical experiment. People in university circles were always mentioning it. A cat is placed in a box where it can't be observed. There is a fifty-fifty chance it will be exposed to noxious fumes. It is impossible to know if it was exposed or not, so it is considered to exist in both potentialities—alive and dead at the same time.

I told him I had.

"Well let me ask you something."

I waited.

"You're a cat. In a box. You're both alive and dead. Right?"

I thought about it. Just a few moments ago I was free. Walking on air. And now I was back in a box, debating my existence. I tried to see the humor in that.

"Until the box is opened," I said. "I think that's how it works."

"Fine. Until the box is opened."

"Okay?" I said.

"Well, here's my question, kid. I understand the observer effect or the Heisenberg Principle, or whatever you call it. But, what does it feel like to be that cat?"

"You mean to be both alive and dead?" I said.

"That's what I mean, kid. To be suspended in between two separate realities, with nothing being either true or false—until, as you said, the box is opened—whatever that means. How does that feel?"

I had no answer. I was high as a kite, and my feeling of ease had just given way like a trap door and I'd fallen instantaneously back into a feeling of confusion. I wasn't sure if he was talking about himself or about me, but the question left me feeling pinned down. It hit me like an accusation. I had lived most of my life as though I were locked away in Schrödinger's box. I was always suspended between two realities, never fully committed, some base level of anxiety, some level of doubt and discomfort about myself always playing faintly in the background like Abbott's Mike Post themes. My novel was in the box, both written and unwritten. And until it was written, I was both a great writer and a complete failure. Even my marriage had always seemed to exist right there alongside Schrödinger's cat. From a romantic distance I was deeply in love, but inside the house, at the dinner table, I sometimes felt like a man standing inside a doorway, not knowing whether he should hang up his hat.

We were both silent for a while, and when it was safe to assume the strand of the former conversation was broken, Abbott began to tell me about his more recent past. He had owned a franchise of Shaolin Kung-Fu schools from the eighties through the mid-nineties, and somehow that had segued into a career buying and selling rare sports cars. This enterprise involved a friend named Denton White, who he described as "an almost lifelong friend." Their business had been plainly named Bodyman's Garage. An aura of mystery surrounded the rare sports car operation, and as he sketched it out, I got the feeling it wasn't all completely legal and that Abbott may have even had his own troubles with the law.

This played into another motivation for Abbott's trip west. Denton White was in trouble and he needed Abbott's help. The two hadn't seen each other for years, and Abbott said he'd only been able to locate Denton with the help of a guy named Harelip Lenny. Abbott had employed Lenny for some other business twenty-something years before hiring him to locate Denton. That first time had been to track down some leads on Lucille, who had apparently been missing for almost half a century. Harelip had been hired after a long period of mourning and doubt, Abbott said. Out of the blue, Abbott had received a bit of crucial evidence that all but proved Lucille *existed*, and it reignited a hope he had all but let go. That was the word he used too. It wasn't that the evidence had proved she was *alive*. He said the evidence had proved she *existed*, and I found that odd.

Just as I was about to put some questions to that word, the Ferrari began to sputter and the conversation shifted back to Denton. I gathered more by tone than anything else that Abbott's relationship with Denton was colored by some kind of rivalry, but beneath that—and he spelled this out unambiguously once the Ferrari was back up to speed—was a sense of both brotherhood and debt. Denton had rescued Abbott from bad situations once or twice, and now was Abbott's chance to repay him.

It was a lot of exposition all at once and I'm sure I've gotten some of it wrong, but the fine details weren't really the main point. The main point was that in all of his years of sleuthing, Harelip Lenny had never been able to locate Lucille. He also could never uncover what transpired—"in linear reality"—between Ravi Shankar's set at Woodstock in 1969 when Abbott stepped through that door of light, and October of 1972 when he woke naked and shivering on the dirt floor of an abandoned miner's shack somewhere south-southwest of Ely, Nevada, with forty-something years of memories and a life that had disappeared. In the reality of the timeline Abbott was living now, he had gone missing for three years. But in Abbott's memory, the missing years between Woodstock and Ely had been decades. The source of those memories was as illusive and impossible to account for as the whereabouts of Lucille and the time-space location of the little diner they had run together, day after day, from their twenties right into their golden years when Abbott had jumped through time again.

6

Before I get into the next part of the story, where things become decidedly strange and unbelievable—and which is bound to cause discomfort for anyone who likes to stick to the pathways laid by clear, evidence-based and peer-reviewed scientific theories—I should probably explain what it was that kept my own mind open to Abbott and the unlikely narrative of his life.

The cynics will assume that the failed writer in me smelled a story I wanted to steal, and it's true. I smelled an opportunity of some sort. Maybe I thought I could steal Abbott's craft, or at least learn something imitable from him. The man had the gift of gab in spades. He was a natural storyteller, churning out one chapter after the next without deliberation. His story chugged forward with a feeling of inevitability. He had everything I lacked—the voice full of authority, the charisma, the confidence, the sense of direction. In his Ferrari, Abbott was one of those drivers who never seemed to look at the road. His eyes fixed on me as if we were drinking pints together at a bar, or they gazed far off in the distance as he collected his thoughts, or they focused on the joint he was rolling, or on his own hands as they waved in the air. He told his story that same way. The narrative might have careened this way and that, weaved in and out of traffic, cornered on two wheels with the engine smoking, threatening to explode. It didn't shake me. He had my implicit trust, and for some reason I believed he would deliver me to some predestination written by the fates and a deep truth I'd spent my whole life searching for would be revealed. I never thought for my safety.

I won't deny that these same attributes also lent Abbott the air of a salesman, even a confidence-man, but I arrested any concern about being conned with my belief that my attention as a listener was the only thing I had of any value to Abbott. Our relationship didn't depend on confidence. Rather, it existed in that quantum state where things are neither true nor false and which, in fiction, is the basic contract between the reader and the writer simply known as *suspension of disbelief*. And as a guy who had sat down day after day for twenty years believing that *The First Chapter* (my attempted novelization of "The First Chapter") would emerge from my personal Schrödinger's box as a finished work, the suspension of disbelief was a gift that I possessed in spades.

In my youth, I'd spent several years on the road hitchhiking from place to place, exchanging the service of suspending disbelief for rides. In the economy of the highway, the driver is the big fish and the hitchhiker is the remora, the sin eater. He is usually taken on as a long-haul passenger for one of two reasons—either the people he rides with are challenged by doubt and want to make him a believer of whatever great truth they are wrestling with at the moment, or they have a story that needs to be heard. In those days, I would sometimes be tasked with staving off disbelief that others found overwhelming. Other times I took in indigestible bits of experience for rumination and offered back small insights. Now and then, drivers could no longer suspend disbelief in themselves and their own basic goodness. I would hear a confession and stare dead on into the most gruesome aspects of a person's psyche and be asked to believe that they were redeemable.

It was natural to me. In my mind, light and dark aspects exist without that solid wall between them that most people so carefully fortify. The boundary is porous, each side bleeding into the other so that I've never clearly defined myself as a good or bad person or as any type of person whatsoever. Under the right circumstances and the influence of the necessary bio-chemicals and narrative triggers, I'm sure I could be capable of everything. I can sense these potentials inside of myself so clearly that I always suspect that people who define themselves in opposition to this or that great evil are hiding from their true natures. Terrible confessions have never revolted me so much as filled me with a sense of sadness and relief. My relief was that eating sins leaves a different and less permanent mar on a person's soul than committing them. My sadness was for the drivers. Their actions had revealed a truth of themselves that could be confessed and forgiven, but which left a mark in the world and on the soul that could never be unwritten.

Abbott wasn't completely different from anyone I'd encountered. He had doubts to wrestle, and great truths to share, and sins to confess, but he also possessed something else that I hadn't experienced before. When I observed myself listening to Abbott, I was convinced that what was truly compelling lay deeper below the surface than the story or even the art of telling the story. Like that fungal wire he had sensed at Woodstock so many years before, it ran through both of us. He was broken, divided, and incomplete, and maybe that was our connection. That fractured part of him was so definite and certain and solid that

I almost felt like I could take my bearings by it. The fracture—our common fracture—was where the story lay. And though the story would often be absurd and unbelievable, the fractured part of him that produced the story was so true that I couldn't pull myself away.

It helped that Abbott seemed to be searching for the truth of the story as much as he was acting as its narrator. He wasn't trying to convince me of anything political or personal or religious. His story didn't strike me as a buttress against harsh insight or an artistic re-framing of some personal failing. Much like Abbott himself, it was the rarest of things in today's climate where all narratives seem to be hijacked as hosts for any number of petty purposes. It was a true story, an adventure, and it would strike me, at times, as something almost epic. I had this wonderful feeling when I was with Abbott and when the story was rolling, of no longer acting as a scavenger, cleaning the rot off the old bones of other men's souls or chewing over and over the same old festering chunks of my own, but that I was acting as a sort of midwife whose purpose was to help bring something beautiful and pure and perhaps healing into the world.

Of course, this should all be taken with a good deal of salt. The entire time I was with Abbott, his medical-grade marijuana was never far away—his special blend of indica and sativa, concocted for subtle, targeted effects that were lost on me. Considering how things ended, even some of those who take me at my word on Abbott have suggested the marijuana made me dull and malleable, and I'm sure it did. But I also had a span of months away from Abbott which provided ample time for reflection and discernment. What I always came to was that Abbott's story was too big and unbelievable to be anything other than true—and even necessary. In my experience, most stories have a way of wrapping around whatever narrative core is most expedient to the narrator's cause. Small stories are sufficient to reflect the world we already see, or to push this or that political or social end, while big stories can't be managed. They have a way of prying the world open and showing it as it really is.

So it didn't set off any alarm bells that Abbott claimed to be a time traveler or that Harelip Lenny had the sound of a made-up character. The way I saw it, these were the grand overtures, the broad strokes that came out of the bigness of Abbott's heart. This was the stuff I believed in, the pure *Truth* of fiction. Later, I knew, conflicting data would fill in the blank spaces and provide depth and texture and form and doubt, and when that happened—I made a personal note—I would not be too hard on Abbott. I would try not to go on about inconsistencies and Occam's razor, and I would try not to destroy his big story with some small-minded, therapy-room word salad like the world had always done to me. I would quiet that little voice that Thomas Magnum was so fond of listening to and I would allow myself to dwell in the greatness of imagination and suspend disbelief as I had done so easily and generously in my younger years.

I even began to have a feeling that not just Abbott, but both of us were traveling toward some personal grail, and that *our* big story would help us find the power to reclaim a lost artifact to our consciousness and repair the timeline that left us wandering lost through the present world.

Part Two

Kung Fu Lunatics

Show me a sane man and I will cure him for you.

— Carl Jung

7

If you've ever tried to have a serious conversation with a mother while her toddler alternately plays happily and tugs at her clothes in tantrum, maybe you can understand my frustration with Abbott and his Ferrari. His beautiful little sports car turned out to be a tyrant. It seemed to grow more agitated by the hour. Between Vermont's Green Mountains and Ohio, it had begun a transformation from an elegant supercar to a jalopy. Finally, it commanded every beat of his story. One misfire and all conversational and narrative momentum would come to a screeching halt, only to have to be slowly and deliberately restored. At times, as Abbott's story edged toward revelation and I hoped against hope that the Ferrari would crest a small hill without balking, I would imagine myself as Sisyphus, coaxing Abbott's story along, trying to draw his attention away from the misfires and sputtering so the story could continue without backsliding once more.

The mountains had become the foothills and now the foothills were giving way to rolling fields of corn and soy, but there were always more hills. At times, I was ready to throw in the towel and get some rest and forget the whole thing, but then without me even being completely conscious of the change, we would find ourselves running down a long stretch of flat, open road with the engine firing right on the money and the narrative would start to level out. Finally, I thought the moment had come to ask Abbott about the door of light he'd walked through and about the missing time, and about Lucille.

"Were the three things connected?"

Abbott was more relaxed now. He reclined his seat back a few clicks and took a breath before reaching into his pocket to pull out his gold Zippo. For a moment I thought he was going to light another joint, and I was going to have to politely decline. But he just held it there in the space between us, bridged between his finger and his thumb.

"You see that, kid?" he said.

He was holding it with the air of a magician about to make a coin disappear. I took a look and tried to signal that I was really taking it in, not sure whether he wanted me to take it from his hand or just examine it with my eyes.

"That's it," he said. He slipped it back into his breast pocket. "That's the only relic that came across with me."

"From Woodstock?" I asked.

"From the other place," he said.

"You mean, through the door of golden light?"

"Not exactly," he said. "You see, I was naked when I woke up in that little miner's shack in Ely, but the Zippo was clutched in my hand." He lifted his hand off the gearshift to show me how tightly he'd been holding it.

I nodded.

"At times, that lighter's the only thing that reminds me I'm not completely nuts. That, and Harelip Lenny. Almost thirty years of intermittent investigation—by a licensed P.I. mind you—and not a single record of my existence between '69 and '72. No traffic citations, no arrests, no automobile registrations, no taxes. Not even—as they say on TV—a parking ticket."

I waited for him to go on. When he didn't continue, I asked for an explanation.

He described to me how it was when he woke up in the desert. The gray dawn filtering through the sideboards of the wooden miner's shack. The smoldering fire he was curled up beside. The shivering. The strangeness of his own body. The feeling of disorientation, and that lighter in his hand. Before he even walked outside to find himself in a desert landscape, surrounded by towering limestone formations, he already had a laundry list of things he couldn't explain. Like, for instance, where was Lucille?

"Let me get this straight," I said. "You walked through a door of light at Woodstock in 1969, and when you woke up halfway across the country three years later you were already married to Lucille?"

"Yes and no, kid. It's actually stranger than that. We had been married for forty years. But I woke up and she'd vanished. That whole life had vanished." He snapped his fingers in the air to show me how quickly it had happened.

He told me when he'd gone to sleep, Lucille had been right there beside him. He'd lit her cigarette just before nodding off. His arm was draped over her and he could smell the Pert Shampoo and the smoke of Pall Malls in her hair. But when he opened his eyes in the miner's shack everything had changed. The only thing left was questions: Where was their little bed? Why wasn't he in the back room of her late father's diner where they'd slept for the last three decades?

"Hold on," I said. "I don't understand where you're getting those thirty or forty years. You disappeared from '69 to '72, right? You were only gone for three."

He shook his head. "That's not the way I remembered it. I sat there in the shack trying to figure it out. Believe me, kid, I did my best to make sense of it. Maybe my mind was going and I'd wandered off, you know? Maybe I'd had a stroke. Maybe I was dead, and the shack was holding my soul in some kind of purgatory. I considered everything."

Abbott thought about Lucille waking in their bed alone, searching for him, calling his name throughout the diner. She would be confused too. He listened for her voice in the wind that whispered through the slats, but it was only wind.

"Lucille?" he called.

He needed to get back to help her open the diner, to warm the grill and whisk the eggs while Lucille put Joan Baez on the jukebox and set napkins and flatware on the tables. Who would carry the big tray of burgers out of the walk-in to thaw, and who would pull the bow tight at the back of Lucille's apron? Who would kiss her cool forehead when she turned her head and smiled?

Whatever had happened, Abbott could figure out the details later. It would be easy enough to find his way home. He could hike back into Death Valley and look for that landmark thermometer that rose thirteen stories into the sky. That couldn't be too hard. Lucille's Diner was just inside the farthest reach of its evening shadow. He would be back by late afternoon and they would have eggs and coffee and a stack of pancakes and sort through the whole mess together. And when the shadow of that great thermometer swung across the black and white tiles, he and Lucille would embrace as they always had. He would kiss her lips. He would put on some Country Joe McDonald and wink at her and hold out his hand and invite her to dance.

Abbott rose off the dirt floor. He stretched his back. He felt good—vital—like he could walk a long distance. But when he swung the door of the miner's cabin open and took stock of the limestone formations surrounding him, his heart dropped. Things were even further askew than he'd first imagined.

The morning sunlight had a filtered, golden quality, like a shot out of a Sergio Leone film, and he hadn't seen that sort of sunlight in over a decade, perhaps two—or three. On the horizon, he could see the dust trail left by a Jeep. It was rising from the desert floor. Even at that distance, he could hear the springs of the suspension and a peculiar sound in the transmission that signaled to him a bygone era. Cars, even old cars, didn't sound that way anymore. Abbott stood there as the Jeep approached—dirty, naked, but unashamed.

The Jeep pulled up beside him. It was driven by a park ranger, a burly-looking man whose face had been scarred by acne in youth but had become rough and swarthy from the sun. The man had the look of a Marine, retired maybe, but still fond of the old haircut. By Abbott's estimation, he was about forty years old. Just a kid.

The ranger shut off his engine and took a moment to look Abbott up and down. He reached for a canteen on the passenger seat, unscrewed the top and took a swig before passing it to Abbott.

Abbott drank. Swallowed. Even the water tasted different, less metallic. He passed the canteen back to the ranger.

"I saw your smoke," the ranger said. "I figured. Happens more often than you'd think. At least once a year I see smoke, and then I find one of you hippies holed up here. Always cold and starving and naked. Always with that same wild look in your eyes. Peyote is my guess. I never ask." He set the canteen back on the seat and took a moment to roll open a bag of Beech-Nut and tuck a wad of tobacco under his lip. "The mind is a dangerous place, friend. I seen that in Nam. You wouldn't believe it if I told you."

Abbott didn't respond, even after a length of silence that would've made most men uncomfortable. The ranger spit an ounce or so of tobacco juice onto the desert floor and changed the subject. "I don't know where you come from or where you're headed kid, but you look like you haven't eaten in a week. Let's get some clothes on you and I'll take you into Ely for breakfast."

It hit Abbot strange. "Kid," the ranger had said.

The word reverberated in Abbott's ears like the shot of a sniper's rifle, the late warning of a life that had already been lost. He knew some of his problems could be solved. The sun would warm him as it passed through the southern sky. An empty belly could be filled. A naked body could be clothed. But if a forty-year-old ranger were calling Abbott, "kid," something had gone terribly wrong. Abbott was anything but a kid. For the last forty years, he'd grown old and happy running a diner with Lucille, the wife he'd loved and adored more than anything in the world.

The ranger hopped out of the jeep and Abbott studied him while he rifled through the back of the truck. The man was a straight arrow. Nothing about him spelled out the type of person who would mock a confused old man.

The ranger walked over and handed Abbott a pair of cutoffs and a t-shirt. "Try these on for size."

Abbot took the clothes and dressed himself and looked out across the spaghetti western morning with a sense of dread. When he caught a glance at his young face in the ranger's dusty side-view mirror as he stepped into the jeep, his vague sense of dread turned into actual horror. He didn't see the content old Abbott looking back at him. He was no longer Abbott who'd worked in silent adoration for forty years as a grill cook alongside the easily blushing Lucille. His face was young. He was, as the ranger said, just a kid. He'd somehow cycled back. He was, once again, that tormented, lost soul of a boy who could not find his proper place in the fracas of the churning world.

He was miserable.

Ten minutes later, as they bumped up and down between the dusty earth and the golden sun toward the paved roads of Ely—Credence playing on the radio, asking Abbott if he had ever seen the rain coming down on just such a day—Abbott had the first in a series of fits of uncontrollable sobbing that would plague him for the better part of three years before becoming a chronic condition, like a malarial fever, a malady that would crop up year by year as if to remind him of everything that had been lost somewhere deep within the jungles of his mind.

8

We were finally getting somewhere. We'd come out of the trees and the story was beginning to open up like the horizon before us. This is probably when I first had the thought that I might draw the story out of Abbott and steal it from him, commit it to memory and write it down as my own. At certain moments it was difficult to sit there beside him. The story, as I said, was curative in its way, but it was also painful, and not only because of Abbott's suffering and the way he brought me into the story to suffer beside him. Listening to Abbott's narrative had a way of magnifying the senselessness of the twenty years I'd wasted sitting in my little room above the garage, rewriting and revising my one brilliant chapter and failing to ever make a dent in a second. His story and his voice—the easy flow and the ring of truth amidst the absurdity—made me wonder if I'd ever been anything more than a poseur.

This point would be hammered home in the coming months. Abbott and I would become separated and his long letters would show me that his ability to write wasn't simply born out of a musical ear and the gifts of good windpipes and cathedral-like sinuses. He could also put words to paper. I would be reading and rereading those letters with marvel and tinges of envy right up until I found myself in this place and the letters, so they told me, went mysteriously missing.

Though I can't capture Abbott's words perfectly, I can still hear his voice in my memory as though he's in the seat beside me, or walking through the darkness, or speaking to me from the creased pages of his missives like Ravi Shankar's sitar spoke to him in those final Woodstock hours.

That's the state I was resting in when the Ferrari's engine started stuttering again. We had just come through maybe thirty or forty miles of level ground and uninterrupted narrative and it was irritating and a little heartbreaking to confront the realization that the delicate strand of the story was about to snap. To his credit, Abbott took a breath and managed to continue. For almost a minute the Ferrari ran without a hitch and it seemed like we might overcome the assault on Abbott's temperament. But just as his narrative began to flow the engine stumbled again and, while we both held our breath, it dashed all hopes of recovery with a horrific backfire followed by metallic banging and grinding. Within seconds, the engine's once perfectly pitched, eight-thousand RPM scream had been replaced by a gallop and hiss that called to mind a steam-powered locomotive, and the 308 was chugging along the highway at a top speed that would have made it unsuitable as a pace car for a foot race. You didn't need to be Mr. Goodwrench to guess the thing had thrown a rod or suffered some other grave and antiquated form of mechanical calamity.

Abbott switched on his warning lights and pulled onto the shoulder where we continued to chug along at a jogger's pace. He let out a long string of profanities from which I gathered—wrongly, it turned out—that he had been married two times since Lucille, and that both linear-time wives had been uninspiring in the sack, lacking in punctuality, indolent, late-risers, full of unending complaints, demanding of time, money and emotional energy, and that still, despite everything, neither of those two wives held a candle to the Ferrari's ability to drive Abbott to the very point of self-destruction. He finished his tirade with a clear declaration of his intent to divorce the vehicle once and for all.

"Kid," he said. "I'm gonna tell you something."

And then he told me a number of things. He told me he rued the day he ever became involved with the dressed-up Barbie car. He said something about trophy wives and putting lipstick on a pig and he told me he should have kicked her to the curb years ago. He hit the horn six or seven times, holding down the last of those soundings far too long, and then he said what was more than clear to both of us:

"We gotta get this bitch off the road."

We had barely crossed into Indiana when he pulled off the interstate. "Change of plans, kid. We'll detour north to Fairfield, Iowa." He said. "I know a guy."

This guy, it turned out, had been Denton White's right-hand man at Bodyman's Garage. Abbott said he was "a helluva guy." Denton, he told me, was a mechanical genius. And though Denton's right-hand man wasn't at quite that same level, he knew his stuff. The right-hand man was more of a craftsman and a psychonaut. He'd traveled with the Grateful Dead right up to the end, modifying VW vans, school buses and utility trucks into moving homes which, once parked, could expand, Tardis-like into two-story residences with pop-out bedrooms and slide-out kitchens or widow's walks.

Abbott told me how Denton and his right hand used to install spinning license plates for purposes of deception. They'd wire cut-off switches for a car's rear lights in case a person had to lose the police at night. Abbott was excited. He described rotating compartments for hauling drugs or hiding cash, and then he went silent for a moment before adding that some of their later clients had compartments made for guns. But Denton and his right hand man had eventually relocated Bodyman's Garage to Fairfield to escape that life, and they took up with a meditative community in the Iowa cornfields.

Denton was a sort of brother to Abbott. He had helped Abbott out of jams and gotten him into others, but he was as true-blue as a man could be. He was the type of man, Abbott said, you could trust with your life. And though Denton wouldn't be around, his right hand wouldn't let us down.

The sun was getting low over the cornfields and it was Saturday evening. I knew how these things went, particularly when you were dealing with old deadheads, retired and desperate for company in the country. If I continued with Abbott, I wouldn't be getting anywhere anytime soon. With the car acting the way it was, we would be lucky to make Fairfield by morning. There would be catching up to do. We'd spend the morning smoking herb and the evening drinking beer. The next morning would be Sunday. Parts couldn't be ordered. The bag of herb would come out again. When the parts were ordered on Monday they wouldn't be in stock. I imagined myself in a weedy backyard holed up in a rusted-out van on blocks for the next week or two living off cornflakes and Snickers bars while my heroic journey to finish my novel returned to stasis, and it filled me with anxiety. I was beginning to like Abbott. I liked him a great deal more than I liked most people, and I was starting to think that his story, or maybe *our* story, might be the way out of the jam I was in. I saw it as a possible answer to the book I owed my publisher and the way out of my legal and financial issues, and maybe even the way back to Laura's heart. But I was also desperate to keep moving. My life was wobbling like a gyro at the end of its spin, and without constant motion I was sure my whole world would collapse.

Abbott's Ferrari sputtered farther and farther from the interstate while I tried to quench all my feelings of empathy and camaraderie and obligation—and even a real desire to see how things might naturally unfold if for once I just let them and allowed our story to continue in its own way. But I didn't have a chance to offer my excuse.

"For years I worried that opening Bodyman's with Quickfoot had been a terrible mistake," Abbott said.

"Quickfoot?" I said.

"Denton," he said, "They called him Quickfoot in the institution. Used to be a fast sonovabitch too, when he wasn't catatonic."

We were traveling on level ground, but the car trouble had him in an uphill mood.

"What kind of institution?" I asked. I tried to sound casual about the question, as if I were asking him something inconsequential, like what kind of cheese he wanted on a sandwich.

"Guns aren't for guys like us," he mumbled "It got away from us, man." He didn't seem to be speaking to me anymore.

A car passed us on the left with its horn pinned down and Abbott didn't even react. He seemed lost in a thought. The Ferrari was jolting and bucking the two of us forward and back like a couple of old cowhands on horseback.

"I miss that guy, you know," he said, speaking into the past, but not mumbling anymore. "Denton was always a piece of work. A real piece of work. But he was my brother."

Abbott sighed. We both did. For a few minutes, we listened to the gallop of the 308 as we bumped and scraped along the secondary road. Even in late summer, the frost heaves of spring hadn't quite lain down. It was a nice evening. The air was soft, a little bit damp with dew, and if you didn't have expectations for the Ferrari, it was actually not bad to sputter down those country roads with the Targa top off and the continuous gallop of the engine. It had an old-timey feel, as if Abbott was not just an aging lunatic perhaps a few days off his meds, but really was a time-traveler, and the two of us were cruising around in another era when things still moved at a pace you could wrap your mind around.

I found myself wondering about Denton, this character shrouded in sadness. Where had Abbott met him? Why had they turned to guns? Was I reading too much into the story, or had their relationship soured? I can't quite say why—maybe it was desperation, or exhaustion, or the last hope of the hopeless—but I half-expected to find some insight in Abbott's real or imagined world. I had this feeling that something in his story might finally bridge the distance between the little island where I'd spent my life, and the mainland of humanity I sometimes watched from the edge of the sea. I imagined a story that could sail me across the water to that confounding place—with its twinkling lights and smoky chimneys, and where sometimes when the sea was glassy smooth, I heard music from across the water that was beautiful and full of joy and haunted me with loneliness.

I didn't have to ask. The Ferrari, like so many of us do, settled into its ill and broken way of functioning as if that was what it had been made for. It seemed it would get no worse and no better and that it might be able to jog along at tractor speed for many years. The two of us relaxed into the new pace and Abbott began to open up about his old friend, Denton "Quickfoot" White. Denton had helped guide Abbott back to the linear world when things looked bleak and hopeless, and he had traveled with him in that new and strange world as a friend for a time. This was before they became competitive arch-rivals in business, Abbott explained, and before they forgot the lessons that had brought them back from the very brink of sanity, the lessons that reminded them that only a very few things in life are essential.

"The problem with time traveling forward," Abbott told me as the car jogged along through the cool Indiana evening—and I think he just meant living day to day, the way we all presumably do—"is that the only landmarks anyone recognizes are in the present or the past.

"You see?" he said, "It makes a guesswork of navigating toward any given future. It's not much different when you go back in time," he said. "You spend your life waiting for things that haven't happened yet. Then, when they finally happen, you're never in the right place. You rush after them and you're always too late. You're like a surfer chasing the last wave."

I took in what he said. It was one of those perfect August evenings. Perfect temperature. Perfect humidity. One of those rare moments in life when you don't have to shiver or sweat and there's no war being fought between the inside and outside of your body. It allowed the things he was saying to penetrate. I had no defenses up anymore. Everything seeped in.

9

Abbott said the beauty of that early Nevada morning was etched in his mind. The signature of the era was written on everything. It was striking. Time isn't just a point in a long series of events with all other things being neutral, he told me. Each time brings forth its own unique palette. Smells, colors, sounds, feelings—they belong to time. It's almost as if the life and struggles of an era are created by Time itself, and not the other way around. We're always thinking about the way we felt *at* a time, he said, as if we're shaped by events. As if we shape events. As if we change Time. But when you actually travel through time, you realize how solipsistic that idea is. We don't give Time any credit. We live with its constant company, and the mood of a time shapes us like the moon shapes the tides.

It wasn't just the Creedence on the radio, or the spaghetti western light, or the creak of the coil springs in the ranger's Jeep. The signature of Time itself was unmistakable. Even as Abbott longed for Lucille, he noticed a hint of nostalgia, an old feeling of hope, a sense of standing on the cusp of change. Waking up in the past was like walking into a childhood home. The smells, the sound of the stairs and floorboards creaking under his feet, the way light slanted through the windows and caught the dust. Time was that home. It sent a surge of memories his way that took his mind off Lucille for a few moments while he bumped along in the ranger's Jeep and tried to pull himself together.

He remembered the last years he'd spent with his parents—golden-gloves matches with his father cheering, his mother singing in the kitchen with a shaky voice that was so full of love and heartbreak that it could sweeten coffee. He remembered drinking a can of Miller and smoking herb with a girl, a sexy little Marxist he'd met in The Village, and hearing Crosby, Stills & Nash harmonize together for the first time, and how the beauty of it all nearly blew his mind.

By the time the ranger parked the jeep outside the drugstore, Abbott's sobbing had quieted. He walked in and sat down at the lunch counter and picked up the menu. He just needed to make it through breakfast. It was going to get easier. He just needed to take things one step at a time.

A kind, older lady walked over, tightening her apron strings. She set down a saucer and a mug in front of him and pulled a notepad out of her apron pocket.

"Honey?" she asked him. She poured his mug full of coffee. "Do you know what you want?"

That was all it took for his mental state to collapse into chaos. He felt so far away from Lucille—age, space, time—it was even further than that. The smell of burnt coffee and pancakes, the sound of the spatula scraping the grill, the ding of the bell whenever an order was filled—it was too much.

A gasp of breath moved up from the top of his chest and he caught it in his throat. He pushed it back down.

One moment at a time, he thought.

He lifted his coffee to his mouth and took a sip to steady his nerves.

His hand was shaking.

"Honey?" the waitress said.

Somewhere along the counter, he heard the clink of a Zippo. He smelled the smoke of a Pall Mall. Something was burning him. His coffee was dripping off the counter, spilling onto his lap.

"Hun? Are you okay?"

He looked at the waitress but he couldn't quite make her out.

"Lucille?" he asked.

He wondered if it had all been a dream, if he'd fallen asleep on Lucille's lunch counter or if he was just now waking up in their little bed. He wished that's what it was. How many dreams had fooled him into making this same desperate wish before? And in how many dreams had the wish seemed equally foolish and hopeless? He wanted to rise onto his elbow and kiss Lucille and throw his apron on and take the hamburgers out of the walk-in to thaw. He wanted to fire up the grill and cook.

Abbott tried to answer the waitress, but when he opened his mouth his chest heaved again and he felt his tenuous grip on his emotional state slip out of his control. His body began quaking and the great fits of sobbing he'd struggled to overcome for the entire trip to Ely flowed out of him without resistance. He collapsed on the counter and he was slipping toward the floor when the park ranger caught him by the arm.

"He's having a seizure," somebody said.

The ranger yelled for an ambulance.

Soon Abbott felt himself biting down on a wooden spoon. He tasted pancake batter. When the EMTs arrived, Abbott had to be sedated and restrained and carried out of the drugstore on a stretcher.

He kept calling for Lucille and then sobbing himself into convulsions, then finding that spoon between his teeth again.

The ambulance delivered Abbott to the local hospital where he was treated for exhaustion, dehydration, and exposure, but when his condition didn't improve after several weeks, an emergency court order was brought before a judge and Abbott was involuntarily committed to the care of the state.

10

About a year before Abbott arrived at Ella Rawson State Hospital, Denton White was wheeled in on a metal gurney flanked by two strong orderlies. He was gaunt and thickly bearded and seated in the half-lotus position. This look, combined with his bugged-out eyes and wide open mouth, lent him the appearance of a monk who had come upon a startling realization and was about to say something incredible. All eyes followed Denton. By the time the orderlies had lifted him from his wheeled carriage and sat him on his bed, a small crowd of support staff had gathered in his room. The head nurse came in and hung a bag of intravenous solution above him. Everybody waited for something important to happen. Denton's Maharishi-like appearance, his meditative posture, and his rhythmic, almost hypnotic rocking, had everyone hanging on the edge of his unspoken sentence.

But after two weeks of uninterrupted rocking, after a thousand little grunts and hums that piqued interest but ultimately proved to be only preambles to more of the same, people began to lose interest. The head nurse who had been standoffish toward Denton from the moment she'd hung that first bag of saline, suggested that his jaw had been dislocated mid-yawn. The same thing had happened to the husband of a friend, she said, though her friend had responded very differently from the hospital staff. Her friend hadn't hung on waiting for anything, and certainly not her husband's next words. The husband's locked jaw provided her with a short but much-needed weekend respite that ended far too quickly. Monday came, and their family doctor pried the man's mouth open and it snapped shut with a clatter of teeth and a groan. Then, to the wife's dismay, it opened right back up again. In the head nurse's opinion, it was likely that something of this sort, and not satori, was responsible for Denton's silence as well.

"Hold on," I said. "Where were you as all of this was going on?"

"I'm getting to that, kid," Abbott said. "Give me a second."

"But how could you—" I started to ask. Then I thought better of my question. I made a noise as though I'd found my own answer. "I see," I said. "Sorry I interrupted."

But something curious was beginning to occur. Abbott's narrative voice was shifting to the third person and it was starting to reveal hints of a developing omniscience. Some of this could be overlooked. Over the years of their friendship, the great portion of these next scenes and observations from the institution could have been related to Abbott by Denton. But then there were other things that I found harder to believe—like how either of them could have known the private contents of other people's minds.

As a writer, or maybe as a composition teacher, the inconsistency bothered me. The first few lapses into the omniscient voice left me struggling to restrain myself, as I did above. I wanted to pull out my grading pen and mark it in red as the narrative blemish that it was. But each time this feeling welled up, I would remind myself of my earlier commitment to suspend disbelief, and my resolution to not assail Abbott's story with Occam's razor, and all those other good intentions I'd whispered to myself in my own private and magnanimous thoughts. And I would let it slide.

I mention this now because Abbott's narrative omniscience and his bird's eye view of events only continued to expand as he got deeper into the story. Initially, it was jolting. But as with the Ferrari and as with most things in life, I grew accustomed to it. In his letters, his omniscience would become so complete that it was no longer worthy of notice. By that time, it had made its way into my mythos. It was as real as the earth and sun and all the proclaimed distance in between. That's the trick that Abbott's story played. It had the steady cadence of a romance scam, drawing me up to the rooftop, out to the ledge, and onto a tightrope stretched across the chasm below. Each step was only ever so slightly more anxious. Eventually, one finds oneself suspended between two points, high above the ground, and there is no logical way to go but forward. I can only acknowledge that this narrative flaw exists. Rather than try to repair what I don't understand, I will continue in the way Abbott told the story to me.

The institution's resident psychotherapist, Doctor Boris Schlotzsky, didn't believe Denton's problem was physical, but after another week without a single word, he conceded that a specialist should be called in to perform an examination and rule out physical causes. The specialist arrived and he received assistance from the head nurse, who told him about her friend's husband while she handed the doctor a series of scopes and stainless steel instruments. The physician, who had recently divorced his wife so he could take his own long and much-needed vacation, perfectly understood the joke. His next action probably had more to do with the head nurse's young and attractive figure than actual medical curiosity, but he pulled on Denton's jaw a few times before shaking his head.

"Nope, the mandibular joint is in perfect place." He stepped back and put a finger to his lips. "Do you think it's possible that... this—" he looked at his clipboard before continuing, "—this... Denton White. Have you considered he might be under the delusion that he is a frog, sitting on a lily pad, and his mouth remains open in anticipation of flies?"

The head nurse threw her head back and laughed far louder than the doctor's quip deserved. Then she slapped him on the arm and told him he was horrible. The doctor allowed himself a little chortle and then put his hand to his mouth and cleared his throat as a way of reminding them both not to get carried away. He completed the examination and then called in Doctor Schlotzsky, the resident psychoanalyst, to break the news of Denton's results.

Denton was mute, the specialist told Schlotzsky. He paused a moment to let that sink in. "No talking cure for this one, I'm afraid," the specialist said, "Though, I have to tell you, Boris, my ex-wife was a big fan of psychoanalysis. Never stopped talking about it. She even practiced a little on me."

And then, because the head nurse was still in the room and he hadn't asked for her phone number yet, he riffed a little. Yes,

Denton was dumb, he said. That sad fact was certain. His elbow found the back of the head nurse's arm before he continued. "But there's also something else, Doctor," he said, pausing dramatically, as though about to say something grave. "There's a strong possibility that, in addition to being dumb, Denton may also be"—he paused another moment before adding the last word—"stupid." With both he and the head nurse glancing sideways at each other and trying not to snicker, the specialist recommended the use of antispasmodics, handed Schlotzsky a prescription, and walked confidently out of the room, remembering only after the door had closed behind him that he'd never asked the head nurse for her phone number.

Schlotzsky wasn't so sure about the specialist's assessment. He hung back and observed Denton still teetering on the edge of his unspoken sentence. The patient appeared to be stuck in a dream well known to psychoanalysts, he explained to the head nurse. It was a dream in which the mouth is opened in terror but the dreamer is unable to find his voice. The Freudian pinched his sparse beard between his thumb and index finger and turned to the head nurse. "Perhaps he is not mute," Schlotzsky suggested. "But only lacks the verbiage to define his experience."

The head nurse rolled her eyes. She liked Schlotzsky a good deal. In fact, whenever the two shared private space, she felt an inexplicable urge to confess all her secrets to him. She felt it even in that moment. But the support staff had played the waiting game with Denton and underneath the look of epiphany, the high cheekbones, the chiseled jaw and the kind eyes, they had found a path to nowhere. In this case, she was inclined to trust the tall stature, the deep voice, and the stainless steel scopes and instruments of the specialist.

Nevertheless, she had Denton wheeled into Schlotzsky's office the following morning, where he was placed on the doctor's chaise lounge to undergo the talking cure.

Schlotzsky wasn't sure how to proceed. Rather than reclining, his new patient insisted on remaining seated cross-legged atop the chaise lounge. Schlotzsky lit his pipe and squirmed from one side to the other in his recliner, trying to escape Denton's gaze and gather his thoughts, but Denton's eyes had the quality of a Renaissance portrait. Without ever moving, they followed Schlotzsky in all directions.

About thirty minutes into his first session, Schlotzsky determined that sitting face-to-face was too confrontational for the delicate work of psychoanalysis. Accepting that Denton would not be the first to avert his gaze, the doctor pulled the handle at the side of his easy chair and fell backward to stare at the ceiling, hoping some intimate distance might grease the wheels of free association.

"Mmm," he prodded, with Denton humming back at him, the patient's eyes now following Schlotzsky even in the doctor's imagination.

In two weeks of these attempts, it would always be Schlotzsky who ended up revealing himself to Denton. When one session ended with the clock striking the hour as Schlotzsky confessed the long and painful process by which his unretractable foreskin had been worked free, the doctor decided to dismiss Denton for good and he conceded to the orderlies and the head nurse that his application of the talking cure may have been premature. Denton was like a dog whose jaw remained locked on a bone even as he starved to death, he explained. His deep oral fixation would need to be loosened at its roots before the talking cure could work its magic.

Schlotzsky gave the go-ahead and the orderlies carried Denton up to the third floor where the head nurse strapped him to a bolted-down stretcher, clamped electrodes on his head, shoved a wad of leather in his open mouth, and dialed up the voltage on her Medcraft ECT Unit. The shock therapy seemed magical at first. While Denton's body arched and contorted against the leather restraints into curious yoga-like postures, his mouth clamped shut for seconds at a time. After a final, one-hundred-and-seventy-volt pulse, Denton went flaccid. His mouth remained shut for a solid fifteen seconds while everyone waited in silence. Finally, it creaked open again. His tongue ejected the leather strap and it rolled out of his mouth and down the side of his cheek until it almost touched the floor. For another minute, he lay there panting. When his humming began again, it was tentative. One of the orderlies suggested that it might just be the tail end of a groan.

Everyone held their breath and crossed their fingers as the head nurse rolled Denton back to his room. But soon it became apparent that things had taken a bad turn. Denton climbed onto his bed, fixed his legs in a half-lotus position, and began rocking back and forth three to four times more violently than before. When the head nurse asked him how he felt, he placed his hands over his ears and hummed at the top of his lungs. His right leg began to twitch, and then shake. Within minutes, it was flapping vigorously enough to send him skipping and bouncing violently across the bed in a way that almost created the illusion of levitation.

Doctor Schlotzsky and the orderlies stood in the doorway scratching their chins and nodding their heads, waiting for the commotion to stop. After twenty minutes, they exchanged concerned glances. After thirty minutes, all concurred that something had indeed been loosened at its roots, though they disagreed on what exactly that was. After several days, they moved Denton to a padded, soundproof room and pumped him full of Valium in hopes that chemistry and time would have a cooling effect on his addled brain.

11

Six weeks later, on February 22nd of 1972, under the cover of darkness and on the wings of ultra-high-frequency radio waves, a medicine almost as gentle and miraculous as the talking cure itself slipped into the facility.

Schlotzsky spent those six weeks hoping for a therapeutic breakthrough that might repair the damage done by Denton's treatments with the old Medcraft machine. Day after day, besieged by guilt, the doctor wove his way through the long hallways of the institution following Denton's ear-splitting hum toward the locked door of his padded room. Schlotzsky never remembered arriving at Denton's door. He could only recall walking toward the door, and then later finding himself standing motionless outside the door with the key poised in his hand, not certain whether he had entered and was leaving or if he had never entered at all. The keyring would be returned to his pocket and he would shamble back through the halls toward his office with the feeling that Denton's Renaissance-portrait eyes were now following him to every corner of the institution.

Even in his home at night, when Schlotzsky retired to his Barcalounger with a shaker-full of dirty martinis and drew his Venetian blinds tight to the outside world, he could still feel Denton's eyes on him. Denton's hum still rang through the hallways of his ears, even as Bob Dylan's *New Morning* spun on the turntable and played at full volume through a set of high-fidelity stereo headphones. Sometimes Schlotzsy would drift off to sleep while imagining himself as a spelunker, exploring deep within his own labyrinthine eustachian tubes, a lantern in his hand and a set of keys jingling at his side. Cautiously, he would move toward the source of the unending noise, finally coming to a door glowing at its edges with light. But always, just as he inserted his key and turned the lock, he would start awake and find himself sticky with vermouth and olive juice in his chair, the repetitive hiss and click of his favorite album spinning in its locked groove, haunting him with the memory of a more tranquil Denton.

Whatever good the martinis did for the doctor's sleep, they extracted twice as much in payment every morning. His first steps into the institution with Denton's hum echoing through the halls would leave Schlotzsky feeling as though he was trapped inside an audio feedback loop from which there was no escape. After several weeks, Schlotzsky considered his predicament carefully and decided it would be the best thing for both doctor and patient if he cut the cord entirely. The specialist might have been right after all, he confessed to the head nurse. Treating Denton with the talking cure had indeed been fruitless. With the sound of Denton's operatic hum echoing in the background, the awkward little Freudian called a meeting of his colleagues and explained that the talking cure, just like any other miraculous medicine, did have its limitations. He suggested they give his patient a few months to cool off before reevaluating. Then he declared Denton a rare and perhaps incurable case, prescribed a strong cocktail of Thorazine and Valium, restored the patient's yard and common room privileges, and did his best to move on.

It was on February 23rd—in the middle of a session, and at some point just before lunch—that Boris Schlotzsky realized he hadn't remembered his former patient all morning. A moment of relief was followed by a moment of confusion which was quickly followed by several moments of panic. The doctor jumped from his recliner mid-nod, rushed through three sets of fire doors, and burst into Denton's soundproof room. He half-expected to find Denton hanging from the ceiling with his legs dangling above the floor or collapsed on the ground in a pool of froth and vomit, having swallowed his own tongue. But much to his surprise, when he arrived at Denton's room his patient appeared healthy. Denton was glowing. His eyes were bright and active, darting about the room as he chatted a mile a minute with a group of orderlies. The lead orderly spotted Schlotzsky standing at the door and guided him back out into the hall.

Schlotzsky's mind flashed back to grade school. He felt as though he were being called out of the classroom for discipline—perhaps for one of his compulsive acts of exhibitionism that he now remembered he'd confessed to Denton during one of those early, unsuccessful applications of the talking cure.

The doctor felt his face flush and then he recovered his composure, reminding himself of his stature as a doctor of psychiatry. It was best to let the orderly speak first, he decided. He covered his mouth with his hand and nodded at the other man with an air of professional superiority. After a few tense moments, the orderly told Schlotzsky his initial diagnosis had been dead on.

"Can you believe it?" the orderly asked him.

Schlotzsky raised his eyebrows. It was hard to believe indeed, especially considering he wasn't sure of which diagnosis the orderly was referring. He pinched his beard and paused as though in session. "Yes, yes, of course," he said. He nodded his head. After another moment, he repeated the same thing over again. "Yes, yes, of course."

The orderly apologized for doubting the doctor's expertise. Everyone had, he confessed. But just as the doctor suspected, Denton had never been mute. He simply hadn't possessed a fitting metaphor with which to define his experience.

The orderly told Schlotzsky his diagnosis had been brilliant. The transformation had taken place the previous night in the common room, the orderly explained. Denton was humming and rocking on the couch, his right leg shaking like it did—like a dog when it's being scratched just right. Same old, same old. There was a commercial for toothpaste on the TV. Then the hour changed over and suddenly music filled the room. Denton turned toward the TV and almost at once his humming and shaking began to slow. The pilot episode of the TV series *Kung Fu*, starring David Carradine, was airing.

As Carradine's character Kwai Chang Caine made his way across the sandy desert in the show's cinematic opening, Denton became transfixed. After a few minutes, his tics had completely quieted. He sat still and absorbed the remainder of the show in silence. When the last of the closing credits finally rolled, Denton stood as if waking from a deep trance. He blinked his eyes a few times, his mouth clapped shut and then it opened again and he started to speak. The previously mute Denton White had become loquacious.

Schlotzsky rocked back and forth and nodded his head as he listened to the orderly's story. At one point, he tilted so far back on his heels that he was suspended for a moment on the edge of his balance. Finally, he fell forward onto the balls of his feet.

"Yes, yes," he said. "I thought as much... Yes, yes, this is quite interesting."

He excused himself and left work early, returning home to celebrate the propitious turn in Denton's case. Filling his shaker with gin and vermouth, he already felt a weight lifting. The eyes of Denton were no longer following him and his anticipation of eternal guilt was gone. He put on *New Morning*, flopped into his Barcalounger, and slept through the afternoon and night without even spilling his drink. In the morning, he woke refreshed, pulled the needle out of the locked groove, showered, clipped his beard, and headed to the institution to resume sessions with Denton White.

The silence was lovely as he opened the institution door that morning, the quiet moments between his footsteps returning the doctor to a forgotten sense of serenity and purpose. Later, as he sat listening to Denton chatter on about *Kung Fu*'s pilot episode, his patient speaking with such enthusiasm he seemed to teeter on the very edge of mania, the psychoanalyst couldn't help but wonder what it all meant. This same man whom the specialist had declared mute and whom the orderlies had dubbed Quickfoot for the violent tremor that had developed after his electroshock treatments, now spoke eloquently and seemed comfortable if not completely at ease in his own skin.

The Ferrari was still sputtering along the side of the road as the sun edged down toward the horizon. One cornfield ended and revealed a farmhouse or a post office, a restaurant, a country store, and then another field of tall corn drew across the scene until the next vignette appeared. Abbott said something about the rising moon and we both admired it for a while. Then he lit another joint and continued his story.

Denton was still mad, Abbott explained. Ultra high-frequency airwaves had blown a partial cure to him, but he hadn't been cured altogether. Abbott told me how one night in the desert, years after they'd met at the institution, Denton shared something he had learned during his institution days. Denton pointed toward the moon and said that all the secrets of eternity were right there. On the light side, you don't think about the light, he'd explained. But on the dark side, the light is all you think about. It was that simple, he told Abbott, and Abbott had a sense of Denton's meaning. Abbott had always kept his pre-institution life to himself, but the comment made him wonder if Denton's experience had been more like his own than he'd ventured to imagine. Abbott had walked through the light Denton spoke of, and he had found himself on the dark side. Now, all he could think about was time.

Sometimes sleep put Denton back on the dark side of the moon. When the orderlies approached in the evenings with his horse's dose of Valium, he often bolted rather than let the Valium pull him into the quicksands of time. The fire doors would swing closed, the institution locking down as the orderlies made chase, Denton leaping over chairs and couches, sliding across tables, bobbing and weaving so that the orderlies fell over each other attempting to subdue him. At the far side of the fire doors, young nurses would stand giggling, remarking how much like a certain handsome movie star Denton looked, and how he moved like an NFL quarterback among the Keystone Cop orderlies. They swore the electroshock treatments must have altered the physiology of his legs. But the head nurse, who had administered the treatments and who had always been standoffish toward Denton, insisted that there was nothing at all extraordinary about Denton White.

It was Schlotzsky who discovered the two things that could calm Denton once he entered an agitated state. When Abbott introduced these into the narrative, I began to understand a certain quality within the story even as I became more doubtful of the story's literal truth. I could see by which ingredients an ordinary institution of brick and cinder, situated in a stark desert landscape, was transformed into a place of healing and magic so much like the legendary Shaolin Temple from the TV show Denton loved. I couldn't identify the precise formula, though I had ideas. I imagined such a world would consist of things like imagination, compassion, expansiveness, a sprinkle of indulgence, an appreciation for metaphor, a compassionate organizing force. It even felt good to imagine myself in such a place. I could hear the voice of Doctor Schlotzsky over the institution loudspeaker—sweet, hypnotic, soothing—breaking Denton out of his flight response with one or the other of his two gentle therapeutic miracles. He would either sing Edelweiss in the original German or hum a rendition of the theme song to the TV series, *Kung Fu*.

"Boris Schlotzsky had a beautiful voice," Abbott said. "It was part of the reason I could open up to him. He reminded me of my mother." Then, in a tone I had to strain to hear, he added something cryptic that I would only come to understand much later. "It would be a shame," he said, "If each of us were stuck living out just one of our potential incarnations."

12

Our conversation was becoming more of a monologue, and I was okay with that. The Ferrari's engine chugged and sputtered. The world moved by at tractor speed. Tall moonlit cornfields parted to reveal rural landscapes of the present, providing short glimpses into lives I didn't want to inhabit and that seemed even lonelier and more alienated than my own. Then the curtains closed, the moon and the headlamps lighting the path through the endless fields, and I slid back into Abbott's narration. We continued to chug along the edge of the hard shoulder while Abbott strained to put a tack in the beginning of his friendship with Quickfoot. It was a struggle with a degree of theatricality to it, but it pulled me right into the story with him. I tried to keep his mind on course the way you lean in toward the kingpin when the bowling ball starts drifting for the gutter. And this is to say two things—that I hung on his words and wanted his strange world to continue opening to me, and also that I already had a sense that I knew where his story needed to go. At last he found the date he was looking for and said it out loud: October 14th, 1972.

It would take a little time for Abbott to get us there. His first weeks at the institution were spent staring out his one small window and watching the hot desert air twist sunlight into a dark and mysterious sea. At times, that giant thermometer he remembered would rise out of those bending waves of light as though it were breaching the surface on the back of a great whale, and then Lucille's Diner would rise with it. Abbott would stand from his bed and walk toward his window and the great whale would dip back below the surface of the desert waters, Abbott sinking too, his chest heaving and that gate in his throat giving way. Orderlies would rush in with a big needle. They'd lift Abbott to his bed and soon he would pass into unconsciousness with his chest still quaking.

When evening came, and as the sun bowed below the distant mountains, he'd sit, sedated on his bed, remembering the golden light bursting into Lucille's diner and blanketing the checkered floor. Sometimes Lucille herself would surface out of the desert mirage, and Abbott would find himself standing in his stocking feet, swaying, back and forth to the music of Janis Joplin or Santana. He'd pull Lucille in tight and whisper into her ear, telling her the same sweet thing he always said—that her waist was so tiny he could wrap his arms around her twice. Lucille would giggle in his ear, and just as he tightened his embrace to prove his point, she'd be gone. Soon, the orderlies would be towering above him with their big needle again. He would be lifted to his bed, drift into darkness, and then the day would begin again.

At times, as Abbott spun his yarn, it seemed that Lucille might not be a person, but the figurative representation of something else that had been lost, not just for Abbott, but for myself too. I kept this to myself. It was clear that Abbott did not intend Lucille as a metaphor.

I even suspected that his wellbeing depended on me taking Lucille at face value. And because my separation from Laura had left such an unanticipated and unresolvable void in me, it was not hard to see her as he wanted, as a literal figure.

And I did see Lucille. I'll be drawn and quartered for saying so, but I had this image in my head of her, not only of her but of great women throughout America and all throughout history, standing just beyond the bending light with their aprons on. They were waving to me and Abbott, and to all the troubled men of the world, and I could feel how necessary these women were, not only to us but to all of humanity. They were our anchors, our centers of gravity. Without them, our world spun in widening gyres like the falcon in the Yeats poem just before everything falls apart.

There was something else too, another thing I'm hesitant to say because it's an idea as hard to hold and as out of time as Lucille standing in Abbott's room with that apron tied around her narrow waist, as out of time as Abbott himself. But it would be hard to talk about what made Abbott feel so kindred to me without mentioning that it was becoming clear that we held in common a fascination with the ideal of romantic love. There was something revealing in that. I'd like to say that Abbott and I shared a deep satisfaction in giving and receiving affection, in captivating and being captivated, that we both had wildly romantic hearts. I could say that our search for Love was a pure search for Truth, that we were not simply fugitives in our own ways, but two men filled with metaphysical yearning, traveling through a world increasingly out of touch with the true internet and possessed by a simulacrum. But that's just the honey. I suppose the Truth, with all its snarling and sharp teeth, is always buried in the simulacrum of some narrative or other. Ours was simply older fashioned, more literate and laborious. Its difference was found in our careful chiseling away of defects, in a level of introspection and curation for which the wider world had no time.

When I listened to Abbott speak, it was hard to be critical. I was taken by the sweetness and simplicity of that image of Lucille in the kitchen with her apron on. And even as Abbott began to theorize about the cold mechanizations of fate and as that falcon drifted further and further from the falconer, so to speak, I began to hear hints of that same tender love he felt for Lucille, expressed in how he spoke of all his characters. That held things together for me. It kept me with him. It became the way Lucille remained in the story even when she disappeared for long periods of narration. More than any LSD-fueled revelation at Woodstock, Lucille had taught Abbott to see the world through the eyes of love.

That world Abbott saw enchanted me. It possessed me. It made me think about my writing and how I'd always fantasized that my big philosophies and grand ideas made the wheel of my fiction turn. For twenty years, I'd struggled to write a second chapter without ever really understanding my first chapter. Right then, as the twilight air of August blew across the two of us, I had the glimmer of a realization that would only crystallize much later when I made the transition from captive audience to captive storyteller and, in the coldness of a cell, this story began to become my own.

I was thinking that maybe there are only two tricks a storyteller can perform. There is the writer who can captivate his readers with his rhythm, his vibration, with the magic carpet of his Tom Selleck voice. Those rhythms play at locked passages and coax open doors in the reader until at last they realize they are in good hands and submit. Then he tells them things and they listen. Dark things. Beautiful things. They lie down and put their hands and feet in restraints and let themselves be poked at and prodded and electrified in the most intimate ways until they are sweetly teased to climax.

But then, maybe there's another kind of writer. This one places *himself* on the table and lets his reader in, unafraid to put his hands in leather cuffs, like Denton White just before the head nurse fried his brain and altered the physiology of his legs. This type of writer submits himself to the world like some lustful Houdini, bound up and boxed in, narrating the tale of his own passion and crucifixion, pen in hand, playing at the locks that bind him as he sinks to the bottom of the sea. And although it was an uncomfortable idea, I thought maybe I'd always been confused about the type of writer I was meant to be. I'd imagined myself as a sage, setting out on a great sailing ship with a message to give to the world. But that wasn't me. I was at my best when I surrendered, when I experienced life as a twig thrown from a bridge into the raging current, left to bob in the waves and, if I survived, to tell my tale. My first chapter had been just a stretching of the muscles, a limbering up, a character—me—looking at the river that's about to swallow him. But I had never thrown myself in. I'd stood on that bridge admiring the limitless beauty of all the potential stories I could write and the years passed and the world waited, and Laura and I grew older and further apart.

13

When Abbott woke from sedation on October 14, 1972, he opened his eyes to find Denton White sitting in the afternoon light at the edge of his bed. As the light grew dim, Abbot remained quiet. He wondered if this young man, who looked about his own new age, had risen out of the same mirage as Lucille and her diner, and the great thermometer he remembered so clearly. At twilight, when Denton had neither moved nor disappeared, Abbott rose to a sitting position and began to sob quietly. Even then, Denton did not move or speak. The two remained like that for several hours. Finally, as if commanded by a force more powerful than himself, Denton stood. He took Abbott's hand and led his new friend out to the institution's common room where he fluffed the cushions of the threadbare couch nearest the TV and sat Abbott down. A few moments later, a familiar song burst through the television and several patients reflexively rose and shambled off to their rooms for the night. *Kung Fu*, the series, had begun.

Abbott didn't undergo the sudden transformation Quickfoot had experienced when the pilot first aired. But there were moments during "King of the Mountain" that Abbott's urge to sob completely quieted. For the first time since waking in the miner's shack outside of Ely, he remembered what it was like to gather a complete breath. In the character of Kwai Chang Caine, a Shaolin monk living as a fugitive in the American West, Abbott saw something of himself that he couldn't quite pin down. Maybe it had something to do with Caine's deep sadness and his feeling of being a refugee in a world where he didn't quite fit, or it was because Caine also carried a message, a story, a past that was impossible for those around him to comprehend. When the hour came to an end, Abbott was far from cured, far from loquacious. He didn't speak a word. But something of Caine's example had steeped into him, much as it had with Denton. He returned to his room feeling that something was slightly different, and as the days of the long month between the first episode and the second passed, Abbott would often find himself looking out at the sunset and reflecting on the character of Kwai Chang Caine, and he would be struck by his own silence.

In January, after *Kung Fu*'s third episode, "Blood Brothers," Abbott began to understand that Denton's appearance in his life was no accident. Forces he did not quite understand had brought him and Quickfoot together for a purpose. They may not have been brothers by birth, but they were brothers. They'd been reborn together in suffering, and now they would grow in this place of healing, and they would become brothers in Shaolin.

Abbott gleaned his first pearl of wisdom from this same episode. One of Kwai Chang Caine's simple phrases had stuck with him, and he began to contemplate it in his newfound silences: "Do not clutch at pain and pain will pass," Caine had said, and Abbott hoped with all his heart that this was true. Yet, as he contemplated, he began to also fear what it meant to let his pain go. The pain was all that was left of Lucille, and Lucille had been the truest thing he'd ever known. Without the pain, he wondered, who would he be, and how would they remain together?

Soon, it was determined that Abbot's sobbing fits had quieted enough that he could be brought to Doctor Schlotzsky to begin psychoanalysis. Schlotzsky explained to Abbott that the talking cure was the most powerful medicine in the psychiatric pharmacopoeia, but when Abbott tried to talk about the subjects he found most curative, Schlotzsky bristled. He steered the conversation away from Kwai Chang Caine and toward the one single subject that interested him—the place Abbott had come from. This was a subject Abbott wanted to discuss as well. If he could figure out where he'd come from, maybe he could figure out how to get back. But the more time they spent analyzing where Abbott had come from, the more it struck Abbott that the "most powerful medicine's" mechanism of action lay in the reverse alchemy of transforming gold into lead.

Somehow, Schlotzsky always managed to reformulate Abbott's most treasured memories into riddles to which only Schlotzsky himself held the answer. These riddles would then be presented back to Abbott and, to gain Schlotzsky's approval, he was expected to struggle earnestly to solve them.

"What kind of riddles?" I asked him.

Abbott waved his hand toward an imaginary scene on the imaginary stage of the horizon. "For instance, there was a giant phallus that rose up one-hundred-and-thirty-four feet and towered over the valley of death. What do you think that meant?"

I thought it over for a few moments, wanting to solve it. I love riddles. "Like maybe hope?" I guessed. "Maybe hope springing up in a place of overwhelming despair?"

Abbott looked at me for a few seconds. He seemed stunned.

"Wow," he said. "You just came up with that right now?"

I was proud of myself. All those years of literary analysis were finally paying off. "I'm right?"

"I wouldn't say, you're right, kid. Not at all." He stopped and considered for a minute. "Well, hope, yes. But not the way you're thinking."

The irony of the situation didn't escape me. Abbott had taken Schlotzsky's place. He was the one posing riddles now, and I was struggling for the solution to win his approval. I wondered if he was taking some pleasure in that, the way I'd always taken pleasure when I posed these questions to my writing students.

"So what did it mean?" I asked.

Abbott looked disappointed.

"You're giving up already? I worked on that one for two years and I already knew the answer," he said. "But alright, kid, The 'valley of death'," was Death Valley, California and the 'phallus' was the giant thermometer outside Lucille's Diner. It was my landmark, kid. It was my way back. But Schlotzsky was a Freudian, you see? He was one-hundred-percent crazy with Freud, and one-hundred-and-ten-percent certain that this 'potent image'—that's what he called it—would provide the insight that would lead to my cure. He wouldn't let it go. He was like a dog with a bone locked in its jaws."

"A thermometer one-hundred-and-thirty feet high in the middle of Death Valley?" I said. "How difficult could that be to find?"

"If every dimension was lined up correctly, it wouldn't have been hard at all. I was thinking the same way."

"You're talking about time?" I asked.

"That's part of it. But time is just another measure of distance, kid. You can't fully understand that until you've walked a mile in my shoes."

Abbott would begin to tell Schlotzsky about the one-hundred-and-thirty-four-foot thermometer that towered over Death Valley. He'd sit up in the chaise lounge, grab the pen and notepad right out of the doctor's hands and scribble a map. He'd describe the thermometer's shadow crossing the floor of the diner every evening. With the gate in his throat locked closed, he'd recall the embrace he and Lucille would share as the sun fell below the horizon, their tender kiss. He would beg the doctor to help him find his way back. Returning to that life, he told Schlotzsky, was the only thing that could bring about his cure.

Schlotzsky always shifted the conversation away from the solid ground of time and topography. In a somber, patient tone that always struck Abbott as condescension, he would explain that Abbott was thinking about the content of his memory in its manifest reality. Abbott was assuming his experience contained an objective truth. To Abbott, this object may be a thermometer. But the thermometer also existed at a deeper level of consciousness. Exploring that level would be the work Schlotzsky and Abbott engaged in together. If Abbott wished to make any progress at all, he would need to anesthetize himself with an understanding that would allow the doctor to poke and prod and eventually debride his psychological wound. He would need to understand that within Schlotzsky's chambers all stories would be considered as objectively false, but *also* as deep symbolic representations of their narrator's mind. All stories, the doctor told him, while shifting awkwardly side to side in his chair, performed the same perverse trick—they converted the great sphere of psychological experience into the plane Euclidean geometry of fiction. They created the illusions of cause and effect and beginning and end. In manifest reality Abbott might speak of a thermometer, while at a deeper, latent level, it was a phallus. It was a virile image rising out of a barren and empty landscape, devoid of the fertility of hope.

It was a tough pill for Abbott to swallow. Impossible. It presented a challenge that Abbott wasn't prepared to undertake. Yet he and Schlotzsky had reached a standoff, and Abbott knew the situation was delicate. To gain freedom from the institution and begin searching for the manifest Lucille in the manifest desert by the manifest thermometer, Abbott needed to find the solution to Schlotzsky's riddle. But to reach that solution, Abbott would be required to talk about his lost life in the gibberish Abbott considered madness but Schlotzsky referred to as latent reality. He would have to talk about Lucille and the life he'd cherished as if it'd been a figment of his imagination, and the object most likely to lead back to that life would be converted into a giant erection. Gold would be converted to lead.

His first attempts were no more than stutters followed by silence. It was in these moments that the Freudian would sometimes break character. He'd place a hand on his patient's shoulder and offer a bit of validation that felt to Abbott like pure empathy. The doctor might nod his head and tug at his sparse little beard and confess to the impossibility of Abbott's situation.

"Such a young heart," he might say, "How can it be expected to handle the loss of a wife of forty years?"

Sometimes he'd even shift the conversation away from his favorite subject—the latent phallus in the valley of death. He'd ask Abbott to tell him what it felt like to wake up in a strange body day after day. At these times, Abbott could feel a kind of healing taking place and, despite their differences in worldview and background and the power dynamic that should have precluded it, Abbott would sense a deep and unspoken friendship developing between them. But the conversation would always return to the giant thermometer in the desert, and Abbott could never convince the doctor to help him find that landmark in manifest reality.

As the weeks passed, Abbott gathered his courage and finally decided to try things Schlotzsky's way, but almost as soon as they engaged the subject Abbott's mouth filled with the taste of pancake batter. He felt a wooden spoon between his teeth, then the pinch of a big needle, followed by a flash-flood of chemicals that rushed through his veins and washed him toward unconsciousness. He opened his eyes in his bed and closed them again. A series of days passed as before. Mirages. Slanted light. Dancing in his socks. Sobbing. When Thursday came, Quickfoot once again materialized on the corner of his bed and ushered him to the threadbare couch and tuned the TV to *Kung Fu*. By the end of the episode, Abbott understood how he needed to deal with Schlotzsky. He moved over to an octagonal table, sat down in a little plastic chair, picked up a crayon, and plotted his escape.

14

It was around this point in the story that the Ferrari finally shit the bed. It went out with a bang, like a cherry bomb in a mailbox, and I had little doubt that if I looked under the thing, the muffler would be opened wide at the end of the tailpipe like a rust-red hibiscus flower. I worried that Denton's right-hand man might be the type to pluck an exploded exhaust from a manifold and perform some sort of junkyard ikebana, and create something striking and pointless that would leave us in awe and delay us in Fairfield for an extra week. But it was dark, and I didn't really care to look under the car, and Abbott was more concerned with getting his 308 off the road and covered in a camouflage of tassels and cornstalks than he was with performing any sort of autopsy.

We heaved and grunted and rolled the thing off the shoulder and pushed it a little way into the field. Something about the Ferrari felt off to me. It felt chintzy, like the body might crack under the pressure of my hands. It rolled off the road with all the same creaks and groans and chafing of rotors as every junker I'd ever rolled off a country road, and when it bumped to a halt, I heard large flakes of rust drop from the underbody onto the ground. The car even had the decaying smell of a junker.

That got me thinking. Usually when an autopsy is circumvented after a suspicious death, there's a reason. I was about to find out that in this regard the 308 was no exception.

"Some Ferrari," I said, once the car was in the woods and we were leaning against the back end catching our breath.

"She sure is," Abbott said. He spanked the rear quarter like it was the rump of a prize stallion and I heard another pound of rust let go and hit the ground.

"She sure is," I repeated.

I walked around and reached in and grabbed my backpack from the floor by the front seat. Abbott popped the bonnet. He pulled out a brown tarp to cover the T-top, then reached back in for a carry-on-sized, rolling suitcase. When I shined my cell-phone flashlight into the bonnet to help him out, I noticed the inside was corroded and flaking in what one might call "juxtaposition" to the shiny, red exterior paint, and there weren't any of the engineering flairs or components that I expected of an Italian sports car. Just bubbling rust, and a suspension spring at each side.

"This isn't a Ferrari," I said. "What is this? A kit car?"

"Well kid, it depends how you look at it," Abbott said. He closed the bonnet and latched it.

"Uh-huh," I said.

"What makes a Ferrari a Ferrari? You know what I mean?" He asked the questions as if the conclusions were established science for men like us.

"I don't know what you mean," I said—though I thought I was familiar with the argument he was about to make.

"Alright, kid. Alright. So maybe this was put together at

Bodyman's Garage instead of in some fancy factory in Italy. So maybe it's got the chassis of a '74 Super Beetle and a 1.8-liter Boxer engine. But when people look at this, they see a Ferrari. Just as much of a Ferrari as if it were the real thing. The mind creates reality. You understand? Even a real Ferrari is just a metaphor for something else."

I wanted to tell him that this "mind creates reality" thing sounded a lot like the gibberish that would come out of the mouth of Doctor Schlotzsky. But instead of arguing, I took his bait.

"The Ferrari's a metaphor for what, Abbott?"

"For success. For vitality. For living your best life. Stuff like that. You name it. Stuff a real Ferrari doesn't make any more or less true than a fake Ferrari. And I would know kid, because at one time I owned the real McCoy. True story, kid—a genuine, Italian-made Ferrari 308 GTS. It didn't change a thing. Same me. Same roads. Same mountains. Same air. Broke down just as often too. I damn near wore out my Triple-A membership with that thing."

"So now we're going to talk about the Ferrari's latent reality?" I asked. The abrupt halt of our trip had me anxious and, more than that, I was worried that if the Ferrari was phony, Abbott's whole story that was going to be my salvation was probably phony too. "Let me ask you something, Abbott. How much of anything you told me has any manifest reality whatsoever?"

We both stood there speechless for a moment. It was dark enough that I couldn't see his eyes, just dark, circular shadows on the lighter shadow of his face.

"What I mean to say is," I began to say. I smacked the bonnet a couple times and waited for the rust to drop off the underbody. "Is, what kind of Ferrari is your story?"

"What!" Abbott said.

"Well?" I said.

"Kid," he said. "How can you ask me that? It's all true. It's all the real McCoy."

He sounded hurt. I had to fight the impulse to soothe him. When I said nothing, he reached in through the tarp and flipped on his headlights.

"All these things I'm telling you—nobody ever believes me," he said, "But I'm gonna show you something that will change your mind." He reached into his pocket and took out his wallet, flipped it open, and pulled a folded envelope from an inner flap. He offered it to me. "Go ahead," he said. "Read it."

I brought it over to the headlights and unfolded it. I expected to see a photocopied title for a real Ferrari with Abbott's name on it and I expected to quickly dismiss it as bullshit. I was feeling sidetracked and conned. I'd expected to be in a fast car roaring west through the night and now I was stranded in the middle of a never-ending cornfield with a lunatic. I was almost to my limit with suspending my disbelief.

The envelope was stationary-sized, the kind used for personal correspondences before all that stuff was done over email. For postage, there was an original ten-cent Mariner 10 stamp from 1975. At a later date that had been supplemented with several Christopher Columbus commemoratives. It was twenty-nine cents worth of stamps. The postmark was dated October 14, 1992—almost exactly twenty years after Abbott met Denton White at Ella Rawson State Hospital.

In orange crayon, which had been shadowed with black ink, it was addressed to Abbott, care of a post office in a New York town I'd never heard of.

Inside the envelope, there were two separate documents. One was a letter of several pages, written in black ink and full of small printed words on both sides. I unfolded that first. It began, "Dear, dear Abbott," but before I could read more, Abbott brushed it aside.

"The other one," he said.

I unfolded the other one. It was a single sheet of lined paper torn from a writing pad. It read, in orange crayon letters, two lines high:

ABBOTT,

YOU WERE RIGHT AF-

TER ALL.

X_____

DR. BORIS SCHLOTZSKY

Along the line, beside the X, there was—presumably—the signature of Doctor Schlotzsky. If the signature was forged, then tremendous effort was made to give it the look of authenticity. I could see that every time the ballpoint had contacted the crayon, the pen had stopped inking. The doctor had to begin his signature over several times. In the top right-hand corner of the page, there were a series of black spirals that betrayed the frustration of a doctor who was used to scribbling his mark without a second thought. I couldn't imagine a forger producing anything so clumsy.

Perhaps the most notable thing about the document was that Schlotzsky had not only signed it, but he'd gone through the trouble to have it officially notarized. The mark of the notary public was from San Bernardino County, California, and it was also dated October 14, 1992. I concluded that whatever this letter of vindication referred to, the letter itself was most likely real.

I didn't see how it had anything to do with Abbott's Ferrari, but it made me curious. I wondered when and in what state of mind the letter had been written. What argument did it refer to, and why had it only been signed so many years later? I thought if I stood there and opened a part of me to the letter, I might see the whole story play out through some internal eye. Sometimes I felt like I could do that, like I could connect to a personal object or a photo and see into events that surrounded it, feel the emotions of the moment, and read the things that were hidden between the lines. I stood looking at the strange document, trying to relax a certain area of my brain and get a read. But Abbott didn't give me much time. Just as a fuzzy image was starting to come to me, he cut off the lights. When I protested, he raised his hand up to shush me and told me to be still.

"You hear that?" he whispered.

I forgot about the letter for a moment and listened.

Abbott was in a hurry. He snatched the document from my hand, grabbed the envelope, shoved the paper inside, dropped it into his blazer pocket, and switched off the headlights. He was nervous about something. I was left holding the letter with the small print he'd told me to ignore. I started to pass it to him but when he held up his hand to shush me again I slipped it into my back pocket. I didn't realize that much like Abbott's Zippo it would soon become a relic connecting me to another world—one that would sometimes seem to have sprung from my own imagination.

"What is it?" I whispered.

"You hear that?" he said. "That's a Ford, four-point-six. A Police Interceptor. No mistaking it."

I could hear the car before he finished speaking. It had been a lot of years, but I'd done enough hitchhiking along highways, often illegally, to know the sound he was talking about. That engine hadn't been altered much since the early nineties, and the combination of the big displacement, the cop tires, and the way the wind moved over the lights in a deep whistle, made a pretty distinct sound. But if I made a call like that, I would've been wrong just as often as I was right.

So I waited.

I was having an internal debate. I wanted to be heading west toward a new life, a fresh start, toward new chapters that might bring Laura back to me. But I was also convinced that Abbott's story was important and I was still thinking that if I stayed with him, I might even discover the very chapters I needed in what he had to say. That made it very hard to leave him. Of course, I didn't know then how long it would take for his story to unfold and that months into the future I would be sitting alone in a little shack in the middle of nowhere, reading and rereading the letter in my back pocket and waiting for a conclusion. I didn't know quite what I wanted to happen next. I sensed the albatross of *Chapter Two* circling above me. It hovered there, its big wings casting a shadow on the empty white page of the future.

I decided if Abbott was wrong about the Interceptor I was going to dismiss him as an ex-mental patient a few days off his meds—a guy who was frankly full of shit about everything. That would be my excuse to walk away, to wave him off as a man as fake as his 308, to forget him. Eccentrics like Abbott were a dime a dozen out on the road. An extended thumb was like catnip for them, it was the whirring gyro that called them in. I'd be riding with another Abbott in a matter of hours.

That's what I was telling myself and maybe at the time I believed it. But part of me knew it wasn't true. It was like Abbott would later explain—things had changed. Eccentrics were disappearing and a wave of homogenization was sweeping through the civilized world. Abbott might blame it on Hollywood, or happiness gurus, or centralized media, or SSRIs. He'd say the lunatics were running the asylum. He would become sidetracked and rant about brainwashing experiments the CIA had run in the sixties, raving about top-secret projects with the names of birds and vegetables and a program called MK-Ultra that he claimed was an established part of American history and was still going on right under our noses. "Stay away from the internet, kid!" he'd tell me, hurling my phone from the back of a pickup onto the highway somewhere in Illinois, and warning me that social media and movie streaming services were just the phase-two rollout of the same old program. They were there to reinforce the mind control and funnel the great flow of free thought into one narrow stream. His eyes would become dark islands in white, churning seas, the same way as when he'd talked about Woodstock.

"You don't understand," he would warn me, his eyes swelling with fury. "The internet is destroying the internet."

And maybe he had a point. Something certainly changed after I disconnected from it all in his little cabin out West. Maybe the internet had us all connected on some garbage level of reality that rendered us unable to sense the deep connections of the true internet—that fungal wire Abbott had witnessed at Woodstock with the rain pouring down and five-hundred-hits of LSD coursing through his genitals. The old models of communication had suffered an extinction event, slowly strangled out by the dust of a cataclysmic meteor. We couldn't see the light or walk into the light or even mention the light. We could only recite talking points and repeat anointed opinions as if trapped at high tea with the queen.

The headlights of the approaching vehicle were starting to flicker through the stalks of corn, diffuse at first, and then, as it came up over the last rise, I could see the placement of the lamps on the grill more clearly. It looked like a Crown Vic, but that didn't mean a whole lot. It could've been a Town Car, an F-Series pickup or a Merc Grand Marquis. All of those vehicles have that same cop engine, and old men and hicks drive a lot like cops. At night, those vehicles are hard to distinguish until they're right up on you.

"Better get down," I said.

We were both standing there, watching the headlights approach, ten or fifteen yards in from the edge of the road.

"Right," Abbott said. He laid down in the field on his belly and put his face to the ground, shielding it with his hands.

I did the same.

I listened to the vehicle pass with the crunch and ping of gravel and a wake of wind that rattled the tassels of corn. I remained as I was until I heard the field become still.

When I lifted my head, the taillights were barely visible. It was impossible to say if Abbott's call had been on the mark or not. I watched the red lights drop below a far hill and rise again, then they dropped out of sight for good.

I hadn't avoided the truth, I told myself. It was more of a thought experiment. The car was now both a police interceptor and not a police interceptor. It was a lot like Schrödinger's cat.

15

I read my mother's email while I was waiting for Abbott. He was still twenty yards or so into the cornfield, swearing at his prostate. It was like we were back in that replica Ferrari, on the road again, struggling uphill. His flow would start pattering against the sod and almost as soon as he breathed a sigh of relief, the sound would break off and he'd be swearing again.

In the distance, I could see the blinking red light of a radio tower. Before I even realized I'd noticed it, my phone was out in front of my face. I'm not sure what I wanted to see, maybe something from Laura or the university or the police or McGee, something that said it'd all been a big mistake and things would be alright.

Since before there were cell phones and long before Abbott pulled over on the highway, I'd anticipated the moment that would change the course of my life. It would be a knock at the door, or an envelope in the mailbox, or an email from a distant relative I had never known. In that moment, this problematic and rudderless life would switch direction and my life's true purpose would become clear.

Abbott growled at me from the edge of the corn.

"Kid, put that thing away. You're ruining your night vision."

Speaking caused his flow to stop and he returned to cursing under his breath.

There was only one new email. It was from my mother. It was written like a letter, with a salutation and with her love at the end, but it made one simple request.

"Call me before bed. It's important."

My mind started running with it. Good important or bad important, I wondered.

Sometimes my optimism surprised me.

Against my better judgment, I called my mother.

"David," she said, "Well I'm glad you decided to call me back."

"Back?" I said. "You sent me an email, Ma."

"Well," she said, "You know what I mean. Sometimes I think I could be dead up in my bed for a week before anyone would know the difference."

"You said it was important," I said.

"Actually, there are a few things," she said.

I sensed my mother's version of the old bait-and-switch beginning. She'd set me up. She had me thinking I was going to get some valuable information, but now she was going to start talking about all of my many failings and, most probably, my ex-wife.

"Can we at least start with the important thing you mentioned?" I said.

"Well," she said, "That Mister McGee was by the house after we talked. It wasn't thirty minutes later, David. Isn't that the strangest coincidence?"

"I wouldn't make too much of it," I said.

"I knew you wouldn't," she said. "But there was something strange about his visit. Some of the things he said. I got to thinking about this monk you're traveling with and how maybe you could write a little story about him. I told Mister McGee about it and he thought it was interesting too."

"Ma," I said, "Please don't tell McGee anything. The last thing I need is that guy tracking me down all over the country. I just need him to leave me alone for a while."

"Well, that reminds me of what I really wanted to tell you. Somebody from the sheriff's department called looking for you. I didn't tell them anything, but they seemed to know you were heading out West. Isn't that strange? I just don't know how they would know that. They even asked if I had an address and phone number for Laura. "

"Probably just a guess. It's a small town. They don't have anything better to do."

"Do you think they could be tracking your phone?

"Ma," I said. "Over taxes?"

"Who knows these days, David. I don't know what to think anymore. Did you use that prepaid credit card I gave you?"

"Yeah, I used it. Just once though."

"Recently?"

"I bought a pack of cigarettes earlier, just before we talked."

"Oh," she said, "You and those cigarettes. Why don't you just give that up?"

"Ma," I said.

"Those cigarettes are gonna get you one way or the other, David. I can see that."

"I'll give it up once I get settled out West. Okay? And I doubt anyone's tracking my prepaid credit card. I don't think they're even trackable."

"Maybe," she said, "but something was strange about that call."

"I'm sure it was just routine," I said."

"The woman asked about—and this is how she said it—*known associates*. You don't think that is odd? She was acting like you were part of some big ring. I told her you're a good person, David. I told her about the divorce, and that you're just going through a rough patch—Laura told me about the drinking, you know. She said she heard that you ruined your little office at the college."

"Oh, please. I knocked over a bookshelf."

"And fighting with other drivers? That doesn't sound like you, David. Why didn't you tell me that's why you haven't been driving? Laura thinks you need to see a therapist."

"Of course she does. She's a therapist herself. She's been indoctrinated. And the thing with the car was an argument, not a fight. It was last year, right before she left me. Maybe she should get some therapy."

It was silent on the other end of the line.

"Tell me about McGee," I said.

"You know me, David. I just want everyone to be happy."

"I know, Ma."

"Maybe if you hadn't lost your license—"

"Mom," I said. "McGee?"

I heard her shift in her bed, and then maybe the sound of her getting her reading glasses off the night table. Maybe she'd taken some notes she wanted to share.

"Well, Mister McGee seems to think he can help you out of this if you just give him a chance. He seems like a nice man, David. I think he really cares what happens to you."

"McGee is alright," I said. "I'll give him a call when I get settled. I have some ideas too."

"Are you still traveling with your friend in that Ferrari? That monk who looks like Tom Selleck?"

"He's not a monk," I corrected her, as if I hadn't made the same mistake. "His name is Abbott. That's a long story. Anyway, we're together, but I don't know for how much longer. He's having car trouble."

"In that expensive car? You'd think a car like that would never give you trouble."

"That's what you'd think," I said.

"Well, I've been thinking about him, David. And not just for your story. That's the other thing I wanted to tell you. I think you should help him find his wife. Remember how you used to be so good at solving those mysteries on TV?"

I lowered my voice. "I think he might be a little crazy."

I pulled my ear away from the receiver to figure out where Abbott was. He wasn't kidding about the night vision. It was ruined. I listened for him and I could hear him grumbling in the woods.

"He says his wife is lost in time, or in another dimension where he already lived a whole life with her. That's pretty crazy, right?"

My mother was quiet for a few moments.

"Mom?"

"It does sound a little strange, David, but I think I know how that poor Abbott feels. Sometimes I swear your father is right here with me, David—I know people would think I sound like a crazy person, but it's true. Sometimes I think maybe I'm with him, wherever he is, or it feels like he's waiting for me up ahead. That's who we need to solve this mystery. Your father. Remember when we used to watch those TV shows? We'd have to tell him to keep his ideas to himself. Not five minutes in and he'd have the whole thing solved. It used to amaze me, you know?"

"But Mom, this isn't a TV show. Abbott could be a complete lunatic for all I know." I suddenly placed one of the Mike Post theme songs I'd heard before in Abbott's car. It was from a show where an experiment goes wrong and a physicist gets stuck traveling through time and fixing things that are about to go wrong. "This isn't like *Quantum Leap,* Mom. People don't time travel in real life."

"Well," she said. She let the conversation fall into silence. It was her way of changing the subject and also letting me know her feelings were a little hurt.

I waited for her to continue.

"I was thinking, David." She said, finally. "You know who you're a little like?"

"Who?"

"Remember that doctor, who used to travel from place to place with the newspaper reporter always chasing him? He was always hitchhiking—such a nice man too. What was his name?"

"That was in *The Incredible Hulk.* You mean, David Banner?"

"That's right. David Banner. He was in trouble too, David. But he always found time to help people. You even look a little like him. Well, I think you do. You know, he was considered a very handsome man in his day."

I could hear Abbott making his way out of the woods.

"Mom," I said. "I should go, but I'm gonna think about what you said, okay?"

"I know you will, David. And don't use that card anymore. I'm going to send some money as soon as I have somewhere to send it to. Just so I know you're eating."

"Thanks, Mom, but I've got some money. I'm eating."

I told her I loved her and she said the same and then I ended the call. I could feel Abbott standing beside me. I had a momentary inclination to tell him about the sheriff's call. And that my mother thought we were being tracked. But I decided it was only my mother's overactive imagination and all those detective stories she was always watching on TV. And I also figured it didn't really matter anyway.

So we just stood there in the darkness for a minute or so. It was nice. It gave me some time to move away from that safe but irritating little planet my mother always took me to, and return to our quiet place on the road where a new story was just beginning.

"Kid," Abbott finally said, "I gotta tell ya."

I turned to look at him and my eyes were still glitchy from the phone. His face was a shadow crawling with light.

"I stop doing my qi gong exercises for a few weeks and my prostate goes to hell. I tell you kid, absolute crap. I used to have a flow like a horse."

He gave me a rough slap on the shoulder.

"Kegels, kid. A hundred a day. Best piece of advice I can give you. Mark my words. You'll thank me in another twenty-five years."

He walked on ahead, his suitcase rolling behind him. I adjusted my backpack and caught up with him. He told me not to worry about a thing. We'd make our way to Bodyman's, and he'd have another car. It would take us as far as we wanted to go. I was in for a treat, Abbott insisted. This other car was sure to be something special.

We set a pace toward I-70 sticking our thumbs out when things felt safe and hiding in the corn when Abbott thought cars sounded suspicious. I never looked. Both realities remained equal possibilities. I put the conversation with my mother out of my mind and watched the stars. Single bright settlements became little towns, became bustling metropolises. Soon the sky was as bright and crowded as the earth below it. The road was empty for a long time. I didn't think of Laura or McGee or my unfinished novel. One of Abbott's suitcase wheels had a little chip in it, or there was a rock embedded in the plastic. It kept spinning around and clicking, then spinning again. It made me think of *New Morning* in its locked groove. It kept me in the story until Abbott began to speak.

16

The contrast was strange. That's what I was thinking as that pebble ticked again and again over the pavement and Abbott started back into the story of Denton and the head nurse. It occurred to me that maybe this juxtaposition was part of Abbott's special gift as a storyteller. All his insanity seemed to press toward the present, setting the story of the past free. The Abbott I stood beside sometimes seemed a little touched—the wide eyes, the conspiracies, the time traveling, the fungal web of humanity. But when he took me to the past—when he talked about Lucille or the years he spent inside the institution, all the churning inside him began to still. The Tom Selleck quality in his voice returned. There was such humanity in it all, such largess in his rhythm and tone. It was an odd trick, and I don't understand how he pulled it off, but somehow the most unbelievable part of Abbott—his alleged past—began to be the ground I stood on.

Without my conscious awareness, my distrust of Abbott transferred to his present self: the qi gong exercises that cured his bladder, his stories about brainwashing and the CIA, this ludicrous insistence that because of some perceptual flaw in material reality, his Ferrari was actually real. That stuff made me roll my eyes. All the things I'd taken at face value began to become suspect. I no longer believed he was being honest with me about where he was going or what his motivations were for offering me transportation and friendship. I suspected wild things. I doubted that Bodyman's was the garage of some deadhead and his mechanical genius friend and I wondered if their business together was far more illegal than he let on. I also wondered if Abbott had plans to make some use of me—maybe as a mule of some sort, or maybe as a contact out West who could be activated later.

I didn't know what was going on, exactly. I just knew I was in a vulnerable position and I was sure Abbott had a sense for that as well. But what I noticed—or what I notice now, as I tell the story—is that the thing I stopped doubting was Abbott's past. I stopped thinking critically about the limitations of time and space and the unlikely eventfulness of his life, and I began to take Abbott's tale of his past at face value.

Even with the benefit of retrospect, it's hard to feel foolish about this. However unrealistic I thought the events were, I liked the story. The characters and their personal dilemmas had started to speak to me and the story made me feel less alone. It's the same glue that makes any story, historical or otherwise, adhere to the consciousness.

Abbott broke the rhythmic click of his wheel with a big laugh.

"That head nurse had it in for Denton," he said.

It was an observation that he particularly enjoyed. He shook his head and let out another laugh, an even bigger one that brought me right back into the story.

"We might've all been better off if Denton could've just kept his mouth shut," he said. "I mean open." He laughed again. "But fat chance of that."

Abbott began to sketch out how Denton's sudden return to speaking had created the final fissure in the head nurse's relationship with her new husband whom she'd already begun to consider a bit of a dunce. Soon she began to like Denton even less than she had before. She'd managed to marry a doctor—not just a family doctor either. She'd married a specialist. Now she was finding that her prize catch wasn't only a philanderer with sleep apnea and poor digestion and several private bank accounts to which she had no access, but he was also grossly incompetent. And as far as the head nurse was concerned, Denton Quickfoot White, with his cornsilk hair and his Jesus beard and his dumb refusal to speak had been responsible for the whole mess.

Now that Denton had shaved his beard and his cornsilk hair and had started speaking in riddles and manically raving about the power of kung fu and the wisdom of Kwai Chang Kaine, she liked him even less. But she did agree with the other nurses on one thing. With his bald head and his brow furrowed, he had begun to resemble David Carradine. He might've resembled David Carradine almost as much as he'd resembled white-Jesus in his earlier iteration. Though she thought he looked more like someone else—a movie actor who she found so dazzlingly handsome that his face would sometimes enter her mind while her philandering husband panted his moist bad breath into her ear in short asthmatic wheezes that left her wishing she had the skills to bring his panting to a more abrupt conclusion.

These were things she could sometimes confide to a few close friends over cigarettes and coffee in the staff lounge, but the thing she would never confide was that sometimes during those uncomfortable moments with her philandering, soon-to-be ex-husband, the face she held in her mind was Denton White's. Soon she didn't just dislike Denton. She despised Denton with a passion so deep that she couldn't take her eyes off of him.

In the mornings, when Abbott and Denton would take their meditative walks around the institution's campus, the head nurse could often be seen watching the two from the third-floor room where Denton had once lain with his pelvis writhing and his limbs strapped down and four-hundred-volts of current running through his head.

Just looking at Denton in the presence of that floor-bolted table would shoot a tingle of pleasure through the head nurse that would send her straight down to Boris Schlotzsky's office to issue a report on the pair's strange behavior. Each time she tore down that long, third-floor staircase, she knew exactly what she'd say. She would list her observations to the doctor. She'd tell him how every day she watched the two walking slowly with their hands clasped at the abdomen. She'd describe the meals eaten in silence, the slow chewing, the half-closed eyes, the inward gaze. And then she'd detail the strange afternoon calisthenics performed under the shade of western juniper at the very back corner of the yard, for which the two would remove their shirts. Finally she would make the case that for the sake of sanity, their television viewing had to be restricted.

But it wasn't easy for the head nurse to address these things to Schlotzsky. It actually proved impossible—not because she was intimidated by the awkward little man, but for just the opposite reason. Schlotzsky had a way of making her feel too comfortable. She might storm down to his office in that familiar fit of rage that she barely understood, take a moment in the hall to adjust her white frock and push up her glasses, bring her knuckles three times against the heavy oak, and then be struck as dumb as Quickfoot in his white-Jesus period when the doctor finally opened his door.

Schlotzsky would stand there scratching his thin beard, and the head nurse would want nothing more than to collapse into his chaise lounge and confess everything. She wanted to describe the way the beads of sweat on Denton's soft skin caught the filtered sunlight; and how his almost pornographic physical presence contrasted with the childlike innocence of his eyes so that when he looked at her she had to scowl to avoid gasping. Or—and this was the confession that most wanted to escape her—she would suddenly want to describe to him the way Denton's animal-like stretches in the shade of that western juniper sometimes recalled to her a time she'd seen lions fucking on PBS, and how that recollection sometimes sent her straight to the ladies room, damp with perspiration, to lift her white skirt and still her own panting breath.

She didn't know why Schlotzsky had this effect on her any more than she understood her strange infatuation with Denton White. It was as if the doctor had managed to purchase one of those sets of eyeglasses she'd sometimes seen advertised in her brother's comic books when she was a girl—the kind that only cost a few dollars but gave the owner the ability to see through several thick layers of women's clothing. But the doctor's glasses had been miscalibrated at the factory and now he saw straight through flesh and bone and gray matter, all the way to the deepest folds of her brain. Maybe it was because Schlotzsky was so gentle and kind and deferential or because, even in her nursing shoes, the head nurse towered several inches above the little analyst.

There was no clear explanation why. But whenever she began to talk about Denton White in Schlotzsky's presence, she felt such strong neurotic, confessional compulsions that it took everything she had to wrestle back the urge to lift the floodgates to her most closely guarded secrets and reveal everything. And this only made her animosity toward Denton White that much greater.

In the end, she wouldn't mention Denton at all. Just the thought of saying his name would leave her in the hallway resisting the rush of warm blood into the capillaries of her cheeks as her lips swelled and her labia became warm and soft and damp. When this resistance failed her—and it always did—she'd have to manifest a little fit of coughing to excuse her blush. The next fifteen seconds would be spent trying not to swallow the saliva pooling in the back of her mouth. But when she looked through those glasses and met Schlotzsky's eyes, she'd swallow anyway. She would swallow so loudly it would echo down the long hallway and out the big doors and could probably be heard at the back corner of the grounds where Denton and Abbott were stretching shirtless in the afternoon shade.

In the end, the nurse's head of steam would amount to nothing. She would barely trust herself to speak. She would make some polite excuse for her presence—maybe a recitation of the cafeteria dinner menu—then nod to the doctor and walk down the hallway and up the long staircase to sit on top of that floor-bolted table, light a cigarette, gaze out the window at Denton White, and try not to think of lions.

17

Abbott stopped in the road, took a breath, and shook his head. There was something unique about Denton, he told me. He had some strange power. A gift. You couldn't spend time with him without feeling something spark to life within you. A calling, maybe. Or some auspicious feeling, a sudden inclination toward great hope. This was even true much later, after what happened when Denton returned to Salt Lake City twisted him into two separate characters and brought something ugly to life which Abbott would come to call "the third man."

I heard Abbott's gold Zippo snap open and shut a few times. Then it opened again and sparked to life.

After another moment, he clicked it closed.

"Denton and the nurse," I asked him, "they left together?" It was just a guess, the kind that so impressed my mother when my father would spot the plot points in a TV procedural, but Abbott was in too inward a state to give me any credit.

"That's right," he said. "Together. Though it's probably not what you think. It wasn't what I first thought anyway."

I made a mental note about that. I wanted to dig into it, but something else was bothering me.

"And you and Denton—were you both found in the same desert?"

"It was even stranger than that," he said.

I looked over at Abbott. He had an unlit joint in his mouth. He must've rolled it earlier.

"We both woke up in the same cabin," he said. "Same feeling of disorientation. Same park ranger picked us up. Denton's last memory was listening to Richie Havens perform a Strawberry Fields Forever/Hey Jude mashup. He disappeared a few hours before I did. He remembered becoming famished and eating an entire plate of brownies a little before the set. That coincidence took us a long time to discover."

Abbott clicked his Zippo open. The flame came alive again. One half of his face glowed orange, the other half black. When the lighter clicked closed the tip of the joint was glowing cherry red.

"The whole thing is almost impossible to believe now," he said. The smoke crawled out of his mouth and played in the air between us. "A few months later—this was after Denton was gone—I walked into Schlotzsky's office and he sat me down on the chaise lounge and looked at me with a serious expression. He looked nervous. He said all our hard work had finally paid off."

Abbott took another drag and passed me the joint. I held it in my hand for a moment.

"You were cured?" I said.

"Not exactly," he said.

I took a small hit off the joint and handed it back to him.

"Let's walk," he said. He pulled on his suitcase and that rhythmic ticking started up again. I was thinking about martinis. I could hear Bob Dylan singing "If Not For You," or "The Man in Me." I was tired, ready to finally get somewhere and relax.

"What was it?" I asked. "Had Schlotzsky found the thermometer?"

"Let's not get ahead of ourselves," Abbott said.

"They found Denton?"

"No," Abbott said.

"What then?" I said.

"Well kid, it turned out that the latent thermometer in the latent desert was never about me after all."

"Who was it about?" I asked.

"It was about Schlotzsky," Abbott said.

"Schlotzsky?" I asked. "How could it be about Schlotzsky?"

"After all our hard work, Schlotzsky finally realized he'd cured himself. He'd been trying to cure himself all along."

"That's always the way. Isn't it?" I said.

"It sure is," Abbott said.

Schlotzsky described the process of his cure to Abbott. For almost twenty years, Schlotzsky had fixated on images like the one in Abbott's fantasy, and for good reason. Some things weren't socially acceptable—the doctor explained while Abbott sat on the chaise and listened—and a person of refinement felt the need to sublimate these things into more acceptable frameworks. Then, in the last few days, there had been a sudden crystallization within the doctor's supersaturated psyche. The internal work had occurred over time, but the ultimate realization hit him like a lead pipe—and it was the long analysis into the latent reality of Abbott's giant phallus that deserved all the credit.

Schlotzsky trailed off before continuing from a different angle. He explained how taboos and their sublimation were often the launchpads for leaps in arts and sciences, historical shifts in thinking, and progress in civilization. Most great undertakings would not have been possible without some constraint and refocusing of the libido. Taboos often supplied this constraint, but sometimes constraint just led to neurosis.

"Sometimes Abbott,"—he said, in a rare moment of frankness. "The thing is... The thing is, sometimes..." He took a breath and spit out what he wanted to say all at once. "Sometimes trying to be like everyone else just fucks you up."

He tapped his notebook, brought his pen to his lips, glanced up at Abbott and blushed.

Schlotzsky confessed that his study and practice of Freudian Psychoanalysis had been, for him, just such an act of sublimation—a very positive act, perhaps, and he was certain many patients had benefited—but it was sublimation just the same. What Schlotzsky had discovered, finally, through the process of Abbott's analysis, and his—well, both of their—investigations into the latent reality of the gigantic phallus and the flaccid id at the valley of death, was that he was... Schlotzsky was talking about himself now—

"Well, what I mean to say is—I am—well, what I mean is..." The doctor stopped himself and looked away from his patient.

Abbott had been sitting up facing Schlotzsky, but now he laid back, clasped his hands on his abdomen, and looked toward the ceiling to make things easier on his nervous analyst.

Schlotzsky cleared his throat.

"I'm closeted, Abbott—I mean I was... closeted." Finally, he just committed himself to blurting it out in one fast sentence. "What I mean to say is I'm—" His fast sentence came to a screeching halt and he reduced his voice to complete it in a hushed tone —"I'm *a homosexual*."

Schlotzsky let out a nervous little laugh and continued.

That he never really knew he was in the closet was the damnedest thing. He was just really drawn to Freudian analysis, and in the bedroom with women he—

What he was saying, he said, was that he was coming out of the closet. The latent reality of Abbott's image had cured him of a neurosis that had persisted for most of his lifetime. That was gone now. His years of heavy martini drinking, the sleeping in his easy chair to the repetitive sound of spun-out records, the strange mix of fear and arousal he felt at the sight of a snake, the shame he felt when Kwai Chang Caine removed his shirt. Yes, yes, he admitted, he had been watching *Kung Fu* at home all along. And then there was his habit of drinking all fluids through a straw—how had he not seen these classic signs of the dis-ease that always accompanies repression? It was a testament to repression's power is what it was. But the fact that he had finally arrived at this insight after almost two decades of analysis—this certainly demonstrated the more than equal power of Freudian therapy.

Schlotzsky cleared his throat and adjusted his posture with an air of dignity before stating in no uncertain terms that the time had come for him to move on, but he was willing to stay at the institution as long as Abbott needed him if that was necessary.

Abbott sat back up on the chaise lounge. He considered the doctor's offer for a few moments while the doctor's posture collapsed. Then, with an uncharacteristic lack of repose, Schlotzsky squirmed in his chair, tapped at his notebook, brought his pen to his lips, and waited for Abbott's answer.

Abbott laid back down.

Kung Fu's third season was over, and Denton had escaped the institution. Abbott had the sense that neither the series nor Denton would be returning. He thought he might have learned all he could at Ella Rawson State Hospital—from *Kung Fu*, from his time with Denton, and from Schlotzsky. Denton had restored his faith in friendship. Caine had shown him that the pain of lost love could be carried with dignity and strengthen the spirit. And the hours spent in the office with Schlotzsky—the hours when they hadn't been discussing giant erections—had taught Abbott to navigate through the most treacherous storms of life. Together, they'd mused over the questions of age and death, passion, love, debility, longing, impotence, and the prison of the passage of time. It was Schlotzsky who taught Abbott that one shouldn't look for material solutions to spiritual problems. Abbott's time at the hospital, that place that had been his and Denton's Shaolin Temple, had been fruitful. It had been necessary. But Abbott also knew that it was time to venture outside the terrain of his mind and seek some material solutions to his problems in the manifest world. It was time to leave Schlotzsky and the institution behind and open a new chapter.

He was still weighing out how to answer the analyst when Schlotzsky spoke up again.

"Do you know Carl Jung's story of the golden scarab?" Schlotzsky asked Abbott.

Abbott was confused, suddenly nervous. He stopped breathing. He felt like he was crossing an icy river with only a few steps left to the far bank, and now the doctor had thrown Jung on top of him—Jung,

Freud's student turned nemesis who Schlotzsky abhorred. Under the weight of both of them, the ice would certainly crack. He shook his head to answer Schlotzsky and listened for those first sounds of ice ripping at the seams like overstretched fabric.

The doctor began a story.

Schlotzsky told him that Jung once had one of those rare patients who, without some intervention of divine providence, are incurable. The doctor took a long breath and let it go, as though setting something down he'd been carrying for a long distance.

"One hundred percent incurable," he said.

Abbott winced. Was Schlotzsky talking about him?

The patient was a highly educated woman, Schlotzsky continued. This woman couldn't access the possibility of transformation because transformation would require a change in her thinking. She had an answer for everything. She was brilliant actually, and she believed the knit of her intellectual fabric was flawless.

"She was so reasonable that she could not be reasoned with. Do you understand, Abbott?"

Schlotzsky was silent for a moment. At the very edge of his vision, Abbott could see that the doctor was shaking his head.

Abbott imagined himself walking carefully across that icy river again. In his mind, if he could reach the far bank he would receive his walking papers and begin his new life. If the ice broke, he might tread water in the institution until he drowned in hopelessness.

He didn't speak.

"My friend," the doctor said to Abbott, "miracles do not happen every day."

"I know this," Abbott said.

The doctor shifted his position again and sighed. After what seemed like minutes, he continued the story with a tone of fatalism. He told Abbott that one evening Jung's patient came to him with a dream that had lodged in her mind. In the dream, someone had presented her with a golden scarab, an expensive piece of Egyptian jewelry. It was an important dream, Jung thought, but it would make no difference. He was certain its promising virility would be gelded, as always, by the woman's cutting rationalism.

"In situations like this," Schlotzsky explained, "an analyst is hamstrung."

He took another breath and Abbott heard him shift in his chair again, and then he continued the story.

While Jung sat listening to the drone of the woman's voice, no doubt watching the clock and counting down the minutes of what seemed to be another wasted session, he heard a persistent tapping on the window behind him. His patient continued. She couldn't understand, she told Jung, why she derived such pleasure at receiving the piece of jewelry. It was something she felt she'd wanted—needed—for a very long time. When she woke, she was heartbroken. Now that wonderful gift would be left forever behind in the dream world.

Jung was distracted now. He could only listen with one ear. He was trying to reason through what might be causing the tapping he heard at the window, which seemed to get louder by the moment. Finally, he had to excuse himself to check the window.

Schlotzsky stood, and Abbott could hear him walk to his own window and, though Abbott dared not follow him with his eyes, he somehow knew that the doctor was gazing out over the yard of the institution to the houses of the nearby town. As the doctor continued, Abbott could hear by the sound of Schlotzsky's voice that the doctor remained facing the glass.

"This esteemed analyst," Schlotzsky said, "Freud's most insightful and influential student, had the good sense to investigate any phenomenon that called out for his attention. He understood that maintaining focus is a fundamentally different act than repression. You see, dear Abbott, when Jung opened the window, something landed in his hand. And when Jung looked in his hand, he'd understood the significance immediately."

Schlotzsky became silent and Abbott wondered if he should risk breaking the silence to ask what was in Jung's hand. He couldn't decide. Finally, Schlotzsky gave him some direction.

"You are wondering what was in Jung's hand?"

"Yes," Abbott said.

"Jung closed the window. He walked over to his patient and took her hand in his. 'Here is your golden scarab,' he said. He removed his hand, and in the woman's palm was a scarabaeid beetle of gold-green color, just like the piece of jewelry she had lost in the dream."

Abbott heard the doctor turn from the window and begin to walk toward him. The next moment the doctor was standing above him, looking directly into his eyes.

"You see? Schlotzsky said. "The insect had arrived at the window just as she spoke of her dream. It was there to assist with the session. It was the miracle Jung had been waiting for. It shattered the woman's neat little world."

The doctor stood where he was and waited for Abbott's reaction.

Abbott didn't know what to do. He thought of the peaceful way of

Kwai Chang Caine and breathed deeply, making his hands rise and fall, counting his breaths to keep a calm mind. As his hands fell the seventh time, he heard the doctor take a dry swallow. He thought he heard the sound of fabric tearing as he imagined a short, hopeless life, treading in the icy black waters of cinder blocks and psychotropic drugs. He wondered if Schlotzsky thought that without the intercession of a miracle, he would remain incurable. That was the question on the tip of his tongue, but Schlotzsky didn't give him time to ask. He leaned over Abbott and took him by the shoulders.

"You, Abbott! You were my golden scarab!"

Schlotzsky gasped for breath as he fought back his tears. Then the tears came and, covering his face, Schlotzsky explained that it was the image Abbott brought to him, that gigantic phallus towering over the valley of death, that had torn apart the tight weave of the doctor's mental world.

"Life is too short," Schlotzsky went on, "We have to chase after what we love—however impractical or illusory, and however uncomfortable. You taught me that, Abbott"

Schlotzsky brushed his eyes with his sleeve. There would be no more Freud, he said, and there would be no more Jung. There would be a stage show in Vegas for the doctor and a discharge for Abbott. When the paperwork was completed, the doctor would be resigning his position and both he and Abbott would be free to chase the great story told in their hearts. *This*, Schlotzsky declared to Abbott, with the sound of authority and certainty finally returning to his voice, this was the closest anyone could ever come to approaching sanity.

Abbott sat up. The doctor took his hand and looked at him with his face beaming, then he pulled his friend of several years in close and hugged him with everything he had.

18

The lights of I-70 were becoming visible on the horizon. Abbott used what was left of our walk to spill a few details about the dark period of doubt and confusion he experienced after he left the institution and headed back to the Mojave Desert to search for the giant thermometer and reunite with Lucille.

He didn't find what he expected. What he found was despair. What he found was doubt. But he also found that beneath that doubt and despair, as far down as it penetrated, were always more layers of hope and faith. Soon he would encounter deeper levels of despair and deeper layers of doubt, but if he kept traveling he would always find hope again. And even through the blackest of doubting darkness, he would still catch pinpoints of light that kept his faith alive.

Sometimes the light would be a flame—that gold Zippo he carried, which had somehow leapt across time and space with him. He would find it in his hand while he sat in the darkness somewhere in the frigid night of Death Valley, a landscape he would traverse in its entirety, searching for that towering landmark, searching for the lost diner, the lost love, his lost life. But Abbott would hitchhike the surrounding highways and find nothing resembling the one-hundred and thirty-four-foot phallus he remembered. He would ask everyone he encountered. It didn't matter if they seemed kind or lonely for conversation or if they seemed irritated by the very fact of his existence. He asked because he had to—because the compulsion could not be repressed.

Mostly there were no words. Amusement was common, as if he'd told a good joke. If he pressed, he might be met with a barrier of cynicism and distrust that seemed to him the sad legacy of a country that had lost its mind fevering for gold. There would be no thermometer, but Abbott would see some beautiful and strange things in that desert.

A man with a wooden leg like a pirate who picked him up in an old Ford F-500 would beam with excitement when he heard that Abbott was looking for massive objects in the shape of a man's engorged penis.

"Cocks?" the man asked.

His voice betrayed a level of anticipation that filled Abbott with nostalgia for Schlotzsky and the days at the institution when a man could speak of these things without any sense of embarrassment.

"If you want to see gigantic cocks," the pirate said, downshifting and turning his truck around at the first pull-off, "I know the place you're looking for."

The man drove southwest out of the valley, babbling on about the transformative powers of the Mojave, about lights in the sky, about giant stones that crawled through the darkness on their bellies. He told Abbott about a mystical boulder in the Mojave that sheltered an underground room where a man had been visited by an alien from outer space who told him how to build a machine that could rejuvenate the human body—a sort of time machine, the pirate said. It was a tall wooden dome with sixteen sides and an electrical coil, like the one designed by Nikola Tesla. It was called the Integratron.

When Abbott heard this, he grabbed the pirate by the arm and squeezed.

"Does it send people forward or backward?" he asked.

The pirate looked down to where Abbott's hand was gripping him and Abbott released the man's arm.

"The fuggin Integratron?" the pirate said. "Only backwards."

Abbott considered for a moment. "I think I need to go forward," he said.

"Well, the Integratron is a nice structure, kid, but if you need to actually get somewhere, you're better off with a fuggin Ford. You might even be better off with a fuggin Chevy."

"It doesn't work?" Abbott said.

"Fuggin George Van Tassel," the pirate said. "Every time I see that fugger he's just a few minor tweaks away from a viable, working time-travel device. He wants to go backward. Fugger wants to live forever. Meanwhile, life's dragging him one step at a time toward one certain end."

"I feel that way too," Abbott said. "I want to get to the end. Except I only want to get there faster."

"Well kid," the pirate said. "I got good news and bad news." He pulled a gallon water jug half full of brown fluid off the floor and shoved a plug of tobacco in his mouth. "Life's gonna drag you that direction whether you fuggin like it or not. Kickin' and fuggin screamin' or rowing merrily down the stream." He took the cap off the jug and spit in a stream of brown fluid from a half foot away. "If you have some fuggin patience and maybe a bit of a sense of humor, you might even enjoy yourself a little. Soon enough," the pirate said, pointing to his face. "You're gonna look like me. You'll get there eventually, kid."

Abbott looked at the pirate. He was old. About Abbott's real age, the age he was before everything had gone terribly wrong. He felt for the gold Zippo in his pocket and laid his hand on top of it.

"Is that the good news or the bad news?" Abbott asked him.

The old man laughed. He shot another stream of saliva into the jug.

"Happens in the blink of an eye, son. So let me pass on some fuggin advice that I paid for by the pan full—by the fuggin shovelful. But I'm gonna give it to you free of charge, see?"

He looked on the floor by Abbott's feet, at the Idaho potato sack that contained all Abbott's worldly possessions.

"You don't look like you could afford what I oughta charge you for it, anyway."

Abbott met the man's eyes for a moment before turning away. He looked out across the flat desert—at the parched floor, cracked and dry like the old man's skin. Far away, he could see the light bending into that dark desert ocean. He recalled how sometimes, in the institution afternoons, Lucille used to emerge out of those waters like a mythical Lady of the Lake, with Abbott's entire lost life taking shape behind her. Now he hoped that would happen again, that at any moment the giant cock that the pirate had mentioned would peak over the horizon. He imagined the trusty old F-500 approaching as the red tip of the thermometer became visible and slowly revealed its full height. He anticipated the excitement that would overtake him as the diner materialized below, the morning shadow tilting away, pointing toward Lucille like the compass in Abbott's heart that was forever calling him home.

The pirate interrupted him. "You ready?" He said.

Abbott nodded without taking his eyes off the horizon.

"Don't dream your fuggin life away, kid."

Abbott wondered if that was it. Was that the advice, or was the man just observing Abbott's lack of interest in anything but what lay just over the horizon?

"You understand, son?" The man asked him. "Don't waste your life in some mineshaft digging for the fuggin gold that's gonna change the perfectly good life you already fuggin have. Look at Van Tassel and his fuggen Integratron. Wasting all his time tryin' to recover all the fuggin time he's wasting tryin' to recover all his wasted time. You wanna know where you'll discover the best fuggin time machine you're ever gonna find, kid?"

Abbott took a moment to look away from the horizon.

"It's dangling right between your fuggin legs!"

The pirate took a moment to let his point sink in, then he slapped the dash with his hand and continued.

"That's right, kid. Your fuggen cock! And there's nothin' more miraculous than when that thing stands up straight in front of a woman. Doesn't matter if it's three inches high or a full fuggin link of kielbasa, or—what'd you say you were looking for?—even if it's a tower in the fuggen valley of death. It's a time machine that blows that Integratron to fuggin smithereens. And Jesus fuggin Christmas, kid—if you love the woman, then that's the icing on the fuggin cake. That time machine'll take you forward, backward, and everywhere in between. Anywhere you wanna go, kid. It'll take you to fuggin outer space if you let it. It's the original fuggin rocket ship, kid. You understand? You think it's some sort of coincidence that NASA had to build a gigantic fuggin cock to take us to the moon? You get me, son?"

Abbott's eyes began to well up. Then his chest shook and that gate in his throat burst open. He started quaking with sobs. If the only way to recover his lost life would be through loving another woman, he wasn't sure he wanted to get there. The pirate reached over and pulled some napkins out of the glove box and Abbott took them.

"Jesus Christmas, son," he said. "What did I fuggin say?"

"Lucille," Abbott managed between sobs, "I just need to find Lucille." He focused on the horizon again and tried to regain control of his chest.

There was no thermometer. The man with one wooden leg drove Abbott out to see the Trona Pinnacles, huge stony formations that reached up from the earth like the clutching fingers of long-buried giants. They were rough and beautiful and majestic in a way that would've made Schlotzsky swoon, but they didn't compare to Lucille and they didn't point Abbott in any clear direction. The old man reached back into the glove box and pulled out a flask of rum and the two men sat on the flatbed and passed the flask back and forth in quiet admiration for a while before anyone spoke. When half the flask was gone, Abbott told his story.

The pirate sat there and listened. Even after Abbott had finished speaking, the other man was quiet. He took a few sips of rum.

"A hundred and thirty-four-foot thermometer?" he said. "Well kid, if it's not out here now, it's gonna be. It'd fuggin fit right in."

"Patience," Abbott said. "I know."

The pirate talked a little. He told Abbott that for years after he'd lost his leg he would dream about it almost every night. He'd look down and it'd be there again. He'd be happy. Running and skipping and clapping his feet in the air like a loon. Then he'd slowly become conscious that he was dreaming and he'd realize that to wake up, he'd have to lose his leg all over again.

"The old tin can doesn't let you welch on the mourning process, see?" The pirate tapped his temple a few times. "You can drink rum all day and it'll just wait for you. Patience. See? It'll collect what's owed in your fuggin sleep."

Even when he was awake, he'd sometimes sense that his leg was still there. But soon enough he'd realize his mistake and he'd get angry at the world for taking it from him. The old man said he knew a little about what Abbott was experiencing. But at some point, the man told him, he'd had to make a decision—he could mourn the life he'd lost or embrace the life that remained. Once he'd made that decision, all the energy of his leg flowed elsewhere and he found contentment again, perhaps even more so than before. After the leg went, he said, his erections became harder than stone. He pointed his finger to the landscape towering over them. "Harder than those pinnacles," he said.

"You think I should let go?" Abbott asked him.

The pirate took another sip of rum. "Naw," he said. "Go and find her, kid. Some things in life, you gotta chase after even if they kill ya. Some things are more fuggin harmful to let go than to hold onto."

Abbott nodded. He secured the latch on that gate in his throat and tried not to sob.

"But if you change your mind, kid, I know a few cathouses—a few women that would cure you right fuggin quick."

Abbott shook his head.

"I know," the man said. "A young kid like you—and I know you're not really a young fugger, but I mean you got years ahead for miles and miles. You need a quest. You're looking for an adventure—something extraordinary. But this Lucille—this woman of yours waiting for you in the future—I think she'd want you to smell the roses—at least a little bit. I mean you're a hell of a good kid, Abbott, but I'll tell you something. No woman wants to marry a fuggin monk. Trust me on that."

Abbott nodded. He felt the skin on his cheeks stretching. It felt odd, a first for his new, young face. He was smiling. He was also drunk. Strange, he thought—he had recovered a little piece of his lost life after all. He sat and admired the pinnacles for thirty minutes or so over the remaining rum, then he thanked the pirate and grabbed his potato sack and set out into the desert to try to recover the rest of what he'd lost.

The pirate wasn't kidding. The valley was full of a magic that spoke a language Abbott didn't quite understand. He saw strange lights in the sky that sometimes seemed to follow after him. He came across bighorn sheep, dead and bloodless with organs removed as if by a surgeon. There were shadowy figures shaped like men that moved like nothing from this world. Far away he heard coyotes baying. Sometimes the coyotes seemed to follow just at the edge of the darkness, as if he had strayed from the pack and they were watching after him. He saw the strange stones the pirate had mentioned, some of them larger than himself. In the night, they would come to life, crawling on their bellies across the cracked earth like men desperate with thirst. In the mornings, he would follow along the snail trails that marked the slow deliberate effort of the stones, and he'd wonder at their patience.

In a desperate moment, he drank the bad water from Badwater Spring, not so much out of thirst, as out of a strange hope that the discolored, salty water might bequeath supernatural powers or visions to those bold enough to drink it. But the water only burned his throat and disturbed his stomach and made Abbott wish he could find the Integratron and travel back in time to the moment when he was debating whether or not to drink the water, so he could tell himself that the idea would turn out to be exactly as stupid as it sounded.

The towns Abbott came across were ghost towns, towns that had sprouted up with purpose and great promise and had seen good years when men dug down into the soul of the earth to uncover precious elements. But then, just like that, the precious elements had been exhausted and fortunes had changed in the blink of an eye. Abbott spent nights in several of these towns, sleeping on the dirt floors of abandoned adobe huts with sunken roofs, passing time in the darkness, moving between doubt and the flickering light of his Zippo. Clicking it shut, resting in darkness until it seemed Lucille had never existed and there had been no giant thermometer—that there had been no shadow, and no Lucille's Diner, and that there had been no black and white floor for that shadow to sweep across like a broad and happy broom. His memory of Lucille and his very faith in the past he'd shared with her would begin to turn to dust before his eyes. He would watch it swirl around the floor, rise with the wind that never quieted, and make for the window to escape into the night and join the forever-lost memories of the valley and the stones that followed after them. Then that gold lighter would click again, the flame would dance, and he would remember that he was sane.

Many nights, Abbott would fall asleep as the wind made its rounds again and again through one of the many ghost towns, in and out of doors and windows, searching for the old citizens and life and music that had disappeared without reason or warning and had left an emptiness that the wind could not fill. Now there was only Abbott and the memory of Lucille he held close to him and the stones that came to life in the night to make their sad, slow way on their bellies through the dead streets and the long, flat expanses of the playa.

Sometimes he would wake and lift his arm to see if Lucille was there, so he could shake her eyes open and tell her the strange story of his horrible dream. When she wasn't there, he would tell her the story anyway. She always giggled about Schlotzsky. She loved Schlotzsky. And she rolled her eyes at the antics of Denton. She said Abbott must have looked handsome so young and fit again—and so like the man who had first walked into her father's diner confused and hungry for pancakes and wondering what year it was. She would smile and tell Abbott she was happy to wait for him, right there in the diner where they had first found each other. She told him that someday she would like to be found by just such a man.

Abbott always sobbed when Lucille said that, and he promised that he would not stop searching for her, and then his eyes would bubble with bad water that poured into his mouth and did at least provide the supernatural grace of sleep. In the morning he would look across the ghost town where he'd spent the night and wonder if somewhere, in the eternal landscape of time, his life with Lucille remained like that—a sad and unfinished story where once life had thrived. Then he would overtake the stones that had crawled through the desert all night on their bellies. He would marvel again at their patience and wonder where their snail-like efforts would take them.

19

We walked through most of the night. A few hours before dawn we reached the on-ramp to I-70 and stuck out our thumbs. After a short time, an old pickup driven by a pair of hillbillies stopped and we jumped in the bed. The moon rose in the sky and the cool air swirled around us and we pressed our backs against the cab to sit where the air was most still. Abbott looked different now than in the Ferrari. The light shifted on his face and his hair tousled in the wind and I caught a different impression of him—sadder, more broken, less gregarious, older. Then his face flickered as if it were a television receiving signal from two different stations, and I saw him as a much younger man. He struck me as a character out of a tragic legend, a timeless spirit one meets on the lonely roads of America when hitchhiking late at night, long dead or undead and doomed to wander the earth in the same circles, forever in search of a lost love he will never find. I imagined him repeating this life over and over, and I wondered if I was stuck there with him, if the two of us had met and would continue to meet like this eternally, or if he was the type of spirit who had accepted his curse with an attitude of benevolence and now traveled these long American highways telling his story over and over to steer men like me from a similar fate to his own.

One of the hillbillies, the passenger, tapped on the cab window and slid it open. He handed us a couple of bottles of cold beer. I took a few sips and felt a small rush of clarity, deciding right then that the worst future was the one in which nothing changed. As that was decided, it seemed I could now let go of all my worries about what lay ahead. Either I would find my way and things would get better—in which case I should be hopeful—or things would continue to get worse, which meant I should enjoy every remaining moment of my declining life to its fullest.

I started to share this insight with Abbott, but then I changed my mind. Instead, I began to tell him about *The First Chapter*. I crafted the story in a way I knew would speak to him. I told him that every day for years that novel had seemed to twitch at the tips of my fingers and yet I could never bring it into the world. Its absence haunted me the way a phantom haunts an old house, always there in some sub-atomic form but somehow never able to physically materialize. I described myself sitting in that same chair above the garage, keeping vigil, waiting for the chapters to reveal themselves on the page. Twenty years—and yet with each passing year I traveled fewer paragraphs into chapter two. I struggled forward but I always turned back, taking the first chapter apart and rewriting it over and over until it was exactly the same as before. Sometimes, I told Abbott, it drove me crazy. The world saw me as a failure because a man is defined by what he has done and not what he knows already exists, fully formed in his future. As far as I was concerned, *The First Chapter* had already been written. It would exist. It already existed. I just didn't know when.

I looked to Abbott for a sign of acknowledgment or commiseration, but he only sipped his bottle of beer and swallowed, keeping his eyes on the dark road behind us where the sun would rise, as if keeping a vigil of his own.

"I became a bit of a joke around the college," I said. It was an admission I'd never made before, not to Laura or even to myself, though it wasn't exactly a secret either. It'd been eating me from the inside. "Everyone else was important. Published papers, symposium invitations, awards. I had nothing to show for myself but a single chapter that had long since been forgotten by everyone but me and my agent and the publisher who was suing me for my advance. Then Laura stopped taking me seriously too. I noticed it at department parties. A couple of the more distinguished professors would flirt with her while I stood, hands in pockets, shouldered out of the conversation, feeling like Laura was smiling to punish me. I was an eyesore, a lump on the floor to be skirted on the way to the bar. They couldn't understand what Laura saw in me. I had no accolades, no awards, and no new chapters. Nothing to offer. You either walked around me or you ended up scraping me off the bottom of your shoe."

Abbott cleared his throat.

I stopped speaking and waited for him to offer some insight.

"Did it help your writing?" he asked.

I thought I heard humor in his voice, but you could hear anything you wanted in Abbott's voice.

"It made it unreadable," I said. "Pretentious. Overwritten. I had too much to prove. I wanted my novel to be the best thing ever written."

"That's the third man," Abbott said. "He was doing the writing for you."

He'd mentioned this man before. I couldn't place him, but I got the gist of what he was saying. The third man had a way of railroading things toward the very end he materialized to prevent. He was the guy Laura left, not me.

~~*~~

I spilled my guts until dawn. Interstate 70 ran through Indianapolis and we continued west on 72. I told Abbott about my legal and financial troubles, about the repossession of my house which had been bought with that first advance and refinanced twice over the years to supplement my meager income as an adjunct composition teacher. I told him about my big financial crime, which had been too sloppy and brazen to properly call embezzlement—though they were calling it that anyway—and the blaze of glory that had ended my employment and sent me out on the road. I showed him the cheap, phony ID I had ordered on the darknet under the name "Daniel Wilder," which was just a touch more edgy than my given name and shared the same initials to avoid a complete identity crisis, or that was my working theory anyway. I even showed him my small bundle of embezzled cash that had originally been a large enough bundle to fund my trip west and keep me going through a twelve-month stint somewhere in solitude. Of course, the third man—I told Abbott, getting a better hold on exactly who this guy was—tried to turn the twelve-month bundle into a more luxurious twenty-four-month bundle by playing the stock market, and now I only had a bundle good for six months of beans and rice in a rented room somewhere in a down luck town that time forgot, or perhaps in Mexico.

All I wanted to do was finish my novel. That would satisfy my debt to my publisher and maybe it would fulfill the promise of my premise to Laura too. If it was a good novel, it might make enough to repay the university the embezzled funds. And if the critics liked it, maybe it would even stop my mother from constantly naming off occupations that she thought I might be good at—things like shoe salesman and yard care technician. I knew my plan was straight out of a win-the-girl-back Hollywood script, and success would require me to survive starvation and avoid arrest long enough to produce an actual novel that would garner an impossible number of book sales. In short, it was a terrible plan, but it was all I had.

Abbott thought about it for a while, and then he told me about a place he still owned in the foothills of the Rockies on the outskirts of a small city. The place was a head clearer, he said. It had clean water and electricity but not much else. No internet. No phone. Not even a mailbox. He asked to see my phone and I gave it to him. "This is for your own good, kid," he said, and then he hurled it out of the pickup bed. I watched it sail through the air and land skidding and bouncing on the dark highway, the fracturing screen picking up glimmers of light. All I felt was a sense of release. Now I was ready to write, Abbott told me. He gave me the address and some directions, scribbling it all down on the back of his gas station receipt while it flapped in the wind and dawn chased us down from the road behind us. He couldn't go with me. He needed to get to Bodyman's in Iowa and recover the Ferrari from the cornfield in Indiana, but he would meet me at the cabin soon enough, he promised. It could be a few weeks, a month maybe, but when he arrived the two of us would continue west to find Lucille. He had some solid leads, but he needed a car and he needed to head north for a bit to meet with Harelip Lenny and figure out some details.

The sky grew lighter by shades. Finally, we were crossing the Mississippi. The truck slowed at the far side of the bridge as we approached the junction of Routes 36 and 61 in Hannibal, Missouri. From there, Abbott would continue with the hillbillies north toward Iowa City to meet Bodyman in Fairfield, and I would travel west on my own. The truck stopped and I hopped out. A huge bust paved into the hill at the opposite side of the interstate caught my eye, glowing orange in the morning sun. It reminded me I was standing in the birth town of Mark Twain. I remembered how Huck Finn had faked his own death before running off with Jim to seek freedom and change their fates. It was a sign, I thought. What a place for my journey to really begin. I could imagine the brilliant future ahead of me—writing long chapters in Abbott's little cabin in the shadows of the mountains, sipping strong coffee morning after morning until I finally placed the final page on a big stack of pages and bundled up the manuscript. I could see Abbott approaching from far off, a plume of dust in his wake, as I sat ready, novel completed, waiting for the next phase of life to meet me. In my imagination, Abbott wasn't driving the Ferrari anymore, but a Western car for a new adventure—a copper Firebird or a black Trans Am. Abbott would pick me up and the two of us would continue west, me with a completed novel and him with a solid lead, a map with a deep red X on it. We would be on our way to reunite with the women we had lost.

I stood there in the road and we said a few words to each other. Then I watched the truck pull away, disappearing down the road like Laura's car had done a year before. Back then, I stood watching impotently from my little room above the garage, but the feeling was different now. The whole world was teetering on the cusp of change. I felt the sun rising behind me, heating my back as I began to walk, its warm fingertips painting my silhouette onto the road ahead.

20

On October 14, 1992, Boba Savage and his Happy Accidents were returning northeast along I-15 after performing at a secretive union ceremony between a former Hollywood action star and the action star's former male masseuse. The troupe had become fashionable among certain Hollywood circles, and these trips from just-off-The-Strip to just-off-The-Boulevard were becoming more commonplace. Savage enjoyed the time on the road. The troupe had purchased a hot-pink, touring coach and now found themselves traveling round trip through the Mojave once or twice a month. For Savage, the novelty of Death Valley never grew old. Whenever their tour bus dipped into the salt pan of the valley, a bittersweet nostalgia would overtake him, and he would recall the quixotic earnestness with which his most memorable patient had spoken of his lost life.

Boba Savage had also left a life behind him, and though he had never been confident enough about the permanence of his new vocation to fill out the paperwork and make his *nom de guerre* legal, the name and the career path had stuck. In the twenty years since leaving Ella Rawson, the professionally trained Freudian had graduated from backup dancer to lead act, and he now managed and choreographed his own, all-male cabaret.

For years, memories of the old life had remained mostly dormant, but lately this landscape brought to mind a letter which he'd carried with him for so many years and now stored at the bottom of the first makeup box he'd purchased for himself with a feeling of liberation and hope. Though finer boxes had long ago taken that first one's place, Boba still opened that original box now and then to reconnect himself with the long and sometimes painful path he'd traveled. The changes in his life had been so drastic over the last twenty years that he sometimes needed to remind himself that those days in Ella Rawson State Hospital with Abbott were not a figment of his imagination. Even simple memories like the constraining tweed suits he'd once worn and the mildewy smell of his old, oak desk were so distant from the person he had become that they often seemed like details from a story he'd heard somewhere or read as a child. Whenever that seminal image Abbott had first presented to him and the work the two had done to uncover its latent reality entered his memory, he found it nearly impossible to believe that such recollections were actual products of the past and not some fiction he'd dreamed up as a catalyst for his own emancipation.

Upon returning to his luxury Vegas condo after one of these recent trips through the Mojave, the old doctor would dig to the bottom of his old makeup box where he had tucked away Abbott's short document and unfold that single page to read it once more, word for word as he recalled the events of his life. In this way, he would ensure that he was still of sane and sound mind, and living in manifest reality where the line of causation traveled a single line from past to future in only one direction, and that his steady transit of this line had formed his identity. Sometimes that line of causation would fill him with nostalgia and the old doctor would dig back into his makeup box for one of his many bowls of glass or marble or clay or wood—whatever fit his mood—and stuff it with a moist bud of marijuana. He'd sit on the big, brass bed that he'd bought on a whim, after a breakup, when the only album he wanted to listen to was Bob Dylan's *Nashville Skyline*, and he would smoke and let his mind drift and recall his days with Abbott.

Over the years, as the cult status of his all-male cabaret exploded, and Schlotzsky found himself traveling more and more often through that lonesome valley, its spirit of emptiness had a way of clinging to him. It was something that became progressively difficult to shake. The more that emptiness clung to him, the more he found himself scouring the infertile landscape, cracked and weathered and caked like dry makeup, for a sign of life and hope that could rejuvenate his failing libido. That old image, the erection towering one-hundred and thirty-four feet high over the desolate landscape, would flash into his mind and he'd find himself smiling with a strange and hopeful sadness.

It occurred to Schlotzsky that only now, in his own sunset years, could he understand the suffering and heartache his favorite patient had experienced when he had been cast out of the idyllic life of his imagination. As old and worn and desirous of youth as the doctor was, had he woken from a dream to find himself back at the institution with all the difficult trials that followed on the heels of his liberation still ahead of him—had he to look forward to the failed loves, the lost loves, the loves that collapsed under the guilty burden of their great sensual pleasure, those first desperate and disappointing friendships, the decade long estrangement from his family, the secret shame that overshadowed every early joy in that new life—he would've been terrified. Looking backward, he could relive it all with the sweetness of nostalgia, but he wouldn't have wanted to travel that hard road again. This thought could overwhelm him until the dry landscape grew cloudy and he realized once again that he had failed to understand the friend who had set him free.

The travel-coach was making a right turn off the exit for Baker, California as Schlotzsky wiped his eyes with the sleeve of his tunic. The troupe had only been traveling a few hours, but at his age, Schlotzsky welcomed any opportunity to stretch his legs. And things being what they were, he preferred the bathrooms of diners and gas stations to sitting over a swishing chemical hole in a moving bus. Schlotzsky had long ago learned to deal with the stares and the comments of the inland locals that would've kept him in the bus in his early years as a performer. The truth was that anything he had to endure from these cretins of the valley was bound to be less damaging than the knocks to the head he took in the coach's small restroom with Freddy at the wheel.

Freddy was a handsome twenty-three-year-old who'd flattered and fucked his way into The Happy Accidents but didn't seem to have the rhythm for dancing. They'd made him their driver, but he didn't have much talent for that either. He was always turning away from the road to flirt with the troupe and his main talent seemed to be forgetting he was piloting a twenty-ton bus, and then turning and jerking the wheel in abject terror as it slid off the shoulder of the interstate toward the dry and open and rutty desert.

Schlotzsky had been lost in thought. The sound of the air brakes as the bus came to a halt brought him back to the present. He stood up and filed toward the front of the bus with the rest of the troupe, looking at the name of the restaurant they'd chosen for their evening meal with a smile.

"Big Bun?" he said to Freddy.

The driver turned and smiled back at Schlotzsky, and the smile sent such a wave of pleasure through the old choreographer that he once again concluded that Freddy's employment with the troupe—barring the very real possibility of some disfiguring traffic accident—was an ironclad reality for at least the next fifteen years.

"Carly wanted to see the world's tallest thermometer," Freddy said. "Would you look at that?"

Freddy pointed over his left shoulder and then closed one eye, lining his hand up with the phallic monstrosity before moving it up and down slowly in a gesture of caress.

"I think it turned Carly on," Freddy said.

Schlotzsky leaned over Freddy and followed the red lights up the shaft to where the thermometer sat at a middling ninety-six degrees.

"You've gotta be kidding me," he said.

"It's brand new," Freddy said, "I was hoping for something bigger, weren't you?"

Schlotzsky followed the shaft of the thermometer back down to where it met the ground in a few tons of concrete. "I'll be damned," he said. He traced the direction of the shadow before looking behind him to check the sun's proximity to the horizon and then he gathered his tunic in his hands and ran off the bus.

"Boba, where are you going?" Freddy asked him, pointing in the other direction. "Big Bun is over there."

"I have to find Lucille," Schlotzsky shouted over his shoulder. He was already heading east, his brisk walk turning into a trot as he took off in the direction of his shadow.

It was close to midnight, at a filling station in Topeka, Kansas, when I first read Schlotzsky's letter. My long day of travel from Hannibal, Missouri, had been strung together with a series of rides from regular old strangers, and our easy, mindless talk had restored me with a sense of normalcy that was almost narcotic. I took a second ride and a third. The day wore on, the sun moving from rear windows to overhead to low and blinding on the horizon so that the visors had to be flipped down as the slightly rolling hills became the plains—but my conversations with drivers didn't change. Naturally, there was a bit of improvisation, but every conversation traveled across the same phases and phrases to reach the same final points. It wasn't just the drivers either. I couldn't help myself. At each conversational juncture, I found myself responding just as I had in the previous vehicle, as if the two of us were rehearsing a scene from a play. By around midnight, when I reached Topeka, the repetition was triggering a familiar experience of claustrophobia and déjà vu that put me right back up above my garage rewriting my first chapter. I couldn't put a finger on exactly what was causing it, but I found myself wishing I could bring Abbott back into the story to break me out of the loop.

After seven or eight rides, I got off at the filling station in Topeka to get a cup of coffee and a pack of cigarettes. When I reached into my back pocket for my wallet, I felt the letter there and I saw myself standing in a cornfield, in a time that now seemed like a lifetime ago, debating the existence or non-existence of an approaching police interceptor.

My dear, dear Abbott, it began.

Part Three

A Man of Letters

When the sun comes up, I have morals again.

—— Elizabeth Taylor

21

Something startled me awake. For a moment, I thought I'd drifted off in the passenger seat of Abbott's 308 and it had been a backfire, a sudden lurch of the chassis. I opened my eyes and turned to my left, almost expecting to see Abbott with one hand on the wheel, the other pulling on the gearshift. I could almost hear that musical voice dropping down to a grumble as his storytelling shifted from its big gracious strokes to the petty feelings that sometimes consumed him when the car began to misbehave. For a while I laid there silently, breath shallow, the eyes in my ears searching the blackness, listening for the sounds of keys jingling, scratching for the lock. Sometimes I even thought I was back home in my bed with Laura. My hand would reach out searching for her only to find a cool mattress.

This happened at least a couple of nights a week during my stay at Abbott's cabin. I might lay there for a few minutes, a half-hour. It didn't matter. Whatever amount of time I waited, when I finally turned to check the clock, it always read 3:08. It was strange and I don't know what you call it. Coincidence? Synchronicity? I might start awake and lay there in the darkness, imagining an entire life unfold. Abbott had returned from his trip to Bodyman's shop in Fairfield. He'd picked up a new car and chased down leads with Harelip Lenny. I would close my eyes again and enjoy our adventure—dust flying up behind us, Mike Post themes playing loud through the stereo, the two of us in some classic car with a big engine, charging toward our lost women and the magical lives we should have been living all along. Finally, I'd open my eyes to check the time.

It would be 3:08.

Most nights, sleep didn't return. Dawn cracked and I rose and switched on the lamp, dug through the drawer of Abbott's writing desk, pulled out Schlotzsky's letter, and unfolded its map-like creases to read it once more. Once I was satisfied that I was of sane and sound mind and Abbott had not been just a figment of my imagination, I would refold the letter and return it to the drawer for safekeeping until the next morning. Then I would sit quietly until the birds began to sing, percolate some coffee on the stove, and begin writing.

For the first six weeks or so, I felt like I was getting somewhere. Abbott's cabin was stocked for the apocalypse with non-perishable supplies. There was plenty of food and plenty of coffee and very few distractions. I returned to *The First Chapter*, but I worked differently than before, eschewing the keyboard and cursor for furiously scribbled notes. Half my notes were fairly journalistic, dedicated to Abbott's story and my impressions of him. The other half related to a treatise on time travel. It wasn't only about time travel. There were other elements too, ideas taken from simulation theory, Platonism, Buddhist philosophy, Judeo-Christian theology, even a touch of Flat-Eartherism and other stuff I was catching on late-night AM radio. I was telling myself this theory was purely fictive, a representation of Abbott's worldview. But deep inside I began to wonder if it might contain a deep truth that could shake the non-fictive world into a new era of consciousness.

I would scribble for hours at a time, draw diagrams, sketch out possible plot lines and character arcs, and in the afternoons I would clean and cook or chop wood or walk about the property, wandering as far as I thought I could before encountering people. The one thing I didn't do was read, even though Abbott had a small library of the type of modern literary fiction I should have enjoyed. But reading didn't provide much of a distraction. I found that the books I had previously loved no longer spoke to me. Something about them didn't capture this new era. I couldn't define "this new era," but I had a feeling sometimes, while trying to give myself to those old stories, that a few fundamental laws of reality had been shaken askew and, by some strange application of the Mandela Effect, most of humanity had shifted into a new reality and only a few of us remembered enough to be confused. Other times, in a more pedestrian way, my alienation from literature made complete sense. It was me who had changed. I was now much older than my literary heroes, and the same stories I once looked to for clues about the experiences that lay ahead and who I might become, now only contained the same faulty information that had led me to my current state of ennui. It seemed that if a man my age was to find any semblance of adventure and hope on the horizon, he would have to manifest it himself, almost out of thin air.

As the weeks wore on with no sign of Abbott, my writing began to stall. I would go through my notes from beginning to end only to find myself going through them again. At times I would be confronted by the haunting feeling that I was still up above my garage, that my actual place in the cosmos was not geographical but temporal, and that time was no longer moving. It seemed that I would be held in this prison of timelessness, away from the people I loved and the grace of change until *The First Chapter* was complete. I could flee my job, my debts, my legal troubles. I could escape all the externalities that plagued me, but my life would revolve around this one internal point of purgatory until the book was finished. The novel would be my act of penance, but it would also contain my confession.

I had virtually zero contact with the outside world for the first several weeks. The cabin had minimal electricity and no internet or TV, just the little AM radio that only got reception at night. In the mornings, scribbling notes, I would be thankful for that. But when afternoon approached and I laid about in silence as the sky grew dark, I often cursed Abbott for tossing my phone onto the interstate. I would suffer a brief and desperate thirst for connection, for even just a little news from outside my small universe, delivered to me by the counterfeit internet that Abbott loathed. Finally, I became lonely and distraught enough that I walked a mile or so to the nearest little town and, using a technique we had agreed upon the night before I first arrived at Abbott's cabin, I called my mother. She had always been such an antagonist to me, but in these new circumstances our relationship began to change. She became the person I would call when I started to feel disconnected in my solitude and when my head would become so full of my treatise on time travel that I needed to feel some sense of ground and continuity.

I suppose I had a similar feeling to what Schlotzsky had described in his letter. The road that connected the present to my past had been severed by a fault line behind me, and I was having trouble connecting the self whom I found at the cabin to the past I thought I had lived. The present didn't make sense to me anymore, and when my mother informed me that Laura had taken up with a memoirist and was speaking about me as if I'd lost my mind, I began to wonder who I actually was. I didn't know if my experiences still aligned with anyone else on earth, or if I now existed in my own box where everything I believed about myself was both true and false. I suppose this explains the dating and desperation that would soon govern my life. Laura had always been the one to polish my image and reflect it back to me in a way I liked to recognize. Without her to hold me in place, I could almost feel my self-concept bleeding into the void that surrounded me. It was as if my very skin had been flayed away and my skeleton had begun to dissolve in acid. I was alone in the forest, and I needed someone else there if only to hear me fall.

22

I shouldn't have begun thinking about Laura before the book was finished. It put my writing in a holding pattern and sent my mind into a tailspin. My whole misadventure had begun for the purpose of finishing *The First Chapter*, but after hearing the things Laura was saying to my mother about me, I was saddled with such a persistent feeling of alienation that all I could think about was forgetting Laura and forgetting my book. I wanted to set the past aflame and start everything over on a clean ream of paper. I wanted to write myself as I truly was, to cut loose from that old stale character, that person that time and struggle and bad circumstances and mistakes had scribbled out in indelible ink without my consent. As a writer, I knew characters could only be redrawn in this way through the type of curiosity and hope that came with love. So, about eight weeks after I arrived at Abbott's cabin, I put down my notes and began becoming a regular at the little town library and turned my attention to online dating. Maybe it was selfish and cheap to use someone else's mind as a platform on which to build a new self, but I wasn't really conscious of what I was doing. Like a drowning man, I was reaching for anything I thought would keep my head above the water, even if that happened to be another drowning body.

I retrieved a few of my best photos from a cloud service and knocked my short bio out of the park and dusted off the cheap fake ID which had cost me a fortune, and which I had hoped would be the beginning of a new and adventurous life on the lam but which probably couldn't have passed the sniff test of a liquor store clerk. Still, I thought I felt something begin to change. Just like that, I was no longer David Wilson, failed novelist. I was now Daniel Wilder, aspiring novelist. It wasn't a dramatic difference, but it was just the fresh start I needed.

The truth is that online dating felt far more natural to me than writing ever had. I never had much luck with the cold approach, the opening line at the bar, but the internet suited me perfectly. Soon I found that though I'm socially awkward in person, I had no trouble reading cues and responding appropriately and even charmingly through online messaging. A little wit here. A sprinkle of self-deprecation there. A clever innuendo thrown in like a CAPTCHA to identify myself and filter out the women who couldn't read deeply. The game was obvious to me. I might acknowledge a double entendre and respond with the sort of ambiguity that gradually forked a conversation into a language of shared experiences and private jokes. The following night, I'd find myself looking into the eyes of a lovely woman across an expanse of white tablecloth, like the clean page of a new first chapter just waiting for a few of my choice sentences. I'm sure it helped that we were all stranded in a little chain of bedroom towns outside a single small city that was a few hour's drive from the nearest bigger city. I was a new fish in a stagnant dating pool.

My first dinner was with a woman in her thirties, fresh out of a dull marriage, dressed to the nines, and bursting with the desire to be known as only someone new could know her. She took me to a bar in the back of a Chinese restaurant and we shared scorpion bowls, one after the next, flirted for hours, made out in the parking lot. I felt the return of a familiar old self. I remember how the big night sky seemed to stretch on forever as I walked back to the bus station, how the air seemed so soft and welcoming, as if I had opened the door to a room glowing with fire.

There were a few women like that over the next months, while I waited for Abbott's return to my life. I let them in so far and then held them at a distance. I wanted to remain as long as possible as they first saw me, idealized, before the angle shifted and the language became more critical, before time took its toll on passion, before some unguarded remark about an ex-husband or an ex-lover clued me in to the role that would be waiting for me down the road. I found it odd that they thought me so engaging, but I also found engaging them had a tonic effect on my psyche. I'd become bored with myself after twenty years of sitting alone, pouring my heart out into one chapter, reading and writing the same fifteen pages over and over again, the first sentences of chapter two never more than a thin wire of text traveling along a road that went nowhere. But with each new woman, all it took was dinner and wine and one good chapter and all the wonderful possibilities of new love opened up right there across the table from me. I learned to welcome these women into my new story as though we were writing it together. It was a trick I performed over and over again, without conscious intention. Entire cities could spring up overnight and hold form for several weeks before crumbling slowly and painfully into rubble. It would become increasingly uncanny to watch, and as the weeks turned into months and my mother reported calls from creditors and collection agencies, from my agent, from law firms, from Laura, and even as she reported visits from the police and Mr. McGee, I remained entranced by the very hopelessness of the repetition. Each relationship shared the same predictable beats, and each woman recited the same weirdly identifiable lines. It was almost as if I'd written every scene myself. And yet every first date still presented a fresh start, a new chance at true, deep, and undying love, and even if there was no way of moving forward, my motives always felt pure.

My mother listened to my dating stories with a mixture of tolerance and lurid curiosity. Now and then she had a few words of reproach. She'd wonder if I was ready to be dating again and where I found the money. Or she'd warn me to be safe. She'd say that I didn't know what kind of women these women were, that they could carry diseases "or worse," whatever worse was. In my mother's opinion, the most worrisome thing about the fading, thirty-something-year-old beauties I found myself dating, was that even if they weren't disease-ridden or worse, they were bound to be complicated with all sorts of baggage. My mother was an old-fashioned sexist. She solidly believed that the best women were snatched up by their mid to late twenties, and anyone older than twenty-eight, unless she was a widow, had probably reached that age as a single woman either because she was a basket case or—and my mother would never use this word herself, though it was clearly the implication, spoken in the quietest of unspeakable whispers—*((a slut))*. And that was an ironic thing to suggest to me. Sure these women were divorcées and floozies with eighteen-wheels worth of baggage trailing behind them, but that also described her son to a tee, and with the aid of my many brief, intense encounters, I was starting to think of myself as rather lovable.

My attraction to "age appropriate" women was something I wanted to chalk up to my own maturity. But I knew that wasn't it. Sometimes, sitting over coffee and croissants with a new first chapter opening up, I would think it had to do with a depth of life experience that I shared with women who had been out in the world for a few extra years. But I knew better than anyone that the experiences of life don't really deepen with age. They don't slowly build toward some terrific crescendo and then go pouring forward off a cliff of great change. They just repeat themselves over and over again, lapping at the side of your boat until you fall asleep. If anything, a thirty-something-year-old woman might have been able to relate to me on that sad point, but age and change were such touchy subjects to women in their thirties that any foray into that conversation was like lighting a cigarette in a room with a gas leak. The thing that made these women such incredible lovers and such a good match for me wasn't something that could be spoken out loud. It had to percolate in quiet semi-consciousness and explode to life in the bedroom. We were all circling around mobius strip storylines, trying to find a way out of the loop as the clock was running down, and our connection to that most distressing truth in life—the mutability of flesh combined with the immutability of character—was best communicated non-verbally.

In a word, it was desperation that connected us. We were desperate to escape ourselves, desperate to be seen for the rare and precious gems we knew ourselves to be. And sometimes, in the night, in the dim light of the cabin or on the couch after several glasses of wine, or in the kitchen with dinner plates stacked in Abbott's sink, we could see each other for the perfectly cut stones we were. And even in the morning, when the blinds came up and as the coffee dripped into the pot and we backhanded flies off last night's dishes, that vision of the night before might persist. It could sometimes persist for days. At times, it seemed that a locked door had opened up again, that the love train had one more unscheduled stop, that we both had been given one more chance to get things right. I know this because I talked about it with more than one woman. It was one of those conversations that repeated as if on script. And then, after recurring arguments, after another turn around a track with red flags flying, after a few days of hopelessness that left us pining alone and unable to rise from bed, it was this illusion that brought us back together. Each time it came up, that same conversation, that same convincing speech of mine about love and chance and time would seem to occur spontaneously, organically, out of the truth of my heart, out of nowhere. Only gradually did I see, as more conversations repeated themselves right on script, that each relationship was no more than a fainter echo of the last. Rather than try to trace that echo back to the sound of the initial voice, I blamed the women, the dating sites, something in my character that drew a type. And I began to look for a woman like my mother suggested, one who was younger and not so world-weary and could come in fresh enough to break the cycle.

My date with Naomi began like a promising first sentence. I booked a room in the city and met her at a café under the polite pretense that we would visit the exhibit of a modern artist we both said we liked. After cappuccinos and a little conversation, she wanted to go directly to my hotel. We walked through the streets, the air cool with hints of winter, with hints of the snow that would soon become constant. She was so small and sweet that she seemed even younger than her twenty-four years. At first, I worried that she might be an underage girl looking for an adventure. I teased that I needed to see her ID, and then quizzed her on her birth date. She was hurt, but she liked it when I told her she would be thankful for her youthful appearance when all her friends were wrinkled and sagging and she still looked barely the age she was now. Her face blushed and she linked her arm in mine. She pulled herself close, standing on her toes to kiss my cheek. I felt the sweetness in her young lips, soft and free of injected collagen, and it was easy to begin thinking that the rest of her would be equally human.

I wondered what she wanted of an old man like me, and I concluded that, like all of us, she just wanted to be seen. She had something the boys her age didn't recognize, something that went right over their heads. A man my age could appreciate the glowing gifts of her soft skin and her soft eyes and all that vital warmth that hadn't yet been dissipated in false starts and false hope. We had not yet reached the hotel and I already found myself imagining breakfast in front of a big window with the blinds thrown open and sunlight streaming in. I could feel the cool morning air, smell fresh orange juice and coffee and toast, and eggs with plump yolks as orange as the sun. I saw myself lighting a cigarette and looking out on the landscape of late autumn while Naomi tasted everything and smiled. In my mind, I saw her as a child playing in the snow for the first time. A feeling ran through me, absent the usual dread of the impermanence of everything, and it went jogging down roads I barely remembered were inside of me.

As we checked into the hotel, I thought I caught the man and woman at the desk eying me with suspicion. I wondered if, as I had, they thought Naomi was too young. One of them walked into a back room and picked up the phone. Was she calling the police? I was beginning to feel awkward. We went up the stairs, Naomi's shiny hair bouncing on her back. She headed down the hall and I followed in the trail of her shampoo. I unlocked our door and Naomi put her bag down on the bed and smiled at me. She was so small and young and her smile so pure that it stung me with guilt. I suggested we go to dinner and I asked her what she liked. She liked pizza, she said. She sat down on the bed and leaned back on her hands. Her blouse fell open at the top, those purely human breasts of hers resting against the thin calico like two small children lounging in a hammock. She patted the bed beside her, signaling me to sit, but I remained standing. I leaned back against the bureau. What other kinds of food did she like, I asked. She told me she liked lots of things—cheese sticks and chicken fingers, for instance. She liked milkshakes and French fries. She pulled out her phone and started looking for restaurants, scrolling through photos of world cuisine until finally she gasped. She said the name of an American chain restaurant with a big beatific smile on her face. It was the kind of place where you sit down and order from a waiter after a day of shopping in an outlet mall. She showed me photos of their food, breaded and fried and served in a colorful basket.

After dinner, we walked back to the hotel. I bought two bottles of wine and chugged a few glasses in the room. I tried to make conversation but I couldn't do it. I was bored of myself. I was old and I didn't really understand why I'd come. This new character had lost his lustrous veneer and I was bored with him and I was sure I was boring her too. I had nothing of value to offer Naomi. She lounged on the bed, now leaning back on her hands, now reclining on her side, now on her stomach with her head resting on her hands and her feet kicked up behind her. I leaned on the bureau again, refilling my wine, knowing what was expected of me but unable to give myself permission to act. Once, I even sat down next to her. I could feel the warmth radiating off her skin and through her shirt. She looked up at me, that electrical layer just beyond the skin connecting with mine. I stood up as though shocked, as though scared. Poured more wine. Finally, I told Naomi I had to go to bed. I lay down with my clothes on and my head heavy with wine and I fell asleep.

I startled awake in the night like I did sometimes at Abbott's cabin. Naomi was sitting up in bed, watching television in her bra and panties. A late-night host was interviewing an actress who looked to be about Naomi's age. Naomi was giggling along with the studio audience, her big eyes soft, her face charmed, even delighted, her thumb gently rubbing the remote control, caressing the side, reaching up to read the buttons like braille, waiting awake for me like the sweet wife she might one day be. She glanced down and I closed my eyes, breathed heavily for a few minutes, and then I turned over and slept some more.

Early in the morning, I woke again. The TV was still on. Naomi was flipping between a reality cooking show and a teen romance movie. She'd taken her bra off and moved under the covers. Those breasts, as soft and human as her lips, were just barely peeking out above the sheets. My cock had filled with blood in my sleep and for a moment I thought about making love to her, but the scene struck me as so sad. It was more desperate than anything I'd experienced with women closer to my age, perhaps because Naomi was still young enough to be blind to our desperation. I propped my head up and watched TV with her for a bit, making a few comments about the food. Did it look better than pizza? Better than chicken fingers? She smiled and changed the channel and we watched men and women her age play at being teenagers, kids for whom the world was an oyster, an unopened book which contained between its covers not some collection of disappointing first chapters, but the pearl of all pearls.

An hour or so later, Naomi got up and walked around in her panties for a little bit. Her young face bore that look I'd seen too many times in the past few months and I was ashamed to be responsible again. I watched as another beautiful city crumbled, as she opened her eyes to the reality of me. Another train was announcing its final stop at a dead-end town. Another promising chapter was failing at the limits of my creativity. She took a shower, sat down on the bed in a towel, and we looked at each other for a minute or so. There was nothing to say. She got dressed and we hugged awkwardly at the door and I watched her as she walked down the hall and as her shiny long hair bounced down the stairs, and I never saw or heard from her again. In my experience, a woman will never forgive a man for not making love to her when she is right there naked, even in spirit, before him. And in the broad view of things, the world being what it is, unfolding so often without half the promise of its premise, I have to think a woman is right to find that so unforgivable.

I left an hour later, found an internet cafe and took my name off the dating sites. I was emotionally bankrupt and so many first dates had all but exhausted my six-month bundle of cash anyway. I made a new resolute decision to live on canned beans and coffee until *The First Chapter* was finished and I could make good on my debts and build the life that Laura would want to come back to. Then I got on the bus and returned to Abbott's cabin with an inescapable tragic feeling taking hold, a sense of hamstrungness that was also somehow quieting. The city grew distant as the sky turned a darker shade of gray, and then, slowly, the snow started falling, right on cue.

A week later, word from Abbott finally reached me. It was a hopeful moment, and I needed hope just then. Whatever fresh life dating had brought to my life had now evaporated and my writing returned to its old repetitive pattern. The communication came via a circuitous route worthy of a spy novel. Our intermediary, a former detective who was now a bar owner in Salt Lake City, knocked on Abbott's cabin door one morning and introduced himself as none other than Harelip Lenny—though he didn't seem to have a harelip. He told me only two things. Abbott wanted me to travel to Salt Lake City to visit Denton White in the hospital, and when I arrived, I would find letters from Abbott that would explain things in further detail.

"Can I tell Abbott he can count on you?" Lenny asked. He loosened his scarf and took a sip of the coffee I had made from Abbott's apocalyptic supply, which somehow had begun to run low.

"Count on me for what?" I thought.

Lenny raised the mug again and I looked at him through the rising steam, still unable to find any sign of a harelip. Outside it was gray and snow was floating in the air, blowing from the trees or falling lightly. It was hard to tell. It had been snowing on and off in little flurries since Naomi and I had parted.

I nodded at Lenny. "Of course," I said. What I didn't say, is that I'd exhausted most of my small bundle of writing cash in my months-long frenzy of online dating and now I wasn't sure how I would manage my trips to Salt Lake City. "He can count on me," I said. "Of course he can."

Lenny placed a small paper bag on the table and labeled it with his voice. "Expense money," he said. On top of the bag, he laid a slip of paper with the name of the hospital and Denton's room number and labeled that one too: "Address."

I nodded.

Lenny stood and took a last sip of coffee. He set the mug back down with a clunk. Then he clapped me on the shoulder and walked out the door. His Power Wagon pulled down the long driveway and the snow blew around for a moment in a stronger flurry. Then it settled back to its floating way, and I was alone again.

23

I didn't know what to expect when I arrived at the hospital. I wasn't sure if I'd find Denton tucked away in some psychological wing, strapped down with electrodes on his head and his leg shaking violently, or bald and wasting away in a cancer ward, or sitting with a vacant look in an electric wheelchair with a straw for a steering wheel, a quadriplegic victim of some horrible misfortune. I only knew he'd been there for quite some time and that it was important to Abbott that I visit.

I stopped at the reception desk and told the woman that I was a family friend of Denton White's. She checked the name on my fake ID against a ledger on her computer and let me go up. When I walked into the room, Denton appeared to be sleeping. He had a tube down his throat and a few IV lines coming out of his arm that circulated his blood through what looked like a dialysis machine. An older nurse was hunched over him. She turned around with an embarrassed expression on her face that made me think I'd interrupted her changing his catheter or removing his bedpan. I excused myself and stepped back into the hall.

A few minutes later, the nurse came out and introduced herself as Doreen. She asked my name. I told her it was Daniel.

"Daniel Wilder?" she asked.

"Yes," I told her.

I waited for her to explain, but she just stood there looking impressed and taking stock of me. Finally, I asked her how she'd known who I was. She told me that a stack of letters had been piling up over the last couple of months. They'd been addressed to me, in Denton's care. She said I could find them on the table by his bed.

"We've all been wondering when the mysterious Daniel Wilder would arrive," she said. She looked me up and down and smiled like I was a real specimen of a man.

I thought about my appearance. It had been a long trip to the city, and I was damp and cold from my walk from the Greyhound Station to the metro bus and from the bus stop to the hospital. I was sure I looked exhausted and poorly put together. But maybe she was noticing my exhilaration from the brisk walk and my excitement at reconnecting with a storyline I'd almost given up as lost. I was beginning to feel like a man with a purpose again, on an adventure. I liked thinking that she was noticing some of that in me, and I liked hearing the word mysterious in front of my new name, even if the name was ordinary and so much like the one it had replaced. Maybe Doreen was onto something.

I smiled back at Doreen and then nodded toward the door.

"What exactly is wrong with him?" I asked her.

"Well..." she said. Her voice trailed off and she seemed to fall into an internal debate about how to answer my question. "Not exactly anything. Hypothermia-induced deep catatonia, if you want to put a name to it. That's what we're calling it anyway, but we don't know—exactly. He was found in his home several months ago on a wellness check. No vitals. Cold to the touch—I mean like ice."

She opened the door to his room and waved me in. She gestured toward the machine I'd thought was doing dialysis. There was a steady pattern of clicks and buzzes and beeps.

"We warmed his blood up with that thing and he came right back to life," she said.

"Fit as a fiddle for a few days. Talked our ears off. Crazy stories that had us all in stitches. Then one morning we came in and he was quiet as a church mouse. Just staring off into space. A few days later his body started to go hypothermic again, so we rolled the machine back in to keep his blood warm. He's been like that ever since."

"He's in a coma?" I asked.

"Not quite," she said. "It's complicated. Denton can respond to some stimuli. The specialists think it's a case of stupor."

She walked over and brushed some hair across Denton's forehead and I thought I saw him smile slightly. His left leg started to twitch. It was sad to see this man who Abbott had portrayed as so full of energy and spirit now returned to the stasis that had haunted him so many years ago at the institution. It struck me that I wasn't the only one trapped inside a narrative arc, as in procedural television drama where only the minor characters and plot elements change. Denton was trapped in his own show. Perhaps all of us were.

The nurse tapped a tall stack of envelopes sitting by a flower arrangement. "Letters are right here."

She told me, without a hint of irony, that she'd give the two of us some time to catch up and then she left the room.

I walked over and sat down by the flowers. I picked up one envelope after the next. Each had my new name printed across the center in uppercase letters. But I saw my name a little differently now. It did have some mystery to it, I thought—Wilder. I lifted the top envelope up and read Abbott's name in the upper left corner. I felt a little jolt. The next envelope was the same. Only the postmarks were unique, each stamped from a different town in Nebraska, Nevada, New Mexico, and California. I studied Abbott's envelopes for a while and then I sat there looking at Denton.

I wished I could catch up like Doreen said, maybe hear about Abbott from Denton's point of view and about the life that kept rendering him silent and still. I thought about that for a few minutes, and then I returned my attention to the letters and began to organize them chronologically, putting the one with the earliest post date on the top and so forth, building a mental map of Abbott's trip since we parted ways in Hannibal. Once they were organized, I tore open the first envelope, and even just seeing the salutation almost startled me to tears. "Dear David," it read. I had a sense that fate couldn't help but bring Abbott and Denton together again, and that this time I would be there with them and maybe, this time, we could all be healed together.

24

Abbott's letters confused me. I'm not sure what I had expected. Maybe I thought time and distance and the written word would change his story somehow, and that the act of putting it down with pen on paper would bring him back to earth. I half expected that he would lift the veil of fantasy from his fable and lay it out straight for me in plain terms. And that didn't happen. Instead, the letters were replete with his signature flights of imagination, fantastic with characters and coincidences and events that defied reality. They would've been completely unbelievable had I not been sitting right beside Denton myself and had I not come face to face with a hospital staff as baffled by the aged Denton as I was incredulous of the young man in the letters, the man who, even in his youth, had struggled against stupors that could swallow him for weeks or months at a time.

The letters began with a backstory that fleshed out the Denton I had first known from the institution. Denton's trapeze artist father had fallen to his death while his mother was still in her first trimester. In his absence, her psychological state began to unravel, and after Denton was born, she vanished forever into the darkness of heartbreak, addiction, and insanity. Denton was raised in Salt Lake City by his grandmother, Rose White, and when his strange stupors began to manifest, Rose enlisted the help of a doctor named Henry Sharpe. Rose had been something of a nanny to Dr. Henry Sharpe. She had cared for him as a child, alongside Denton's mother, and the grown Sharpe had later, through some curious coincidence that strained belief, become physician to both Denton and the young Boris Schlotzsky. This curious connection between Schlotzsky and Denton had only been uncovered in their final session, Abbott wrote, and before the doctor had the chance to pry into the meaning of the coincidence, Denton disappeared in the night with the head nurse and the mystery remained unresolved in the doctor's mind.

In my imagination, I put together the timeline, watching Henry Sharpe grow from a boy and go off to study pre-med. While Denton's mother walked the high wire under a big tent in far-off places, Sharpe's nose was buried in books. I could see Boris Schlotzsky too—a precocious child maybe eight or ten years ahead of Denton, and growing up across the city in a world that would not connect for many years.

By the time Sharpe completed his residency and returned to Salt Lake City, he already had gray in his beard and he was going prematurely bald. He was one of those men who becomes old in his twenties and then seems to remain the same age for the remainder of his life. When Rose saw her old ward so affected by his studies and his chosen profession it made her sad for the past, but it also made her smile. Even as a child, Henry's conscientiousness had been such a burden to him that Rose used to warn him that his constant second-guessing and indecision would drive him to an early grave. It didn't please her to see this burden she had recognized early in his life continuing to weigh on him so heavily, but it was a comfort to see the child she had cared for in the man he had become.

Dr. Sharpe's treatments for her grandson, whenever he could decide on one, struck Rose as a combination of tomfoolery, witchcraft, and pseudoscience. But she knew Sharpe's heart was in the healing. He didn't call for specialists or view her grandson's odd curse as an opportunity to make Denton the guinea pig in a young physician's ambitious vision. He didn't argue for long-term admittance to a university hospital while his eyes rolled back to review a subtext of wires and tubes and the extensive and meticulous testing that might lead to a sizable grant and publication in a medical journal and distinction in his field. Sure, Henry Sharpe's results were unpredictable. One day he was Jesus Christ himself, raising her little Lazarus from the clutches of death, and another day he was a useless, bumbling fool. But what he lacked in consistency and self-confidence, he more than made up for with his gentle heart and the strict confidence with which he kept Denton's strange affliction a family affair. It might have been due to her upbringing, but Rose's very presence in the same room with the handsome doctors at the LDS hospital made her skin crawl with suspicion. They were everything Henry Sharpe was not—thick with blond hair, and overflowing with confidence, and full of youth and ambition. Rose didn't trust them and she didn't like the way they looked at her grandson.

I lowered the letter and sat there for a few minutes, listening to the steady rhythm of clicks and beeps and the tidal flow of Denton's blood as it washed back and forth through those warm machine estuaries.

I let my imagination go again. I tried to open myself to that magical reality where Abbott lived, but it was just too absurd to accept without scrutiny. I found myself becoming suspicious, wondering what his endgame was. I thought of the woman who Schlotzsky had mentioned in that last meeting with Abbott, the one who needed the golden scarab to enter the treatment room and set her free. I supposed like her, I was trapped in a world of my own construction, afraid to break free. I wanted to reimagine myself and stitch together a new and beautiful quilt from the old fragments of my life, but I just didn't have the skill to do it on my own.

My mind kept drifting. I'd find myself listening for pebbles against Denton's window, or for the sound of Abbott's footsteps approaching, for his return to my life, for the moment when he would waltz into the room and command us to rise and embark, to wake us both out of our slumber with a few choice words. I had this conflicted sense—and it had grown stronger in Abbott's absence—that as with Schlotzsky, his story was the door to my emancipation, to my new life, maybe even the door to my Lucille. I was stuck in a world that had no use for me, where I'd exhausted my options and my credibility, and where I didn't fit. Everything I took up followed the same repetitive pattern. But now, as I sat with those letters, I could see a door forming, maybe the same way Abbott had seen his own door rising out of the mud all those years ago at Woodstock. I was the one knocking now. I wanted Abbott to open that door again and write me into the story that existed just across the threshold and pull me through.

At some point, my mind quieted and began reading again. I read as if doing research for a future trip, as if the letters were a travel guide of sorts, like one of those Lonely Planet books I would've bought to whet my appetite when I was younger and full of wanderlust and possessed with absolute foreknowledge that I was born to go interesting places and do great things. I tore into the next letter. This one told the story of Rose's only child, her daughter Lila who was Denton's mother. I watched Denton, with his one foot twitching in the hospital bed, a smile gracing his face for a brief moment, and then a frown. Was he there too, I wondered. Was he stuck in Abbott's fourth dimension, watching it all happen with me: his mother's adolescence—the jazz, the swing dancing, the promiscuity, the stint in the mountains waiting for the apocalypse with a Mormon sex cult... Was he in bed next to me or right where I was imagining him—trapped in Abbott's letters, sitting at the kitchen table of Rose's big Salt Lake City home with a warm glass of milk and a grilled cheese sandwich? If I relaxed my mind, I could see him clearly—his foot, even then, wanting to twitch under the table, having a mind for what was to come.

"And as far as I'm concerned," his grandmother is saying, "for anyone to refer to any branch of Mormonism as a 'sex cult—'" I watch her put her hand on her hip to finish her thought "—is one-hundred-percent redundant." Rose had some experience with these things. She'd grown up in a fundamentalist sect of the Mormon Church and when she became pregnant, she escaped to the city with Denton's unborn mother in her womb.

She goes on. She tells him about his mother's later love affair with the trapeze. How more than anything she felt as she watched her daughter high flying among circus heathens—more than the sharp pang in her gut at the sight of those revealing costumes, and more than the twinge of anxiety she felt at her daughter's proximity to well-built men, coarse with animal beauty and dripping with sweat

188

and testosterone—was a sense of relief. She'd never seen Lila more grounded and at peace than when she was sailing through space in the hands of Denton's future father.

Of course, having never experienced her own heart opening to a man, Rose couldn't foresee the romance that would develop between the two aerialists. She hadn't accounted for the destabilizing effect which would follow her daughter's loss, or the way that magic carpet that grounded her even in flight would be pulled right out from under her when Denton's father was no longer in the world to catch her.

"But if you're going to go off and ruin your life, Denton," she is telling him, as she tops his mug off with warm milk, "I guess it's better to do it in the name of love than by withering away up in the mountains, waiting for the end of the world with a bunch of brainwashed hippies."

The letters didn't explain why Rose reacted so energetically when her grandson developed an interest in photos of barely dressed women. It seemed like a natural enough interest for an adolescent boy, but I could extrapolate why Rose might become concerned. Either Rose's own relationship to sexuality had been marred early on by her life among religious fanatics, or she feared Denton, who shared her daughter's obsessive tendencies, might spin off on some romantic infatuation with a woman who was out of his reach and disappear into that same dark land where she'd lost her daughter. The letters would later prove the second concern to be prescient, as a mother's concerns often are.

When Denton was a child, Rose had struggled to orchestrate his diet, his sleep schedule, and moderate his appetite for ideas. She'd read his moods like tidal charts, pulling books full of fantastic, paranormal, or abstract subjects from his hands at bedtime, replacing them with Bronte or Jane Austen—women who might build a bridge for him to the world of emotion, and who had their heads rooted firmly in the concerns of the world. Sometimes she'd awaken in the night to blood-curdling screams and rush in to find Denton tearing at the covers with bulging eyes, or running about his room, or crouched on his bed like a cat. A flashlight grown dim from failing batteries would be setting on the floor next to a contraband book.

"What is it?" she'd ask him.

He'd point about the room and hide his head in her night dress. The walls were crumbling. The bed was burning. Snakes or demons were slithering on the floor or crawling up the walls.

Rose would stroke his head. When his breathing became heavy again, she would collect the flashlight, pick the book up from the floor, and return to bed.

Rose's concerns didn't waver as her grandson approached adolescence, but the books that concerned her began to change. All through Denton's childhood she'd looked for some hobby to pull him out of the complex labyrinth of his mind and ground him in the physical world. She'd bought modeling sets, sculpting clay, pushed him toward rocketry. Nothing took. His internal world pulled him back with its gravity and threatened his well-being. It drew him in and dragged him down and held him motionless as though in quicksand, until the grandson she knew had disappeared and only Dr. Sharpe, with his drugs and his witchcraft had any hope of fishing him out.

The first worldly objects Denton ever developed an interest in were scantily clad young women—and Rose was quick to tell him, in the sternest voice she could muster, that they were not objects at all. In his early teens, after she'd found him pouring over the lingerie section of the Sears Catalog, Rose panicked. She snatched the catalog out of his one free hand and turned his room upside down until she found two years of back issues. She hid the catalogs under some floorboards in the attic and tried to deflect her grandson's growing curiosity by apprenticing him to a clockmaker.

For a while, she was hopeful. When Denton would remain in his room for long hours, she'd climb up to the attic expecting the worst and find the catalogs under the floorboards, undisturbed. But soon she noticed Denton wasn't sleeping. One night, she walked into his room and found him lying in bed beside a flashlight and a stack of books full of equations. His eyes were wide open and his body was cold and he seemed to have lapsed into what Dr. Sharpe referred to as a state of trepidation. She stood to leave the room and heat some blankets in the clothes dryer, but Denton called her back. He was babbling. He grabbed her night dress and asked her if she'd ever considered that an Einstein–Rosen bridge could connect space-time in an infinite universe. Could she imagine it? Identical moments of eternal recurrence stacked on top of each other. Time would be like an image seen through two opposing mirrors.

Rose took a breath. She told him no, frankly the idea had never occurred to her.

Denton babbled on, his eyes opening wide and then shutting tight. He confessed that he'd been having a recurrent nightmare. A watch that had stopped keeping time had been brought to him for repairs. Inside, he saw that a strange insect was stopping up the works. He picked up his magnifying glass to look more closely. But every time he looked through the lens, a cloud passed between the big skylight that lit the workshop and the sun. So he turned on his jeweler's lamp and looked again. But now he could see that it wasn't an insect. It was a smaller version of himself, also sitting at a work table with a jeweler's lamp, also looking through a magnifying lens at a stopped-up watch.

He pulled at Rose's night dress and buried his face. It hadn't been a cloud blocking the light, he told her. That wasn't what was coming between himself and the sun. It had been his own enormous eye peering down at himself through what he had always thought was a window to the sky but which was actually a magnifying glass held in his own hand. It was a wormhole through which he could observe himself repeating his life, infinitely, forever.

Rose took the flashlight away and shut it off. She stroked her grandson's head.

"Really Denton," she said. "You need to stop with all this voyeurism." She felt him clutch her night dress more tightly in his hand. "If you ever become trapped in a universe where you can hide on a rooftop and secretly watch yourself watching yourself forever," she said, her voice becoming stern, "I hope you at least have the decency to respect your own privacy."

She sat on the corner of his bed until he fell back to sleep. The next day, she told the clockmaker he wouldn't be returning and found him a job at a machine shop. He did well there for the better part of a year. But eventually he found his way down a rabbit hole that led him to the ancient art of alchemy. Recognizing the telltale look of obsession returning to his eyes, Rose asked him to quit the metal shop and found him a better-paying job with an electrician. But this led Denton to discover the work of Nicola Tesla and soon he was spending sleepless nights in Rose's basement attempting to reconstruct a Tesla coil out of her household appliances.

Finally, Rose threw up her hands. She climbed into the attic, dusted off the old Sears Catalogs, and left them by Denton's bed. For the next week, he snored peacefully and woke late. Before Rose could plan another intervention, Denton's draft number came up. It was a shock to both of them. Childhood had passed in the flash of an eye. It had camouflaged itself as a great, never-ending struggle, and only now that it had ended did the two of them fully appreciate its sweetness. Rose put some milk on the stove to warm and melted some butter to grill a sandwich. Rather than worry about losing another child, she soothed herself with the thought that at least in the army Denton would have a regimented schedule and exhaust himself with physical exercise and be discouraged from any sort of thinking at all. And although she couldn't imagine anything more immediate and concrete to ground a man in the world than war, she just hoped her grandson wouldn't end up burning villages in Vietnam.

When Doreen entered Denton's room again, I'd almost entirely forgotten myself in Abbott's letters. I came back to the clicks and beeps, the whooshing of blood, and then I saw Doreen standing over me, looking at the pile of opened letters.

"Good reading?" she asked.

"Yes," I said. "They are. My friend is a good writer."

"What's in them?" she asked. "Are there any clues about Denton's condition? We've all been watching those letters pile up and dying of suspense."

"There's a little bit about him," I said. "It seems like this might be something that's troubled him since childhood." I considered whether to tell her about Denton's time at the Ella Rawson Psychiatric Hospital, but I didn't want her to think we were a couple of lunatics. "Abbott is a friend of mine and an old friend of Denton's, but I never met Denton before today. I don't even really know what I'm supposed to do here."

Doreen nodded and gave me a look as though to extract anything that I was withholding.

"I probably know less about Denton than you do," I said.

"Are there any clues about how to treat him?"

"Not really," I said. "Warmth, I guess. But you have that covered. Maybe kindness?"

"Of course," Doreen said, pushing some of Denton's hair aside.

I told Doreen I'd give her some space and then I gathered the letters up and shoved them into my pockets. I asked if she could recommend a place nearby, or somewhere close to the bus station where I could get a good meal before taking the bus back to Colorado.

"Try Alice's Restaurant," she said. "It's right down the street. Heaping helpings of home-cooked food, and great coffee. You'll love it. And you can sit and read as long as you want and Alice won't bother you."

I thanked her and headed for the door.

"Daniel," she said.

I turned around and stood in the doorway.

"Maybe the answer to why you're here is in those letters."

It caught me a little off guard, and I stood there taking it in for a few seconds. "That's what I've been hoping," I said.

25

I was under the impression that it was illegal to smoke just about everywhere in America, but apparently Alice had found a loophole, or she didn't care.

"Smoking," I said.

The waitress led me to an elevated section in the back corner and handed me a menu. She was young and pretty. I ordered coffee and she bounced down the stairs. I watched the people in my section talk, wave cigarettes while smoke gathered them in a sort of complicity. Sometimes they were surrounded by thick gray clouds, and then the smoke would clear and they'd emerge like characters at the end of a good story. It was pleasant to watch, but it also reminded me that I needed to call my mother. I figured I'd order my meal and then sneak out to use a payphone if I could find one, and avoid the awkwardness of waiting in front of an empty table. I'd make the call and then come back to eat and sit over a coffee and enjoy the day's one cigarette. It was a good plan, but I got antsy waiting for the waitress and I needed something to do. I lit up a cigarette and leaned back and blew out a big white plume.

When the waitress returned, I told her what I wanted. She smiled as the list got longer. It had been a while since I'd eaten anything other than Abbott's apocalypse rations, and now I had my little bundle of expense money. When I was finally done ordering she asked if I was expecting someone.

"It's just me," I told her.

"How sad," she said. "Don't you hate to eat alone? For me, it's the worst thing."

Noel, her name tag said. I told Noel I sometimes preferred it, which was true. Her name had me thinking about Laura. I had this memory of coffee brewing as the two of us danced to Christmas songs in our kitchen and snow fell outside. It was an ancient memory and could've been from ten or fifteen years before. I couldn't place why it came to me just then. Maybe because of the name Noel or because another Thanksgiving was about to come and go, which didn't really mean anything to me personally, but I knew it meant my mother would be lonely. I took another long drag and blew my smoke off to the side—Noel didn't look like a smoker.

"Noel?" I said. It was unusual for me to call a waitress by name, but I wanted to hear the word and live in my memory for a little longer. I asked her where I could find a pay phone.

"I can bring a phone to your table," she said. "I'll put your order in and be right back."

"Like in an old truck stop?" I said. I recalled phones brought to the table from truck stops in the early nineties when I'd traveled the country by thumb.

She smiled and said she wouldn't know, and then she went bouncing down the stairs again. I couldn't help but think of Naomi, about our happy meal on the terrace that had never been, and the way her shiny hair had hopped on and off her shoulders as she left the hotel, floating in the air at intervals and then falling on her shoulders with all the weight of our confusing night together.

The phone was one of those old, five-pound things with a touch tone pad. Noel plugged it in under the table. I dialed my mother and let her phone ring once. After a minute, I called and hung up again. I had ten minutes or so before my next call, so I finished my cigarette and tried to relax in the afterglow for a few minutes, just watching other people talk. Then I picked the receiver back up and called the pay phone outside my mother's local supermarket. I liked to imagine she enjoyed the intrigue of this system we used. It was like a scene from one of the television mysteries she was always watching.

"Hi David," she said. "Is everything okay?" She didn't sound like her usual self. Her voice was flat and far away.

"Yeah Mom," I said. "Everything's okay." I asked her if she was okay.

"Where are you?" she asked. "What's all that noise I'm hearing?"

I told her I was at a diner.

"I tell you," she said, "traveling here and there, eating in fancy restaurants. Nobody would ever believe you're broke and hiding out. It's more like you're on vacation, living the life of the rich and famous."

"Are you sure you're alright, Mom?" I said. "You sound funny."

"You're not meeting another one of those women, are you, David?"

"No Mom," I said. "I told you I was coming to visit Abbott's friend, remember?"

"That's right," she said. "Denton White. The lunatic. How is he?"

I told her what I knew. The hypothermia followed by a short recovery, followed by the lapse back into catatonia or coma.

"It doesn't sound like there's much hope," she said.

"Ma," I said. "Why would you say that?"

"People don't usually come out of those things, David," she said. "And if they do, they're never the same."

"But I told you about the institution, Ma. Abbott says it's happened before. They think it might be psychological."

"Just now you told me they found him on a wellness check with no heartbeat. I tell you, David, sometimes I think they're going to find me that way too."

"They brought him back, Ma."

My mother sighed. "Well, I don't know what to believe anymore, David."

There was something in her voice I couldn't identify.

"Mom, are you sure something's not bothering you," I asked again.

"I just don't know what to think," she said.

The line was quiet for a few moments while I tried to figure out what was going on. I could hear the sounds of the supermarket parking lot. Cars. Shopping carts. Children nagging. A mother scolded her son. "Jimmy," she said. "Enough!"

"I had a dream about you last night," my mother said.

She was always having dreams that foretold things. At least she believed they foretold things.

"Something bad?" I asked.

"Your father was there," she said.

"Oh," I said. "Mom? Is that what's going on?"

"Do you remember when we used to go to those Olde Home Days? During the summer?"

"Yeah, Mom. Of course."

"You'd win all the races. Remember that? Your father loved that egg and spoon race. He used to hang his tongue out of the side of his mouth whenever he concentrated on anything. I always worried that he'd bite it off. I really did, David."

She took a moment to laugh. There was sadness behind it.

"Well, it was such a simple dream. We were standing by the pig roast. You were barely more than a baby, and I was holding you in my arms. Some other kids were taking rides on a pony and you got it in your mind that you wanted to ride that pony too. I was worried, David. You know me. But your father said, 'Oh Mary,'—you know how your father always was. So I put you on the pony. I wanted to walk right beside you, but your father put his arm around me. He said you'd be fine. This girl—I mean, I say girl, but she must have been at least twenty-two or three—she was leading the pony by a rope. I was so nervous. I was sure you'd fall."

Her voice trailed off.

"Mom?" I said.

"I just looked away for a second, David. When I looked back, you were on this enormous horse—I mean giant—like one of those horses that used to be in the Budweiser commercials. Do you remember those? The Clydesdales? But now you were older and the horse was galloping away. I started crying. I wanted to run after you. But your father held on to me and kissed the side of my head. You know what he said?"

"What did he say, Mom," I asked.

"He said, 'Mary, it's going to be all right.'"

I heard her fight back tears.

"He talks to me like that you know? I just wanted to tell you that I think he's watching out for you."

"I know, Mom," I said.

"There's something about this Abbott character that reminds me of your father a little bit. Sometimes I think—well, David, I don't even want to say it or people will start thinking I'm one of those crazy women— Anyway, I should let you go, but if there's any way you can help that man—"

She stopped speaking and I heard her fighting tears again.

"Okay Mom," I said. "I will. But are you sure it was just the dream that bothered you?"

"I don't know, David," she said. "I guess I've been thinking about that sad man searching for his wife, and she is lost out there somewhere, waiting for him to come home."

"About Abbott?" I said.

"Have you already forgotten about him?"

"Of course not," I said. "That's why I'm here."

"You told me you would help him find her when he comes back."

"If he wants my help. Sure Mom," I said. "But for now, there's nothing to do about it. I just have to wait for him."

"Nothing to do about it?" my mother said. She seemed disgusted with me all of a sudden. "You don't know what it's like to lose someone you love like that. If your father was still alive—"

"Mom," I said. Sometimes she forgot that I had lost someone too.

I wanted another cigarette. I looked at my pack sitting on the table, at the butt in the ashtray. I never seemed to learn anything.

"That nice man, Mr. McGee came by again yesterday afternoon, David. He just wants to help, you know?" Her voice began to break. She took a moment. "I feel like my world keeps getting smaller," she said.

"I'll be home soon, Ma," I said. "I just need to finish my book first."

"Finish it already, David," she said. "This has gone on too long."

"Okay," I said.

"David," she said. "I should go. Elaine's coming over later. I have cleaning to do. I'm sure you remember Elaine. She's—well—anyway David, I should go."

Noel came with the food but I wasn't hungry anymore. I tried to return her smile but I didn't have it in me, so I told her the food looked delicious. I lit another cigarette and sipped my coffee and just savored the loneliness of it all. Finally, I put down some cash for the bill and I left without a word to go catch the bus back to Colorado.

26

I tore into the next envelope as soon as the bus came up to speed on the highway. I regret that I can't reproduce at least portions of the letter here, not because I'm concerned about my ability to tell the story accurately, but because there was something so beautiful and compelling about Abbott's voice that I am afraid I will not capture. The letters themselves seem to have vanished, pulled perhaps into that same void where Abbott lived for decades and where so much of my own life has also vanished. Their disappearance became just one more piece of evidence in a case against me that never saw the inside of a courtroom, that big inquest that felt like it would be the end of everything and then, like so many other stories in my life, fizzled out and went nowhere.

I can see the events of that letter as clearly as if I were there myself, standing on the stoop with Denton, in that late spring of 1975, when Rose opened the door and gasped to see him. Perhaps it's so easy because I've seen that look in my own mother's eyes so many times. I'm looking right at her, even as I tell this now. My mother? Rose White? I'm not sure which. Her face is a mess of emotions. It's the face of a woman who's suffered in doubt and anger and heartache. She doesn't know whether to scold the young man standing on the stoop or wrap him in her arms and never let him go. Last she heard, he'd been discharged from the army. He was getting on a plane. Now, after going missing for almost five years, he's shown up on her doorstep looking like he's been dropped there by the postman, packaged up and sent straight from the jungles of Vietnam. He has the appearance of a man who's been spat out of a tunnel deep below Saigon City, or a prisoner, escaped from long captivity in a bamboo cage, or as if a land mine in the paddy field of a burning village had exploded and her grandson had been ejected—ejected from the village and ejected from the war and ejected from sanity itself, which never really held him by more than a few fingernails anyway.

Like any good mother, Rose put her own feelings aside. She noticed a familiar desperation and pain in Denton's face and she saw in him the child she'd known since infancy. She warmed some milk on the stove and sat in the kitchen while Denton did his best to fill her in on where the years had taken him. He ranted about government conspiracies, German doctors and sexy nurses, about Chinese monks who roamed the American West planting seeds of great wisdom. He told her he'd been to Woodstock, woke in a cabin, wandered the desert; that he'd been kidnapped, thrown in a truck and shipped to an institution where he'd been strapped into a chair and electrified, and that in the swirl of chaos and seizure that followed he'd found a calm place and he'd seen the future. He told her about Abbott, the friend who he'd met at the institution and who had appeared again and again in his visions of what lay ahead. Rose just sat and listened. To her surprise, she found that she wasn't alarmed by her grandson. What she felt was a sense of relief. Her sweet boy was alive, and the war hadn't changed him at all. When Denton finished his rant and fell into silence, she led him to his old bedroom and sat with him until he drifted off to sleep.

It didn't take long for the glint of mania to return to Denton's eyes. Soon, he began rising early to practice calisthenics in the courtyard or to sit cross-legged and suck in big breaths of air in front of the rising sun. Over foul breakfasts concocted of fruits and vegetables that he mixed up in Rose's blender, he would speak with wide eyes about the supreme ultimate art of kung fu. Or he might try to engage Rose in discussions about the television series *Kung Fu*, which they watched together on Saturday evenings, Denton with unblinking attention and Rose distractedly, while working on a crossword puzzle or fumbling with her crotchet—which was supposed to induce relaxation and reduce her blood pressure but actually just seemed to aggravate her rheumatism and wear out her eyes.

In the mornings over breakfast, Denton might frown at the bacon and sausage on Rose's plate, telling her that the consumption of animal products divorced the human spirit from the harmony of the natural world. He'd take big slugs of his foul-smelling elixir and smile like the child she'd missed so much. His rants were music to her, like old songs almost forgotten. She'd ask him to tell her more about his elixir, never mentioning the persistent odor of garlic on his skin or the strange orange hue that now seemed to govern his complexion. And that old music would continue. He would raise his glass, proclaiming his beverage was the liquid prophylactic to every ill of the modern world, the childish smile Rose loved flashing across his face. He'd swear its daily consumption could counter the damage from the polluted air, the erratic pace, the mental disturbances caused by materialism, and the brain toxins accumulated by reading newspapers and watching television advertising.

Rose noticed something new in Denton's smile too. In these moments, while he talked of kung fu or his monk-like diet, his smile was relaxed and genuine in a way she had never seen before, absent that usual quiver at the corners of his lips that told of a deep and inconsolable unrest. In this dietary nonsense and his odd oriental exercises, it seemed that Denton had finally discovered the thing she always knew he needed, an activity to keep his hands busy and distract his troubled mind. When Denton vanished after the war, she had imagined the worst. She had imagined him struggling alone in some dark room, forever lost in the same personal hell that had swallowed his mother. But now there was hope. Denton had found a hobby capable of maintaining his precarious balance in the world. Rose considered it her duty to encourage Denton as much as possible, and feeling that her own time in the world was limited, she went to the local bookstore and bought him a copy of the first martial arts book she could find—*The Tao of Jeet Kune Do*, by the famed martial artist and cinema star, Bruce Lee.

This was in late April of 1975, and the book came at a crucial moment for Denton. The last episodes of *Kung Fu*'s third season were airing and a rumor had been circulating that the series would not be renewed. The book smoothed what could've been a turbulent time in Denton's life. Within a month of *Kung Fu*'s final episode, Denton's obsession would shift seamlessly away from David Carradine's traditional kung fu and onto Bruce Lee's modernized art of Jeet Kune Do.

The character of Denton's calisthenics began to change and become more vibrant. Rose watched as he hopped around the living room on his toes and danced about on the back porch with a feeling of contentment. She was beginning to feel a call of her own. Her interest in the physical world—always tenuous, except inasmuch as it was rooted to her grandson—was beginning to vanish. She would wake sometimes in the night to the sound of Denton snoring peacefully from the next room and it would be her that would watch the physical world crumble and rearrange itself into the ghosts and demons and snakes of her past. The old hurts she had overcome and those she'd never been able to let go replayed on the stage of her bedroom. Characters flickered before her, reenacting scenes from a play that had been full of joy and pain and which she had deeply loved. And as those characters dissolved into daylight and she heard her grandson rise and begin the breathing exercises that she still found ridiculous, she nonetheless entertained the hope that in her absence, the martial arts would bring the lasting peace and balance and structure to Denton's life that had evaded Rose and her daughter but which she had always wanted to endow to him.

It was a bitter cold night in November of 1975 when Rose called out to Denton in the hours before dawn. It had been evident since his return home that his grandmother lacked the steel-handed grip on life that Denton remembered her by, but he was not prepared for the abruptness with which she would pass. When he arrived at her bedside, Rose took his hand. She told him she was bored with the world and instructed him to follow his own path through life. "Promise me you won't waste your time living out other people's expectations," she said. He squeezed her hand and promised. A few hours later, she gave his hand a final squeeze from her bed and looked up at him. "This better at least be interesting," she said. Then she closed her eyes and died of old age on the spot. The loss rattled Denton to the core. Rose had been his champion and confidant since infancy. Now he looked about his grandmother's bedroom—at the profound emptiness, at the cold world outside, at the ice crystals spidering up the single-pane glass—and he felt some vital thing inside him begin to falter.

Denton had always been a reptilian sort of creature. When his emotions ran cold, he had a way of becoming progressively inanimate until finally the cold pressed down on him and held him frozen in place. Rose had a way of bringing him back to the sunlight. When Denton was threatened with one of his static periods, her spirit had always warmed and lightened him. But now, with his grandmother gone and *Kung Fu* canceled and the dead Bruce Lee leaving only an enigma of a book and five kung fu films that Denton had not managed to find playing anywhere within five hundred miles, Denton felt one of those old states begin to overtake him. Time began to slow as a storm loomed in the distance. There was the small funeral, a few visits from Doctor Sharpe—knocks at the door that Denton didn't have the energy to answer. He would lay in his childhood room thinking about the great curse of time. When Bruce Lee was teaching in Hong Kong, Denton had been running scared through the jungles of Vietnam. When Bruce Lee was in Seattle, Washington, Denton had been getting his brain cooked somewhere in the deserts of Nevada. Now he was certain he was in the wrong place again.

Rose's attorney sold her home as Rose had requested and he presented Denton with a check. The sum was significant. It came with a short note that reminded him, once again, to follow his own path in life. Denton deposited the check and, not being able to find the energy to figure out what to do next, he checked into the first motel he could find, a cheap place on the south side of the city. He decided to wait for the universe or his dead grandmother to give him a sign. Not knowing how long it would take, he slowly gave in to the cooling of his emotions. He slept later into the morning, limited his waking hours, ate only once a day, and sought to preserve his life force and his grandmother's small fortune until the day when Rose's voice, like a clap of thunder, would wake him to a more auspicious time and tell him what to do.

His breath slowed and his voice weakened. His heartbeat became shallow and light, and his extremities all the way to his torso remained at room temperature. Soon he was held in the clutch of an icy hand that pulled him toward something cold and dark and endless and familiar and which lacked all the promise of death. He watched the light push against his thick drapes and drip onto the floor only to be pulled back into the darkness. He waited for someone to appear and pull him out of the deepening gray, to bring him some warmth. Maybe it would be Abbott or Schlotzsky or Doctor Sharpe or even the head nurse, who had led him away with all the implicit promises of a lover but in the end had left him cold. He knew he should call someone, but he couldn't find enough energy to pick up the phone. Days passed like breaths and he felt nothing except, now and then, a sense of reverence for beauty and sadness and for the very plasticity of time. He cooled further until even his own icy coolness felt like nothing at all, and though his room temperature remained at sixty-two degrees, somehow Denton White cooled from the inside out and entered into a state of self-induced, cryogenic suspension.

27

When I put the letter down, the sky was becoming dark. The bus was moving through barren fields of stiff, shivering grass. We dropped down a slight hill and what was left of the gloomy sunlight disappeared below the horizon, only to rise again as we crested the next. I remembered how as a child I sometimes walked long distances through the forest, drawn by some promise I saw in the light just over the next hill. I'd scramble up ravines, cross little streams, expecting the forest to open onto something new and life-changing at any moment. I never knew what I was looking for—maybe a passage to some undiscovered place that would fit me like a glove, a little kingdom of my own, where I'd find a chair waiting for me among people who had been anticipating my arrival for a long time. But it was always just more hills. Always promise followed by heartbreak. And though I'd never connected the two things before, I remembered a dream I started having around the time my marriage began to disintegrate. I'd be walking through the forest like in that first memory, not knowing where I was but not quite lost either. Then I would see that light I'd always followed when I was a child—losing it in the terrain and then finding it again. I would begin to run toward it and the forest would open to a trail, and the trail would open to a clearing, and then I would look across a field of grass covered in diamonds of dew and I would see my childhood home.

Maybe it was some combination of that memory and the long bus ride that turned my thoughts back to Schlotzsky—aged and looking back on life and crossing the Mojave in his travel coach. And then I thought of Abbott sleeping in dusty ghost towns, of Denton who had disappeared from Abbott's story and had now appeared in my life. I felt as though I missed them all. And by that I guess I mean that I missed Abbott or my time with Abbott, but I was happy to at least be back inside the story. I felt the story playing on those strings that Abbott talked about, that fungal web that lay below the skin and muscle and sinew that he had described with his eyeballs threatening to jump out of his head. I could hear the faint music of some truth that was in all of us just waiting for the right person or situation or series of events to draw it out. I thought about the women who had walked across my life over the past months, the lines I had asked them to read for me, their sad exits at the dark side of the stage. I wondered if anyone would ever touch the places a good story could touch, if I would ever find anyone who had a bit of Lucille in her or if I simply had lost the ability to make those deep connections like Denton had lost his awareness and Abbott had lost his bearings and we'd all somehow lost our proper place in time.

As the gray dusk turned to blackness, I began to wonder if watching the passage from day to night along the road would always recall Abbott's story, if I would forever remember its chapters by the slant of the light and the depth of the darkness. A few passengers switched on reading lights in the seats ahead of me and I did the same. I pulled the next letter from the stack, but I didn't open it just then. I was still thinking about Lucille. I was remembering how Laura had been so fresh in my mind when Abbott first told me about her, and how I'd wondered if I would, in my own way, search my whole life to find Laura again. I wasn't so sure I hadn't been doing that, if that wasn't the reason I'd kept hearing each woman I dated reciting the same tired lines. It was easy to see it that way—as if I had directed the scenes and cued the lines from offstage, encouraging each actress to reproduce the energy of lightning striking, and to embody the feeling of a great story on the edge of unfolding. And then, when I discovered they were not and would never be Laura, I abandoned them.

I wondered if Abbott had that problem too. I thought about setting down his letters and writing him to ask about it, but I had nothing to write with or write on and I didn't know how to reach him. It was curious that Abbott had not really talked about the allure of women, or sex, not even in relation to Lucille. He had never described her to me—not her body, her face, her lips. That was all conspicuously absent from his story, and it seemed to me now that a man who chose not to associate his lost wife with her concrete form and instead held onto the energy of their moments of intimacy and the truth of their story together, might end up in a situation kind of like my own.

28

In mid-June of 1976, Doctor Sharpe received a call at his office. At the other end of the line was Ray Cook, the owner of a rundown motel on the south side of the city. He told Sharpe that Denton had been a resident at the motel for the past six months and now Denton's credit card had expired.

Sharpe asked Ray what that had to do with him.

"Well," Ray said, "Maybe you oughta come down and see for yourself."

The door of room 113 was open when the doctor arrived. Inside, Ray Cook was relaxing in a chair by the window, sipping an iced tea through a swirly plastic straw. The AC had been turned off and a box fan had been set on a small table to the side of Denton's bed, blowing over Denton White's body at the highest setting. The room was cool.

The doctor looked at Ray and Ray gestured toward Denton.

"Sweating like a cold bottle of beer," Ray said. "What do you make of it, Doc?"

The doctor walked over and placed his hand on Denton's head and pulled it away. He was as cold as ice. In the past, he'd witnessed states that sent Denton's temperature below what normal bodies could handle, sometimes falling as much as twenty or thirty degrees, but he had never seen or even heard of a body dropping below ambient temperature. It didn't make any sense. He stepped back from the bed and wrinkled his brow, not sure what to do next. That old indecision was acting up again. He stepped forward and placed his fingers on Denton's neck, finding a spot a little less cold than the frozen tissue that surrounded it.

"You might have to wait a minute or two," Ray said. "Ticker needs a good winding-up, but it's still working as far as I could tell." Ray slurped the iced tea out of the bottom of his glass and knocked his heel against the AC unit where he was resting his feet. "Feel that cool breeze, Doc? Pretty much makes this thing a redundancy."

After a little over a minute, the doctor felt one shallow pulse from Denton's neck. He raised his eyebrows and stepped back again to debate his options.

"What made you call me, Ray?" he asked.

Ray gestured with his head. "That note by the phone."

Sharpe walked over to the bedside table to look at the note. His name and number were written in a shaky hand that requested he be called in case of emergency. He looked back at Denton and shook his head.

"I'm not sure what to do here, Ray," Sharpe admitted.

"Do anything you want, Doc. But if you want to keep him here, I need a new credit card on file. And I gotta ask for some compensation for the mattress. That one is ruined. Soaked up all that moisture like a sponge."

Doctor Sharpe considered the situation. Bringing Denton to his office was out of the question. He had only one treatment room and Denton might require months to recover. His home was off limits as well—he valued his privacy too much. He could call an ambulance and be free of the whole weird problem of Denton White for good—but what about Rose? Her foremost concern had always been to keep Denton away from mainstream medical establishments. Sending Denton off in an ambulance now to be admitted to a hospital and poked and prodded like some freak of nature almost as soon as Rose, who had done so much to keep Denton clear of those places, had passed away—it seemed a decision that lacked integrity. And besides, he cared for Denton. He'd known him since he was a boy—and as Sharpe had spent most of his adult life pining for a woman who'd never returned his affections, he had no child of his own. Whether he liked it or not, Denton was the closest thing he had to a son.

"Let's get him out of here," Sharpe said. "I'll pay you a hundred bucks to help me move him."

"Plus something for the mattress?" Ray said.

"Sure," said Sharpe. "But you never mention this to anyone."

The motel owner took in a long, last slurp of air and melted ice from his swirly straw and swung his feet down from the cooling unit.

Ray helped the doctor roll Denton up in a wad of bedclothes, and then Sharpe pulled up to the door of 113 and they slid him into the back of the doctor's Cutlass. Ray hopped in and they secreted him away to Rose's old house. It was empty now, boarded up, bought by a real estate developer who was awaiting a permit for demolition. Sharpe pulled a big ring of keys out of his pocket and opened the door, and the two men lugged Denton's frozen body up the stairs and unfurled him unceremoniously on his old bedroom floor.

Ray Cook stepped back and tilted his head in thought. "What do you think goes on in the mind of a man in that condition, Doc," he mused. "Do you think he shivers in his dreams, or do you think in his dreams he is always warm?"

Ray's unexpected show of empathy caught Sharpe off guard. Something about Ray's callousness had been holding the doctor together. But now, in the same place he'd just unrolled a cryogenically preserved body, he saw the boy he'd cared for since childhood lying frozen on the bedroom floor. He turned away to compose himself.

"Ray," he said. He reached into his pocket and pulled out a wad of bills.

"Yeah Doc?"

"Please don't speak of this to anyone."

"Who would believe it, Doc?" Ray asked. "It'd be just like it was with the UFOs. They'd send me away again."

Sharpe's eyebrows raised at that last word. Again? Perhaps he could trust Ray. He turned around and counted two hundred dollars into Ray's open palm and then showed him to the door.

29

While Denton continued to thaw out, Sharpe collected supplies from his office and waited for dark. Then he returned and set the place up to facilitate Denton's recovery. It took a while. Putting things in order was always a problem for Doctor Sharpe. There were always so many decisions to be made, and each decision would grow into a branch that led to the next decision. One wrong decision at the beginning of a series of decisions might theoretically lead him toward a catastrophe which could've been easily avoided by just one extra moment of consideration at a key juncture.

Sometimes it seemed that every moment was a key juncture. It could be torture. Awful things could result from something as simple as storing syringes in an upper drawer as opposed to a lower drawer, or vice versa. This chronic case of analysis paralysis was, in fact, the key reason Sharpe had never employed a nurse. The last thing he needed was to be under the eyes of someone who could observe him struck suddenly motionless in the middle of writing a prescription, or to catch him standing still and silent as a porcelain cat, with his right hand on the bathroom doorknob—captivated by one of the minutes-long deliberations that possessed him at unpredictable moments, dozens of times a day. Now that he was getting on in age and could've used the assistance of a young nurse, it would've been even more dangerous to employ one. He might be thought senile, reported to the medical board, and lose his license.

Once the room was arranged, Sharpe tried to settle on a treatment plan—another difficult task. He looked at his longtime patient thawing on the floor, his face frozen, lacking clear expression—a poker face—and Sharpe's own head nodded at the burden of each critical decision that lay before him. A few minutes later, he was startled from his stupor by an insight so obvious that it seemed impossible that it had never occurred to him before. Maybe Denton's affliction wasn't so odd after all. Perhaps it was just a more virulent strain of the same paralyzing condition from which Sharpe himself suffered.

The thought gave him courage. When he looked at his past in this new light, the whole long series of events—all the movements of fate and the complex web of decisions that had led him to Rose's house as a child, sent him across the country for a medical degree, and led him back again to the same bedroom where he'd long ago played as a doctor with Rose's daughter Lila—they all made perfect sense. He saw himself standing in front of Rose holding a doctor's bag, a young man, anxious with perspiration and falling hair and aged prematurely by the burden of life and death, by the heavy responsibility of diagnosis and the looming possibility of misdiagnosis, and the further possibility of adverse drug interactions and contamination and cross-contamination and a thousand other things. He saw himself returned as a family doctor, no longer a sweet-faced and curious gynecologist to the young Lila whose path had since diverged. In her place, is a small child, fragile and cold.

The very sight of this child fills Sharpe with ambivalence and self-doubt. But Rose had faith. She called him back though his treatments were often ineffective, though she often found him frozen in deliberation or shaking his head and mumbling to himself in an empty room. Perhaps Rose, who had known Henry Sharpe since childhood, had seen what had been invisible to the eyes of the doctor himself—that of all men, the similarly afflicted Sharpe might be one of the few physicians capable of understanding her grandson.

Sharpe snapped out of his stupor into one of those rare states he could never seem to hold onto for very long: he felt decisive. He was certain of his place and purpose in the universe. He was sure he knew exactly what to do. With bolstered confidence, Sharpe found the strength to drag Denton's frozen body to the bathroom tub. He filled it with cool water, hoisted Denton over the side, and then began raising the water temperature degree by degree. After several hours, Denton's veins softened and his heart reached a cadence of ten beats per minute. Sharpe hooked him up to an IV drip of warm saline and continued to raise the water temperature. The process took most of the night. At daylight, he hauled Denton onto an adjustable gurney, wrapped him in an electric blanket, added some glucose to his bag of saline, and fell asleep in a chair beside him.

30

I fell asleep for a while and when I woke up the bus had pulled off for a midnight breakfast at a truck stop along Interstate 80. I sat down and when the waitress asked me what I wanted, I ordered all the same things I'd ordered at Alice's Restaurant the evening before. She went to put my order in, and I opened the next letter, more so I wouldn't feel awkward sitting alone than because I wanted to begin reading it just then. I looked over the first few lines—salutation, then straight back into the story. A few weeks had passed in that old Salt Lake City world, and the letter had Doctor Sharpe walking through the door of Rose's old home carrying a bag of fast-food hamburgers and fries, and a pint of Breyers ice cream. He climbed the stairs and walked into the bedroom to find that Denton was not there.

I set the letter down and got my waitress's attention to ask if I could add a slice of apple pie *a la mode* to my order. Ice cream sounded like just the thing to finish off the spread I'd ordered, and as Abbott had been fairly generous with the bundle of cash he'd sent along with Harelip Lenny, I could afford to splurge.

"You got it, hun," she said.

She wrote it down on a slip and clipped it in the kitchen window, and for a moment I let all the different worlds converge, imagining she was Lucille and Abbott was in the kitchen and maybe I was sitting in the past, in the diner with the two of them, reading a letter sent from a future where Abbott detailed the whole saga to come. And if it had been true, what could I have said that would've made any difference at all? Maybe I'd simply mention how beautiful a day it was—though it was cold and snow was falling and it was midnight. I might tell them to hold this moment in their memories to keep them through darker times, though those words would undoubtedly come across as the words of a mental patient.

The food put me in the present again—a bunch of plates with overcooked steak and hash-brown potatoes and fried eggs and bacon and sausage. Then a mug of burnt coffee, a big glass of orange juice from concentrate. The apple pie, the waitress told me, was warming in the oven.

I topped everything with ketchup and Tabasco sauce and dug in. Every bit of it was delicious. It had me thinking about Naomi again and the wonderful breakfast I had imagined enjoying with her, but that we had never shared. The thought put me in a world where I'd been spending a lot of time lately.

"Hun," the waitress asked, setting down a plate of warm pie, "do you want me to top off your coffee?"

She'd caught me staring off into nowhere, hurtling through the past, thinking about exactly how far back in time I would go if I had a chance to choose. She didn't wait for my answer.

"There you go," she said.

I picked up the letter and read until they called us back onto the bus, and then I got on the bus and stared out the window, into nowhere for a while, and then I read letter after letter.

Denton was up and out of bed. That was a good sign, Sharpe decided. His patient was making remarkable progress. Sharpe had weaned him off IV fluids, and he had retired the electro-stimulation device that he had been using to rehabilitate Denton's atrophied muscles. Only a twinge of anxiety overshadowed the doctor's certainty that Denton's absence from the bedroom was a good omen. He walked back down the stairs to the foyer, checking rooms, one by one. At last, he heard a persistent thudding coming from somewhere close. The sound was arrhythmic, like a heart in spasm. He opened the basement door and descended the stairs.

When he reached the landing, Denton's back was to him. Denton was shirtless and covered in perspiration. Sharpe saw that his patient had turned an old three-legged chair on its side and fastened it, chest high, to a post. The legs were facing outward and Denton was bobbing back and forth in front of it, striking the legs with his forearms and punching the bottom of the seat with his fists. His arms were covered with welts and his knuckles were tinted with blood.

"Denton?" Sharpe asked softly.

His patient spun around and winked at him while throwing a sideways kick to the seat of the chair, connecting with a final, solid thud.

"Doc!" he said. "Look what I've made! It's a wing chun dummy!"

Denton tossed a towel over his neck and walked over to where a book lay open on the basement workbench. "Come check this out, Doc." He waved Sharpe to join him.

Sharpe stood next to Denton and set down the fast food and ice cream. He recognized the book as one of two—the second was a conspiracy book by Gary Allen—that he'd packed with Denton's things from Ray Cook's motel. The book was Bruce Lee's, *The Tao of Jeet Kune Do*. Denton flipped through the pages, explaining the exercises and the philosophy of Bruce Lee's fighting art—a man who Denton exalted as a cinema star, a modern sage, and perhaps the greatest fighter to ever live.

"I want to tell you something extraordinary, Doc," Denton said.

"Extraordinary?"

"Extraordinary!" Denton repeated. He pulled the towel off his neck, threw it on the workbench, and returned to knocking his forearms and palms against the repurposed chair.

Doctor Sharpe stood at the bench and leafed through Bruce Lee's treatise, keeping a careful watch on his patient. He was torn. On the one hand, he wondered if Bruce Lee's obtuse theoretical ideas might endanger the manic proclivities of his patient. His forehead wrinkled with concern. But then he remembered Rose White's long-held belief that Denton needed to interact with physical objects to remain sane, and his eyebrows reversed the creases in his brow into an expression of hope. He couldn't deny that Denton's muscle tone was improving. His spirit was light. Sharpe decided to take a wait-and-see approach.

After twenty more minutes of exercises, the two went upstairs to eat, taking seats in the front room, on the big sill of the boarded-up bay window. Denton devoured his quarter-pound burger and fries and slurped down a quart of Coke without saying a word. The former vegetarian had woken from cryogenesis hungry for meat, carbohydrates and grease. This return of appetite was another reason to be hopeful, Sharpe thought.

"Where's that ice cream, Doc?"

Sharpe slid the carton toward him and pulled a couple of spoons out of the fast-food bag. He handed one to Denton and disposed of his leftovers in the empty bag. Condensation was dripping down the outside of the ice cream carton, the same way it had formed on Denton's cold body just weeks before.

When Denton opened the container, the edges of the ice cream were soft. He moved his spoon around the rim, took a scoop of melted cream and pulled the spoon through his mouth and shivered.

"Wow, this hits the spot, Doc. What a sensation!" He pushed it back toward the doctor. "You gotta try this!"

Sharpe scooped some cream onto his own spoon and tasted it. The rush of mint took him somewhere he'd been before. "Oh, that *is* pleasant," he said. He took another scoop and tasted it more deeply. He felt neural pathways open up, a rush of emotional pleasure, and then, for a few moments, he forgot about Denton entirely. He became lost in the memory of an old, unrequited love, a Dutch widow whom he had spent half his life pining over. Her memory was the place where all roads of sensuality and emotion eventually seemed to lead him these days. He swallowed the cream, letting the old regret finish with sweetness, and slid the carton back Denton's way. "Denton," he said, not quite knowing how to broach the subject delicately, "you said you had something extraordinary to report."

"Extraordinary!" Denton said.

Sharpe waited for his patient to elaborate. His eyebrows raised again, involuntarily. Sometimes they did that, as if they were a medical instrument more sensitive than his conscious mind. He wondered if there was something ominous in the involuntary expression, but after a few moments of careful analysis he decided that it was nothing—just a reflex from the after-rush of the mint and the memory.

"I don't know if you'll believe this, Doc," Denton continued, "but I think I know why I'm here. I think I know my purpose."

Sharpe felt his forehead smooth out. Hadn't Sharpe had a similar revelation regarding his own purpose, just weeks before, while he sat in near-despair on the floor of Denton's second-story bedroom? If Denton was a lunatic for thinking such a thing, then the doctor had to admit he was a lunatic himself.

"I believe you, Denton," he said.

"You believe me, Doc?" Denton said. He handed Sharpe the ice cream and stood up with a long sigh, took a few steps, then ran his hands through his hair and sighed again. "Because when his apparition appeared in the basement, I thought, 'Nobody is *ever* going to believe this.'"

Sharpe's eyebrows were acting up again. He wrestled them down and composed his face.

"When who appeared to you, Denton?"

"Well, Doc, a few hours before you came, I was going through some of the movements from the book." Denton snapped his arms into a few fighting positions and nodded at the doctor.

Sharpe nodded back.

"Out of nowhere, this intense heat flowed into my palms. Burning heat, Doc! Right here. Right in the center of my palms. Then, just like that, my hands were on fire. Fire, doc!"

Denton let out a howl and jumped back into a low crouch, slashing the air with a series of strikes and yelps.

"You following me, Doc?"

Doctor Sharpe nodded again. He felt his eyebrows twitching.

"I'm trying, Denton," he said.

There was something painful about Denton's pantomime—but in that sweet way that so confused the doctor. It reminded him of a kabuki performance he'd seen years before. He remembered how he'd intended to invite the Dutch woman he was still pining for, but he'd lost his nerve. He'd ended up sitting beside her son instead—a former patient, now grown, who had become something of a colleague and a friend.

Denton stopped the kabuki and came back to the window for a scoop of ice cream and caught his breath.

"It was him, Doc," he said.

"Who?" the doctor asked again.

"It was Bruce Lee, Doc. He spoke to me."

Denton took another bite of ice cream, swallowed, and shook his spoon in the air.

"I know it sounds crazy, Doc, but he was right down there in the basement with me."

Denton went on while the doctor fought to keep his face composed, struggling between the sadness of memory and his concern for all the daunting variables of the unformed future. Denton told the doctor how the heat built in his hands until his clenched fist delivered a bolt of lightning that sent him staggering back from his wing chun dummy, and as he picked himself up off the floor, a low blue flame remained that glowed with the figure and face of his hero.

"It sounds crazy, Doc. I know that," Denton said. His face, if it had been an instrument like the doctor's eyebrows, would have been registering something far outside its normal range.

"It does sound crazy, Denton," Doctor Sharpe said. The spirit of his memory was still with him. "But perhaps we all sometimes wish we could speak to people who are no longer with us."

"So you understand?" Denton said.

Doctor Sharpe nodded. "You said he spoke to you?"

"He instructed me," Denton said.

Sharpe listened as Denton went on. It sounded delusional, but no more delusional than many of the doctor's own thoughts, and the more the doctor got on in years the more he wondered if it was only our delusions that brought beauty to the world anyway. Denton's communion with the dead Bruce Lee didn't alarm him. The alarm came later, when Denton began talking feverishly about the Illuminati, running up the stairs to his bedroom and returning with the other book that Sharpe had brought from room 113 at Ray Cook's motel—Gary Allen's *None Dare Call it Conspiracy*. A half-minute later Denton was standing in front of the doctor with his face again registering something beyond its normal range.

"You know who I'm talking about!" Denton said. He held his spoon pointed at Sharpe for a few moments, and then bent down and dug deep into the bottom of the pint of mint ice cream to mine the last of the chocolate chips.

"The Mormons!" he said, "The American wing of the Illuminati." Denton watched for his doctor's reaction while Sharpe did his best to remain composed.

Bruce Lee's death had been far beyond suspicious, Denton told him. It was something that had troubled Denton as he had passed into darkness with the manual of Jeet Kune Do beside him, and six months of sleep had done nothing to change his mind. Bruce Lee had been eliminated as part of the same Church of Latter Day Saints conspiracy that had robbed the world of John F. Kennedy and Martin Luther King. There were powerful forces out there who were intimidated by big ideas and big thinkers, and though Denton White didn't exactly place himself among such luminaries, he believed it was his calling to—

In the calmest voice he could muster, Doctor Sharpe asked Denton if he thought this idea was the best thing for his health.

"Probably not," Denton admitted.

But Sharpe had only a moment of relief.

In fact, Denton told him, if he carried out his plan—and he assured Sharpe that he would carry it out—he fully expected to meet a powerful resistance from the Latter Day Saints. Death threats and attempts on his life were to be expected. And because the Illuminati were in league with the elite overlords of the city and because they had the police on their payroll, Denton could expect resistance to come from all quarters—both from legal and more unscrupulous avenues.

Sharpe took the spoon from Denton and scraped the melted ice cream at the bottom of the carton. The chocolate chips were gone. He barely tasted the mint. He shook his head just slightly, and then he decided that he had no choice but to decide everything would be all right. Much later, he would look back on that odd conversation and shake his head more vigorously— at both his miscalculation in the timing of the impending disaster and at Denton White's strange prescience.

31

The next few months would put Doctor Sharpe's wait-and-see approach to the test. Denton obeyed Bruce Lee's directive and used what remained of his inheritance to purchase the dilapidated Palace Theater on the south end of the city. His martial arts instruction had begun on the small screen, in an institution. Now it would continue on the big screen. He restored The Palace into a Kung Fu Theater and acquired prints of Bruce Lee's five films, one for each of the theater's five screens. Not having enough money left to hire employees, he staggered showtimes so he could man the concession at the beginning of each show and still manage to float between projectors to change reels. He bought himself a set of nunchaku and mimicked Lee's choreography from the projection rooms. Once he mastered a sequence, he would occasionally appear on the stage and perform in front of the projector's flickering light while the movie played and Bruce Lee fought in synchrony beside him.

The community ate it up. There was no Mormon backlash, no death threats. Instead, Denton enjoyed his first brush with something akin to public acceptance, even adulation. For several months, it seemed like he'd found his calling. An article appeared in a local paper, along with a photo of Denton White side-by-side Bruce Lee's *Game of Death* poster—the theater owner striking an identical pose to his idol and uniformed in an identical yellow tracksuit. Young people looking for a novel experience flooded the theater to dig this eccentric place with its eccentric proprietor and they endowed the Palace with a sense of hipness. The *Tribune* picked up the story and, in their review of Denton's theater, even they would have to admit that something about the place simply jived with the times.

Denton didn't know what to make of it. He had been anticipating the resistance he'd seen in his vision, and now it was a little upsetting to brace against a force that wasn't there. He read the *Tribune* article in disbelief. He knew the paper's history—Illuminati control giving way to the power of the Roman Catholic Church, and the strange connections to the Jewish community and the political elite that could be traced all the way to Washington. But the review of his cinema was glowing. Their portrayal of him was sweet. They'd even printed his damning accusations about the Illuminati and quoted him on Gary Allen who he claimed as a source of inspiration almost as important as Bruce Lee.

While the article may have been suspicious and destabilizing to Denton, across town it was soothing the uneasy mind of his physician. Doctor Sharpe had been suffering from disturbing dreams ever since the day Ray Cook had called him to his roadside motel. Denton's subsequent visions, his theater purchase, his obsession with the Illuminati—these things had done nothing to alleviate the doctor's already troubled sleep. Sharpe was certain he had violated the very foundation of his Hippocratic Oath. He had intended to save Denton. Now he wondered if he'd only succeeded in shepherding him back toward a world of chaos. Sharpe himself was exhausted. He'd never been a man of action, exactly, but in the months that followed his intervention, even as Denton threw himself into the restoration and opening of the Palace Theater with tremendous energy, Sharpe was finding that he lacked the will to make up his mind about anything. It was as if holding back the powerful waves of indecision and second-guessing for those long weeks of Denton's treatment had drained a shallow well of decisiveness that was intended to be rationed out in teaspoons over an entire lifetime.

Now he wondered if the *Tribune* article should restore his confidence in himself. He read it over morning coffee and tried to come to a solid opinion about the matter. He would raise his eyebrows and conclude, decisively, that it was a positive development. But no sooner would he remove his reading glasses and set them down, than he'd knot up his brow and begin doubting himself and slip his glasses back on to review the article again. Finally, he was settled. He thought Denton came off rather well—far closer to a charming eccentric than a certifiable lunatic—and he decided his own neurosis had led him to judge Denton too harshly. Even the quotes about LDS conspiracies and the Illuminati, when taken in the context of the theatrical persona of Denton White, somehow now seemed endearing.

Doctor Sharpe sipped another cup of coffee while he read through the rest of the lifestyle section. He could now stop all his senseless worrying. At last, he felt completely relaxed. He stood up and folded the paper and flopped it back down on the table with a note of finality. He was satisfied. He decided to put Denton and Ray Cook out of his mind and reserve what remained of his decisiveness for the years ahead.

The doctor's resolution was wildly successful. In fact, he happened to be reflecting on his most recent victory of action over indecision at the precise moment that Denton hobbled into his office, not two months later. Earlier that morning, Sharpe had been looking down the throat of a female patient in her early fifties who was suffering from chronic streptococcus infections. Most physicians would've prescribed antibiotics and sent her on her way, but Sharpe's mind went to the Dutch widow he had so dearly loved, and he wondered if something else was at play. He'd decided to trust his intuition. When he asked the woman if there was some deep emotion she had been keeping to herself, the woman began to sob. After spending the better part of his morning listening to her heartrending story, Sharpe told her to begin journaling and was convinced they had thwarted a festering cancer. Yet, it only took one glance at the emaciated and confused-looking Denton White to shatter his hard-won confidence. A shudder of panic coursed through the doctor and he feared he had wrongly encouraged his patient to lower her defenses. He was certain she'd return to him with a tumor in a matter of weeks.

As for Denton, it seemed fame had been a merciless taskmaster, and now the poor child was a wreck. The *Tribune* article had filled his theaters to bursting, first with fellow martial arts buffs, and then with strange, dispossessed loners like himself, looking for their tribe. Finally, as droves of hipsters flooded the Palace in search of the latest fad, Denton struggled to keep up. He sprinted from the concession to the projector rooms, to the stage and back again, performing Bruce

Lee's choreography to a cheering crowd perhaps a half-dozen times a night. When the stress made him anxious, he relaxed himself with marijuana. He swallowed handfuls of aspirin to relieve the pain in his lower back and spoonfuls of throat syrup to recover a voice that had grown weary from shrieking and yelping and was beginning to falter at its upper register. One night, while executing a spinning back kick, he pulled his groin. Unable to sleep, he smeared himself with Bengay and tried to quiet his mind by pondering the precepts of Jeet Kune Do, meditating on using no way as a way, and on having no limitation as his only limitation, and so forth. But all the thinking only gave him headaches, and he wasn't sure that was a coincidence. The same migraines which had once plagued his martial arts idol had now begun to debilitate him. He became sensitive to light and soon he was spending most showings lying on his back in the dark projector rooms with his eyes protected by a thick, damp cloth.

The fertile soil of exhaustion and anxiety was watered by the liberal doses of marijuana, and paranoia began to take root. Progressively unable to meet the demands of his crowded theater and on the brink of mental and physical breakdown, Denton began to wonder if this road to exhaustion had been planned and paved by the New World Order from the beginning. Perhaps this was why they had published the glowing review in the *Tribune* which brought the very notoriety that continued to fill his theater to the bursting point. The lack of anticipated resistance had sent him soaring toward the sun. Now, with his waxen wings melted, he was plummeting back to earth, and like the perfect sucker he was, he hadn't thought to pack a parachute. He began to believe he had come so close to merging his spirit with that of his master that he now shared the same curse that haunted

Bruce Lee's family for generations and had killed his hero dead at the age of thirty-two. The proof of this was in his dreams, which had again become plagued by the demons and dragons of his childhood. These were the same frightening figures that had relentlessly pursued Bruce Lee after he refused to take his prophesied position among the Illuminati and had instead devoted himself to the martial arts and acting.

Denton became certain that the devious plot of the New World Order was now reaching its completion. It would soon take him out, just as it had destroyed Doctor King and JFK and his mentor. Fame was a door that opened with surprisingly little resistance and led, on its other side, to a long, anxious fall through a great nihilistic void.

"Doc," he said, jolting Sharpe out of a spiral of self-doubt, "I need your help."

Ever since Denton could remember, Doctor Sharpe's vote of confidence had seemed to brace him up. At times, he just needed some guidance, an external voice to project itself over all his internal chatter and tell him to do the thing he already knew needed doing. Now, as he walked home, he decided he would close down his theater for the two weeks of rest that Sharpe had recommended, and even if he wasn't willing to teetotal his marijuana use, he would cut back to using it only in the evenings.

It was good advice. After only a few days Denton felt as though he was thinking more clearly. His sleep was less fitful, his bad dreams had subsided. But soon he was tortured by a new anxiety. If the price of admission to the world of health and sanity was closing down the ticket booth to his theater, Denton would very soon be broke. On their own, the films of Bruce Lee couldn't draw the crowds night after night. His business model required his full commitment to the path of Jeet Kune Do. It demanded the very performances that drove him toward physical and nervous exhaustion. Without Denton White breathing life and moment into the films, even the greatest martial choreography of all time would soon grow stale. He needed to come up with a new gimmick or he would lose his theater.

Ten days later, he was sitting in his dark basement office listening to The Who and contemplating the way of no way. The basement was full of old pinball machines from another era. There were a few in his office that he'd barely noticed before, covered in junk and dust, stacked with old reels of corrupted celluloid and vintage movie posters. He'd never had a moment to look through any of it and now that he had some free time, he was curious.

Denton stood and began to clear off one of the old pinball machines, but what he found stopped him in his tracks. It was a poster for the 1952 film *Love is Better Than Ever,* featuring Elizabeth Taylor in the sexy getup of a Rockette dancer. He blushed and turned the poster over. Then, realizing his grandmother was no longer around to admonish him, he flipped it around for another look. After standing and admiring it for several minutes, he moistened a cloth, cleaned it off, and pinned it up on the wall above the pinball machine. When he flopped back down in his office chair, an idea began to crystallize. He saw a happier version of himself, a version that had not been stunted by the sexual hangups of his grandmother. In his vision, there were bells and flashing lights. He could see himself, full of vital energy, playing pinball with Elizabeth Taylor poised above him. He closed his eyes to see it more clearly and then opened them again. The poster was crooked. He couldn't think. He climbed up on the pinball machine to rehang the poster and came face to face with Liz Taylor's leotarded pelvis. Blood rushed to his head. His vision went dark.

When he woke up on the floor, The Who record was fully spun. He rubbed his eyes and stood up, hitting the back of his head on the bottom of the pinball machine. There was a flash of blinding light and as it cleared Denton saw the vision of a pinball parlor in his theater lobby, bells ringing, colored lights flashing, and a whole troupe of Rockette dancers doing some kind of cabaret act. He saw them hunched over pinball machines with deeply curved lower backs and their round bottoms tilting side to side. Others were twirling their boas and posing on top of the machines in four-inch stilettos to the cheers of a crowded room. It didn't make a whole lot of sense, but the vision was clear. It was even clearer and more immediate than the apparition of Bruce Lee.

Denton extended the closing of his theater for an additional week and put his adolescent trade skills to work. He was certain that his apprenticeships as clockmaker, machinist, metal fabricator, and electrician had been honed for this purpose. He refurbished the old machines, altering their simple components into complex systems of chain reactions that triggered flashing lights and electromagnets and conveyors and alarms and bells and music. When he was satisfied with his creations, he had a group of old patrons help him move them upstairs and he reopened his theater.

Denton half-expected to find a whole troupe of Rockettes waiting at the door as he pulled aside the velvet rope at his grand reopening.

But the Rockettes he had seen so clearly didn't come. Instead, young Mormon boys poured in. They were blond and big-eyed, innocent to the addictive charms of Denton's new-fangled machines. Their unsuspecting parents bought them tickets to movies they would never see. The boys would stand in place for hours, enraptured by the bells and flashing lights. Soon they were cutting school, looking for lawns to mow and leaves to rake, or lifting coins out of their father's pants pockets like junkies. Angry parents and truant officers were showing up at Denton's theater in the middle of the day to drag kids off to school by their ears.

There had always been rumors that Rose White had left Mormonism to become a Pagan, and when her daughter took up with the circus, most people assumed the rumors had been true. Now the old rumors were given new life. Rose, they said, had raised her grandson without ever banishing the devil within him. Rose's heathen grandson had grown up free of the controlling influence of Mormonism, and now his godless machines were drawing their own sons away from the Church as well. The Latter Day Saints had turned a blind eye to the art of kung fu. They'd been able to look past the conspiracies of Gary Allen. They knew there was a conspiracy afoot. This much had been known for thousands of years and it would've been strange for a man of Denton's obvious intelligence not to sense it. But the conspiracy that Denton dared call conspiracy was just a diversion, part of the long con of the greatest conspiracy of all time—that of the penultimate conman to draw the minds and hearts of humanity away from Truth itself. These were the talking points that flooded the churches and burst forth from the pulpits and cooled the first wave of Salt Lake City's pinball fever, and ultimately led to the empty lobby and empty screening rooms that sent the Palace Theater plunging back into the red.

Soon Denton was back in his cool basement office. If he wasn't going to lose the theater and his entire inheritance, he needed a new plan. Denton put The Who on the record player, then he sat down and put his feet up on his desk to think. The pinball machines had been moved upstairs, but Elizabeth Taylor was still pinned up and hanging crooked on his wall. Denton looked at her with one burning question on his mind—Why had The Rockettes never arrived? What detail could he have missed? He closed his eyes and tried to see the vision again. He listened for the voice of Elizabeth Taylor to tell him what to do. Nothing came. He opened his eyes and asked Elizabeth Taylor the question directly, but she just stood there in her skimpy outfit and looked coy and said nothing. He lit up a joint, took a few hits, and closed his eyes again. Finally, Liz Taylor began to materialize behind his eyelids. He focused his mind and strained his internal eye and he could see that she was gesturing him to take his feet off the desk. Now she was rolling off her stockings. She twirled them in the air and draped them over his neck. She sat down on his lap and crossed her legs, uncrossed them, crossed them again. Now she was caressing his cheek, whispering in his ear. She was telling him the things she wanted to do to him, and the things that she wanted them to both do, together.

Denton clasped his hands behind his head and rested back against the wall. The last piece of advice his grandmother had given him before slipping off into her final sleep was to be happy and do what he loved. He considered that for a moment. There were only two things Denton White had ever loved more than kung fu. The first, he'd been passionate about since adolescence—he loved to admire the curves and crevices of women clad in skimpy attire. The second had remained dormant for most of his life and was just now beginning to flower—he wanted to expose The Church of Latter Day Saints for the corrupt arm of the Illuminati he knew it to be. Between these two loves was a tension, because Denton knew that Rose would've been horrified by the first passion, but the second was undoubtedly born of a seed she had planted deep within him. Behind that one, she would've thrown her full support. He decided the idea germinating in his mind was more or less a wash as far as his grandmother was concerned. In fact, as a struggling theater owner in the very Mecca of the Latter Day Saints, he could not think of a better way to exact retribution for all the trouble the Mormons, the Illuminati, and the New World Order had brought to his and Lila's and Rose's lives, than what he was thinking at that very moment.

The idea was perfect. It was time for Denton to put aside the subjugation of his more instinctual drives. He would stop sublimating his nature with obtuse philosophy and deep ponderousness, with the calisthenics of Bruce Lee which were, quite frankly, inimitable. He would put aside his practice of jeet kune do which had driven him to the point of physical exhaustion, and he would forget the Chinese movie star whose chiseled body and cinematic charisma sometimes made Denton feel as physically imperfect and socially awkward as the cryptic aphorisms of Lee's *Tao* made him feel feeble-minded. He recollected his grandmother's dying wish once more and, between the prior moment and the one that followed, his course was settled. If the vision Bruce Lee had bestowed on him could not be realized without his life descending into chaos, and if the world could not properly repay him for his artistic and mechanical genius by making The Rockettes appear out of lights and bells and dust, then he would have to follow his heart in a different direction. He would transform the Palace into something new, something breathtaking. The Palace was about to become the region's most artistic, stunning and illustrious—it was about to become the region's *only* pornographic theater.

32

"I don't trust doctors, Ponchito,"

That's what John Sullivan told Carlos Rubinstein on their way out to the Porno Palace. He rattled off a list of medical terms: chronic, recurrent, remission, relapse...

"These words have no place in a man's vocabulary. You catch my drift, *amigo*?"

Carlos cracked the window of the squad car and listened to the wind whistle, sipping a few quick breaths of fresh air.

"*No bueno.*" Sully said, "*Comprende?*"

Carlos opened the window a little further and watched the buildings pass, block by block. In his mind, he was already tucked away in a room of his own at the University Hospital where a sleep study would provide three weeks of paid leave and much-needed respite.

There was no question that the two men were meant to be partners. Either man, if he had been pulled aside and asked if fate had interceded in their unlikely collision, would have nodded in affirmation—Sully with a note of contentment, certainty, and even hope, and Carlos with a wince of pain. But the odd pair would've disagreed on what exactly the universe wanted of them, and they would've told entirely different versions of how it had thrown them together.

In Sully's mind, their eventual connection was prophesied by a parish priest in New Orleans who really hadn't foreseen anything. Rather, much like Sully's half-Mexican counterpart, the priest just wished to return to a life of peace, absent of the lawman's diatribes on manliness and chivalry and things related to the protection of women's virtuousness, and from the cruel stories Sully told to him in confessional—served to him like a cold, stale sandwich, garnished not with the complex flavors of conflicted remorse which was the confessional's *reason d'être*, but with an odious pleasure that made the gentle priest shudder.

The other thing the priest wished to escape, and not without a sense of conflict and remorse—because his desire to be free of this thing made him feel petty and mean and lacking in Christian charity—was the awful smell of John Sullivan's feet. Sully's feet had developed an incurable fungus, an infestation that could only be described as biblical. Perhaps it was intended as a divine punishment for Sully, or a trial for one of them or the other, or perhaps for both. For over a year, the priest took on the challenge with this in mind, handling this new member of his flock with the patience of Job and with the same kindness and humility that Francis had shown the lepers of Assisi. But on an unseasonably warm day in November when John Sullivan entered the confessional with his feet kicking up an August-level odor, the priest finally reached his breaking point. Unable to face the thought of rinsing and blessing Sully's feet even one more time, he confessed to himself and his God that he lacked the strength to fulfill his Christian duty to the malodorous lawman and he threw in the towel once and for all.

He sent Sully west with a promise that somewhere in the

high and arid desert he would find God's grace and his incurable foot fungus would be cured. When the lawman balked at the suggestion, the priest—who had a sense for the superstitious fetishes of Irishmen—lied outright. He said the Virgin Mother herself had come to him in a dream and told him as much. Then, probably because of the August-level odor and because the priest was fond of show tunes and because the new Andrew Lloyd Webber album had found its way into his hands and his heart, he stole a bit of inspiration from the biblical story of Joseph and the coat of many colors given to him by his father, Abraham, and he told the lawman to keep his eyes out for Jews. In the desert, the priest falsely prophesied, Sully would meet the young Jewish outcast in a colorful coat, and through their friendship he would find both absolution for his old life and a gateway to something wholly new and beautiful.

This desperate climactic embellishment would both sell the story and seal Carlos Rubinstein's fate. Carlos was half-Jewish. His father had been a sports writer, and his mother was a Tacuate Indian and the eldest daughter of a midget luchador. Carlos' parents met when his father traveled south to write an article on the legendary lucha libre fighter, El Santo. His journalist father had intended to reveal the heart of a fighter who had never appeared unmasked in public, but fate had its own plans. When he arrived one evening to interview Carlos Rubinstein's grandfather, he was welcomed to the table and served a plate of *chilaquiles* by the little man's full-sized daughter. Over the next weeks, it was the writer's heart that revealed itself, while the article went unwritten and the secret depths of the legendary El Santo remained unplumbed.

The poncho that earned Carlos his nickname was, in reality, a denim jacket. It was big on Poncho, a Christmas gift that had been hand-sewn and colorfully adorned in traditional Oaxacan embroidery by Carlos' mother. But where the other officers saw a short Mexican man wearing a poncho, Sully saw someone different—the man in the colorful coat whom he'd left New Orleans to find. For several months after arriving in the city, Sully tried unsuccessfully to manipulate his way into the squad car with Carlos. He sewed mild seeds of discord between Carlos and his partner and nudged his own partner—an old-timer who'd been shivering through an unusually cold Salt Lake City winter with the cruiser windows locked fully open—claiming that they were broken—toward retirement. But in the end, it turned out Sully's efforts were unnecessary. Fate intervened. Carlos Rubinstein's partner was photographed cavorting with prostitutes inside the Porno Palace and Sully's partner took sick with pneumonia and died. After sharing only two months together in the squad car, it didn't sit well with the Irishman that Carlos would be abandoning him for a sleep study, just when they'd been assigned to the Porno Palace and things were about to get interesting.

"Chronic insomnia, Carlito? Come on, *amigo*. Leave the chronic conditions to the *muchachas*." Sully laughed and slapped Carlos on the thigh. "We've got heads to crack. Am I right?"

Carlos remained silent. He was reflecting on something, someone, on an image that calmed him at moments like these.

Carlos' new partner claimed to be descendant from a long line of Irish bareknuckle fighters. He was a big man who thought himself something of a white knight in a world that was losing its way in regard to the divisions and definitions of men and women. Sully could be big-hearted, and when Carlos was able to brace his olfactory senses

244

and squint through the horrible odor that followed Sully around like a devoted dog, he sometimes caught a glimpse of the gentleness and capacity for friendship that his grandfather had told him existed, often in remarkable quantities, in the very men most practiced at violence. But the brutality he sometimes witnessed in John Sullivan, and which the code of his profession required him to defend and sometimes conceal, made it impossible for Carlos to accept the hand of friendship that Sully was forever extending to him. Now, he was haunted by the knowledge that their new assignment was sure to bring out the worst in Sully—for nothing incited his Irish partner more than men who disrespected women. Carlos was certain that this fact was the reason their captain, under pressure from the city fathers, had chosen to put Sully on a beat that had driven so many of his officers to distraction and disgrace. In the illicit temptations of the flesh, John Sullivan was pure, stoic, and incorruptible.

"Come on, Ponchito. Ditch the sleep study and lay down the law with me" Sully patted Carlos' thigh a little softer than before. "Women are delicate, *amigo*. They need to be treated with care. But a man? Ponchito, if a man is sick, he's sick, and if he's well—well, it's settled then, isn't it? Look at me, *amigo*. On March 17th, I'd had enough. Woke up and decided my trench foot was cured. Gone for good, Ponchito. *Adios*. Just like that." Sully snapped his big middle finger against the meat of his thumb. "And have you heard me speak a word about it since?"

Carlos sniffed and cleared his throat. It was a dry day, early morning, and all he could smell was sulfur. He'd spent enough time in the squad car with Sully to know that doses of sulfur were applied liberally to his bare feet, twice a day. By lunch, the spongy smell would take over, and then it would be sulfur again through the afternoon. Sometimes Carlos imagined a future of days like this extending almost into eternity. Fate had brought him there and fate was his only escape. He could close his eyes at any time, day or night, and sleeplessly visualize the long voyage of the infectious spore that had brought John Sullivan to Salt Lake City and into the very car where they now sat. Carlos had become a host for fate, the same way John Sullivan's feet were a host for the spore that infected them. And fate, like disease, could be suppressed, ignored, beaten down with drugs or alcohol, but like sleep, it could not be forced against its will. Fate had its own mind and Carlos knew this with the same certainty that he knew there was only one thing that could make his sleep problem go *adios* for good, as Sully said. But Carlos' patience was wearing thin, and even while he knew the sleep study would not ultimately find a cure for his insomnia, the three full weeks quarantined in a glass room away from the feet of John Sullivan would provide the respite he desperately needed before he could return to his humble role as a proper host to fate.

"It's just three weeks, partner," Carlos said. "It's not like I'm leaving you for good."

"Don't leave me, Carlito." Sully rubbed the smaller man on the head. "You're my lucky charm, *amigo*. My salvation."

He parked the car on the street where a group of Mormon protesters were keeping a twenty-four-hour vigil outside the Palace.

"Let's just get the lay of the land, Ponchito. Today's a fact-finding mission. Tonight, I'm gonna come back and crack some heads while you sleep."

The partners got out of the car and walked toward the protesters. Along the street, the lamp posts, parking meters and benches were all plastered with the same fliers that had led Sully to be assigned to the job. Each featured a candid photo—of fellow Mormons, of formerly upstanding citizens, or of beat cops who had been entrusted to wrestle back the future of the community. All of them had succumbed to the pull of the theater and strayed from the path of righteousness. Now they were displayed in mock mugshots, faces burning with iniquity and guilt, the word "LOST" depicted below them in flames, setting fire to what John Sullivan declared to be—categorically, of all the offenders—weak chins.

"You'll never see this jaw tacked to a pole like that, Ponchito" Sully said, squeezing his own thick chin between his finger and thumb.

Carlos crossed the street to get a look at the theater and gather a few breaths of fresh air while Sully held court with the Mormons—mostly women at this time of day. His partner's voice boomed with vibrato, paused to hear the complaints of the women, and then boomed again.

At the front of the theater, thick red curtains were drawn over the windows. Though Carlos had heard rumors of what went on behind them, he had never seen it for himself, not even from across the street where the Mormons picketed. But now that he stood there, he felt something. A pull of sorts. He lost himself for a moment. The sounds of traffic and the voice of John Sullivan faded until everything fell silent. He closed his eyes. He could hear his blood moving through his veins, one swoosh, then another, then another. Then he saw it, the fateful spore that had infected his partner's feet was blowing across his inner vision. It was both the cause of his partner's foot condition and the cause of Carlos' chronic insomnia—that disease about which the finest doctors in the city understood nothing.

Sometimes, in the treatment room after a night of listening to sounds in the dark, and while his physicians scratched their chins and guessed at causes and solutions for Carlos Rubinstein's sleep problem, the little cop would visualize that strange and colorful spore, blowing miles over the sweltering bayou. In his mind, he followed it airborne and glinting in the sun. He saw it fall in the stagnant air of afternoon to rest briefly between the eyes of an alligator, and as the reptile weaved through murky water and tall grasses Carlos watched the tiny, fated puffball get swept up in a hot evening wind. Carlos rooted for the spore's survival even though he shouldn't have. When he saw it dip toward the swamp, he held his breath until it rose again above the tall grasses and sailed past the pole houses of cray-fishermen to land on the deck of a smuggler's boat and travel through the night toward the lights of New Orleans.

Over the long, sleepless months Carlos Rubinstein had spent trapped in the stuffy cruiser with Sergeant Sullivan, this vision of the spore's path had crystallized around a character who was the very antithesis of his partner. She was young and pretty and naive and she had squirreled away money earned through odd and menial jobs to buy passage from the bayou to New Orleans. The city was to be the place where her life would take a new form, and as the smuggler's boat that carried her sputtered across Lake Salvador, she climbed to the deck to sit and dream of a job waitressing in a little café. She would have a simple apartment where she could make toast with jam, a morning now and then to sit on a bench and toss the ducks crumbs from the heels of her bread. She sat on the deck and watched as the lights of the city grew closer and soon she was commanded by the captain to disembark. When she stood, she took up the fated spore in the hem of her summer dress and carried it with her into the city.

When Sully's brutality haunted Carlos in the night and Carlos' heart began palpitating in his chest and rattled him with the anxiety that he and Sully would be connected forever, he would sometimes imagine his pretty friend walking down a cobbled street. He would watch her sundress swoosh like a metronome from the left leg to the right. It was not a leering sort of feeling he had at these moments, but an admiration that calmed him. Soon he would find that his breath spilled in and out of his throat to the shift of that dress and the click of the young woman's heels on the cobblestone, and even if he didn't sleep, he would begin to relax. He knew the spore was still caught there in the hem of that pretty summer dress and that it would eventually infect the feet of John Sullivan and send him west to doom Carlos to this very restlessness. But in those moments, he didn't care. In that microscopic spore was the fate that had sent Sully off the streets and out of New Orleans, and in this was the cause of Carlos Rubinstein's sleep disorder that the cleverest doctors in the city could not figure out how to cure.

When Carlos Rubinstein could understand how to execute his part in this strange path of that bayou puffball, he and John Sullivan could at last go their separate ways and his salty city would be ready for the girl of his dreams to arrive. This was something Carlos Rubinstein knew for a fact. Yet even in his sleep-deprived and possibly delusional state, he knew better than to mention this to his physicians. They could never understand that the root cause of his affliction was a spore that had blown into New Orleans on the hot winds of the bayou and commenced a path of predestination by infecting the feet of his brutal partner. And without understanding this, they would never comprehend the procedures that would be necessary to actuate a cure.

For a precious few moments Carlos felt perfectly still, even sleepy, then the voice of John Sullivan startled him from his daytime dream and he found himself back on the sidewalk.

"Ponchito," Sully barked, "*vamos!*"

33

Denton White entered the world in the tangled net of his own umbilicus, as if his father's fall from the trapeze had not stopped dead at the circus floor, but had continued through space and time only to be arrested months later by the womb of Denton's mother. He wasn't breathing. His mother lay motionless, over-medicated and unmoved. She watched with blank eyes as her son was cut free and hauled up by his tiny ankles. After a few moments, his heart started and the mucus cleared his lungs and he sputtered to life with his first anxious breath. But the feeling of being ill at ease never entirely left him. Rather, throughout his childhood he only learned more ways it could be defined. Denton was out of place. He was alienated within a world that only he could see, and he was haunted by the ominous foreshadow of something approaching from the future. It was a pervasive state, an image ghosted onto the screen of his life which only faded during periods of deep stupor and rare moments of forgetting. And since Denton left his grandmother's home as barely more than a child, he could count these rare moments on his fingers.

One day in Vietnam the rain and the gunfire had ceased simultaneously, and out of the blue and cloudless sky a big heron swooped down and perched for what seemed like an eternity on the barrel of his M21. That short, peaceful interlude somehow made bearable both the hell that had transpired before and the hell that was approaching. The same quietude would revisit him during the institution evenings when he sat watching *Kung Fu* with Abbott, and later again in the afternoons when they practiced together under the western juniper. At the Palace Theater when *Enter the Dragon* played to a full house and the crowd cheered and his nunchaku whirred though the shimmering air of the projection room, Denton forgot for a short time the feeling of being out of place. More recently, forgetting had embraced him during the long days he spent rearranging the guts of pinball machines in his subterranean office, with only Liz Taylor and the sidewalk's shadows and his phonograph player to keep him company. But although Denton felt at home within himself in these moments, his feeling of homelessness within the world of people always pervaded.

Considering the circumstances, the unseasonably cold winter of '76 should have been a rough time for Denton. His pornographic theater had made him a pariah, and the city had turned against him. Mormon Bishops and Elders were petitioning the city's elites to act aggressively, while rank and file Mormons were picketing on the sidewalk outside the Palace. Even his poor grandmother, he was certain, was kicking at the door of her casket or scratching through the dirt to confront him in the night with hollow eyes. In the films he showed, she would have told him, women were treated like objects. They were used for pleasure. This was not artistic performance, she would scold him. It was exploitation. For Denton to simply consume the sinister material for his own voyeuristic pleasure was to participate in each performer's undoing. But when he chose smut as his very livelihood and began to provide a platform for its dissemination, he had made himself complicit in every sordid action that took place in every film he showed. It might as well have been Denton himself performing the lurid, salacious acts that took place on screens of his theater.

Denton knew that even if his grandmother's words only existed in his imagination, they should have sobered him. At Ray Cook's motel, he had passed into unconsciousness waiting for Rose to pipe up from beyond the grave and tell him what to do. Now, when he finally heard her voice telling him what *not* to do, he was consciously choosing to ignore her. The situation normally would have driven Denton toward depression and stasis, but he had never felt less alienated or more at peace. He had long anticipated the Mormon backlash, and he didn't find Rose's arguments convincing enough to disturb him. For one thing, he thought the women treated the men in the films like objects too. The bald truth was that it was precisely this that made the films so sexy. It actually seemed to Denton that the women derived *more* pleasure from their objectification than the men who objectified them. He saw it in their more expressive faces, and in those hypnotic sounds they made which drew him in like a good plot. At times these sounds seemed to arise from that same quiet place that had graced his own life in only those few rare moments. Their bodies also betrayed a receptiveness to sensuality that was wholly lacking in the men. And though he knew, not being a woman, he could never speak authoritatively on these subjects, he also knew, by virtue of being himself, that his grandmother's last suggestion was preposterous.

It wasn't that Denton didn't wish Rose's point could be true. Denton desperately wanted to connect to a woman as closely as the actors in the Palace's films, and he often imagined this was the case. But the fact was that Denton had never actually touched a woman in any intimate way. Even in Vietnam, in those jungles singed with dioxin and rife with smoke and death, where his friends, if that's what you called the men who died beside you, accepted every offer to escape mortality with open arms, Denton had remained, for better or for worse, Rose's grandson. He could not have touched anything delicate and soft in that place without it killing him. And that inhibition had persisted. He felt it with the head nurse after she unlocked the gates of the institution and took him away to unlock his heart. And during that unusually cold winter, as Salt Lake City's prostitutes began flocking to his newly opened Porno Palace to warm themselves in his lobby, he still felt traces of that same danger. He felt it even as he made the shivering women fresh pots of coffee and offered them free range of his popcorn and candy. And when he began handing them rolls of quarters to pump into the pinball machines that had been going mostly unused since he'd switched his venue, that feeling was still there. Something in the outcastness of the prostitutes made them feel kindred to Denton and he wanted them to feel welcome and at ease in his theater, but he dared not touch them. It seemed that his grandmother's accusation, though an arousing idea, was likely to remain the forever unfulfilled subject of his fantasies.

When he considered this during his initial screening of *The Devil in Miss Jones*, sitting quiet and alone in the back of the theater, the thought brought Denton to that rarefied place of forgetting that had been visiting less and less since his grandmother's passing. He let his chest fall in synchrony with the performer's breaths, felt the warmth and dampness of Barbara Bourbon's body against his own, smelled the sweet fragrance of her skin, pulsing off of her with every beat of her pounding heart. For a moment he slipped away entirely, as if back into the void from which Doctor Sharpe had rescued him. He recalled that vacuous place—his centuries-long existence as a cast iron hinge on the door of a New England farmhouse, and then waking suddenly to the smell of coffee and finding his old doctor sitting beside him, flapping and folding the Salt Lake City *Tribune*. His eyes fell back onto the screen—but it was no longer Barbara Bourbon he was imagining.

During that unusually cold winter, there had really only been one thing that reliably brought Denton to that place of forgetting, and he was intensely aware that it was not a thing at all—that *she* was not a thing. She was a person, in fact, a woman. Her name was Tasha. She was a young prostitute who had been coming by for coffee and warmth. Denton had tried to engage her in conversation once, but he had just ended up asking her out for coffee. His question made Tasha giggle. She stood there sipping her Maxwell House coffee, sweet and extra blond, just the way she liked it. Denton looked at the Styrofoam cup he had just handed to her and then back at Tasha. The amusement in her bright eyes set him to a fit of blushing. He opened his mouth and began stammering and he couldn't get out another full sentence, but the way she had looked at him would haunt him for weeks. He would wake in the night out of a dead sleep to imagine those same eyes looking into his own from beside him in his bed, and he would wonder what that look had intended to say.

Over those long sleepless weeks, he came up with a plan to woo Tasha away to a private place for a few moments, where he might find the courage to speak to her. Finally one night, after several unsuccessful attempts to use spoken language, Denton managed to capture Tasha's attention through gestures and stammering. She followed his wagging hand until they entered the back room of his once-bustling pinball hall. Dusty machines banked the walls, their colorful lights twinkling and flashing in a way that created an electric, neon atmosphere in the otherwise darkened room. Tasha looked around at Denton's elaborate creations as Denton gently coaxed her. And though she only acted in kindness that first time, only to protect his sweet, artistic soul, she took the roll of quarters she had seen in Denton's pocket and mistaken for desire, and she began to play.

Since childhood, it had always been that when Denton's life began to come together in one aspect, there would be something just over the horizon, getting ready to crumble things into chaos. Tasha had a way of making Denton forget about the outside world and about this curse, and it seemed Denton had the same effect on her. After Tasha made some gentle inquiries about the inner workings of Denton's pinball machines that achieved her purpose and restored the awkward proprietor's ability to speak, Tasha found that the two had an uncommonly easy time conversing. Much like Denton, Tasha had been raised under the roof of a strong older woman. Her Granme, as she called her, had been the same sort of champion Rose had been for Denton. From a young age, Tasha had been encouraged to look past the smallness of the world that surrounded her and dream of big things—a life that would suit the enormous energy and desire that her Granme recognized within her.

Sometimes Denton's conversations with Tasha would take place in his cool basement office where she would visit him before they began their evening work, but these were always sedate, almost formal affairs. The most intimate facts were always betrayed over pinball.

When Tasha played pinball, Denton would become entranced. The way she arched her back and thrust her hips into the machine, at times reaching down to adjust a torn stocking, or perspiring and pulling off a faux fur boa, or the way she tossed her hair and the air around him became full with her—it was almost too much. He couldn't focus. And yet all of it—the noise of the bells and buzzers, the flashing lights, the smell of her skin beneath the scent of fruit and vanilla, the little grunts and gasps she made—it all somehow drew him deep into her world until he felt like he was there with her. He was in her Granme's kitchen making cucumber and mayonnaise sandwiches. He was sweeping porches, yellow with pollen. He was hand-wringing clothes. He was on his hands and knees, scrubbing a porcelain bath. And then he was watching Tasha scrubbing a porcelain bath. He could see her with cut-off shorts and chipped, red toenails, bending over the edge to scrub the far side of the tub, her heels lifting off the ground, her calves and her hamstrings tightening. Then he was back in his theater, watching her lower back arch, and her pelvis thrust against the pinball machine. This thing that he had made with his own hands was bringing her joy and forgetting. For a moment he was back again. He was in Tasha's Granme's house as Tasha leaned over the bathtub. He heard her little grunts, a little shriek of glee as the lights flashed and the bells rang. Then they were on a boat crossing Lake Salvador. Her dress was blowing against her in the wind, silhouetting her figure. She was different then, she told him. She was hopeful. She was naïve. Denton watched her on the boat as the city lights grew closer. He wondered if, like him, she was a virgin.

As the unusually cold winter of '76 melted into spring, the other girls began to discover the joys of Denton's pinball hall. Soon the back room was wall to wall with fast women looking for that same sort of escape that Denton now found only in the presence of Tasha, and Tasha only found in the controlled chaos of Denton's intricately fashioned machines—and in her conversations with Denton. The other women also seemed to find what they were looking for. Dressed in their tall boots and high-cut skirts, the strange magic they worked on those machines and those machines worked on them had an equal effect on the spectators who were attracted in droves. It wasn't long before the bumping and grunting of the working women at Denton's pinball machines began to become as popular an attraction as the theater's lurid films. Men who bought tickets for a story-rich film like *A Dirty Western* would unintentionally forgo the exposition after passing the pinball hall and becoming entranced by the women and the noise and the flashing lights, and after sitting down as the film moved toward climax they would have to whisper a plea to a fellow viewer to catch them up on the plot.

When Denton finally moved the pinball machines out to the front lobby as the unseasonably cold winter transformed into a summer of violent electrical storms that brought torrents of rain running through the streets, it wasn't, as reported in the *Tribune*, just to antagonize the Mormon picketers whose numbers, which had dipped into the low single digits, now increased with the temperature. Because Denton wouldn't speak to the paper, the article quoted Denton from a former interview in which he had ranted about the Illuminati and blamed a far-reaching LDS conspiracy for the deaths of Bruce Lee, John F. Kennedy, and Martin Luther King. Indeed, the Mormons had come for him, just as he had prophesied to Doctor Sharpe all those many months ago while brandishing a spoonful of mint chocolate chip ice cream, but Denton had already put aside the theories of Gary Allen. Those things were said at what had been a bad time for him. He had spent the better part of a year in a deeply disturbing sleep. His theater had been struggling in nascency. He had been smoking too much marijuana. And visions were reaching across that timeless and endless space to assault him in the middle of the night.

Rereading those quotes for a second time, he no longer felt the same sense of injustice. Instead, he recognized that he had made scapegoats of the Mormons. He had seen in them and their tight-knit community, something that his life lacked—that sense of belonging and of being born again into the right time and place that had always been foiled by his bad timing. Now that he had found his place on earth, that resentment melted away. He harbored no ill will toward the Latter-day believers and he had no desire to go to war with them. Over the past few months, in that back room among the pinball girls who fawned over Denton like a kid brother, and beside Tasha for whom he felt a strength of feeling that he had only ever felt for ideas, and with the patrons who viewed Denton as a mechanical genius and an artistic visionary, in that room of reclaimed people and reclaimed machines built of reclaimed materials, Denton had reclaimed the sense of warmth and belonging that had evaded him his whole life. It was a sense he liked to imagine he felt for the first time—if only for a few moments—while resting and gasping on his mother's chest. Now, even as the Mormon picketers gathered on the other side of the brick and the glass, Denton had the feeling that his theater existed inside a reality they couldn't see. It was not just a palace in name. It was his castle, his fortification against that strange and confounding place of curated and cultivated humanity that made up the outside world and which he could never seem to understand. And it was only there, within the Palace walls, surrounded by the dregs of society and his fellow outcasts, that Denton had finally begun to feel at home. Denton had found his tribe. He had built his palace. He had men and women he cared for now, and he wanted to protect them.

～⊛～

Day by day, the Mormons were becoming more aggressive. Some nights, an angry group of men and women would join arms and blockade the entrance and deride The Porno Palace's clientele as godless and perverted. Soon they were bringing cameras. Flash bulbs went off as patrons with hats tilted low were taunted to smile for their photos. The clearest mugshots were printed up on fliers and stapled to telephone poles with the word "LOST" in bold, red letters that appeared to be exploding into flame. By early August, many of Denton's patrons had been scared off. His whole world was threatening to devolve into the old chaos.

It was only at this point that Denton brought the pinball machines to the front lobby. He installed heavy, red velvet curtains in the street windows and drew them back for just a few minutes between showings. In those few minutes, the blacked-out theater would burst forth with its own flashing lights. The pulse of strobes and the whirl of sirens and the glimmer of mirrored balls that spun and glimmered like diamonds would reveal a horde of sensual women, comfortable in their own skin, in tall boots and high skirts, midriffs bare, rear ends high in the air like cats in heat, or exposed thighs rubbing up against cool metal. In their bodies could be witnessed that orgiastic ecstasy of complete forgetting that few Mormon couples knew but all had, in their weaker moments, awake in their bedrooms with a lingering feeling of unfulfillment, imagined and dismissed, and then reimagined more vividly. It would only be with great effort that most would push this lusty yearning far down within themselves where it would exist moist and warm and held on the edge of germination and it would be reserved for God alone and sought, unrequited, in prayer.

The life of the flesh required a delicate balance for the Mormons. In the protected confines of the community, and with the prohibition of such exciting influences as alcohol and caffeine, this delicate balance could be maintained sometimes indefinitely. In the old days, the novelty of polygamy had provided for the men—in theory—some promise of respite from their unanswered longing, and one would imagine the women suffered most often from fits of sleeplessness and frustrations that tangled the bedsheets. But the novelty of polygamy had rarely provided the men the answer they were truly seeking, and often after a night with a new bride that had been no more satisfying than any other night with an old bride, a Mormon man would wake from a restless sleep in a tangle of bed sheets and wonder exactly what it was that he longed for. If nothing else, the end of polygamy had provided the modern generation of Mormon men with a clear reason for their dissatisfaction in the bedroom. Their self-inquiry could now stop solidly against the bedrock of the problem of monogamy.

Though it was not the intended result when Denton moved his pinball machines to the front lobby, this delicate balance of the life of the flesh had been upended. The intended result had been purely Pavlovian. At the age of nine, after Rose had wondered out loud if a dog might be a good companion for her grandson, Denton had entered into a deep study of Pavlov. Now he had the idea of installing an electric whistle on the outside of his theater, and he began sounding the whistle a few moments before the curtains were drawn back at the front windows. After a few days, The Latter-day Saints proved themselves eminently trainable. In the minutes-long frenzy of good Mormon wives correcting the wandering eyes of their husbands and as mothers protected their sons from lusty thoughts by burying their innocent eyes deep within the darkness of their own breasts, Denton's patrons could enter the theater unmolested.

Unfortunately, this system would not save everyone. That fact would become more evident as the hot summer nights wore on and Denton cut the air conditioning, and the pinball girls shed their already sparse outer layers of clothing to within a hair's breadth of the decency laws. The resolve of the picketers would be tested to the breaking point, and many would stare toward the lights a few seconds too long and become entranced, dropping their picket signs on the sidewalk to join the crowd of Denton's outcasts at the other side of the glass.

These spontaneous conversions did not go over well with the Mormons. In Old Testament days, the Almighty Father would have set fire to the whole block with a wave of his hand, but in the common era this sort of thing was done with far less showmanship. The heads of church met with the city fathers, offering alms and beseeching them to take action, and God's long arm descended through the offices and institutions of the State, eventually tapping the shoulders of Carlos Rubinstein and John Sullivan to rid the city of Denton's den of sin.

34

It was almost morning as the bus moved along the foothills toward Abbott's cabin, and as I opened the last letter, I wasn't sure how I felt about Abbott's chapters coming to an end. His story was bringing the ideas of fate and destiny to the forefront of my imagination again, and I was growing impatient to leave my repetitive life behind and start the adventure that would unite Abbott and me with Lucille. I hoped that I might finish that final letter and hop off the bus and walk back to Abbott's cabin to find him waiting there for me, sitting on the front porch with a mug of coffee in his hand.

The trip to Salt Lake City and Denton's company had been a welcome change. I guess I was lonely and bored with myself in the same way that had led me to start dating. My money and Abbott's supplies were running low and I wasn't any closer to finishing my book than I had been for the last twenty years. It was beginning to look like my haphazardly laid plan to write the great American novel, buy my freedom back, and earn Laura's love again had been a failure. Abbott was my Hail Mary. If we could find Lucille together, there would be a story in that, and between my notes and his letters, a good number of chapters had already been written.

I looked at the salutation and the first sentence and then lifted my head to watch the horizon, the long expanse of snow and scrub that ran flat and free to the boundary of the foothills. On the road, the painted lines counted off the time while I rested my head against the cool glass and meditated on the long path of interactions and intricacies that had led me, Abbott and Denton to our present moments—our semi-subversive lives, the complex paths determined by our strange proclivities, the way we all seemed to brush up against the standard American life only to be repelled by something within or without us that bounced us back into the intricate works, off this bumper and that, as if caught within one of Denton White's fantastic pinball machines. I even wondered if Abbott truly wanted to find Lucille, or if he just wanted to search for her and arrive again and again to the cusp of finding her, to the very threshold of that golden door, only to step back every time. But I suppose that was my modus operandi, both with *The First Chapter* and with the first chapter of my adult life that seemed to keep repeating. I confused all Abbott's characters with me from time to time, which I suppose is natural when one becomes invested in a story.

The bus hit a series of ruts bouncing my head against the glass and I returned my attention to the final letter. It was a short one by Abbott's standards, and after a few sentences I came to the painful realization that the story of Denton White would not have the space to conclude in its pages. I would be left waiting for more, hoping new letters would arrive at the hospital and that I could somehow retrieve them. I was suddenly hit by a wave of self-pity, feeling alone and stranded and loathed by whatever universal powers had formed my life. I wished I had the strength to hold the doors of those letters from closing. I didn't feel like there was enough of me left outside the story to fool myself or anyone else into believing I was real. It was even becoming difficult to believe that my voice was capable of making sounds that vibrated outside my own head.

I thought of that old miner who brought Abbott to see the Trona Pinnacles—his story of a lost leg that still existed in happy dreams where he moved through the world without hindrance. Abbott's stories were my lost leg, and like that miner, I felt the dream ending and I didn't want to wake up. I suppose all that isolation hadn't been good for me. I had no friends to reach out to and my mother was the only one connecting me to my past. In Abbott's letters, in his whole story, I found the burnt-out relationships of my life in surrogate. I began to feel like I'd been there through all the events that Abbott spoke and wrote of and even through others, events I'd imagined myself to fill in the portions of the story Abbott didn't have the time to tell.

I picked up the letter again as the bus swayed in the winds and it began to snow. Denton was back in Doctor Sharpe's' office. He was a mess again. A wreck. I put the letter down and pictured him there, sat with him. The snow blew around the wake of the bus, big light flakes that would become smaller through the morning until they covered the evening in white, in sheets as they say, in reams. I hoped that like that first snow on the bus back from my night with Naomi, this one would be a harbinger of some change in my life, another surprise meeting that would fill me with purpose, another visit from Harelip Lenny. Maybe it would be Abbott this time, and I'd find him sitting on my porch just as I'd imagined him.

Doctor Harry Sharpe observed Denton out of the side of his eyes while pretending to take down notes. He'd been trying to make sense of the younger man's addled state for the last several minutes, and now he had an idea. His eyebrows raised. He rejected the idea with a shake of his head, considered it again. He couldn't help noticing how much like a Benzedrine fiend Denton appeared. Agitated with wide-eyed intensity. Verbose in fits and starts. Benzedrine. He remembered it well. It was one of the more wonderful substances in the pharmacopoeia. Half the doctors in his graduating class wouldn't have made it through medical school without it. But he was pretty sure it had fallen out of vogue.

The doctor momentarily lost himself in a memory of a wild night many years before and then he found himself smiling. He wasn't thinking about the wild night anymore. His mind had returned, as it so often did, to his own personal Rome, the Dutch widow to whom he had only professed his love at the very end. Mildred Schlotzsky had been the mother of an early and particularly memorable patient and the most beautiful woman he had ever seen. Lately, everything made him think of Mildred Schlotzsky, of the sweetness of his longing and the waste of all the years. Now, and more to the point, he remembered the terrible and unending sleeplessness she had caused him. He glanced sideways to study his patient again and wrote a single word down in his notebook. He read it back to himself to see how it hit him, and then he put the pink end of his pencil to his lips, raised his eyebrows, and nodded.

"Yes," he thought. "Yes."

He thought of Mildred's son again, who was grown now and a doctor of psychiatry. Maybe Denton's case wasn't so simple as that one word. There could be other interpretations—and given Denton's history, it might make sense to be more concerned. He thought about excusing himself to make a call and shook his head. He was already so indebted to Boris Schlotzsky—consulting him would be beyond the normal threshold of professional courtesy, and the balance of their friendship was already far too heavy on Sharpe's side of the scale to add the burden of a personal favor.

He thought again. What if the symptomatology Denton was presenting was the manic phase in what might be an extreme case of slow-cycling manic-depression? That was a sobering thought. He recalled Denton's case—his progressively worsening cooling periods, the deep sleeps that brought the boy closer and closer to the very edge of death. It was a state Sharpe had never found detailed in any of his many medical texts. He thought about the cold and nearly complete stasis he'd witnessed at Ray Cook's motel and shuddered as he considered the way an equal and opposite bout of mania might present itself. He looked at Denton, then back at the single word he had written in his notebook. He remembered the absolute insistence of Denton's grandmother that he keep her grandson's strange disorder out of the medical literature. Many times, with tears threatening—only threatening—to stream down her face, Rose had made the doctor swear to reveal Denton's condition to no one, and Sharpe had promised her his confidence. The boy, she told him, just had a way of feeling the pain and potential of the world more deeply than most—and perhaps this was true. Sharpe considered how

Denton's last state had come on the heels of Rose's death. It had been almost like a period of mourning, but more powerful, more extreme. Then he tapped his pencil on the word he had written and nodded his head once more. He was thinking about Mildred Schlotzsky again, but the smile had transformed into sadness.

"Denton?" he said.

Denton snapped to attention. A look of hyper-vigilance flashed across his face.

Doctor Sharpe looked down and read the word in his notebook to himself and cleared his throat.

"Would I be correct in assuming a beautiful woman has recently entered your life?"

Denton blushed. "Tasha?" he said. He looked confused. "But how..." His voice trailed off.

It really was a brilliant diagnosis, Doctor Sharpe thought. Nail right on the head. He gave Denton some time to collect his thoughts.

"But she's a..." Denton started. He couldn't bring himself to say the next word, because the word was ugly and mean and Tasha was so much more than that. He turned his palms over on his thighs and studied them in silence.

"Do you have the feeling that she is somehow beyond your reach?"

Denton held the doctor's eyes for a moment before looking down at his hands again. The blush returned, this time it was a deeper shade of red. Through Denton's t-shirt, the doctor could see the pounding of his patient's heart.

"How long did you say since you last slept?" Doctor Sharpe asked him.

"From the first day I saw her I was restless," Denton said. "After she spoke to me, I started waking up in the night and thinking about her until morning. Once she started playing pinball, I had a hard time sleeping at all. Now, as soon as I start to fall off to sleep, I see her with another man and I jolt right back awake. I can only sleep for seconds at a time."

"Pinball?" the doctor said.

Denton nodded his head at his hands. "Can you give me something, Doc?"

Doctor Sharpe gave his notebook a few more pensive taps with his pencil. There she was again—Mildred Schlotzsky, as beautiful as ever. "I think I can, Denton," he said. He pulled a thermometer from his breast pocket and told Denton to open his mouth. He had something to say and he didn't want to be interrupted. "I can give you some advice."

For the next few minutes, Doctor Sharpe tried to tell Denton the things he wished he could go back and tell himself when he was younger and hopelessly taken with Mildred Schlotzsky. She would eventually—

"Had it been two years already?" he wondered to Denton out loud.

But Denton couldn't answer the doctor, both because Denton had a thermometer in his mouth and because he didn't even know Mildred Schlotzsky. Well, she had died. Not that death alone was exceptional. "We all will die," Doctor Sharpe had to concede. But the point was, Mildred died alone, without him—or, not exactly. He was right there at her bedside, of course. He was her doctor, after all. "My point is," he told Denton for the second time, "My point is," he said, doing his best to come to the painful point which was really very simple. "My point is, we loved each other, but we were both too stubborn and proud to admit it."

He took a moment to appreciate how hard a thing it was to say, even now, at his age, and even without Mildred there to possibly reject him. "To think of it now—we could've avoided all those nights of lost sleep. Maybe Mildred wouldn't have gone so young. Maybe I wouldn't feel so much like I'm stuck on this earth serving out a life sentence. Maybe instead of twisting the covers into knots every night, we could've been making love for the last twenty years."

Doctor Sharpe took off his glasses and pinched at his eyes. He walked over and opened a drawer. With his glasses back on, he pulled out a copy of James Joyce's *Ulysses,* and flipped through its pages until he found a paper pressed flat near the center of the book. He handed it to Denton and pulled the thermometer from his mouth and glanced at the numbers mindlessly. One-hundred-and-eight degrees, he thought to himself, without being particularly alarmed. The boy had always run hot and cold.

Denton looked over the letter.

"Dear Harry," he read out loud. Seeing that it was written with a woman's penmanship, he read sweetly and melodically. "I loved you from the moment I saw the tender way you handled my sweet Boris's foreskin. Yours always, Milly"

It was Doctor Sharpe's turn to blush. "It was strictly professional," he said. "The point is—" He winced, realizing he was coming to the point for the fifth or sixth time now. "The point is, that letter was given to me by Mildred's son, only after Mildred's death. You understand? Now I can do nothing about it but tie knots in the bedsheets for the rest of my life." He winced again, realizing that Boris's role in delivering that letter was just one more thing that indebted him to the younger Schlotzsky. How would he ever balance the scales?

"Doctor?" Denton said.

Sharpe snapped his head in Denton's direction. He was feeling edgy all of a sudden.

"What exactly is your point?" Denton asked him.

Doctor Sharpe's eyes fell on his notebook. The word he had written down somehow returned him to the present moment.

"Denton," Sharpe said, "If you *love* this woman, let her know. Don't wait. Whatever happens is better than the alternative. Better a few sleepless weeks in heartbreak than a sleepless lifetime in regret."

Denton nodded his head. It was good advice and he knew it. He stood up and took his doctor's hand. His mind was made up, he told Sharpe. He would tell Tasha that night.

I put the letter down—I think that's the way it must have happened, though I'm not certain whether the next part was my embellishment or a flourish of Abbott's. Neither of us could have known what Tasha was thinking or doing, and yet I clearly remember her in a tiny apartment across town, talking with her roommate over a bowl of shredded wheat. The two friends were working through Tasha's confusion. She was feeling something strange in relation to Denton. He had presented her with a gift on her birthday only a few days before and Tasha had felt something she didn't recognize. The feeling made her want to disappear forever, to find a new city again, somewhere where she knew no one. She had been trying to stay away from the Palace and make sense of it all, but after only a single day, she began to miss Denton. After a second day, the powerful draw she felt to the theater was hard to resist. During a walk to the pharmacy, she lost herself in a memory and came back to the present moment only as she approached the ticket booth and heard the shouts of the picketers. She turned around and walked briskly in the other direction. But later that evening she found herself walking toward the theater again. She was losing her mind and she wasn't sure what was happening to her. It was a hard thing to explain to her roommate. Something was pulling her in the direction of Denton White and resisting that pull took conscious and vigilant effort.

She explained to her roommate what she had felt when Denton drew the cloth off her gift like some sort of magician. It was a strange confusion in her stomach and a rush of blood through her body that felt like her first shot of moonshine.

Her roommate, a young Russian woman who had come late to their occupation and had once been in love, lit a cigarette and took a drag before passing it to Tasha. Tasha took a drag, exhaled, and dismissed the whole thing.

"It's nothing," she said.

But her roommate disagreed. She told Tasha she thought it sounded a lot like butterflies.

The gift Denton gave Tasha was a pinball machine, built specifically for her. It was painted red and shaped like a stiletto, and had been covered in a velvet blanket. When Denton pulled it away, Tasha stood speechless in the Palace's cool basement, Liz Taylor watching over her from the *Love is Better Than Ever* poster's crooked position on the wall. She waited for the butterflies to pass while Denton reached into his pocket slid a quarter into the machine, and then Tasha began to play.

The ball rolled down the ramp and she hit the paddle hard, making a row of Rockette dancers kick up their legs. A slew of bonus balls was released, bouncing chaotically off the bumpers, and when the synthesized voice of the machine said her name to cheer her on, Tasha felt another new sensation, this time in her chest, a sensation that was translated by her more worldly friend as the feeling of her heart melting.

Tasha told her roommate that she hadn't handled the melting of her heart well. She had become flustered in a way that was usually characteristic of Denton. She excused herself, claiming she had eaten a bad burger earlier in the day and she was feeling ill. She had not returned to the Palace since that afternoon.

"Darling," her roommate said, snuffing out the butt of their shared cigarette in the bowl of shredded wheat that was now finished, "I hate to be the one to break it to you, but you have all the signs of a woman in love."

35

I arrived home to find the same empty cabin I had left behind. There was no Abbott waiting on the porch, no Harelip Lenny, just steps covered with perfect, untrodden snow. I put some coffee on the stove, sat down and sketched out the details of my trip, and afterward I slept the rest of the day and through the night. In the morning, my usual vigil of sitting at Abbott's table with a pen and pad was too excruciating to bear. My better half was trapped—or so I came to think—in Abbott's world. Returning to that world was all I could think about, so I decided to give up the façade of writing. Instead, I tried to pass the time by reading novels from Abbott's small library. For the next several days, I lay on the couch and started one book after the next, but I couldn't find anything that captivated me. The part of me that could commit myself to fiction had gone missing. The stories refused to come to life. So I began rereading the letters Abbott had sent me, and when I came to the end of the letters I would start again from the beginning. I was stranded. There was nothing to do but wait for Abbott to return, or hope he would send another messenger to retrieve me.

During a trip to town to call my mother, I had an idea. I rented a postbox at a shipping store under my alias and called the hospital to ask Doreen to forward any letters that arrived before Christmas to the box number. I told her I would make another trip at Christmas. Then I walked home and began spending my days waiting for the mail to come. I didn't have much faith that any new letters would arrive but I had a lot of hope and at least the hope gave my days some structure. Around ten in the morning I got out of bed, then I drank coffee and read letters through the early afternoon. When the sun was low, I showered and dressed and set out on my long, hopeful walk to the shipping store, pulling my coat tight as the cold and darkness encroached on the afternoon. Sometimes I would imagine myself like a character in a Jack London story I'd read as a child, a small, black dot on a windswept tundra traveling toward a distant light.

I know that's a little dramatic, but that's the way I was. I was like an actor fully committed to a part, like a hopeless lover waiting by the phone, trapped between the polarities of dejection and life-changing love. I was like myself sitting at the keyboard for all those years, waiting for the next chapter to be delivered through my fingers. With each walk to town, I was more convinced that a letter would arrive, and each time I returned to the cabin I expected to find Abbott or Harelip Lenny waiting for me on the porch. It didn't register that these hopes were only a new rendition of my old hopes and that the black dot traveling across the windswept tundra was but a simulacrum of myself within another simulacrum, in which I had simply replicated my old life in a new place with another name. In each simulacrum, hope combined with inaction and repetition to produce the illusion of moving toward something life-changing. Time was the path of hope, and if I could only remain patient, it was hard to take a wrong turn. When my patience wore thin and I lost faith in the path of time, I began to let my beard grow and the mirror comforted me with the evidence that something was happening even if, day by day, everything seemed the same.

Two or three weeks went by like this. My beard filled in. I drank coffee. I walked to town to check the mail. Now and then I called my mother. By that time, official charges had been filed against me. The case was represented by several imposing folders of documents. These frightened my mother terribly when a lawman came and thumped them on her counter. But as I said, the case ultimately went nowhere, though it still hovers over my head and will most likely remain poised there like a guillotine for all of eternity. Of course, my mother made sure to list off the charges in those folders on a regular basis. Embezzlement. Unlawful use of a computer. Disturbing the peace. Making a public nuisance. Evading arrest. The list went on and on with a slew of fluff charges to make things look daunting and to encourage me to take the plea deal which the lawman told my mother would be generous. Her calls would begin with brave, happy intentions and always lead to that long list of charges, followed by tears.

Laura had lost faith in me, or my mother thought so, because Laura had stopped calling. But of all people, Laura would've understood what I had done. Our breakup, and then her divorce papers had been the catalyst for everything, and I was certain that at some deep level of consciousness Laura hoped my crazy plan would pan out. Not that my mother wanted to hear any of that.

"You told me it was unpaid taxes," she would say in a hurt voice, "You never mentioned embezzling money from the university."

I would reply that it wasn't a lot of money and that if I knew they would trump up the charges like this, I would've made it worthwhile.

"And they were so good to you, David. Letting you do that little job for all those years when, let's face it, David, you only really ever wrote that little first chapter."

And then she would tell me how I wasn't raised that way, and she couldn't understand what possessed me, and I would begin making excuses for myself. But she was right—she couldn't understand. I'd chosen between leaving everything behind and the slow annihilation that came with accepting myself as depicted in one small chapter of a book I had not written—though I suppose leaving had not been the solution I was hoping it would be either.

Sometimes the conversation would recover. She'd tell me that the supermarket was hiring, or that so-and-so down at Meals on Wheels told her there was an opening at the hardware store and it had good benefits. A year in jail wasn't the end of the world, she'd say. And then she'd tell me I could have my old room back when I got out. Or she'd bring up Mister McGee who still visited her for coffee like clockwork. He thought there was a way out of this, she said. And while I appreciated McGee keeping my mother company and being a calming force in her life, I told my mother it wouldn't be any use for me to get in touch with McGee until Abbott and I found Lucille.

It was during my daily walk to town, on a day that I was feeling particularly trapped by the small perimeter of my life, that I began to think of the story of Denton White as a portent of transformation. After spending a few months in relative isolation I'd begun framing everything with phrases like these—harbingers, portents, tundras, and distant lights—which I know is ridiculous, but I also thought my insight was technically accurate. Between Abbott and me, the letters maintained an open channel of communication, and they also held open a channel to the alternate reality I found so intriguing. But I was beginning to understand that back in 1976, when the events were taking place for the first time, the episode in Salt Lake City foreshadowed both reunion and transformation for Abbott and Denton. The way I saw it, if Abbott and Denton hadn't reunited, Abbott would have remained ignorant of the events in Denton's life. And if the events had not been transformative and important, Abbott would not have been able to retell the story in such vivid detail.

As I approached the edge of the tundra, I had an intuition that another letter, or several letters, would be waiting for me in my postbox. It was time for Abbott to reenter the story, and I could feel it. In my dramatic language, I knew he was about to throw off the lines, let go of the past, and sail through time by dead reckoning. That was the only way he could reach the future that was waiting up ahead. It struck me that when the moment came, when that happened and the letters finally brought the Salt Lake City episode to a conclusion, the Abbott and Denton of the letters would reunite in 1976, and the three of us would reunite at the Salt Lake City hospital of the present day.

I was just mounting the steps to the shipping store when I felt an ember somewhere inside me spark to life and begin to catch fire. I stood there for a moment just feeling the heat build. I understood it now—the story in the letters and all of this waiting had been warming the hearth for a bright fire that was about to visit all of our lives. I took a few big breaths as if fueling the fire with a bellows, and when I looked at my reflection in the glass doors, standing there, bearded and covered in snow like a man out of a Jack London story, I could see that I had started to glow. In the dark glass before me, I saw the stark trees and the overcast sky of my background reaching toward the brightening light in the center of my chest as though reaching for the sun. I opened the door and walked toward my little postbox, knowing I would find it stuffed thick with the final chapters of Abbott's story.

Part Four

The Spiral Notebook

You weren't satisfied with *de nom de plume*. You developed this whole persona to create the kind of playboy you envisioned writing cheap pulp so 'you' could devote yourself to serious writing.

— Thomas Magnum, Magnum, P.I., Season 7

36

Tasha walked toward the Palace in a wool peacoat and her second prettiest dress. Her four-inch heels clicked along the pavement and her dress followed just behind the beat, tapping one thigh and then the other, the snare and then the high hat. It was jazz. In herself, she recognized something of the mindless multitudes she sometimes watched from distant corners and often envied—tired workers burdened with responsibility and lives they didn't choose, moving with the thoughtless march of soldiers through dreadful or lovely marriages, through jobs they loved and hated, from the fourth of July until they counted down to Christmas and from Christmas to the first day of spring.

But Tasha wasn't marching, exactly. She felt the rhythm of her life pulling with the backbeat, but also some force greater than herself, some music about to break over the beat and take the reins. It was as if the star of her future had risen in the night sky and while it was invisible to the naked eye, its light in her soul was nearly blinding. For years, her life had been marked by an internal resistance that expressed itself outwardly in the tension between her shoulder blades, in the restrained expressions of her face, in the hardness of her lips that should have been young and soft and welcoming. The compass of her soul had been pushed down into some dark burrow in her gut. In strange rooms with strange men, it was the only part of her she never exposed. In her Granme's kitchen, it was there. It watched over her from the ceiling, hovering above the iced tea and lemons, above the mayonnaise and cucumber sandwiches. It swirled with the pollen she swept from porches, traveled with her through the Bayou, soared above her as she crossed Lake Salvador. Then sometime between New Orleans and Salt Lake City, it was gone. But as she walked toward the Palace Theater in her second prettiest dress she could feel that her soul was with her again, above her again, and she surrendered. Her pace picked up.

I could feel what Tasha was feeling. As soon as I'd opened my postbox that afternoon, I'd known my time at Abbott's cabin had ended. I shoved the big envelope into my jacket, turned up my collar, and trudged across the imaginary tundra and I didn't stop walking until I reached the bus station. Loose inside the envelope, there'd been a short note from Doreen: no change in Denton's condition. Stuffed in with her note there were three thick envelopes from Abbott, all postmarked two or three days apart, and when I sorted them chronologically, I noticed the most recent one bore the postmark of a town in Utah. I felt something in my chest and then a few palpitations, and for half a minute I had to remind myself to breathe. When I was collected again, I had come to the realization that Abbott was quite possibly on the road to meet me or already waiting for me at the hospital.

This realization made it difficult to focus on the reading. I would begin thinking about the big reunion ahead and then I would have to clear my mind and let myself be drawn back into the story—in which there was also a big reunion ahead. After a couple paragraphs I would find myself thinking about the car Abbott would be driving, about Mike Post themes, about how good it would feel to smoke a joint after all the months of forced abstinence, about everything we had to say to each other. I drifted in and out of the sentences and had to reread the first few paragraphs several times. I rubbed my beard and tried to get control of my mind, tried to stay on the beat. It was the first time in a long time that my concerns were in the present and the future instead of the past, and as I read about Tasha marching toward the Palace it struck me what a precious thing our futures are, how we could give ourselves away moment by moment to anything and anyone, allowing our present to dissolve into a thousand identical pages, how we would write first chapters one after the next and dole out our future in teaspoons rather than invest ourselves in an unworthy narrative.

All the threads of Abbott's story, and possibly my story too, were about to converge and suddenly I could not hold my focus for any length of time. It was maddening and enthralling all at once. For this reason, the final letters did not cement word for word in my memory in the firm way of the earlier sections and there may be a greater number of elaborations and inaccuracies in my telling. Any issues in the narrative are also partly due to the strange way my own life was about to intersect with that world and make the separate threads very hard to pull apart.

Tasha was confused as she approached the Palace. She was thinking about butterflies and the feeling of her heart melting, and she began recalling other moments in life when that same confusion was present. She reached the theater and placed her hand on the lobby door, noticing a police cruiser parked out front between her and the jeering group of Mormons. The butterflies were back, but it wasn't Denton who was flashing through her thoughts right then. It was someone from another time, long before Denton, before the truth that once drove her forward was pushed down so that she could keep moving along in her own way. As she stood there and the bell rang outside the theater and the curtains began to open and men rushed around her and through the doors, it occurred to her that the butterflies were the truth. They had come back to her like an old friend she barely recognized.

That thought was in her head as she met his eyes through the glass and felt a third sensation she could not name. She dropped her gaze and turned to walk in the opposite direction, slowly at first and then faster, wobbling on her four-inch heels as she put distance between herself and the theater. Her heart was the bass drum now, beating hard enough that it blocked up her ears. She couldn't determine whether she was feeling joy or fear. Her cheeks were warm. Her hands and neck were tingling. She felt a light go on inside of her, a candle began to flicker in the hollowest and darkest part of her chest. She'd been away from herself for a while, and now she was home—but she couldn't figure out where she'd been.

She took a few steps into a dark side street to compose herself, to catch her breath. When she looked up, an imposing figure was standing at the edge of the darkness. She stood motionless for a moment and then the figure spoke her name.

"Tasha?"

John Sullivan was just a few feet away.

37

The story went from Tasha to Doctor Sharpe's office without any break or narrative segue. This was uncharacteristic of Abbott's writing. He was rushing, or so it seemed to me. When I reached the next paragraph and Doctor Sharpe placed the phone down on the receiver for a second time, and for a second time lost himself in thoughts of Denton, it struck me that Abbott could have been writing about any of us. We were all lost in the same thought, that same anticipation that our story might be about to jump out of its tired groove and unfold in a new and surprising way. It even occurred to me that Abbott's writing was being challenged by that same anticipation. Perhaps, at the same moment I was reading his letter, he was rushing toward Salt Lake City from a different direction.

For Doctor Sharpe, it was not just Denton who was in his thoughts. It was also Rose White to whom he thought his promises were implicit, and Lila, his childhood playmate whose mind had been destroyed by a strongman's jealousy and the violence and heartbreak that had caused. Sharpe worried that something of the future might be written in a person's DNA, and that encouraging Denton to declare his love to Tasha had been terrible advice. He remembered the lovely Polish widow from whom he kept his love a secret for so many years, and then he thought of her son.

Boris Schlotzsky had been among his first patients. He had mentored Boris through medical school and the two had enjoyed a long friendship, but it had been many years since either of them had dropped a line on the other. Sharpe thought Boris might be able to ease his mind.

He picked up his phone a third time and then put it down.

The trouble was that he wasn't sure if he was indebted to Boris Schlotzsky or if Boris Schlotzsky was indebted to him. This trouble began when Mildred Schlotzsky, the beautiful Polish widow that Sharpe had spent half his lifetime pining for, brought in a six-year-old Boris to consult the doctor about a delicate issue. It had been discovered by the school nurse that the boy's foreskin would not retract. Doctor Sharpe was a Jew, as were most of his patients, and outside the covenant of circumcision he had little experience with foreskins. Yet Sharpe was about to become a big-picture man. Where many proponents of Brit Milah would have seen an opportunity to expound on the wisdom of Judaic tradition and circumcise the boy, Doctor Sharpe saw an opportunity to spend time with young Boris's lovely mother.

Not that his opinion would've mattered. Mildred stopped that conversation dead. She raised one finger to her lips, silencing Sharpe instantaneously, and then she explained to the doctor that she would not have her young son sexually traumatized by the barbaric practice he was certainly about to recommend. The doctor put his hand to his chin and tried to listen, but before Mildred Schlotzsky had even finished marking her boundaries, he had already fallen deeply in love.

Mildred ordered Boris to undress and the doctor inspected his member with an air of solemnity. He poked around a bit, sighed, thought to pull out a magnifying glass, thought better of it, and then put his hand to his chin and made his prescription. The only way to see this problem through, Doctor Sharpe told Mildred Schlotzsky with an air of gravity, would be to work the foreskin free over time. It would take months of consistent effort and the three would have to meet regularly.

Mildred agreed, and at the last of young Boris Schlotzsky's nine weekly checkups, Doctor Sharpe was no closer to declaring his romantic interest in Mildred than he had been on that first day they met. Still, the procedure had been a success. Their work together had brought forth the large and beautiful and fully intact penis the mother had wanted for her son, and a lifelong friendship had developed between Boris and Doctor Sharpe. The doctor even became somewhat of a father figure to the boy and steered him toward a career in medicine—even if the procedure Sharpe recommended had virtually preordained that Boris would later take up the study of Freud. Now both doctors lived with the same guilty feeling that they owed a deep debt to the other. Shortly after Boris's eighteenth birthday, when Sharpe performed his circumcision—free of charge—they both felt the matter was settled once and for all. But in the end, each became more confused than ever. Neither could determine whether the second procedure had deepened the debt from the first, or cleared the books for good.

❧

Doctor Sharpe picked up the phone again and dialed Ella Rawson.

It was the most recent number he had for Boris Schlotzsky. As the line opened, it brought up the same old feeling that had been the crux of their friendship from the start. Henry Sharpe was both excited to hear the voice of his friend and yet troubled by the thought that the call might place him further in Boris Schlotzsky's debt. Had Schlotzsky answered the call and heard Sharpe's voice on the other end, Schlotzsky would've been feeling exactly the same thing. But the call was answered by a woman, and when Sharpe introduced himself as Schlotzsky's childhood doctor and an old friend, the woman told him what she'd heard of Schlotzsky's new life. She told the doctor briefly about the cabaret act in Vegas and gave him the number that Schlotzsky had left for former patients—mostly in the chance event that Abbott or Denton reached out to him—and she informed him that Schlotzsky was now going by the stage name Boba Savage.

Sharpe hung up the phone with a feeling of dread. The scales were undoubtedly forever tipped in Schlotzsky's favor. He put on his hat and took it off several times. He could see that his medical intuitions were consistently flawed, but he couldn't decide whether, in this most recent case of Denton White, the flaw was in his initial recommendation that Denton declare his love for Tasha, or in his present and intense desire to jump into a cab and travel to the Palace to correct the initial recommendation. His more conservative second opinion would be for Denton's continued silence on the subject of love. He suspected that whatever decision he made would be wrong in the end, and though he thought there must be a way around this inevitability, no matter how many times he placed his hat on his head and returned it to the hook on the wall, he just couldn't see his way around it.

38

At the sleep laboratory in a quiet wing of the university hospital, Carlos Rubinstein was lying in bed with a snorkel and mask on his face, floating deep beneath a heavy dose of Valium. He wasn't under any illusions. While he didn't see his case as completely hopeless, exactly, he was still certain that there was only one possible cure. A successful treatment wasn't something that could be achieved by elaborate tests with electrodes and rubber tubes and the ridiculous mask and snorkel they planned to suction to his face every night for the entire twenty-one days of his stay. Even so, he swallowed his horse pill, requested a can of ginger ale, and begrudgingly strapped on his diving gear and climbed between the sheets.

He felt like they were sending him to explore the underwater wreckage of a lost city rather than simply cooing him off into the deep, drug-induced rest he'd anticipated. But he laid back and closed his eyes and soon his mind was drifting toward New Orleans. His limbs twitched a few times and then he jolted as he tumbled backward off a gunwale and slipped below the surface of Lake Pontchartrain. He imagined himself swimming deep underwater, following a glowing blue light—the spirit of the pirate Jean Lafitte himself—as it guided him through a world of sunken merchant ships full of skeletons and treasures.

The light led him back to the surface. It rose above the water, traveled south, high over the lights of the crescent-shaped city, descended toward Lake Salvador, and hovered over the smuggler's boat he had imagined so many times. He saw the girl in the summer dress. Lafitte, he knew, was a guardian angel to the smugglers, and the way the light circled the girl and glowed around her head, seemed to suggest that she was now under his protection as well. In this blue light, the fifolet of Jean Lafitte, Carlos found a kindred spirit. It was comforting to travel with Lafitte. The smuggler's life had also bound him to a place and to a cause, though there was a difference, Carlos reminded himself, in that Lafitte's destiny shackled him eternally and Carlos hoped to one day be free.

Carlos Rubinstein knew his insomnia would eventually abate. Fate would run its course. He would sleep. His partner's feet would heal. His path had become intertwined with John Sullivan's and it would resolve in its own time. It would not last forever, but the timing of his emancipation couldn't be electrically detected or observed under a microscope or caught on time-lapse video in the middle of the night as Carlos sat straight up in bed and gagged at the very thought of sulfur. Still, he did often wish there was some way of knowing when the cycle would end. Waves of agitation would pass over him and leave him to wonder if Jean Lafitte, doomed as he was to certain and eternal restlessness, was the freer spirit. And then as he continued to float and dip through Lafitte's world, his desire for his bonds to be severed waned. He began to wonder if it was only in eternal bondage that a soul found solace.

He opened his eyes to stare at the ceiling and fretted over this thought for a period of time which was unquantifiable. It blended with every other night he had lain in bed considering the same question. At last, he came to the same answer he always came to: Fate would have its way. This spiritual fact could remain invisible to the world of the rested for an entire lifetime, yet to anyone deprived of sleep for a long enough duration, it would reveal itself indiscriminately. It was a fact that did not weigh on John Sullivan with the same heavy hand because John Sullivan had not yet been laid low enough to uncover it, but Sully in all his strength and bravado could no more outrun fate than Carlos could. Once Carlos had served his purpose, the bonds of fate would release him from his sleeplessness, and perhaps that sleeplessness would sit by his partner's bedside for a time. Carlos would move along in his own way while his partner slowly and sleeplessly came to understand that it was not in willfulness that a man found his true strength, but in resignation.

As that first restless night of the sleep study passed by, Carlos became more aware of his fellow sufferers. He heard the rustle of bed sheets and the low murmur of their voices through the thin walls of the research wing. Sometimes there were soft, lonely voices, heavy and resigned and troubled like his own. At other moments they would sound out in painful lament and become angry before quiet negotiations would begin again. Insomnia, he came to realize, was not a disease that affected pessimists. Some men could spend ten sleepless hours in bed, believing hour by hour, night after night, that in the next moments the soft embrace of true rest would come. Others believed a short walk through the halls would set their minds at ease. Not one man thought his sleeplessness could last forever. Had he believed such a thing, he would have risen from his unrest and begun to work.

He could've mastered particle physics, written symphonies, sculpted masterpieces, or designed cities. But instead, each man whiled away the dark hours waiting for sleep with a faith that was almost religious.

◈

Carlos slept a little more than an hour before waking with a start to a familiar smell. He opened his eyes to find the feet of John Sullivan resting on the bed beside him. He rubbed his eyes and looked at his partner with confusion. When his doctor first mentioned the sleep study, Carlos had envisioned an all-expenses paid vacation, complete with room service. He'd have his own nurse, extra helpings of potatoes, all the Jell-O he could eat. He'd been so excited when he first checked in, that he hadn't even wanted to sleep. But now when he woke up to find his partner sitting beside him, he didn't even flinch. He knew how fate worked. You could outrun fate in a dead sprint, settle in a new city, change your name, change your occupation, start a brand new life. The next morning, fate would be leaning back in a chair at your bedside with its smelly feet resting on the mattress beside you. It would try to lift your spirits.

"*Amigo*," Sully said, seeing that his partner's eyes had opened. "They say this insomnia is all in your head."

When Carlos said nothing, Sully assured him that with enough willpower, all things could be overcome. He pointed to his own feet as an example, swung them down and stomped the ground a few times sending little puffs of sulfur into the air. "See that?" he said. "*Adios amigo*." He waved his hand in front of him as if performing magic and sent a waft of air in the smaller man's direction that did seem less noxious than usual.

Maybe Sully had a point, Carlos thought. Then he remembered
fate and his own sleeplessness and he decided it was only his
resignation and possibly the horse's dose of Valium making everything
seem more bearable.

Carlos pulled off his mask and diving snorkel. "How did you get
them to let you in," he asked Sully.

Sully clinked his finger against his badge. "Police business, *amigo*. I
said it was an emergency."

"Is it?"

"Of sorts," Sully said.

The bigger man put his feet back up on the mattress and continued.
"Last night, at the theater," he said, "I saw a girl I used to love."

"To love?" Carlos asked. He sat up on his gurney. "Who?"

"I've never told you this, *amigo*, but I wasn't always the kind of man
you see now. Before all of this, back before the trench foot, back before
the girl and what came after, I had—one might say—a more pleasant
disposition. I was naïve is what it was, *Ponchito*. I thought a girl on a
bench throwing crumbs to ducks would always be the same sweet girl
on a bench. But the world is cruel, *miho*—you must know that—why
else does a man lose sleep?"

"Yes," Carlos agreed, "the world is cruel."

"She's ashamed to see me now, but it's my fault, *Carlitos*. I strung
her along. I didn't know her situation, see? Her grandmother was sick
and in need of care. I thought she'd be on that bench waiting for me
forever. Ah! *Miho*, this trench foot has been my penance! I thought
I could make other men—bad men, you see?— pay the price for my
mistakes. But the price was mine to pay. I see that now. Before I came

here, a priest in New Orleans told me to look for you *amigo*, and now I need your help. The priest said you would be the one to help me."

"He said to look for *me*?"

"He told me to look for a man of the desert with a coat of bright colors. And aren't you a Jew, *Carlitos*? And a Mexican? A man of the desert—and look at that jacket Carlos…"

The colorfully embroidered jacket was hanging on the door hook. Carlos looked at it in disbelief. All the time Sully had been in his life, Carlos had thought it was the spore that connected them, but the blame for his suffering lay just as squarely on his mother. With this realization came another: the woman of his sleepless dreams had not come to the city to escape his brutal partner, but so that Carlos could reunite the two together. He threw off his bedclothes and stripped out of his gown and began to dress.

"Whoa there, *amigo*, what's your hurry?" Sully said, "Destiny will wait for us. We'll go tonight. You came here to get some sleep. So sleep, *compadre*. I'll be back this evening. I need you at your best, *amigo*. *Comprende*?"

Carlos nodded his head and put his gown back on and got in bed. Once his partner was gone, he closed his eyes. He was standing in the desert in his mother's jacket, the wind blowing in his face. On the horizon he recognized the wiry figure of his partner, his body moving in its easy, cocky way. He studied the distant silhouette, trying to discern if it was moving toward him or away. He watched his partner for a minute or more, but before he could come to a conclusion he'd fallen into a deep, peaceful sleep.

39

I was already on the bus back to the city when I opened the second of the letters and came to the final fateful meeting of Tasha and her hopeful suitors at The Porno Palace. We still hadn't reached Fort Collins. It was late evening. Snow was falling, as was typical during my time in Colorado. It began in the afternoons and fell through the night, or it began late in the mornings and fell through the afternoon, or it fell for days at a time. And when it stopped, there were always moments when the sun shone bright and all the sins of the landscape were forgiven and if you were of that mind, you could look out over everything, clean and white like a bed made fresh for a new woman. In those moments you could believe just about anything you wanted to believe. The bus was in those moments, traveling inside them, the first vehicle across a new and soft world, and because we were traveling with the storm or the storm was traveling with us, we stayed right there on the cutting edge of hope for those first several hours, through Fort Collins and all the way to Laramie.

As the Salt Lake City story reached its conclusion, it was hard not to feel the disappointment of anti-climax, but the bus ride helped with that. It had me in a reflective mood, thinking in the sort of metaphors that cure everything. No matter how disappointing an ending, I remember thinking as I looked through the falling snow toward distant, twinkling lights, the future is always a new chapter, an unwritten road. And even knowing as I did that this was no more than a platitude, in the beauty of that moment on the warm bus with my few tired traveling companions nodding off against the cool windows, or seated beside lovers, or mothers, sipping bus station coffees and communicating, it seemed, through religious silences, that platitude filled me with longing for what lay ahead.

In this same spirit, I knew it wasn't so much the ending of the Salt Lake story that was important. What was important was that it came to an end so that the next story could follow on its heels—so Abbott could appear. And as I was reflective and thinking in metaphors, even this informed me in some important way, though I don't want to go too deeply into that for risk of stacking platitudes on platitudes. Suffice it to say, I felt emboldened and unafraid in a way that I hadn't experienced for such a long time that it felt like a completely new experience.

Of course, this was just a fleeting feeling in the broad schema of my life, like Sharpe in a moment of certainty before the return of his haunting indecision, but then sometimes I suppose it only takes a moment of visitation by a foreign self to change the course of one's life.

The letter started with Sully arriving at the hospital to collect Carlos. It was evening, and Carlos felt rested for the first time in forever. The two men got into the cruiser, and after six or seven blocks of riding with the windows closed, Carlos noticed he wasn't gasping for clean air. He'd been waiting for this moment for so long, and now that it had arrived, it wasn't quite the moment he had expected. He already missed the past. He already missed the insomnia and the smell of sulfur and the long nights dreaming about the future girl he once believed he was put on earth to save. Now that the end was near, he wished he could suffer in hope just a little bit longer.

They parked the car and offered a wave to the picketing Mormons, unaware that maybe twenty or thirty blocks away, in some ordinal direction, Doctor Sharpe was standing on a sidewalk trying to decide whether or not he should hail a cab. At the moment, he was leaning toward *yes*. But when he stepped toward the street and raised his hand and no cab had appeared after half a minute, he had time to reconsider. By the time Sully flashed his badge at the ticket booth and pulled open the lobby door, Sharpe had taken a step back on the sidewalk and his forehead was wrinkled in debate.

The actual meeting, the moment when everything shifted, took place in a heartbeat. Tasha was playing on the pinball machine when Sully and Carlos walked in. She was wearing her prettiest dress, shod in leather ankle boots with clean new laces and two-and-a-half-inch heels. She was dressed like the girl John Sullivan had seen on the bench that first time, the girl who liked sweet tea with extra lemon and day-old baguette. She looked different in some ways, older, her face no longer so round, her cheekbones sharper, more striking, but she was Tasha for certain. She was the girl he had sat beside on countless afternoons, keeping his distance, keeping conversation polite, eating corned beef sandwiches, eating bowls of gumbo. And because he was a big, dumb, Irishman, with a big, dumb Irish heart, and because when he sat beside Tasha it was difficult not to consider things he didn't think it polite to consider, he'd sat beside her for months without ever asking her the question that was truly on his mind. And then one day she wasn't on the bench anymore. A fortnight later, his feet began to itch. He tried to find Tasha, asked after her here and there and heard things he didn't want to hear. Soon he was angry. Big boils formed on the soles of his feet and halfway to his knees. They burst with puss and boils formed again, the wounds weeping powerful, sulfuric tears ranker than the water that flowed out of the anus of the earth at Badwater Springs, the water that Abbott had once drank seeking visions or transport or death. The itch drove Sully to despair, despair drove him to religion, and religion had driven him, in the watercourse way of fate, to The Porno Palace.

Tasha bent down low, leaning over the machine. She arched her back, straightened up and thrust her hips against the machine, hammered on the paddles. A siren went off as the Rockettes spun round and round and a small cannon shot a dozen balls at different angles. Her name rang out in the pinball hall while five or six other women turned momentarily to cheer her on. Sully and Carlos watched her, enrapt.

At that same moment, in the projection room, Denton White was busy trying to wrap his mind around the Russ Meyer movie, *Up!* which was supposed to be something of an art film. He couldn't—though the elements of the film certainly intrigued him. The first fifteen minutes portrayed an S&M-loving Adolph-Hitler-in-hiding murdered by a piranha in his bathtub. It was a brilliant revenge fantasy, but when the police came in to solve the assassination, it puzzled Denton. He just couldn't buckle himself in and accept that this was a crime that needed solving, particularly with so many attractive diversions around town. As the film progressed and the beautiful hitchhiker, Margo, played by voluptuous Raven De La Croix, found her way onto the set and drove every man in town to lusty distraction, Denton found himself beset by sadness and even guilt. His mind, like it so often did, went to Tasha. He saw her arriving young and hopeful in New Orleans and encountering a wholly different world than the one conjured by her innocent imagination, and for the first time in his life, he found his voyeurism distasteful. Mid-movie, as Margo was assaulted by a lumberjack—a caricature of masculinity competing on equal ground with Margo's big, damp eyes and overlong lashes and body reeking of fertility—Denton turned his eyes away in shame and sadness and thought about the one-word diagnosis Doctor Sharpe had written down in pencil.

Of course, as was characteristic of the curse that had haunted him since birth, Denton's timing was problematic. He left the projection room and reached the pinball hall only as the lobby door was released from John Sullivan's big hand and swung closed. He remained standing in his pinball hall listening to the girls tell him of the great romantic scene he'd missed—the reunion, the way the eyes locked on each other, the embrace that should have been reserved for film. As they clutched their chests and cooed and pouted at the sublime beauty of it all, Denton held the lobby door in his own throat tightly closed and, for the first time in many months, he deeply missed the old friend who he had left behind at Ella Rawson. Abbott was the only man he knew who might fully understand the forces moving in his heart at that moment, the tragic sadness that felt as though it might crystallize within him and remain there for many years to come.

He stood still for a long time. Finally, Tasha's roommate who had come late to the occupation and had once been in love, stepped forward to comfort him. She recognized all the signs and symptoms of his heart breaking. Not knowing what else to do and not considering the consequences—acting strictly on impulse—she stepped forward and grabbed hold of the hair at the back of Denton's head and pulled him toward her and kissed him deeply. Her lips pressed into his, parting slightly. Her warm breath filled his mouth with the taste of coffee, and then her tongue touched his and another world opened up, one that was timeless and thoughtless and absent of anxiety. She kissed him while the world of shame and regret and memory dissolved. And then the two of them were in the projection room while the final twenty minutes of *Up!* played out, a kung fu showdown between two naked vixens, followed by an epilogue sung by a nude chorus. Denton never found out who killed Hitler. He didn't care. His world was the scent of vanilla, the taste of strawberry, the wet, warm breath of coffee heating his body even as it wanted to return to ice. The credits rolled. The theater went dark. The crowds made their way to the pool hall and finally filtered onto the street while Denton and the Russian woman lay panting, their bodies connected or separated by a thin film of perspiration. They didn't speak. They lay like that for almost an hour, touching each other, reading each other's unwritten chapters with their hands, until finally Denton stood and dressed. And while the young woman, who had come late to the occupation and had once been in love, lay on the floor noticing the signs of her own heart breaking for a second time, Denton walked out of the theater without even a goodbye.

40

Denton hit the street and kept moving, determined to remain in the world of instinct and intuition, to stay ahead of the coldness that threatened to overtake him once and for all. He walked east to State Street, passing by Regent Street which, in the late 1800s, had been the site of the city's original Red Light District and had once given rise to an era of powerful madams who had found a place among the city's political elite. At State Street, he turned south, following the old route of the Lincoln Highway. It was the route traveled by the riders of the Pony Express as they galloped in from the plains, fresh from dodging Comanche arrows, saddlebags bursting with sacks of tender correspondences. He had no idea where he was going. He let his body or some reptilian part of his mind guide him like a divining rod. He was fleeing the ice storm behind him, staying one step ahead of whatever was chasing him down. He reached Route 171 and turned west with the flow of traffic, and because the sound of the passing cars calmed him, he continued along the shoulder.

After some time, a car stopped and he got in. The driver twisted the dial on the stereo and handed him a Budweiser and said hello and then he turned the dial back the other way and drove. Soon they passed the great lake and Denton remembered a story he'd once heard.

It was the story of a heartbroken young man who'd stolen a wooden dinghy and attempted suicide, rowing out and setting fire to the craft miles offshore. But the lake was so full of salt that the man could not manage to drown himself, and several days later he washed up on shore, alive and covered in the tiny shrimp that had sustained him and he was wrinkled like a piece of smoked meat. People said the salt and the shrimp had an enduring protective effect on the man's body. The young man had been preserved, and though he looked far older and more world-worn than his years, he would live on, ageless for another century. The story went that the man was still alive, and was now enjoying the permanent evening of his life after traveling west, as Denton was, and striking gold somewhere in California.

A few hours later, Denton was walking again. Another car stopped. Another beer. Another few hundred miles on the Lincoln Highway. Gradually, Denton got the feeling he knew where he was going, though he didn't know exactly where that was. It went like that all night—cars, walking, a few cigarettes, a joint shared with another vet, two or three lines of cocaine, a couple of pills. He traveled south through Ely which, years ago, on his way to Ella Rawson, had seemed a ghoulish, haunted town of crooked windows. Now it looked straight and prim and sleepy. His driver steered a couple of clicks west toward Warm Springs and asked Denton if he wanted to continue. Denton nodded, fell asleep.

Soon he was walking again. He looked up at the thousand uncrossed stars and smelled the air of a familiar place and he felt like he was finally getting his bearings. He turned off the main road and headed through the desert and walked in the starlight. He was either completely lost or he was listening to the very voice of the universe. After two or three miles, he walked over a rise and saw the distant miner's shack in the starlight and realized where he was and he wondered why he was there. As he got closer, he saw that smoke was billowing out the chimney. He didn't question it. He walked to the door and pushed it open. His eyes took a moment to adjust. Across the one room of the shack, sitting on the dirt floor, rocking back and forth in front of the light of a fading fire, he saw Abbott. He was clutching that gold Zippo in one hand with the other covering his eyes. His whole body was quaking with sobs. It was a disarming scene, but the thing that most caught Denton's attention was Abbott's mustache.

In the weeks before the head nurse sprang him from one form of imprisonment right into another, Denton had begun to catch glimpses of the future. He might close his eyes and catch one brief, blurry scene, and then the light would begin to flicker and the screen behind his eyelids would go dark. He saw enough to understand that Abbott would play an important role in his future. In these scenes, he always saw his friend shirtless, and always wearing a thick mustache. He often saw the two of them on a stage, or in a gym.

He had almost lost touch with those visions. For the long months in Salt Lake City, that world had lain dormant and forgotten, but now, when he saw Abbott's mustache, the screen far back behind Denton's eyes flickered. Some dust appeared, a single hair danced across the screen, and in the dark theater of Denton's unconscious the camera grew bright and the movie began to roll. He sat down next to his old friend and took it all in, half a lifetime in a matter of minutes—beautiful, sad, at times heroic. Then he opened his eyes and looked at his friend shivering with sobs. He rose and added a few scraps of wood to the fire. A different movie rolled—this one from his memory, while his eyes remained open. Schlotzsky was chiding Denton for his purposeful ignorance, for his refusal to scrutinize the memories of that terrible place he declared it was Schlotzsky's job to help him forget. "A man with no past," he told Denton, "becomes trapped in the very place he is trying to forget."

But there were things Denton would never tell the doctor, things he was sure the doctor had no way of metabolizing, poisons of the mind to which Denton had developed resistance, antibodies, enzymes, something which had allowed him to survive beyond what he thought endurable, but which the doctor, in his quiet, linear little life, could never sustain. Schlotzsky could not have understood because understanding would have demanded that he endure the unendurable, and before the doctor's understanding could have been of any use to Denton the doctor would have been dead.

"What becomes of a man," Denton asked Schlotzsky, as a method of deflection one time when the doctor was about to pry into a vat of poison, "who is so lost in his past that he cannot look forward?" The doctor nodded as if he understood what Denton feared, even though Denton was only asking out of concern for Abbott. "Well that," the doctor said—and his answer would end their session— "that is a recipe for a crippling depression."

Denton sat with Abbott until the storm of Abbott's sobbing had calmed some, arising and falling in intervals. Then he went out into the dawn and gathered some wood and refuse to heat the cabin. When Denton returned, he fed the fire again, first with the candy wrappers and weathered papers and boxboard that he'd found littered around the cabin, and later with old pieces of wooden signs, then with shakes that had fallen from the roof, and finally he fed the crumbling hearth with the big tree-trunk stools that had been sawn years before in some other place and were brought in by a vagrant or a wandering hermit or a prospector who had long since died, or had been institutionalized, imprisoned, or had moved on.

It was as the first signboards were broken over his knee that Denton began speaking to Abbott. He sketched out a future that would be every bit as colorful, rewarding, and inspiring as the past from which Abbott could not release his grip. He reminded his friend of the training they had done at the institution, of the way they had mimicked the movements of Kwai Chang Caine during their afternoon exercise periods, how they had meditated on the pearls of wisdom scattered throughout each of *Kung Fu*'s episodes. Denton told Abbott that their lives had a purpose, that some deep connection had drawn them back together because there were verses written in their fates. There were no coincidences, no chance meetings, no wrong turns, no lost years. There was only the gentle hand of the universe coaxing them forward, pointing toward the future, and directing them to go forth and heal others with the wisdom of Shaolin.

By the time the first stool was rolled onto the red embers of the smoldering shakes, the two had confessed their deepest secrets to each other. Denton had talked Abbott off the ledge of the past and Abbott had, for the first time since he had first woken in that cabin years before, an idea of a future that might be worth reaching. That first stool, a tree stump that had endured years of desert heat and sunlight, crackled on the embers for a minute or two and then burst into a flame almost as white and surprising as lightning. It lit the room like daylight, and suddenly Abbott could see everything. There would be a school. It would be a fleck of gold in the sluice of the world. It would be a place of brightness and clarity, of healing and deep educational purpose, and it would bring to others the tremendous richness that he and Denton had received from the television series *Kung Fu*. The two of them would bring the legacy of this great way to the masses the same way Kwai Chang Caine had first brought it to the wildness of the early West.

Around noon, when Abbott and Denton were leaving the miner's shack, Doctor Sharpe had just finished his fourth cup of coffee and he'd come to a decision. He stood up, put on his hat, and hailed a cab. He stepped in without a second thought, closing the door behind him with a solid thud. Then, in a voice so authoritative that it startled the doctor that it was his own, he requested the driver take him directly to The Porno Palace.

The driver, a young Mormon fresh back from a mission in Brazil who had known the draw of sultry women, glanced in the rearview mirror and remained silent. He knew his way to the Palace by heart.

Sharpe exited the cab on the curb and after knocking several times on the lobby door, he gave it a pull and found it unlocked. The past haunted him as he searched the theater. He recalled pulling his Cutlass into Ray Cook's Mountain View Motel and opening the hotel room door to find Denton frozen on the bed. He remembered the few desperate minutes he had searched for Denton in Rose's abandoned house with the foreshadow of regret darkening his every step. He opened the screening room doors shouting Denton's name, checked the basement office, found it empty, and finally walked up the steep stairs to the projection rooms, dreading in some way that he might find his old patient, the grandson of his beloved childhood caretaker, hanging from a pipe with his belt around his neck.

Sharpe opened the door labeled "Projection Room 1" and the light from the hall revealed something that startled the doctor in a completely unexpected way. A beautiful, naked, young Russian woman lay soundlessly weeping on the floor. She was flat on her back, tears streaming down her face. Occasionally her soft, white chest would heave and sink again. This striking sight moved the doctor so deeply that all his years of loving in silence and mourning in silence were shaken loose at once. He collapsed to his knees on the floor beside the woman and began weeping for the suffering of both of them.

The woman, who had not noticed Sharpe enter, who had in fact noticed very little for almost twelve hours, now sat up. Finding the old, kind-looking doctor distraught, she was struck by a long-latent mothering impulse and she brought his wailing head to her bare chest and cooed to him in Russian. The scene was so strange that after several minutes the two came to their senses and began laughing, then crying again at intervals. And when the spasms finally did subside, the odd couple weren't ready to part. Sharpe, without a second thought, invited the woman to accompany him home. She cried, then laughed again, and then she accepted his offer, feeling in her body a sensation that even she, who had come late to her occupation and had once been in love, could not name, but which she would later identify for several friends as her ego giving way to the intercession of fate.

41

The final letter, as I said, was postmarked from a town in Utah, which I had never heard of and don't remember. It didn't begin much differently than the others. I hadn't been able to make myself open it on the bus. I'd just sat there turning it over in my hands, staring out the window until we finally pulled into the Greyhound terminal in Salt Lake City. I suppose I was worried it would be a goodbye, an end to a story within and without the letter, and I wasn't ready for either to be finished. I tucked the letter back in my pocket and walked to Alice's Restaurant through the snow. When I arrived, the diner was warm. It smelled of coffee and fried eggs. Alice herself seated me, took my order, brought a phone over to the table and went to get coffee while I dialed my mother's home number once, and then again a minute later. I set the letter in front of me and looked at it, turned it over again on the table, and then just sat there staring at my fake name.

"You don't see many of those nowadays," Alice said.

She put a napkin down in front of me and I looked up at her while she filled my mug with coffee. She was beautiful—I mean in the way old women are sometimes beautiful. Her face was marked by a mix of kindness and maybe loss, or sweet resignation. I had a word for it, one word, but I couldn't find it. I kept looking.

"Most people don't take the time anymore," she said.

"Serenity," I thought. That was the word. I'd always hoped one day I would find that for myself. Not the shallow happiness that most people were chasing after, or riches, or fame. But *serenity*.

I gave her the most sincere smile I could muster and nodded in agreement.

"Do you want some cream and sugar, honey?"

"Yes," I said. "Thanks."

"Be back in a moment, sweetheart," she said. Then she pointed at the table. "There's a napkin there for you if you need it."

I thanked her again.

When she walked off, I finally opened the letter. Like the others, it started with a salutation, and then the story continued more or less where it had left off. Abbott and Denton hitchhiked into Ely together. They had lunch at that same drugstore counter where Abbott had broken down years before, where he had lain convulsing on the floor with a spoon of pancake batter in his mouth. I tried to discern a difference in the writing. And maybe the letter seemed a little more thematic than the others. It spoke of the way innocent beginnings often splintered into something more complex and layered. Then it described how the two friends, in the realization of Denton's dream, had been forced to play roles and become different people. In the movie that played behind his eyes at the miner's shack, Denton had foreseen himself as a character much like Kwai Chang Kaine. The film he had visualized was pure art, and Denton played the beautiful, heroic, and inspiring lead. He was the film's star. But to see that film to completion, another Denton would have to take the helm and do the dirty work. This person would be slick and convincing and a little seedy. He'd be the salesman, the money chaser, the guy who kept the studio afloat, and Denton began to think of this persona as The Producer. Sometimes late at night, after putting six or seven Mai Tais down the hatch at the karaoke bar of a Chinese restaurant while a half dozen fading beauties took turns singing yesterday's hits, the tension between The Star and The Producer would become so volatile that a third character would appear like a grotesque offspring of the first two characters, and this third man's presence would threaten to derail the whole project.

In the morning, as the haze of Mai Tais cleared, the first Denton would often wake to find himself in the bed of some strange woman, once beautiful, her voice sexy and horse with cigarette smoke and full of the sadness of country songs. He would rub his eyes and rise and return to his hotel where he would attempt to beat the third man out of himself with calisthenics and breathing exercises and with his spinning nunchaku, bleeding with perspiration until the chastised third man finally skulked back off into the future, and the restored Denton would act surprised to have seen him and happy to have him gone, as if he didn't know that the third man had been the future all along.

That was the way Denton came to think of the third man—a relic of sorts, conceived in the past and aching to be born. Beyond that, his ideas about the third man were vague and impressionistic. He sensed the third man frozen within him, a bad egg or a zygote, cryogenically preserved but also somehow maturing because time itself was maturing. Or the third man was a consciousness stored somewhere in a vat, a brain in formaldehyde waiting to be stimulated, distant in time in space and destined to intersect with a disturbing future that Denton intended to avoid.

Schlotzsky had warned him about the past and Denton hadn't listened. He hadn't traveled into the past with Schlotzsky to geld the third man and now that man was coming for him. The third man was the self who had lurked in the background, hiding in the shadows at the corners of his room, who perched on the corner of his bed and warned him to remain silent. That man had grown fat on unspoken words. For years, he'd been there, feeding on Denton's deep and corrosive anger with his mother for abandoning him. He'd been thriving in the deep disappointment Denton felt with his grandmother, Rose, who had exited the world with a few words of advice and had refused to guide him from the other side. He'd been feeding on Denton's humiliation from the betrayal he felt when Tasha left the Palace with John Sullivan at the very moment Denton felt safe enough to reveal his heart. When the head nurse, after luring Denton away from Abbott and Schlotzsky with a caress that implied romance, sat up straight in the darkness across from him, separated by a side table, and a phone that never stopped blinking red, and three feet of empty space—when she mumbled a few words to the motel room darkness in an accent he didn't recognize, and then fell back onto the bed and abruptly started snoring again, Denton remembered feeling the third man stir within him. "Men vil come," she'd said, and the men did come, but that was days later, when he was no longer expecting them and there were more men than he'd imagined, and when they came, the third man escaped farther into the future, deeper into the vat, while the first two men were left languishing, chained by dark and fear.

The third man had nourished himself with unspent time, that

relentless and indifferent force that revealed, with the turning of its pages, the same cruel story over and over again. He was full of the self-loathing the first man felt at his own weakness, and with the necessity that the first man's weakness had created for the second man. When this drove the first man toward annihilation—in booze, in the cigarettes he chain-smoked, in the women he followed out of smoky bars—the first two men retreated and the third man began to emerge. The third man was an uninhibited charmer. He was a spender, a braggart, a Don Juan who projected Tasha's betrayal and his mother's abandonment and Rose's death and all the cruelty of the world onto the easiest and most needy women he could find. The third man would love these women, sometimes quickly, in the space of a night, sometimes fully and desperately with all the care and kindness and understanding the world had never shown to him. But the third man's love was just a ruse. Soon enough, he would turn and punish the world and all the women who had abandoned him. He would punish the innocent man who was still capable of love and who the world would never allow to fully become by leaving each one of these women, abruptly and alone, just as the world had always done to him.

Over time, Denton began to remember where he'd first met the third man. He'd travel back in his mind through the haze of Mai Tais, through the motel rooms blinking with red, through the institution shock treatments, and then further back to where they'd met in the dark world of power he'd seen in all its terror after he'd eaten a plate of brownies and dropped acid at Woodstock. It was a world that had always lain in the shadow of the first man, and though he was certain Schlotzsky would have corrected him, he came to think of this world as the world of the id. The id ruled the night. It ruled his dreams and fantasies. The id was uncovered over time, through investigation—Schlotzsky had told him as much. The id asserted itself through careless mistakes. It followed, Denton began to suspect, that the dark land of the id revealed the future.

❧

"Sorry that took awhile," Alice said. She put down some packets of sugar and some cream and noticed my coffee was mostly gone. "Oh! I guess you couldn't wait. Want me to warm that up for you, sweetie?"

I put the letter aside. "Please," I said.

She filled my mug to the brim and kept on pouring while a few ounces spilled over the rim.

"I'm sorry hunny," she said. "What am I thinking?" She put the pot on the table and patted her apron. "I don't have a cloth. Would you mind wiping that up with your napkin?"

I saw the coffee pooling around the phone and realized my mother was probably already waiting for my call at the supermarket. I told Alice not to worry about it and picked up the phone and started dialing. Alice sighed and walked off. After a few rings, my mother answered.

"David?" She sighed much the same way Alice had just sighed. "It's about time," she said. "I was starting to worry."

I told her I was sorry. And then I told her I was sorry again because it'd been a while since I'd called.

"Well, anyway," she said, "I'm glad you called, I was just thinking about you when the phone rang. Isn't that funny? I was thinking about you and that friend of yours."

"You were thinking about Abbott?" I said.

"The one you said looks like Thomas Magnum," she said. "That monkish friend of yours. Have you heard any more from him?"

"He sent some more letters," I said. "I'm reading the last one now."

"What a strange coincidence," she said. "Sometimes I think—well, I know you're going to think this is crazy—but sometimes I think we're all connected."

I told her it wasn't strange.

"Well you know me," she said. "Of course I was thinking about your father at first, and then I started thinking about that story your friend was telling you and I did some research on the internet. And you know what, David? It seems like maybe those things Abbott told you aren't so unbelievable after all. Maybe he's telling the truth—or some version of the truth."

"Maybe," I said. I wanted to ask her if she thought the whole thing was just too far-fetched. Like, why was he writing to *me*? I hadn't given it that much thought before. It had just been something I took for granted, but now as the story was reaching the end and I zoomed out, it seemed weird. We'd only really known each other for less than a day.

"Anyway," my mother said. "What did the letters say? Is he coming back for you? Has he found his wife?"

"I'm not sure, Ma. So far, the last letter is more or less a bunch of psychobabble. Things I don't understand."

"What kind of things?"

"Stuff about personalities fracturing into separate parts and how the future is within us, but hidden deep in our minds from the beginning... And then some things about how maybe we could all see the future if we were willing to face it. I'm not sure I understand what

319

he's trying to say. It's weird—even to me."

My mother made a humming sound and then she was silent while she thought it over for a moment. "It actually makes a lot of sense, David, if you could believe what I've been reading on the internet. But if I told you, you'd probably think I've gone batty." She laughed. "Where are you anyway? I hear a lot of noise in the background."

"I came to see Denton again. I'm at a diner in Salt Lake City."

"Out to eat again? I tell you, David, you're living the life of Riley!" She stopped a moment to let out a little incredulous "goodness!" before asking me if there'd been any change in Denton's condition.

"I don't think so," I said.

"Well, like I said before, I'd expect the worst if I were you."

When I didn't say anything, she reconsidered.

"I'm sorry," she said. "I probably shouldn't say that."

"Well, you're right, Mom. I don't know why I came here. I got the letters and I had a sense that this is where I should be."

"You just up and left that little cabin? Just like that, David? What about your novel? Will that *ever* be finished?"

"I don't know, Mom. I got the letters and I just left."

"Well, you certainly won't be eating out at fancy restaurants every day if you don't find a way to make some money. I'll tell you that much. The only eating out you'll be doing is eating out of a soup kitchen."

I stood up and pulled my pack of cigarettes from my pocket and set them down on the table. "Mom, last time we talked you were adamant that I should help Abbott. I have to choose one thing or the other for now."

She sighed again. "I guess you're right," she said. "I just wonder what you're going to do with yourself. You're not getting any younger you know. I just wish you'd finish that novel. Elaine's son's husband—he's gay you know, but he's a very nice person—anyway, he just published a little book on labradoodles. Have you heard of them? It's a new breed of hypoallergenic dog. I mean it's just a little, self-published book, but he has an author page on Amazon and lots of good reviews. I think even you could do something like that."

I placed the phone down carefully and turned away to light a cigarette so my mother couldn't hear, and then I exhaled and picked back up the receiver.

"Anyway," I said to change the subject, "what did you find out on the internet?"

"Well, I know this is going to be hard to believe," she said, her voice seeming to lift a little out of the shadows, "but this isn't just a bunch of nonsense, David. These are all established facts, stuff that's come out over the years. So just bear with me. Hold on a moment while I get my computer in front of me."

There was the sound of the phone being put down, and then silence. I took a few more drags off my cigarette and sipped my coffee while I waited for her to come back. I'd come to accept that on days when I spoke to my mother, I was going to smoke two or three cigarettes. A minute or so later she picked up the phone again.

"Okay," she said. "Are you still there?"

"Still here," I said.

"I don't know where to begin," she said. "One story I read was about climate manipulation and cloud-seeding in Vietnam. They did that to rain out the North Vietnamese. Did you know that? Way back in the sixties. That part is public record, but this is where it gets strange—people think the government might've used the same technology to make the rain at Woodstock."

I took a drag and exhaled. Sipped some more coffee.

"I guess that has nothing to do with anything, but during that same time—I don't know if you're aware of this or not—the government was doing all kinds of experiments with LSD and mind control. People were disappearing, David, being drugged and brainwashed, put in facilities, trained in ESP and remote viewing. Do you know what that is? Anyway, it's all on the internet. Anyone can read up on it. Maybe Abbott and Lucille were part of the experiments. Maybe they spent time at one of those facilities together and their life together was in a place like a dream world, a place they would meet during remote viewing sessions. Does that seem possible? Of course, their memories would have been erased before they were released back into the world. They did that too, you know—at least that's what I've been reading."

"Sounds a little out there," I said, "but I guess everything about Abbott is pretty out there."

"I wish your father was here," she said, "He was always so good at solving those mysteries on TV. Do you remember that?"

"I know, Ma. I wish he was here too."

"Let's see... What else did I come across?"

I took a last drag of my cigarette while my mother clacked her keys and clicked her trackpad. I thought it was good that she was excited about something.

"Have you ever heard of MK-Ultra?"

"Abbott mentioned it once," I said. I remembered the rant clearly because it involved well-known terrorists and criminals and assassins who had apparently participated in these programs. The historical facts in Abbott's story were toeholds that helped ground it in reality. "It was mind control stuff, right?"

"Yes, that's right." I heard some more clicking. "There was also something called Monarch Programming that they experimented with for a while. Some sort of hypnosis that turned people into sleeper agents. There used to be movies about that when I was younger. Do they still make those? But anyway, that's where the information gets iffy. Some of these people on the internet are absolute crackpots, David! To think I was worried that people would think *I'm* crazy!"

"Well, who knows what to believe anymore," I said.

"Isn't that the truth," she said. "It's enough to make *all of us* crazy."

Alice came with my breakfast and put it down in front of me. She saw that my coffee was half empty, warmed it up, wiped up the spilled coffee with a damp cloth, shook her head, and walked away.

"I think you need to finish reading that last letter, David. Maybe Abbott hasn't just been traveling around the country like you think. I mean, if he was a test subject, wouldn't they want to check in with him now and then? Do you think you could be in danger?"

"I doubt it, Ma."

"Now I'm going to be worrying about you. Who knows what you've gotten yourself into this time."

I started picking at my breakfast. "I don't think they'd let Abbott send me letters from a secret government facility, Ma."

"I have no idea what they'd do, David," she said. "I used to think I understood some things, but now I just don't know what to think."

42

I ate some eggs and picked up the letter again. The narrative took a break from Denton's fractured personality and began to detail that same period in a less impressionistic way. Denton and Abbott were traveling the western United States, giving martial arts demonstrations to build startup capital and develop a following for the next phase of Denton's vision—a nationwide network of kung fu schools with the Palace Theater in Salt Lake City at its center.

These demonstrations began as ticketed events, performances in church basements or high school auditoriums in towns where people had little access to entertainment and would pay a few bucks to see something new. But the two soon discovered they could make faster money when their performances appeared more spontaneous. They might walk into a local boxing gym and Abbott would begin jumping rope or hitting a speed bag. Denton would throw a towel around his neck and act as Abbott's trainer for a time before breaking off on his own to perform a Bruce Lee routine with nunchaku, or he would howl and yelp and strike the heavy bag with his one-inch punch. His aim was to attract a degree of attention and derision. Once he had achieved this, he would climb into the ring and call Abbott up for a demonstration.

Denton had an instinct for the pace of a two-man show, and theirs was meticulously choreographed. Abbott started with a flurry of punches. Denton's hands rose languidly and fell back down to his sides. Abbott stumbled. The audience laughed.

It went on like this, scaling up until Abbott lost his temper entirely. Denton remained composed. He brushed aside the clenched fists of the golden gloves champion with an attitude of nonchalance. At last, with Abbott breathing heavily, Denton countered Abbott with a series of finger strikes, stopping him abruptly in his tracks. The bigger man would teeter in place for a second or two, a confused look earning one last laugh before he crumbled to the mat and the laughter changed to gasps.

A skeptic would always emerge after Abbott was revived with smelling salts, a wise guy who would look at Denton's wiry build and carnival barker's jaw and rightly conclude that he was being conned. But Denton would caution these men. He was an expert in *dim mak*, the art of the death touch, he explained. It would be too dangerous for a regular boxer to tangle with him. He would convince his challengers that it was in their own best interest to engage in combat with Abbott instead. "Standard boxing rules," Denton would suggest, adding that to make things more entertaining, somebody should collect bets.

It was in these moments that Abbott shined. The elegant movements he practiced with Denton under the institution's juniper tree fused with his childhood training as a golden gloves champion to produce a style that bore a striking resemblance to the *Jeet Kune Do* of Bruce Lee. The local boxers never knew what to make of Abbott. He was a big, beautiful specimen of a man with a lean body and a Stonewall Riots mustache. While men placed wagers, he danced about with the lightness of a ballerina, lowering himself into graceful postures, and the men often wondered if he and Denton were a couple. But when his opponent moved toward him, he became a boxer, dropping back and bouncing on his toes and letting his long arms fall momentarily to his sides as if his hands held the weight of two iron balls. His body bobbed and twitched at the command of a still and massive center, coiling at every advance, jabbing counters, threatening to set those iron weights whirling at the first lapse of attention.

The men outside the ring always became silent, watching the match with awestruck intensity. "That's it," Denton might coach Abbott from the corner, his hands resting theatrically over his lower abdomen in his best imitation of Kwai Chang Caine, "Remember, Abbott, the willow does not contend against the storm." And then the ill-fated skeptic who had gotten into the ring would shoot a glance to the friend who was cornering him—the one who had encouraged him to take on the big, dancing bear in the first place—as if to say, "Why me?"

It took a little over a year for the pair to earn the money required to renovate the Palace Theater for the third time. They gave it new life and a new name, and soon students were pouring into the reborn and re-christened Shaolin Palace. Some of them were old friends, people who had known Denton and his theater through one or all of its previous iterations. It was a brief time of return for Denton. He returned to an old feeling of belonging and a sense of being among his tribe. But Abbott began to experience a growing unease with his position in their new enterprise whenever the two went on the road. It was his name that was troubling him. The name was a talisman given to him by his father. It had been meant to remind him to live his life as a leader, a straight man, to avoid suffering the same thankless humiliation of playing a clown in the world that had led his father to Marxism and eventually led to his blacklisting and subsequent life as an undistinguished garmento.

The thought festered in Abbott's brain. He began obsessing over the same ideas that had plagued his father with bitterness: meritocracy and the unequal distribution of materials and status. He had no ownership stake in the Palace or the corporation, just a percentage on memberships and a minority share on the wagers. Disagreements about money and respect began to infiltrate his and Denton's every conversation, and Abbott came to think of himself as the downtrodden proletariat and Denton as a vampire who exploited him. In his letter, he wrote about recoiling when he spotted a magazine cover in a city news shop that featured Denton dressed in the costume of a Shaolin monk, leaning casually against an Italian sports car. The cover story celebrated Denton's martial prowess and business acumen. Abbott clenched his jaw and read the article from beginning to end while standing in the store. By the time he returned the magazine to the rack, he had reached the painful conclusion that he had failed to meet his life's one directive. His father would have looked on him with a mixture of sorrow, disappointment, and shame.

The following morning he approached Denton while Denton's mind was still swimming in the self-loathing always brought on by a night of Mai Tais, women, and cocaine. Abbott offered to sell his portion of their memberships and named a price. Denton accepted.

By the time Denton had pieced himself together again, Abbott was gone. In many ways, Abbott had been gone for months. The deeply romantic man, the caring friend and happy fool had been replaced by a man who had become as bitter and humorless as his father before him.

In the years after he left the Shaolin Palace, Abbott defined himself in his own right. This was the period during which he became known as *The* abbot, using his name to his advantage to build his own small chain of schools. There were bumper years for both Abbott and Denton—years of flashy cars, magazine interviews, local and regional TV spots. Some years it was hard to say which of the two was the more prominent figure in the tiny kingdom of kung fu. But then, almost overnight, nobody cared for kung fu or Ferraris anymore. Mixed martial arts and suburban utility vehicles entered the scene and the entire country moved toward practicality and away from mysticism.

The two old friends reached out to each other from across the country and found themselves traveling in the same boat again, stuck with sky-high overhead and unpaid bills and over-inflated egos. Neither was ready to accept that the gravy train of kung fu had made its final stop. They covered overhead by liquidating assets. All the accouterments of wealth were slowly pawned as they hunkered down and held their images together with knockoffs and a façade of stoicism. The friends began speaking regularly again, and soon they started a sideline enterprise building kit-cars in upstate New York. The shop, called Bodyman's Garage, would find a temporary footing among left-behinds like Abbott and Denton and briefly flourish under an insurance loophole called *agreed value* before almost costing Denton his life when he fell into debt and was forced to engineer a fleet of transport cars for a crime family out of Philadelphia. But finally, the debt was paid and Bodyman's fell flat and was downsized and relocated to a junk lot in Fairfield, Iowa where Denton and his right-hand man would make a decent living doing custom work for old deadheads, and Denton would take up Transcendental Meditation and quit Mai Tais and cocaine mostly for good.

It was around the time that Bodyman's was just starting up as a kit-car business that Abbott received Schlotzsky's letter. He sat with it at his kitchen table, reading it over and over, flashing back, mourning Lucille but also mourning the sad disappearance of the Abbott with two Ts, the young man who'd crafted the original document in orange crayon with such sweet earnestness twenty years before. The affirmation of his time travel should have brought him a sense of solace. He had been right about the giant thermometer all along. But now he looked around at the life he had fallen into and he realized he was no different than Schlotzsky or any of his doubters. At some point, he had lost faith in himself.

That night, he was troubled by a dream in which he searched feverishly through a dimly lit house of labyrinthine halls without really knowing what he was looking for. When he woke, he set out across the country. Schlotzsky had written that the diner Abbott had spoken of was not to be found, and Abbott didn't doubt him. In his own heart, Abbott knew it wasn't yet time to reunite with Lucille. Abbott needed to reunite with the better version of himself, the man who had loved Lucille and lost Lucille and for whom love had once been the whole of everything. It was the only way he could be sure Lucille would recognize him when they finally found each other again.

The trip was slow. The original Ferrari 308, the real McCoy, gave him nothing but trouble the entire way. He was waylaid in Akron. He was waylaid in Omaha. By the time he began to climb the long mile up toward Denver, only four cylinders were properly firing and his mood had become darker than the Black Hills to the north. The real McCoy, floundering and faltering as it was, and out of place in the American West and out of step with the times all over the country, had somehow begun to seem symbolic of Abbott's general relationship with life. The car would finally break down on the sad road back from Baker, California, where he'd seen the thermometer he'd long remembered and where in the absence of Lucille he'd experienced what he could only define as an emotional implosion, as though a vacuous internal structure had collapsed into the sudden recognition of its own emptiness. He would have his 308 towed to Des Moines where it was sold to a real estate developer for a song, and then he would hop on a Greyhound back to New York with nothing but his clothes and a pocketful of car cash that he would burn through in a matter of months.

But the long ride did him well. For the first time since he'd left the institution, he felt a sense of freedom and hope that was generated from his own heart. Though he knew he would have to return to New York and hustle to make a living, he also knew he would remember he was only a player in a game of his own invention. He wouldn't lose himself in the game again. He wouldn't forget that his true identity wasn't defined by the number of kung fu schools he owned or the karate magazine covers with his face shining like the face of the fake

Rolex that now hung around his wrist and ticked out a linear rhythm that was more of a fraud than either of the two other faces. He would return to New York and replace the real McCoy with a fake McCoy built by Denton White because truth was only to be found in fiction anyhow, and the truth was that time and all its phenomena were illusions, projections, disintegrating echoes like overplayed records that had lost their dynamic range. And he would love that fake McCoy because the fake McCoy would, whenever he got into the driver's seat, remind him that the reality he was living in was only a cheap knockoff of the reality where he had known Lucille and loved Lucille and because—if he could only keep his eyes on the prize—that reality might someday open up to him again. So Abbott returned across the country on the bus, watching days turn to nights and eating at one diner after the next, coming back to himself with each meal, each plate of eggs, and each cup of coffee.

Shortly after he returned, it became apparent that Denton was beginning to fall apart. That same world of imitation that had directed Abbott back toward a previous innocence was only further corrupting something in his friend. In the late-night clubs and cocaine sales meetings where Denton cooked up insurance scams and made deals with small-time drug runners and crooks, Mai Tais slipped down the hatch, one after the next, and the third man began to reemerge stronger than ever. It was as if the third man had spent years waiting for Denton, and now he was determined to make up for lost time. Abbott returned to his institution-era relationship with kung fu, taking up daily practice of the animal forms and Qi Gong.

He found meaning in the small classes he now taught in church basements that he drove to in his misfiring car. His breathing and movement exercises were putting him back in rhythm with his true self and the true beat of time. He would watch his students practice while contemplating the beauty of space and time, the way bodies moved in relationship to other bodies, following each other, intersecting here and there, separating, and then reuniting when the energy moved them together again. Sometimes he called Denton, or wrote to remind his old friend of the deep world they had experienced together in their days at Ella Rawson. But Denton had lost connection to the practice that had saved them both. He had forgotten their training. Denton was angry at the world and everything it had taken from him and now he felt he had stumbled upon a lifestyle that would force the world to pay him back.

Denton detested the cars he made. On the surface each was eye-catching and polished in a way that confused the non-discerning eye, but beneath the skin was an assembly of odds and ends that could never deliver the promise of that initial impression. In the women who were drawn to men who drove his cars, Denton saw Tasha and felt contempt. In the insurance companies he defrauded, he saw the institutions of the military and the State, which had subjugated his will and splintered his personality into fragments. In the clever compartments he installed to transport drugs and guns in honest-looking cars, he recognized all the noble lies he had ever been sold. It made him consider the secret places he had been forced to build in himself, those places deep within the mountains of his mind where he stored away the toxic byproducts of the truth to protect the naïve world. Each car was an imperfect replica of another car and a perfect replica of Denton himself. When he left one of his creations burning in an empty lot and watched as graceful form was consumed by chaos, he felt a sick satisfaction and a spiritual release. He was getting even with whatever forces had created him.

In these moments, he would often find himself wondering if this was what his mother felt when she abandoned him, knowing every nut and bolt and performance specification of his DNA. He was a beautiful child—Rose had always told him this. But he was not built to meet the painful demands of the world. He would watch dark smoke billow up from a distance and wonder if it was better that his mother left him while the illusion of perfection persisted. She never had to endure the pain of that illusion degrading as Denton's imperfect genetic components reached the limit of their engineering and moved him toward his inevitably sad predestination. She never had to look beneath the hood of her fantasy and witness the child of her imagination be reduced to crass physics, clumsy moving parts, with the entire future written right there in iron, aluminum, and steel, while the cruel world of criticism and measurement subjected it to a fate that even flame could never burn away.

I put down the letter and sipped some coffee. I tried to reflect on the last few paragraphs, but they were beyond me, or nonsensical or my mind was somewhere else. I was thinking about my unfinished novel and all the second chapters that had been tossed. Across the diner, I thought I saw Noel, my waitress from last time, but when I looked more closely it wasn't her. Her hair. Her turn of the head. But not her. And then for some reason I couldn't picture Noel clearly anymore. I couldn't seem to remember if she had been my waitress at Alice's Restaurant or somewhere else. Maybe she'd been a young woman I'd dated, a receptionist behind a hospital desk, a former student. I seemed to remember her from a lot of places, appearing in different moments of my life. I wasn't sure if she had ever been a waitress at Alice's Restaurant. Or maybe she had been a waitress there many years before. Or I had just imagined her being a waitress there. Or was it Naomi who had been my waitress—or was Naomi's real name, Noel?

One of them, I remembered—it was either Naomi or Noel—had told me a story about waitressing in a diner and how she'd loved it so much. Except all of the men were old and unattractive and demanding. I remembered she'd told me that sometimes she had a girlish dream. It was a daydream in which a kind, handsome stranger walked in from some faraway place and, instead of moving on at the end of his meal, he stayed with her—just for a few days at first, and then longer. He continued coming in to have lunch and they talked through the afternoons, her tapping her notepad with her pen, shifting from foot to foot. Sometimes they would eat fries off his plate, dipping them into deep pools of ketchup, and he would tell her that the sunlight clung to her hair as if she were a saint in an old painting. I thought I remembered Naomi telling me that. It had been in the evening at the hotel, just before everything became inhibited and strange. We were sitting on the bed, and her story reminded me of Abbott and Lucille. I had imagined myself there, and I saw that whole life with her. I offered her a cigarette. Or maybe I had been telling her the story of Abbott and Lucille and she said she had imagined me.

When I picked up the letter to read more, I noticed the words had begun to ripple across the page. Entire sentences began to form into waves and then the waves grew bigger, as if a storm was blowing in from off at sea and sweeping across the page. Soon great waves began forming and they curled up and broke at the shoreline of the right margin and sent entire paragraphs spraying off the page and onto the table. I put the letter down and lit a cigarette and inhaled deeply and tried to figure out what was going on with my brain. The cigarette tasted strange, like iodine, or maybe Band-Aids. The smoke left my lungs and hung in the air, moved away and circled back to me, formed a little gray universe that pulled me in. I saw Abbott there, his face, Buddha-like, sitting cross-legged on a cushion as if floating among clouds. He was reciting a sutra, something about love and loss. He was explaining that there were people who belonged to other worlds but got stuck in this one. Then I saw him shifting gears and I knew he was driving a car, a copper-colored Pontiac Firebird just like the one Jim Rockford used to drive in *The Rockford Files*. He was coming for me, he said. He was going to show me the world I couldn't see.

I sat with Abbott and listened for a while and then I heard plates clinking together, breakfast steaks being cut, the scraping of steel on ceramic, and I was back in the diner. My cigarette was burned out in the ashtray. All the words of Abbott's pages were spilled across the table, individual letters strewn like the bones of broken ships washed ashore from the sea. The storm had passed. The page was now blank and tranquil. I picked up my napkin to wipe all the words into my hand, thinking I would put them in my pocket and piece them together later. But as soon as I lifted the napkin, I understood the reason my brain was behaving so badly.

"Don't drink the coffee!" the napkin said. It was written out in big letters in blue pen, and it was followed by another suggestion: "Leave! Right away!"

43

Later, they would try to convince me that I collapsed on the floor at Alice's Restaurant, but not much of anything they said was true. I stood up at my table, strolled toward the bathroom, made a casual left toward the exit, and walked out the door as if it was the most natural thing in the world. Once I'd made it halfway down a side street, I began to run. I bolted until I came out onto a wide boulevard. Then I crossed the sidewalk and waved my hand from the curb. A cab skidded to a halt and hit its horn. I asked to go directly to the hospital.

"You got it," the driver said. He turned and winked at me. For a moment I thought I recognized him, but I couldn't place his face.

"Emergency?" he asked. "Or just visiting?" He must've noticed I was out of breath.

"Both," I said.

"I gotcha," he said. He stepped on the gas and weaved around a block of stopped traffic in the bike lane that hadn't yet been cleared of snow. Once he had rejoined the flow of traffic he turned and winked again. "Sometimes it's one thing or the other and sometimes it's both. Am I right?"

"I guess," I said. I was still trying to place him. "You look familiar. Have we met before?"

"I've got one of those faces," he said. He glanced at me in the rearview mirror and gave me another wink. "Everyone feels like they know me."

I used to feel like I had one of those faces—I was always being told I looked like a cousin, a son, an actor who was rarely a leading man. The comparisons were never flattering. I studied the driver's face in the rearview while the car jerked to this side and that, the driver glancing in the side-mirrors, head-checking over one shoulder then the other, the cab drifting in and out of traffic as though the whole world was lost in a dream, stuck in a current deep below the surface of a cold, calm river, and we were a rock dipping in and skipping across the surface. He spun the wheel and the car drifted sideways through an intersection with traffic stopped on four sides, pedestrians ready on the curb, standing in the morning snow, waiting for the command to walk. It was only as he skidded to a halt at the hospital entrance that I realized who he was.

"Lenny?" I said. I handed him a few bills. "Harelip Lenny!"

"Nope. Just one of those faces," he said, "But nobody's ever accused me of having a harelip."

"No," I said, "That's not—Harelip Lenny doesn't have a harelip either."

"I gotcha," he said. "You need change?"

"Keep the change," I said.

"You were in a rush?" he said, "Right?"

He was right. I got out of the car. The effects of whatever they put in my coffee were coming on stronger now and I wasn't one hundred percent sure the driver was Harelip Lenny anyway. I shut the door and the driver gave me a little salute and drifted out of the lot, his car fishtailing into the main road and then jumping ahead of the flow of traffic again like before, a flat stone skipping across a slow-moving river.

I managed to find my way up to Denton's room through halls that seemed endless, too slanted, too narrow, too high, but almost immediately upon entering I wondered why I was there. Everything was the same with him. Same beeps. Same clicks. Same forced breathing rhythm. The room had the feel of a place that was the opposite of where something momentous would occur. It struck me as a place where nothing would ever change, where negative inertia had reached an eternal nadir. I knew that sort of place. It could've been my little room above the garage, my writing desk, the home I'd bought with my first advance and then impotently allowed to collapse into arrears. Each beep could've been a day of my life sitting in front of a blank page, each breath, an unwritten chapter.

I looked at Denton's body, nearly motionless. The only signs of passing time were the darkening beard on his face, the length of his fingernails, the minuscule deepening of the wrinkles around his eyes. He struck me as a painfully symbolic figure. He was a man who might never do another meaningful thing, a character stuck in a book that stretched ahead with blank pages. But for some reason we all pretended he was alive and right on the cusp of rebirth.

If they hadn't put LSD in my coffee, who knows what I would've done. But I was standing there with the feeling that I was being pursued, that they might burst into the room at any moment and drag me off for reeducation, or whatever you want to call it—as they did later. Under normal circumstances, I'm sure I would've done what I usually do. I wouldn't have done anything. I would've sat down in the chair and thought it over, waited for clarity. But my mind was muddled with LSD, and compounded by a sense of panic and confusion. I could feel Abbott getting closer, almost hear him in my head. An idea kept rising up, this idea that I wasn't David Wilson or Daniel Wilder, but that I was actually Denton White. I was having this delusion that I was the third man, the dark character, and that Denton was the first and best version of myself. He was the David Wilson that I'd left behind, the hopeful kid, the one that had fallen in love and written "The First Chapter."

Somehow I had Denton confused with something that was dying inside of myself, the person I'd been struggling to startle back to awareness for my entire adult life. I looked at him in that bed with his life passing by in absolute uselessness, possessed only of the meaning that others bestowed on him, aging without creating anything, what legacy he might've once had fading into obscurity. I looked at his body—old, atrophied, helpless, neglected—and it struck me that Denton White was a figment of my imagination. He may have also been a man in his own right—I wasn't certain about that part—but he was also somehow a manifestation of a discarded piece of my psyche. When I looked at him, I was ashamed. What had become of this part of myself which had once, even for the length of a single chapter, been so alive and even on fire? He and I had become pathetic together and we both needed a jolt, something to shock us back to life.

My next move, as they say, practically wrote itself. I spotted a defibrillator mounted on the wall behind the bed and I remembered the ECT at the institution and the electric stimulation that Doctor Sharpe had performed at Rose's house. Instantaneously I put together why Abbott had written me about all those things. I was here to revive

Denton White. Abbott had appeared, just as I first suspected he had, to wake the part of myself that could return my life to its proper path. But Abbott could only lead me to this place. He could only show me what had become of the self that had once held all my youthful dreams and visions. I had to choose the path I'd travel on my own. Now, after twenty years of beating around the bush, I was ready to do just that.

I pulled the defibrillator off the wall and switched it on. I heard a voice giving me instructions, telling me to call for help, prepare the patient. I thought I'd gone insane for a moment but it was only the defibrillator speaking with an automated voice to walk me through the steps. I switched it out of automated mode and the voice stopped. I set the current at the highest setting, slobbered some jelly on Denton's temples, hit the charge button, shoved a wad of gauze in Denton's mouth, and let it fire. His whole body straightened, toes curling back, eyes bulging out, and the next moment he looked completely relaxed, as peaceful as a man could be. It was just for that one moment, and then the chaos started. Alarms went off. I hit the charge button and shocked him one more time before the door flew open. Doreen rushed in followed by five or six other people. They told me to leave the room, and it seemed like the best thing to do.

Out in the hall, I felt suddenly lost, out of place. I looked around for some sort of sign that would tell me what to do next, give me instructions like the defibrillator had been trying to do for me in the room. At the end of the hall, a shadow caught my eye, moving across the wall like a big finger gesturing me to follow. I walked toward it. Then I heard my name and I turned. It was a nurse, calling to a colleague, but beyond her I saw that the elevator was rising to our floor, the numbers above it counting upward. I headed down the hall

341

and stood facing the doors. When they opened, Abbott was standing in front of me, his hands in the pockets of his leather bomber jacket, a pair of aviator sunglasses hanging from his zipper at his neckline. I thought he looked good, remarkably good. He was a few pounds lighter than the last time I'd seen him. In better shape. There didn't seem to be as much salt in his hair.

"There you are," he said. He let out a laugh, a musical little Thomas Magnum number which, for a moment, made everything feel like it was going to be okay. He'd had a hunch he was going to run into me, he explained, a faint, internal voice that had told him just where to find me. "Kid," he said, and I didn't listen to the rest of the sentence. A wave of emotion was surging through me, washing away months of ennui, washing away years.

"Abbott," I said, "I might've done something bad... We have to go."

His eyebrows raised and then he put a finger to his lips as though to tell me to remain silent. I heard the sound of footsteps running up behind me, my head jerked back, and then it slammed forward into the closing elevator doors.

44

I t was during my initial interrogation that I began to understand an anomaly of human behavior that I'd previously thought outrageous—the false confession. There was no Denton, they told me, no Abbott. There was no telephone at the diner, no warning about drugged coffee written on a napkin, no letters at the summer cabin I had apparently, according to them, broken into and pillaged. I reached into my pocket to show them the loose letters that had washed off the page and there was only a blank piece of paper. They claimed that I'd been sitting alone, talking to myself in the booth of a Salt Lake City diner. There was no telephone at the table and certainly no smoking allowed. This was second millennium America after all. Those days were gone for good. When I started ranting about conspiracies, I'd frightened the other diners. After the waitress asked me several times to lower my voice and extinguish my cigarette, the police and an ambulance were called.

"I walked out," I insisted. My memory was clear on that detail. I had carefully tried not to draw attention to myself when I left the diner. I told them that.

"You were trying *not* to draw attention?" one of them said. I could see them waiting for me to find the irony, but the irony was contingent on me believing I was ranting to myself like a lunatic for the better part of an hour before having some sort of seizure at the table. I wasn't buying it.

Our differences of opinion continued to accumulate. Every time I thought the list was complete, some other fact would fall into dispute and the gulf between my reality and theirs would broaden. They had found no notes in the cabin, they claimed, there was no record of any online dating, no fake ID. I supposed that meant there was no Naomi either, no long series of women in their thirties left disappointed with broken hearts. I wouldn't have minded if history could've absolved me of that part.

"Okay," I said. "Well, can you tell me what I've been up to for the past eight months?"

That's where their story really began to ask for a level of indulgence. I'd "been unwell," they said. There was a woman in the room and two bald men. The woman told me this part, speaking in a delicate, patronizing way. She talked as though the truth were an infant and it was sleeping peacefully in the room with us and she didn't want to startle it awake. She asked me the last thing I remembered. I told her I'd seen Abbott in the elevator.

"But there is no Abbott," she said. "Remember?"

I looked at her. That wasn't the way I remembered it, but I didn't argue. I wanted to know where their story was going.

"Okay…" I said. I told her the last thing I remembered was visiting Denton White in the hospital.

The three of them looked at each other. It was that look that people exchange when they have to break some bad news.

"Oh god," I said. "He's dead, isn't he? I killed him."

"Relax," the smaller of the two bald men said, "He's not dead."

"He's okay?" I said. "Is he awake? Is he speaking?"

"David," the woman said.

For some reason, I kept looking at her hair.

"You're confused. You're not well."

Her hair was short and the texture and cut was like a man's. I began to wonder if it was a wig chosen from a closet of disguises—not a good choice for her. Or maybe it had been the only choice, the one wig in a closet of disguises that was shared among the three of them. Chivalry had dictated that the men remain bald.

The woman continued her story, delicately, like before, like it was a hot beverage that was overfull and she had to carry it across the room and hand it to me without spilling a drop. Some of it was familiar. I'd been under a lot of stress, she said. She mentioned Laura and I winced a little at hearing that name coming out of her mouth. I don't know why. Maybe I hoped she'd tell me I'd imagined that part too, that Laura hadn't left, that she still loved me, that she was waiting for me in the other room. I might have been more inclined to believe a story like that, but the most painful parts of my life remained as I remembered them, so there was really no incentive to take her at her word. I didn't see any point in switching horses midstream.

Even the way she told it, I still hadn't written a thing in over twenty years, nothing "satisfactory" anyway, which was the way it was written in my contract. I had been using small doses of LSD to stimulate my mind and finish my novel, she said. It was a delicate suggestion, a cautious step.

Yes, I told her. That much was true. "Micro-doses," I corrected her, "a few micrograms here and there. I needed to do something,"

I explained. Finishing the novel was my only hope of saving my marriage. What was I supposed to do?"

"Desperate times. Am I right?" the bigger of the two bald men said.

I looked down at my hands. I knew it was just an effect of light and shadow but they looked like they had blood on them. I pressed my right thumb into my left palm and it felt wet. I was probably sweating, but my mind was addled and I couldn't stop thinking about the blood on my hands, even just the metaphor of blood on my hands. It must've been my way of confronting the human cost of wanting to be a writer, the way relationships suffered and the people I drew close to me always got hurt. Wasn't that what it was? I couldn't stop looking at my hands. I didn't want to have blood on my hands anymore. I wanted to wash them and dry them and just walk away from the whole thing, but I had nowhere to walk to. The bridges were burned behind me. Abbott had been my bridge ahead and I had no idea where he was or if he was even real. I looked at my hands again. Finally, I presented my palms above the table.

"Is there blood on my hands?" I asked.

"Metaphorically?" the bigger man asked.

I looked up and he was still bald. I don't know why I thought that might have changed.

"No blood," he said. "You got lucky, David."

"Lucky?" I asked.

"Nobody got hurt," he said.

"I know that," I said.

But I also knew it wasn't exactly true. Everyone in my life eventually got hurt, emotionally speaking. I looked down, then away from my hands.

The woman spoke again—soothing, the same way as before. "David," she said, "We all know this has been hard on you."

I wondered what part she meant. The twenty years of writer's block? The divorce? The loss of my home and job? All that lonely time hiding out at the cabin and all the failures at romance that she said hadn't happened? The LSD in my coffee? Being arrested or whatever this was, and not knowing which end was up anymore? Or maybe she just meant all of it has been hard—my entire time on the planet and the outlook of getting old and never really accomplishing anything. For a moment I entertained the idea that this was my final reckoning and this room was my own pathetic manifestation of Saint Peter standing at the pearly gates.

"You're not well," she said again.

"I'm not well?" I said.

I wondered why she kept on saying that. I was fine. It was just that someone had put LSD in my coffee and I'd hit my head on the steel door of an elevator. I wondered if I should argue her assertion, but then I remembered Abbott putting his finger to his lips, and I decided it was probably better if I said nothing.

45

Once they realized I wasn't going to buy into their story, they moved me to a little cell with no windows. The lights turned off and I spent the time lying alone in the dark while sounds echoed through the building and filled me with apprehension. I kept nodding off and waking up thinking I'd bitten off my own tongue so that I couldn't be compelled to speak. My saliva would taste of blood and my tongue didn't feel right in my mouth. I'd panic and have to whisper a tongue twister several times to reassure myself that my tongue was still there. "She sells seashells down by the seashore," I'd whisper, and I'd see the image of a beautiful young Polynesian woman walking down the beach with a basket full of shells resting against her hip. It would calm me, and then I'd nod off and wake up thinking about my tongue again.

Then the lights fluttered on and I sat up and waited—I don't know for what or for how long. The lights were big fluorescent tubes. They buzzed and clicked and flickered like they were irritated with me, constantly threatening to go dark or get much brighter. I sat up, cross-legged, trying to focus past it all, trying to bring my mind back to Abbott and visualize him coming for me the way I'd imagined it in the restaurant, to hear his voice telling me how to escape and where he would wait for me, but I couldn't focus. The tube lighting kept distracting me, making every moment feel like an eternity of wandering around on dark, winding roads that always returned me to the previous moment, and I'd start struggling to focus again.

Eventually, they came and led me out of my cell and back to the room. They sat me down at the table and the smaller bald man pointed to the empty surface and asked if I wanted to call my mother. I think he was trying to humiliate me. Or maybe he expected me to see a phone on the table. Maybe he wanted me to dial the phone that wasn't there, as if I were a mime, and speak to the imaginary voice of my mother about all my deepest secrets so they could gather information for their grand inquisition, or capture video to certify my insanity in a courtroom. Maybe he was just having fun with me. But I don't think he got the reaction he wanted. I just sat there thinking about how much cruelty some people have in their hearts.

"No?" he said. "You don't want to talk to your mother today?"

I shook my head.

He pulled out a chair and sat down across from me and folded his hands on the table. We studied each other for a few moments.

"Where are we today, David? A diner? A mountain cabin? Riding through the mountains in a fast car?"

I watched the light flicker on his bald head.

The Ferrari wasn't actually fast. It just looked fast. Of course, I didn't expect him to understand the metaphor.

"Are we still remaining silent?" he said.

I answered him by saying nothing.

"We've still got the better part of twenty-four hours," he said. "It might seem shorter if we talk." He took a package of Wrigley's

Spearmint Gum out of his pocket and folded a piece into his mouth and I thought about his teeth clamping down again and again, just barely missing his tongue. He offered me a piece and I shook my head.

"Why don't you tell me about this Abbott character," he said. He had this look, all three of them did—ghoulish and dead inside like vampires.

The smaller bald man continued asking questions, but even in that room the tube lighting made it hard to focus. My mind kept flying off to other places. I was in the institution with Abbott, watching as he held onto his version of reality for two years under constant pressure from Doctor Schlotzsky. I was in the jungle with Denton, covered in dioxin-laden leaves and camouflage. I was sitting by the air-conditioner with Ray Cook. I was in Rose's kitchen with young Henry Sharpe. I was in the pinball hall watching Tasha play. Sometimes I was with Laura in our new home, pot lids rattling on the stovetop, dinner sizzling in a cast iron pan, and everything looked hopeful. Then I'd come back and there'd be more questions.

Finally, I found myself walking along those dark roads that went nowhere again, but this time Abbott was walking alongside me. I heard his footsteps, and that one chipped wheel, humming and clicking over and over again. He was talking about a brainwashing experiment done at Harvard in the sixties by the CIA. I wasn't listening closely. I couldn't focus. I was thinking about my own problems, wondering if I should part ways with him or risk being infected by his insanity. This brainwashing technique, he was saying, it was supposed to target and dissolve the most deeply held beliefs of its subjects. It was supposed to make blank slates on which the government could write their own stories. It was like the way a round of powerful antibiotics clears the intestines for colonization by fresh parasites. On some people, the technique worked, but other times the ideas survived and were driven deeper. The ideas dug in their heels and became more virile, like an antibiotic-resistant superbug. "Imagine this," he said. "Imagine seeing the same ideas you thought you annihilated thirty years before, refined and expanded and published as a 35,000-word manifesto in the *New York Times* and penned by the hand of a terrorist."

He went on, ranting for some time, explaining that the experiment had later been perfected and had become the template for a beta version which was much more subtle and effective, acting with the power of a thousand targeted vaccines, and that these inoculations were happening right in front of our faces on a moment-by-moment basis every time we glanced at our phones. "The internet is destroying the internet," he said. And then he told me that when I found myself among vampires, I should be careful not to ever tell them what I believe. He said it was the blood they lived by.

When I came back to consciousness of the room, the small bald man was gone and the woman was sitting in front of me, talking with that voice that carried an overfull drink. She kept telling me I wasn't well and that I should really tell them more about "this Abbott character." She said it that way—"character." They all did. She told me if I talked about him, they could help me. What did Abbott think of all this, she wanted to know. Did I have plans to meet him somewhere?

For a while, I just sat there looking at her hair, then she left the room and the bigger bald man came in. He spoke to me like I was an elementary school student and he was the principal. It started out as though I'd done something bad but I was still a good kid and it wasn't my fault, and gradually transformed into one of those talks where I was going to have to face the music for my own good. If I hadn't been committed to silence, I would've told him I understood his frustration. I'd had similar conversations with myself thousands of times with no results. But I didn't speak. I just sat there while he played the bad music I had to face, note by note.

Some of it sounded familiar. He told me I'd left my university job in disgrace—true enough. Stolen money from a scholarship fund—yep. I was being sued by my publisher—I remembered that too. Then he said I'd had a mental breakdown after Laura left. He asked me if I remembered starting a fire at the university, right in the center of the quad.

That got my attention.

A bonfire of books, all with their first chapters torn out—did that jog my memory?

It did sound like me.

"Leaping through flames stark raving naked," he said. "Did I remember that? No? Well maybe some things are better left forgotten," he said.

Regardless, I didn't see what he was all hung up about. It made me think about what a long way we'd come since Woodstock with its naked bodies playing and copulating in the mud by the thousands, mad as hatters, everyone united by the same truth, and not a single bald man among them.

"No?" he said. "No bells?" He cleared his throat and told me it would be easier if I talked to them. "Let's start with this Abbott character," he said.

I looked down at my hands and they were just my hands. There was no blood. I studied them to try to find a trace of blood, but there was nothing, not even around the fingernails. They wouldn't prey on my conscience anymore. I just needed to hold fast to the truth and not say a word about Abbott. I knew if they could get me to start talking about Abbott, the truth would bleed out of me until there was nothing left.

46

I don't remember if they ever brought me before a judge. Maybe I sat before one without even realizing it. At some point, they shook me awake and loaded me in a van and moved me to a different facility. I sat down at a table in another little room and they brought me some lukewarm coffee. Then they paraded a few people through and each asked me more or less the same questions. Did I know where I'd been? Where I was? Why I was here? What could I tell them about Abbott? I kept my silence and at the end of it all, they moved me to another little room with a bed and a small window that at least helped me keep track of time.

I had nothing to do but watch the light change all day. Sometimes they brought a tray with food and cranberry juice and a little ketchup cup full of pills that they watched me pretend to swallow. Then the lights went off and I had a break from the buzz and flicker and the sounds would be more occasional. A voice or two moved by to the beat of footsteps, or a shout was followed by the sound of running. Now and then I even heard laughter or a faint melody I couldn't quite identify.

After several nights like that, Laura came to visit me. She brought in a chair and set it down by my bed right in the path of the morning sun and she was the one who finally got me to speak. I talked to her while I ate oatmeal and sipped cranberry juice. It was like old times, like those early days before we had ever been divorced, those days when my one completed short story was a critical success and we'd just bought our house with my advance on *The First Chapter*.

"Remember how we lived off the advance," I said, "and how I sat by that window above the garage every day and never could write more than a sentence into the second chapter?"

I laughed out loud, happy for the first time in what seemed like months, but she only smiled—sadly I thought. I reminded her of how we used to sit and have coffee, how we might play a game of rummy or fool around a little before I taught my morning class. But Laura didn't think we should be talking about that. She wanted to talk about Abbott and why I'd been determined to help him find Lucille.

"It was just one day," I told her. "Then there were the letters, but we never found Lucille. Not yet. I mean, I'm waiting for him. We will."

"And Denton?"

"Quickfoot?" I said. "I don't know what became of him either. They say he's not dead, but they also say he never existed. Who knows? Do I exist, Laura? Do you?"

"What do you think the truth is, David?"

I told Laura I thought the truth was that she only loved me for my first chapter, and that she'd only left me because she wanted to read my first chapter over again, but this time she wanted other chapters to follow. I told her that it's hard to write a second chapter when the first chapter is so perfect.

She tapped her pen on the spiral notebook resting atop her crossed leg. "It's Doctor Nichols," she corrected me.

I thought about that name—Doctor Nichols. It had been so long since I'd heard her maiden name that now it seemed completely foreign to me. I'd forgotten how much I liked the sound of it—Laura Nichols.

"You're a doctor now?" I said. "I'm so proud of you. My mother didn't tell me that part." I moved forward on my bed and reached for her hand but she pulled it away. "Have you told my mother where I am?"

"We're going to let you make phone calls soon," she said. "Maybe you should call her yourself."

"We?" I asked. The way she said that alarmed me. "You work here? You're one of them?"

"I'll be your therapist," she said. "We'll be seeing each other every morning. How does that sound?"

I nodded my head.

"Good?" she asked.

"Yes." I nodded again.

Good," she said.

It occurred to me what a coincidence that was. I could remember my mother telling me that Laura had taken a job at a facility somewhere out west. I could remember that moment exactly—where I was standing in the road, Abbott cursing at his prostate, my phone ruining my night vision. What were the chances that I would end up in Laura's care all these months later? I wondered if she had been sent here by Abbott to help me escape, but it didn't seem like a possible thing to plan so far in advance. I struggled for a few moments, but I couldn't make sense of it so I let it go.

I was just happy to be with Laura again. I reminded her how I used to take that first chapter apart sentence by sentence and comma by comma like an antique clock full of intricate gears and dials, and how every time I put it back together it was the exact same chapter. I laughed, but she only smiled sadly again and asked if I could tell her more about Abbott.

Had she ever heard of Boris Schlotzsky, I asked her.

She looked at me like maybe I should stay on topic.

"Doctor Schlotzsky," I said. "He was a doctor, like you."

"Yes," she said.

"You've heard of him?"

"No," she said, "I meant, yes, go on."

"He used to work in a facility like this, back in the early seventies. He was a Freudian. Maybe you could look him up."

"David," she said, "Do you know what year it is?"

"2019," I said, "I'm not crazy, Laura."

"David," she said.

"I'm sorry," I said. Then I corrected myself. "I mean, I'm not crazy, Doctor Nichols."

"Thank you, David."

"Schlotzsky was Abbott's doctor," I said.

"So Abbott was also a mental patient?"

"Yes," I said, "From October of 1972 until May of 1975. In a facility in Nevada called Ella Rawson. Maybe it still exists."

"And then he was released?"

"He was never even crazy, Laura. He was just sad. He went back through time and left his wife behind."

Laura straightened in her chair. She uncrossed and recrossed her legs.

"I mean, Doctor Nichols," I said, "Abbott was never crazy."

"So he was sad because his wife left him? You mean he remained stuck in the past?" she asked.

"She didn't leave him," I said. "He was catapulted back through time and he got stuck living his life over and trying to catch up with her. She was probably looking for him too."

"That must've been confusing for him," she said. "For both of them."

"He never got over it," I said. "He's still looking for her."

"Tell me more about that," she said.

I was suspicious about what she was doing. She could've been working for them, trying to get me to spill the beans so they could track Abbott down and stop him from ever reuniting with Lucille. But I thought it more likely that she wanted me to talk about Abbott because she thought it was my own mad way of talking about myself, about us, about my feelings for her. She was listening even though I could tell she thought I'd made the whole thing up. She probably believed I was a little insane, but I wondered if she might also be impressed, because if I had made everything up, at least it was a pretty good story. Even the way we were meeting again like this was a good story. She wanted to cure me, to make me well again. It was such a romantic turn of events that I couldn't resist her questions.

I was also wondering if Laura might be giving me another chance. I thought she might be putting her faith in me as a writer again. I remembered how I'd watched her get into the car below my writing desk that last time, how I'd sat there at the window with the computer screen heavenly white and the cursor blinking below those two words at the top of the page. I remembered how impossible it was to move, how painful it was to watch her pack her bags into that little Toyota I'd bought for her with my first advance, and I remembered how the Toyota seemed to take her away from me under its own power, as though the Toyota was making her decisions for her, because Laura would not have left me like that, glued to my seat and stuck at the beginning of my second chapter. Laura was supposed to encourage me and be my muse.

I knew Doctor Nichols wouldn't want to discuss any of that. She wanted me to talk about Abbott. But I thought there might be more to it than that. She had me thinking about those last frustrating years at my writing desk above the garage, about my progressively bad temper, my depression, my drinking, and the desperately increasing micro-doses of LSD. I could remember how I'd watched her lose faith in me over the years, how she'd loved me for that beautiful first chapter and how there had never been a second. I kept thinking about those two painful words that were on the page the day she left. They were the same two words I wrote every morning. After a cup of hot coffee and two or three cigarettes, I would open the file, position the cursor precisely one-third of the way down the page, center the text, and after eleven taps and a couple of carriage returns those two words would be there haunting me for the remainder of the day.

47

I n the mornings, they let me leave my room to meet with Laura. In the afternoons, when everyone went out for exercise, I stayed in. I watched reruns on the TV in the common room, or I used the computers at the small table in the corner of bookshelves they liked to call a library. I researched the strange things that Abbott told me and that my mother said could be true. Many of them did turn out to be true. There was a giant thermometer in Baker, California. Mysterious rocks moved across the flats of Death Valley. The CIA had run brainwashing experiments using LSD. I even found a group of people who claimed that, as part of these experiments, they had been trained in something called remote viewing. Their consciousness would travel through space and time, though their bodies remained firmly fixed in place. I bookmarked the websites and forums to share with my mother when they finally stopped blocking me from sending out email. Laura kept telling me that would be sooner rather than later, but what I'd begun to notice was that time in the institution didn't have its usual flow, and I had no gauge for what sooner rather than later meant. I wasn't even sure whether I could discern the difference between the two anymore. If it turned out to be later rather than sooner, I wouldn't even have anything to be upset about.

In the evenings, I stretched out on the bed in my little room, and I thought about my new life as a captive storyteller. It was much like the life Abbott had described during the time he and Denton and Doctor Schlotzsky had been together, and that wasn't lost on me. I would lay there and watch the light fade and remember all those years I spent sitting above the garage. I was a captive storyteller in those days too, captivated by the blank page, by my own ambition, by the fervent idealism that demanded I write the truth. And yet I was also a captive audience—captivated by all the whisperings of the outside world. I read and reread those initial reviews even as the years passed into decades. Somehow I expected them to show me the way forward, to reveal myself to me so that I could reflect back to the world the story they thought I should write.

Those evenings, as the light in the room changed without the room itself changing, this one thought would always cycle through my head. The thought was that while I was no longer above the garage or lying alone at Abbott's cabin, the little internal room that imprisoned me remained eternally the same. Only time and space and light had changed. It was just as Abbott once said—every time has its own signature, its own light, its own sounds. The world changes around us, but the struggles at the very core of us remain eternally unchanged.

I didn't think that was something I could talk about in therapy. In a nutshell, it was the reason Laura and I were no longer together. No matter how much I loved her, I could never change the thing about myself that made a future with me impossible. I worried that I was and always would be a man trapped in his first chapter, a character imprisoned by a narrow trope, a predetermined narrative structure as though I were the star of my own TV procedural. Each episode of my life would follow the same arc—only with a new client or a new lover or a new little room. It was a circle, really, and I'd become a man not unlike David Banner or Thomas Magnum or Kwai Chang Caine. I was left sailing back and forth across my own flat earth with no ability to write myself beyond the icy tower of the fourth wall.

Unless I counted Laura as a visitor—and Doctor Nichols made it pretty clear that I should think about our relationship as a professional one—I saw only one person from my outside life once they gave me visiting privileges. Jack McGee began flying out to visit once a month. Jack always visited on Sundays. But because every day at the institution was roughly the same, and because Jack always called on the Sundays of the month when he didn't visit, I came to think of Sundays as McGee Day. In the same way we had a pizza day and a movie night every week to create the illusion that we weren't all living the same day over and over again, I had a McGee Day to remind me that I had a past and that there was a life outside the fences waiting for me if I would only give in and see things the way my imprisoning audience wanted me to.

When Laura first walked into my room, I thought she had come to help me cross a gestalt and move us toward a future together. But I began to suspect that things had become more serious between her and the memoirist and Laura had already moved on apart from me. She was Doctor Nichols now. She didn't seem to like me bringing up our past together. Sometimes she told me that if I insisted on calling her Laura and treating her like my wife, she was going to have to stop treating me as my therapist, but she never followed through on that no matter how many times she threatened me. Finally, when she saw that her threats weren't working, she tried something different. Whenever I began talking about us, she would direct our conversation back toward Abbott and all the characters that inhabited his letters.

Laura became obsessed with Abbott's stories. When I was optimistic, I wanted to believe she was trying to show me that I had a way to move on with my novel. I thought she was leaving breadcrumbs to show me the way back to her heart. When I was pessimistic, my old suspicion set in again. I'd wonder if she was working with the two bald men and the woman with the cooing voice and the man's hair, and that her job was to extract the information I wouldn't give to them. In any case, because it seemed to please Laura, I shared my stories about Abbott and the contents of the letters with her freely. Though as a point of caution and to protect Abbott, I always made sure to obscure certain elements by adding my own artistic flourishes to some events and couching others in metaphor. I knew Abbott had done similar things to protect his memory of Lucille when he finally agreed to speak of her to Boris Schlotzsky.

It began to seem like everyone was interested in Abbott. When McGee visited, we sat like elementary school children at a Formica table in the common room. He could barely contain his excitement.

"Tell me about this Abbott character," he said.

By that time, the lawsuit over my advance had been adjudicated in my absence and it hadn't worked out as badly for Jack as it had for me.

I was liable for the full amount, with compounding interest, including the fifteen percent Jack had pocketed when he made the deal twenty years before, and he was liable for nothing. If we wanted, we were now free to sell my book all over again.

I was happy for McGee. He was one of my few remaining friends and I wouldn't have wanted him to suffer. Good for him that he wasn't legally insane and in debt. Good for him that he was free to walk out through the front door after our visits with no worry that a world of his own invention would come crashing down on his head. I'm not talking sour grapes either. I knew I had no one to blame for my problems but myself, but it still smarted to feel that in every aspect of life I was being left to play the patsy. It had gone that way in my divorce with Laura, and it had gone that way in my relationship with Abbott, and now with McGee. Everyone else's life seemed to hit obstacles, recover, and then continue forward uninhibited, while my tires just seemed to spin in place, sinking deeper and deeper into the mud.

When I tried to explain that to McGee, he said I was looking at things all wrong.

"This judgment is a godsend, David!" he said. "Now we can sell your book to another publisher." It was just the sort of publicity we needed to resell my book for a larger advance, he explained. "This little detour"—that's the way he was talking about my time at the lunatic asylum—"is going to put you back on the literary map, David."

"Oh?" I said.

He looked at my face and sobered a bit and remembered to ask me how I was doing, but he didn't have the patience to wait for an answer. He couldn't contain himself. He smelled redemption and god knows we both needed it.

"David," he said. This is the best thing that could've happened to us. You think Pirsig would've sold *Zen* if he hadn't been completely loony tunes?"

I didn't know the answer to that one. Pirsig was a legitimate genius, not some old mope who'd driven himself crazy with self-pity. And, more importantly, Pirsig had a book to sell. That was my take.

"We don't have a book to sell," I said.

"But we do, David," he said. "We *do*."

"We do?"

He looked at me and shook his head. "I've been talking with your mother this whole time. Has she been telling you?"

"I've heard about it," I said.

"We think you might have a story here. Don't you see? It's fallen right into your lap. This whole Abbott thing—it's just what your book needs."

"You believe me about Abbott?" I asked him.

"It doesn't matter if I believe you, David," he said.

I tried not to be hurt by his deflection, but I had to look away.

"Your mother believes you," he said. He reached across the table and clutched my hand. "Can you make *readers* believe you?"

I considered the question. I wondered if Doctor Nichols believed me. I hadn't thought to ask her. Maybe I didn't want to know. I was actually surprised that my mother still believed me. They'd started letting me speak with her on the phone now and then, but she hadn't been able to come to see me at the institution. She told me it was because of the long flight and her deep vein thrombosis, and she said she would come as soon as her blood thinners did their work and she was cleared to fly. "If my doctor doesn't give me a clean bill of health in

365

a week or two, I'm just going to come anyway," she said. But my guilty conscience got the better of me and I began to wonder if she was a little upset with me for keeping the truth from her, or even embarrassed to have an institutionalized son.

It didn't help that as the weeks went on, McGee would tell me of his visits with her and it sounded like she hadn't really faced the facts. As a way of reassuring my mother, McGee had told her that a lot of great writers had spent time in mental institutions, and she ran with it. She was telling her uppity friends that I was at a fancy writer's retreat and that my novel was sure to be a best seller. By that time, I'd made the mistake of talking with her about my preliminary research on some of the details of Abbott's story. I'd mentioned some of the things I might want to write about, and now when my mother and I talked on the phone, all she wanted to talk about was my book and if I was finally going to finish it after all these years. She wanted to know how much I was writing and how close was I to finishing and to be sure I would remember my father and her in my dedication. She asked if I could send her some chapters.

"Ma," I'd say, "I'm just getting started again."

"You're always just getting started, David. You've spent your whole life just getting started."

I explained that they only let me use the computer for an hour a day, and the institution's computers were complete junk, always freezing up and crashing. But even that was a lie—they had actually cut off all my computer privileges and I wasn't writing anything.

"How am I supposed to get anything done?" I said.

"An hour a day?" She was absolutely flummoxed. "What kind of writer's retreat is this anyway, David? Why are you sharing someone else's computer?"

"Ma," I said.

"You're a writer, David. Shouldn't you have your own computer?"

At moments like that, I'd ask her some questions to change the subject and she'd tell me all the little happenings in her own life. Stories about her and Elaine, like how Elaine had won tickets to a Celine Dion concert and my mother had warned her about driving at night but Elaine had gone anyway and because she couldn't see at night, she'd run her car right up on a curb in the middle of Boston and flattened all four tires. The stories were a good diversion for me. I had even less to talk about than she did. Every day I pretended to take a handful of pills to mark the morning and bedtime and midday. In between the pills, I went through the day's series of non-events that blurred together and passed out of memory almost as soon as they were experienced. I told her about it all: pizza day, movie night, McGee—and McGee was old news to her. She heard everything about me and McGee when he went over for coffee.

When I told her the truly interesting things—the coincidences and synchronicities that she was always so fond of when they occurred in her life—like about Laura being my therapist or how I thought the head nurse might've been the same woman from Abbott's story, and how I was worried she might be planning to take me away to a secondary location like she'd done to Denton, my mother would tell me to just stop it. "If you keep talking like that, David," she'd say, "people are going to think you're a crazy person!"

My mother made a good point. It was clear that if I was ever going to get out of the institution, I needed to learn what I could say straight-up and what I couldn't. And needed to learn another way to say the things that I needed to say but everyone else would think were crazy if I said them straight-up. That was probably what Abbott was warning me about when he'd put his finger to his lips at the elevator. Maybe that's what Doctor Nichols was trying to teach me too, by asking me to stop calling her Laura.

48

"You said you were a writer, didn't you, David," Laura said.

This was during one of our therapy sessions, maybe two weeks after McGee came in all hot about Abbott and the possibility of our redemption as writer and agent.

"I'm not sure if I was ever *really* a writer," I said.

"You don't remember?" she asked.

"That's not what I mean," I said. I laughed and told her that she must remember how it was. Nothing much had changed. My mother and McGee still believed I'd finish my novel. They never lost faith or let me forget that I was supposed to be a writer. "You still talk to my mother now and then, don't you, La—" I caught myself. "Don't you, Doctor Nichols?"

She remained silent—encouraging me, I thought, to continue.

What I remembered most, I told her, was not writing. I reminded her about "The First Chapter," and how that story kind of contained the theme that characterized my whole life. I told her that sometimes I worried that there was nothing more to me than one chapter, that I just wrote it over and over again and it never really changed. I'd never admitted that to Laura before and I was going to let it rest there. I didn't want either of us to have to revisit the pain and frustration of those years. I wasn't trying to place any blame. I understood that was why she left me and I wasn't upset with her anymore. But the silence in the room was awkward, so I went on.

I reminded her again about the little room above the garage and my desk by the window. I told her how I woke up there that last morning, how one of those roosters was crowing—the ones that drove us crazy that whole summer before she left. Did she remember, I asked. But she just sat there listening with her eyes all still and beautiful, so I kept talking. I told her about the little bird that was hopping in the driveway where she always used to park her car. How I knew she had left to help me finish my novel, but it still hurt and I had trouble getting over it. I told her how I'd watched the little bird fly up into a tree and I knew it would soon be time for me to go as well. I stopped talking and she still just sat there looking at me. I thought I saw love, actual love, in her eyes. I wanted to tell her I loved her too, but I knew she would think that was an inappropriate thing to say in therapy.

"What I mean," I said, "is that I don't know if all those years of not writing makes me much of a writer."

She looked relieved. "David," she said. I saw her pause to collect herself and get hold of her emotions. "What do you think would make you a writer?"

That was fairly simple, I said. I needed to write beyond one chapter. It was like Kwai Chang Caine said in *Kung Fu*. I just need to take the first step, then the next—put one foot in front of the other, one word after the last.

When Doctor Nichols said she didn't know who Kwai Chang Caine was, I reminded her about *Kung Fu* and about Abbott and Denton and Ella Rawson and even Schlotzsky and the head nurse.

Some of those stories even made her smile. I remembered what my mother said, so I didn't tell her that I suspected that the head nurse in her facility might be the very same person who once secreted Denton away under the pretense of romance. Instead, I told her about Abbott's Ferrari and his strange ideas about reality and how his Ferrari was supposed to remind him that his whole life was an illusion and that his real life was going on in some alternate dimension where he was still with Lucille.

"It's kind of sweet," I said, "Isn't it? "

She nodded.

But for me, I told her, I guess riding around in that fake Ferrari made me think about myself as a writer, and about "The First Chapter," which had all the appearances of being something literary but didn't have much under the hood. Not anything that I could find anyway—though we both knew I'd taken it apart and rebuilt it hundreds of times.

We sat there again in silence for a while, but I was deep in Abbott's world and she spoke first.

"Maybe you should write about your trip with Abbott," she said.

"You think so?" I said. It seemed like everyone kept telling me that same thing.

"It might be a good place to start, David. It might even be cathartic for you."

I thought about it, about my initial research on the asylum computers and McGee's strange confidence. It wasn't the first time it occurred to me that it was a good story. It was probably one of the reasons that, even now, I couldn't seem to let Abbott go. Everyone seemed to think it was a good story, and maybe everyone was right. It was better than anything I'd come up with over the last twenty years anyway.

"Okay," I said, "I'll try. But I'll need access to a computer. The head nurse says my privileges have been restricted."

"Yes, David, that's because whenever you get on a computer you start researching conspiracies. I don't think that's the healthiest thing for you."

I started to object and then I remembered what my mother had said and I stopped myself. At least Laura hadn't called them conspiracy *theories* this time. They weren't theories. MK-Ultra, Paperclip, Mockingbird, COINTELPRO: they were established historical facts, and I'd proved that to Laura many times.

"I'll stop doing that," I said.

She walked around her desk and reached down. I heard a drawer slide open. When she put down a spiral notebook and pulled out a pencil, I thought she was going to write a note for me to give to the head nurse, but she handed the pencil and notebook to me without writing anything at all. Just left me sitting in front of the blank pages.

"Let's start here. Once you get going, maybe we can revisit your computer privileges. Okay, David?"

I took the notebook and pencil. "Okay," I said. "But what about the TV? It helps me relax."

"I'll think about it," she said. " The head nurse thinks you should spend more time outside in the real world, maybe get some exercise."

"It's an institution," I said. "Outside isn't the real world. It's the same as the inside, just without a roof. None of this is the real world."

I was going to tell her that the only things with any reality in this institution were the stories on TV. If you thought about ultimate reality, the reruns I watched like *Magnum P.I.* and *The Rockford Files* and *The Incredible Hulk* had more truth in them than anything on the news, which was all the head nurse would allow me to watch anymore. But I remembered what my mother said and how Abbott had put his finger to his lips and I didn't push my luck. I was getting that feeling again, the feeling that Laura was giving me another chance to win her back, and I didn't want to disappoint her.

49

I started with the notebook and pencil, sketching some things out in my little room and then talking them over with Laura in therapy. She seemed to like what I wrote. She said she was proud of me and that I was making good progress. I felt the same way. I hadn't even started writing full paragraphs and I had plans that extended out a few chapters. Beyond that, I knew the stories I wanted to share even if I didn't know quite how to organize them or what would become of all the characters in the end.

Not long after I started making notes, the head nurse restored some of my computer privileges. Early each morning, she let me write for two hours, as long as I took my medication and showed her I wasn't hiding the pills under my tongue. It wasn't anything like the long days I used to spend sitting up above the garage, but I didn't have the energy for that sort of work anyway.

I don't know why everything was so exhausting—therapy, watching the light change, watching the shadows on the wall, watching the other patients move in their odd ways through the yard, watching reruns on TV—but I felt so languid. Maybe it was because I never could quite let go of the story I'd lived over the past year. I had this feeling of being stretched across three worlds. I was simultaneously reliving my adventure with Abbott while also existing as a voyeur in his story with Lucille. And then, at the same time, I had my own "recovery" at the hospital to worry about—which really boiled down to acting as though I sincerely believed that my writing wasn't anything other than fiction.

It was a heavy load to carry. If I was going to build an imaginary world, I wanted to make it every bit as beautiful as what had really happened, or even more so. I wanted my story, by being fiction, to circumvent the normal scrutiny—all the second-guessing, the annoying questions, the strange looks and dismissals and all those voices that spoke as though they carried overfull cups of coffee across a room to me. But I also understood I was about to leave Abbott and his story stranded in my pages. If I was going to finish my novel, I would have to lock him up in that same flat world where I had been stuck for so many years. I wanted to be sure to leave an exit for him, a little passage through that great wall of ice so that, if he searched hard enough, he would see that he was free to walk right out of my chapters and into my world again. That was important to me, not only because it seemed like the right thing to do, given my own experience, but also, and perhaps selfishly, because I thought someday I might need Abbott again.

I know it probably seems like an odd way to think. Even as I wrote the events of that year as accurately as possible out of my memory, I found it almost too far-fetched. I kept wanting to get back on the internet and find some form of validation—a newspaper article, a FOIA document, a reference somewhere to one of the names Abbott had mentioned—anything. But there was no chance of getting on the internet. The head nurse had changed the wifi password and no matter how well I behaved for her and how many pills I pretended to swallow and how charming I tried to be, she would not surrender it. She kept telling me it was "doctor's orders," but when I asked Laura, Laura told me that wasn't true at all. She said I was restricted from using the internet on the recommendation of the head nurse.

Sometimes, I would have to put down the writing and sit on the couch and just stare blankly at the TV and retreat into my mind for a while. I'd find myself imagining some sort of escape. I'd see Abbott coming for me, pulling up to the big front doors in a copper Firebird like the one Jim Rockford used to drive. The two of us would bust out of this place with one of Rockford's famous J-turns. I'd see us barreling through the desert, the big engine of the Pontiac humming low, a plume of dust rising in our wake. I'd be rolling a joint. He'd be yammering away. Somewhere in the distance—maybe in a diner or a miner's shack, somewhere in the future I guess—I would see Lucille waiting for us in that golden light that surrounded her, not only Abbott's Lucille but my own Lucille as well—though that was just a feeling I had and it took me some time to actually know what it meant in my own mind. I had this sense that whoever Lucille was and wherever she was, I had to protect her the same way I had to protect Abbott. I had to bury both of them so deeply in fiction that they could never be taken from me. They would exist in plain sight where everyone could know them, and yet they could never be found.

It was a disappointing conclusion to reach. From the beginning, I'd misunderstood Abbott. I'd imagined he'd chosen me for a great adventure. I was to help him find Lucille. But what I came to see is that Abbott had never really lost Lucille. Abbott had himself become lost and Lucille had risen from the desert to guide him. She was the North

Star. She was that point of light that the dying walk toward, only realizing in their final moments that they've been searching for it all along. I guess life is just one long march toward death anyway. Abbott hadn't latched onto me to help him find Lucille. He had merely shared her light with me at a time when I was in danger of losing myself, and when I needed her even more than he did.

I moved from the corner they called the library to the big windows that overlooked the yard. Sometimes I did that when I needed to refresh my mind, or when I burned through my computer and TV watching time and sitting on the couch in front of the blank television screen reflected to me the painful memories of all those years lost at the edge of my second chapter. I liked the window at that time of day—just after breakfast. Most of the patients were out exercising in the yard below, and the institution was as close to quiet as it ever became. I could observe my fellow inmates from a height and distance that provided a little perspective, and somehow that put me in touch with my sanity. It wasn't that I felt that I was of a different ilk than my fellow patients, as though I were Boris Schlotzsky at his big office window or the head nurse lusting after Denton from the third floor. It was something else—a more beautiful feeling, as though I was exactly where I belonged and all of us, doctors and nurses and orderlies and patients alike, had found each other while searching for a cure.

The uninitiated observer would've looked upon the yard and seen a free-for-all, but the patients were all doing their best to perform the complex series of Tai Chi exercises modeled by their instructor, and I have no doubt that each believed they were following the movements to a tee. To be sure, the way the patients performed Tai Chi didn't look anything like the way I'd envisioned Abbott and Denton training together under the western juniper tree. There was a weird rhythm to it, with no evidence of meditative or synchronized movement. Everybody just sort of stood around in a cluster and did their own thing. One patient moved through the group at sharp angles as if connecting the stars of an imaginary constellation while another seemed caught in a slipstream of abrupt repetitive movements. There were those who made compulsive noises, like animals or brass horns, and those who seemed to swim through a great cloud of Klonopin laced with kung fu. One older woman positioned herself in the center of the group and threw her hands in the air and repetitively shouted, "Why do I keep running from my responsibilities?"

Not one of them had any facility for imitation, and they uniformly lacked the ability to mold and un-mold themselves in any prescribed sequence of complex postures. It struck me as a good metaphor for our dilemma. It's why all of us were there. If we wanted to leave, we were going to have to give up the straight and direct path to our own identities and go through the world twisting and stretching ourselves in synchrony with everyone else. That grim insight might have been the one that finally helped me let go of the truth and embrace writing about Abbott in the language of fiction. Fiction can tell the truth without requiring the reader to believe anything. And then, when a novel is finished, its entire world can crumble to the earth and with its decay the ground becomes fertile for another to be born. Fiction doesn't ask you to walk around all knotted up and claiming that everything you read actually happened in manifest terms, and yet somehow, in the end, you are changed. Almost everyone understands fiction. Even in a place as unique as this, there was only one person who came up from morning exercises and went about her daily life while still contorted into a pretzel, and even in this place, everyone thought she was a little nuts—although, admittedly, she was the first of us to be released.

As I watched the Tai Chi that morning, I wondered if it wasn't really Abbott who I needed in that moment, but Denton White. I needed a friend to drag me out of the doldrums and down into the yard, to get me moving again. The longer I watched, the more I saw things that way. I was, after all, in a situation much like Abbott's when he had first been institutionalized. As with his story, both when he told it to Schlotzsky and later when he told it to me, my story had been met with disbelief. Now I had to find a way to make it believable. I had to embrace fiction. I had to write. I could see that now everything depended on me finishing the story, from the first chapter to the second, right up to the last full stop of punctuation. It was what everything hinged on. It was my only path forward.

I thought of Laura in her office readying herself for our appointment, and I was certain it was what Laura was waiting for too. I didn't know exactly what was about to happen, if I would ever see Abbott again, or if we were ever going to find Lucille. I didn't know what kind of future Laura and I would have together. I didn't know if the old reality was about to melt before me and reveal a bright new truth, or if the sun would fall from the firmament and shatter on the stage of the earth like a cheap chandelier. I just knew that when I placed that final period after the last sentence, it would make landfall with the power of an atom bomb, of a meteor. The dinosaurs of my life would stand bewildered and collapse to ash. I got ready. I had to prepare myself. In just a few short moments, everything was going to change

About the Author

In 1991, inspired by the TV character David Banner from *The Incredible Hulk*, Daniel Caulfield fastened on a frame backpack and set off hitchhiking across the country. His trip, full of strange and wonderful and novel-worthy characters, would span hundreds of rides and more than 30,000 miles over the next several years, including stints through Ecuador, Canada and Japan. When an inmate in an Iowa county jail woke him up one afternoon to watch a rerun of *Kung Fu*, he knew it was time to make a change.

The next twenty-five years would be spent training in the martial arts, earning him black belts in Aikido and Brazilian Jiu Jitsu and sending him to the World Championships of Tai Chi push hands—for which he was mentioned in Josh Waitzkin's, *The Art of Learning*. While never becoming 100% sane, he did manage to raise two wonderful daughters, run a Jiu Jitsu school for many years—and eventually write the book you are holding in your hands.

He currently lives in Nicaragua where he spends his days writing, surfing, growing food, caring for a small gaggle of hens and a rooster named Nacho Libre, and scouring the internet for the conspiracy theory that will crack the whole ruse wide open.

Acknowledgements

Thank you to the many people who stabilized and enriched my life while the idea of this book slowly became a reality:

My mother, Patricia, for reading these chapters almost as many times as I have and printing my manuscripts until her printer ran out of ink. Thank you for your encouragement and good advice, for believing in me when no reasonable person should have, and for reminding me that I was always the smartest of all your children.

My daughters, Emma and Sadie, who burdened me with much-needed responsibility and became the best parts of my life, and to Jon and Zara, for adding more wonderful parts.

My brother Mike, who taught me how to write well and read deeply in college after I slept through most of high school. Thank you, Mike. And relax—Mom didn't actually tell me I was the smartest.

Well... just the one time.

To Ben, my younger brother, who has always been a quiet source of wisdom, strength, humor, direction, cold beer, and good music.

To my sister Jen, for reading some of my earliest work and never telling me how terrible it was.

To Josh Waitzkin, my other brother and longtime friend, who put me up at his villa throughout much of the writing of this book, read chapters, encouraged me through early drafts, and endured me with almost as much patience and understanding as my mother.

And to Fred Waitzkin, who became a close friend, confidant, and writing coach, who reigned in my wild writing, embraced my wild living, and taught me that what you remove is never really gone.

To Bonnie Waitzkin, another mother of a crazy son, who may have been my second biggest fan through the early drafts of this novel, and to Desiree, Jack, and Charlie, who shared their home and family with me.

To Dennis Troutman, who edited through a mountain of typos, pro bono, and returned a clean manuscript. (Any errors found are most likely due to later revisions.)

To Alison, who heroically scraped me off the pavement after an awful motorcycle accident and nursed me back to health when things looked very bleak.

To the many teachers who taught me the arts that changed my life: Arnie Dinowitz, Hiroshi Ikeda, Bataan Faigao, William C.C. Chen, John Machado, Marcelo Garcia, and Ailson "Jucao" Brites.

To Steve "Road Rage" Maydwell, as solid a man as the rock he climbs, and to Ezra Jones and Steve Walsh who often reached out through radio silence to say, "How you doin'?" and to share a laugh, a coffee, or a few too many pints. And to Jim Lombara, Carter, Ian (Jr.) and Ian Spenser (Sr.), Matt Durling, Josh Edgecomb, Aaron Shields, Jesse Carpenter, Kerry Carlisle, Mike Tabor, Ian Durling, Aaron Wolbach, Todd Tardiff, and all the unmentioned but dedicated students of Flow Brazilian Jiu Jitsu who made an otherwise difficult decade of my life so rewarding and enjoyable.

And to Angie, the fellow writer who convinced me to finally release this crazy novel to the world and who played secretary through the last 2% of this process, when completing it seemed so overwhelming.

I feel truly grateful to have landed in a place so full of wonderful people.

For that, I suppose I have to thank God.

Made in United States
Troutdale, OR
12/05/2024

25932425R00241